D0950709

SWEET TEMPTATION

"Sizzle, sex appeal and sensuality! Maya Banks has it all . . . This book is on the inferno side of hot, and it shows on every page . . . You will not want to miss out on this story."
—*Romance Junkies*

"An enjoyable tale of [a] second chance at life."
—*Genre Go Round Reviews*

SWEET SEDUCTION

"Maya Banks never fails to tell compelling tales that evoke an emotional reaction in readers . . . Kept me on the edge of my seat."
—*Romance Junkies*

SWEET PERSUASION

"Surpassed all my expectations. Incredibly intense and complex characters, delicious conflict and explosive sex scenes that fairly melt the print off the pages, *Sweet Persuasion* will have Maya Banks fans, new and existing alike, lasciviously begging for more."
—*RT Book Reviews* (4½ stars)

"Ignites the pages . . . Readers will relish Maya Banks's exciting erotic romance."
—*The Best Reviews*

"Well-written and evocative."
—*Dear Author*

SWEET SURRENDER

"This story ran my heart through the wringer more than once."
—*CK²S Kwips and Kritiques*

continued . . .

Titles by Maya Banks

The Sweet Series

SWEET SURRENDER   SWEET TEMPTATION
SWEET PERSUASION   SWEET POSSESSION
SWEET SEDUCTION   SWEET ADDICTION

The Kelly/KGI Series

THE DARKEST HOUR   ECHOES AT DAWN
NO PLACE TO RUN   SHADES OF GRAY
HIDDEN AWAY   FORGED IN STEELE
WHISPERS IN THE DARK

Colters' Legacy

COLTERS' PROMISE

The Breathless Trilogy

RUSH
FEVER
BURN

FOR HER PLEASURE
BE WITH ME

Anthologies

FOUR PLAY
(with Shayla Black)

MEN OUT OF UNIFORM
(with Karin Tabke and Sylvia Day)

CHERISHED
(with Lauren Dane)

Specials

PILLOW TALK

ECHOES AT DAWN

MAYA BANKS

BERKLEY SENSATION, NEW YORK

THE BERKLEY PUBLISHING GROUP
Published by the Penguin Group
Penguin Group (USA) LLC
375 Hudson Street, New York, New York 10014

USA • Canada • UK • Ireland • Australia • New Zealand • India • South Africa • China

penguin.com

A Penguin Random House Company

ECHOES AT DAWN

A Berkley Sensation Book / published by arrangement with the author

Berkley Sensation Books are published by The Berkley Publishing Group.
BERKLEY SENSATION® is a registered trademark of Penguin Group (USA) LLC.
The "B" design is a trademark of Penguin Group (USA) LLC.

For information, address: The Berkley Publishing Group
a division of Penguin Group (USA) LLC,
375 Hudson Street, New York, New York 10014.

ISBN: 978-0-425-25086-0

PUBLISHING HISTORY
Berkley Sensation mass-market edition / July 2012

PRINTED IN THE UNITED STATES OF AMERICA

10 9 8 7

Cover art by Craig White.
Cover design by Rita Frangie.
Interior text design by Laura K. Corless.

ECHOES
AT DAWN

PROLOGUE

GORDON Farnsworth had more money than God. He had connections beyond anyone's imagining. He'd lived his life on the fringe, steeped in shadows, so immersed in gray that he doubted he had any semblance of a soul remaining.

He had power, wealth and information at his disposal. And none of it meant a damn thing because his daughter was dying and he was powerless to prevent it.

She'd been seen by the top physicians in the world, had the best treatment money could buy, and he'd been told the same thing by every one of them.

There was nothing further to be done. His daughter couldn't be saved. The best he could do was make her comfortable for the remainder of her time.

Fuck that.

He wouldn't accept that there was nothing he could do. He'd prevented wars and instigated them. He wielded influence with dozens of world leaders. He could make or ruin an entire country on a whim. And he couldn't save his daughter?

He paced the confines of the dark library where he often

brooded with a glass of Macallen whiskey he'd paid over one hundred thousand dollars for. The fire in the hearth had died, leaving only a few glowing embers.

His phone rang and he yanked it to his ear, barking the order before the other party had a chance to say anything.

"Is she legitimate?"

"Indeed it appears she is."

Farnsworth's shoulders sagged and he sank onto the couch, perched on the edge, his impatience snarling and nipping at him.

"She's been able to heal all manner of illnesses and injuries, but it's at great cost to herself. She's been pushed beyond her limits but she's been successful in all cases that have been presented."

"I don't give a damn what it does to her," Farnsworth growled. "Get her here. I'm running out of time."

There was a lengthy pause and Farnsworth didn't like pauses. They never meant good news.

"I anticipated your order, sir. When I was told the results of her testing, I knew you'd want her there with all due haste. I gave the order to go in, remove all evidence of her existence, silence those who had any knowledge of her and, of course, to retrieve Grace Peterson and have her taken to you."

He didn't like where this was going. His gut knotted and his lips tightened in rage.

"What the hell happened then? Where is she? When can I expect her? Elizabeth doesn't have much time!"

There was a deep breath. "She escaped, sir."

Farnsworth exploded to his feet, spit rimming his lips as he puffed out his fury. "Escaped? She escaped? What of this terrible toll? What of her being weak and fragile after so much healing? How does one small woman escape highly trained operatives?"

"There was a miscommunication, sir. Our intel was wrong. The room we thought she was being held in was empty. One of the explosions leveled the quarters she had been moved to, and she escaped in the confusion."

"Your intel was wrong. Miscommunication. Confusion. What the fuck am I paying for? A bunch of goddamn amateurs?"

"We're tracking her now. We won't fail you, sir."

"Goddamn right you won't fail," Farnsworth raged. "I swear to you that if my daughter dies, you and everyone you hold dear will suffer. I'll extinguish your entire family, and you'll watch while it happens. And then you'll die a long painful death. Do you understand me?"

"Y-Yes sir."

Farnsworth cut the connection and held the phone for a long moment, tempted to hurl it through the window. Only the knowledge that he had to act fast for his daughter's sake gave him the impetus to place his next call.

He waited as he went through a series of numbers and security codes until finally the connection was established. He didn't wait, didn't exchange pleasantries. Grace Peterson had to be found, and she had to be found now.

"I need Titan," he bit out. "I don't give a goddamn how much it costs. You get me Titan."

CHAPTER 1

GRACE Peterson drew the blanket tighter around her and huddled in the dark. She stared blankly at the star-filled sky. The mountain air was cold. Not just chilly, as it had been as dusk had descended, wiping away the comfortable remnants of a sunny afternoon. It was frigid.

A low moan escaped as her muscles tightened and protested not only the cold, but the weakness inflicted upon them by so much death and sickness. Pain had long since lost any meaning to her. What she felt couldn't really be considered pain. It was worse. She couldn't feel anything but the desolation of hopelessness and despair. The knowledge that she would probably die from the horrors inflicted upon her. And perhaps she deserved it, for she hadn't been able to help all who had been thrust upon her.

Her escape had been a fluke. An explosion had decimated the cell where she'd been held. She'd managed to get out before the men charged with her care had been able to respond. Or maybe they had perished. She couldn't bring herself to feel any regret. They'd shown her no regard. She'd been treated like an inanimate object. Some magic wand they waved at a wound or an illness and expected her to make it all disappear.

She hated them for that. Hated them for their callousness. For using others as they'd used her. Pawns. Objects to provide them with information. They weren't even people. Just numbers.

Another shiver rattled her teeth and settled deep into her bones. She simply couldn't imagine ever being warm again. She curled her feet farther into the blanket and tucked the ends securely under her chin.

She was severely weakened by all she'd been forced to endure. For all she'd been made to heal. Even now she didn't know where she'd found the strength or the will to make her escape when the opportunity had presented itself.

But now she'd run out of strength. She had nothing else left. No reserves. And her resolve was faltering just as everything else had done.

Closing her eyes, she tried to find some solace. Some measure of peace.

She missed her sister, Shea. Ached for the comfort of her touch. The brush of her mind and the image of her smile. She hadn't ever really understood and hadn't ever taken Shea's decision for them to separate seriously. Until the day she'd been captured, and she realized that if they'd been together, they would have both been taken.

Shea had always been determined to keep Grace safe, but now, Grace was equally determined to keep Shea as far away from her as possible. Grace was hunted. She knew her pursuers were probably in these mountains already. They could be a short distance away.

And so she'd slammed the door shut on her sister, and the void hurt every bit as much as the bombardment of sickness and pain she'd absorbed. Not having Shea there was the worst sort of loneliness. She'd severed the telepathic link between her and her sister, and her worst fear was that it was permanent. She'd never get it back.

In a way, she supposed it would be a blessing. If she lost

her abilities, she could have a normal life. But so would she lose the ability to make a difference in someone else's life.

She closed her eyes, exhausted by the weight of responsibility, sorrow and regret. She hated that she wasn't stronger, that she'd crumbled under so much stress. But the ailments had been thrown at her, one after another. Broken bones, horrible bloody wounds, tumors, diseases, and the list went on and on. The most horrific experiment she'd undergone was when it had been demanded of her to reach inside the mind of a woman with a mental illness and heal her.

For three long days Grace had known what it truly was to be insane. She'd lived the woman's existence while the woman had gone away cleansed of the darkness in her brain. Twice, Grace had tried to kill herself, not because it was what she wanted, but because it was what the illness dictated. In the end, she'd been restrained, unable to do even the basic necessities for herself because the fear had been too great that she'd find a way to end her life.

She was hungry, but the thought of food made her stomach twist into knots. She drank water from nearby streams frequently, because she knew she had to do something to keep her strength up. And no matter that she bore the knowledge that she would likely die, she couldn't bring herself to simply give up. Not yet.

Quietly, she turned over, rearranging the blanket in the fruitless hope she'd somehow find greater warmth. Eventually she'd have to reach out to her sister, but if she did so now, Shea would see the horrific shape Grace was in. Shea would come. She'd put herself in grave danger. Grace would never be able to live with herself if Shea was sacrificed because in a moment of weakness Grace gave in and tried to reestablish the link with her sister.

Silent tears slid down Grace's cheeks, briefly warming her skin until the chilly air turned them to ice. She angrily scrubbed them away and hunched lower, furious with herself for allowing despair to control her.

She was stronger than this, and she'd be strong again.

She just needed time to recover from her ordeal. Maybe she'd never be the same as she had been, but she wasn't going to give in. If she died, she'd die running. She'd die standing up and fighting. She refused to die in some laboratory where rats were treated with less disdain.

A distant sound froze her to the bone. She went so still that even her breath sounded like a roar in the night. She pushed the blanket over her mouth, trying to quell the noise, and she stared into the trees, trying desperately to see through the thick curtain of night.

Someone was coming.

THEY crawled through the mountains under the cover of dark. Rio knew they were close. They'd been closing in on Grace for days now, but somehow she'd managed to elude them just when he was sure they'd come upon her.

He adjusted his pack, slipped on the infrared goggles and scanned the area ahead, looking for anything giving off a heat signal.

There were several smaller forms. Animals. Even a larger shape that must have been an elk or a deer. Nothing that resembled a human, though.

He'd given orders for strict radio silence. They weren't the only ones who sought Grace. But he was determined to get to her first. His gut told him they needed to catch up to her before dawn. The hairs on his nape rose and apprehension slipped down his spine. It wasn't that he feared confrontation. In truth, he'd savor killing the bastards who'd made Grace and Shea's life hell over the last year.

It was the knowledge that she was in danger and that he and his men needed to end this game of cat and mouse.

Beside him, Terrence, his right hand, melted into the dark just a few feet away. Rio continued a path farther up the mountain. There were any number of nooks and crannies a small woman could hide in, and so he carefully scanned the area, looking for any heat source.

Where are you, Grace? I know you're here. I can feel you.

And it was true. There was a distinct prickle, the same awareness he'd experienced the first time he'd seen her on the surveillance footage. The last time anyone had seen her before she'd disappeared.

He'd known beyond a shadow of a doubt that he would be the one to go after her and bring her back to her sister. Safe and alive.

Since that time, he'd tracked her movements with uncanny accuracy. He and his men hadn't left a stone unturned in their search for her. They'd gone back to the house where she'd last been seen and had broadened their search from there.

It had taken weeks, but now they were following a lead into the mountains of Colorado, and Rio was sure they were close. His gut was screaming, and he never ignored his gut. It had kept him alive more times than he could count.

He paused when he heard a noise in the distance. He turned, scanning the area, and then he saw the infrared images of men he knew weren't his moving stealthily through the trees.

Damn it.

He curled his hand into a fist. Where the hell was Grace? He didn't have time to play hide and seek with the men who were after her. He needed to grab her and get the hell out.

He pulled his rifle from over his shoulder and silently moved in the direction of the heat signature. Ideally he didn't want to shoot up the whole damn mountain and leave bodies lying everywhere. He'd rather find Grace and make a stealthy exit, but the savage part of him relished spilling a little blood.

A cry in the night froze him momentarily. He lifted his head to capture the faint echo as it died in the distance. It was a feminine cry, one that sent chills chasing down his spine. There was a hell of a lot of anguish, pain and fear in that one small sound.

Grace.

He began to run, closing in on the source of the noise. He ripped the goggles from his head, needing to see his surroundings better. A hundred yards ahead, Terrence fell in beside him and they charged the remaining distance, guns up and ready.

They slowed when they reached the edge of a drop-off that overlooked a small valley below. The moon shone down, reflecting off the smooth rock floor, and Rio's gut clenched as he saw Grace Peterson backed to a steep edge that plummeted hundreds of feet into a riverbed.

He sensed the grim determination in her that she wouldn't be captured again. He knew without doubt that she'd jump before ever going back. Her fear and desolation were like a tangible scent in the air. It tightened every one of his muscles, gripped his heart and squeezed relentlessly.

He had to get to her before the idiots forced her over with their stupidity.

Dropping down onto his belly, he pulled his gun up and put the crosshairs on the man closest to Grace. The stupid fuck had his hand held out in a placating manner, but in his other hand was a gun and it was pointed directly at Grace. His entire posture screamed menace.

Rio squeezed a shot off. The man dropped like a stone, and suddenly his comrades hit the ground and turned in the direction of the gunfire.

"Hell," Terrence muttered as he got into position. "Thought we weren't engaging?"

"Cover me. I'm going in," Rio bit out.

Before Terrence could protest, Rio scrambled over the edge and rapidly worked his way down until he reached bottom. Above him, Terrence squeezed off round after round, the sounds echoing harshly in the night.

They had a limited amount of time before someone came to investigate all the gunfire. He turned and immediately searched for Grace again. To his horror, he found her just as the edge gave way under her feet and she plummeted over the side.

He lunged forward as more gunfire erupted. This time,

Terrence wasn't trying to scare them. They dropped like flies as Terrence put them down one by one while Rio flew to the edge.

Trusting his man to protect his back, Rio focused only on trying to see how far down Grace had fallen or if the worst had occurred and she'd gone the entire distance to the riverbed.

He dug a flashlight out of his pack and dropped to his belly. He pointed the light down and made a slow sweep. As he pulled it closer to the side of the cliff, the light bounced over a tattered sneaker. He yanked the light up to see Grace lying limply on an outcropping. Her feet dangled over the side and her slim form barely fit the ledge. But she hadn't fallen more than twenty feet.

Breaking radio silence, he called for immediate assistance. His men would have to lower him over by rope, and he'd have to haul Grace up over his shoulder. Provided she was still alive. He wouldn't consider any alternative, though. She hadn't made it this far to go quietly.

As he was pushing to his knees, Terrence dropped down beside him, flashing his own light over the side.

"Diego and Browning have our sixes. Decker and Alton are scrambling to get here," Terrence said. "I'll lower you over with rope so you can get Grace."

"All dead?"

"All dead," Terrence confirmed.

Rio couldn't waste time lamenting the mess they'd made. Grace was the priority and then they had to get the hell out of here before everything went to shit.

Terrence yanked out a coil of rope with a rappel hook on the end and quickly fastened it around his waist. He took several steps back, dug his heels into the soil and then wrapped the extra length around the base of an aspen and set the hook into the bark. He tossed the other end to Rio.

Rio secured the flashlight to his leg, pointing downward so his descent would be illuminated. Then he secured the end of the rope around his waist, yanked to make sure it

was securely knotted and then edged backward until his
heels hung over the side.

Just before he started downward, Decker and Alton hit
the scene. They rushed past Diego and Browning, who
were standing watch, and each grabbed one of Rio's hands
to help him over the side.

They leaned down as he made his descent, holding on to
his wrist until he had sure footing and he was certain that
Terrence could support his weight.

The light bounced crazily as he continued downward.
He glanced over his shoulder to see Grace still lying on the
small ledge. He just hoped to hell it held both their weights.

He pushed off the side of the cliff when he reached her
and lowered himself enough that he straddled the outcropping. Immediately he pressed his fingers to her neck, feeling for her pulse, and was reassured by the steady thud.

"Grace. Wake up. I've come to get you out of here but
I need your help."

When he didn't receive a response, his lips tightened in
frustration. At the top, Decker and Alton shone their lights
down. He dug his feet into the side, finding purchase, and
then he carefully let go of the rope to slide his arms underneath her limp body.

Mentally counting to three, he hoisted her up and then
arranged her over one shoulder so he could hold the rope
with a free hand. He held her tightly, his arm a steel band
over the backs of her legs.

"Pull us up," he called up to his teammates.

Toe over toe, he dug into the side as the rope inched
higher. His muscles bulged with the strain of bearing both
their weights. The rope cut into his skin and his fingers
were numb from his grip.

Let me die. Please.

At first he thought she'd said it aloud. It startled him into
stillness. His toes dragged as they hoisted him higher and
he had to scramble to regain his footing and assist them as
they pulled him and Grace the remaining way.

He was suddenly swamped with desolation so acute that

he couldn't breathe. Pain. Fear. Regret. Hopelessness. And weariness that went soul deep.

He knew then that he'd heard Grace's innermost thoughts. He was feeling what she felt. And her sorrow was so great that it staggered him.

Her tears were locked inside her, but he felt each one. Memories of all she'd endured flashed through his mind until he had to close his eyes to control his reeling senses.

I won't go back.

Her voice whispered through his mind, so broken that he wanted to bellow in rage. He wanted to crawl up over the side of this damn cliff and rip apart the savages who'd pursued her so relentlessly and kill them all over again. The men who'd broken her spirit and made her even now want to die rather than endure more.

He knew that Nathan Kelly had been able to communicate with Grace's sister, Shea, telepathically, but he hadn't considered how or that he and Grace might be able to communicate the same way. It hadn't been important at the time. He'd been gripped by the urgency to find her and keep her safe. Nothing else had mattered at that moment.

Tentatively, he reached out with his mind and spoke gently and reassuringly to her.

You'll never go back to those bastards, Grace. You're safe now. I'm here to help you. Don't give up. You'll get through this.

There was nothing but silence, and he clenched his jaw in frustration. How the hell did you communicate with your mind? How did he even know if he was able to talk to her the same way she'd just spoken to him? He didn't even know if she was cognizant of the fact that he'd picked up on those desperate thoughts.

His teammates' faces came into view as he neared the edge. Their expressions were tense as they hauled him the remaining distance. Diego pushed forward while Decker and Browning held tight to the rope and he took Grace from Rio's grasp.

Free of her weight, Rio hoisted himself over the side

and he rolled to his feet. Terrence let out a light huff, his only indication of the toll the rescue had taken on him. Rio quickly untied the rope and issued orders for his men to dispose of the bodies and then to be prepared to bug out.

They were in the middle of nowhere, no backup, no helo, their vehicles at least two miles away.

He strode to where Diego had laid Grace carefully on the ground and he dropped to his knees beside her.

He pushed the hair out of her face with gentle fingers and frowned at the deep shadows under her eyes, the paleness of her features and the deep lines of fatigue etched into her forehead. Her expression was grim even in unconsciousness.

Not knowing what possessed him, he found himself leaning down to press his lips to her forehead.

You don't give up, Grace. You're safe now. I won't hurt you and I won't allow anyone else to do so either. I'm going to take you home.

CHAPTER 2

SUNLIGHT warmed her face, though she was in the grip of a pervasive chill that was bone deep. It hurt to shiver and yet she couldn't do anything else.

It was as if there were weights pressing over her eyelids, preventing them from opening. Or perhaps she simply lacked the strength to do the simplest tasks anymore.

Pain crept over her, through her, puzzling her with its intensity. It was new. Fresh. And then she remembered falling over the side, sure that death had finally come to claim her.

A soft moan escaped before she could call it back, and she chastised herself for that momentary loss of control. Such a lapse could get her killed.

Grace. Grace.

It took her a moment to realize that the person calling her name wasn't saying it aloud but in her mind. She recoiled, wanting nothing to do with the distant voice. And then she was surrounded by strength. Warmth. It flooded into her veins, so comforting that it shook her to her core.

"Grace."

This time it was said aloud. A deep, rough, slightly accented voice. Just a hint of another world, one she couldn't place.

"Wake up, Grace. Let me see those gorgeous baby blues."

Her brow wrinkled and she tried to process her surroundings. She was afraid to open her eyes. Afraid that she'd be right back in the hands of monsters, forced to do their bidding. The mere thought made her want to weep. She wasn't strong enough to endure more.

A gentle hand stroked over her cheek and carefully pushed away her hair, tucking it over her ear. Such warmth and tenderness. It was like rain to a sun-parched desert. She soaked it up, desperate for any comfort.

It took everything she had to conquer her fear and open her eyes. Sunlight stabbed through her vision, momentarily blinding her.

"That's it," the man said in a low voice. "Come back to me, Grace. I need you to wake up so we can figure out how badly you're hurt."

At the mere mention of injuries, pain screamed through her body. Her eyes flew open and her lips parted. Her breath rushed out, her chest jerking violently with the effort.

Fear nearly paralyzed her when her gaze met with the dark eyes of a man staring intently at her. She let out a cry and tried to bolt, not even realizing that he was still holding her.

She tumbled to the ground, landing with a thud that knocked the breath from her and sent agony tearing through her body again.

The man above her cursed vehemently and he immediately knelt beside her, running those big hands over her fragile body.

"Damn it, Grace, I'm not going to hurt you."

"I won't go back."

She barely managed to stammer out the defiant vow. It hurt to talk. It hurt to breathe. She felt broken. Something was broken. Her ribs, an arm . . . She couldn't even decipher what was wrong with her. There was simply too much to process.

She stared up at him in panic, knowing she didn't possess the strength to escape. Tears gathered at the corners of her eyes. She could do nothing to *prevent* him from taking her back.

A deep shudder rolled through her body, and the tears that had threatened slowly slid down her cheeks.

"Grace, I want you to listen to me."

His voice was calm and oddly soothing. The tone mesmerized her as did those dark eyes that refused to look away from her.

"My name is Rio. I've come to take you home. To Shea."

Her pulse leapt and her throat tightened. "Shea?" she croaked. "Is she all right?"

What if it was a trap? What if he was using information about her sister to lull her into a false sense of security?

He touched her cheek, his fingers infinitely gentle on her skin. He didn't look like a man who had an ounce of gentleness in him. He was big and menacing. A warrior.

Dark skinned, like he'd spent many hours in the sun, uncaring of the consequences. His hair was pulled back into a ponytail at his nape and his eyes were as dark as night.

"I spoke to her myself," he soothed. "I promised her I'd find you and protect you. We're the good guys, Grace. I realize you may have a hard time believing that or trusting me, but we're here to help you. Shea is safe and she wants very much to see you again. We've all been worried about you."

More tears slid down her cheeks and a quiet sob hiccupped from her throat. "I don't want her to see me like this."

Something like understanding flashed in his eyes. He touched her face again, wiping at the moisture on her cheekbone.

"I need you to tell me where you're hurt. We have to move you. We can't stay in this location, but I need to know what we risk by moving you more than we already have."

She glanced around, slowly taking in her surroundings for the first time. Her breath caught when she saw the others. Warriors. Like this man called Rio. Stern and forbidding. How was she to *know* she could trust them? What choice did she have?

They were away from where she'd fallen the night before. How had they managed to find her and how had she survived the fall? Her memory of the event was hazy. She could only remember that moment when she knew she would likely die.

She'd thought that a lot lately. Pondered her mortality as calmly as she might consider what shoes to wear. And yet she was here and alive. Broken but not defeated.

The men were facing away from where she and Rio were positioned. Watchful and wary. Guns up, their stances rigid as if they sensed danger in the very air.

"Grace," Rio prompted. "Talk to me. I need to know how bad it is."

She briefly closed her eyes and then reopened them, focusing once more on his face. She licked her lips. "I hurt."

"I know you do," he said quietly.

"The fall. I think I broke something."

She centered her attention on her body, paying attention to where she hurt and how it differed from the residual pain of the endless torture she'd endured. Her breaths were strained. Shallow and painful.

"Ribs," she managed to gasp out. "Think I have broken ribs. And my arm. It hurts but it's growing numb. I can't feel my fingers."

"Yes, I can see," Rio said as he carefully picked up her hand.

He turned his head and nodded at one of the men. She tensed when the big burly man closest to Rio hovered over her. He was a mountain. Arms bulging with muscles. He barely had a neck as thick as he was. Legs like tree trunks.

"She's lost feeling in her fingers," Rio said as if discussing something as mundane as the weather. "We'll have to set the break."

Her pulse exploded and she tried to sit up, but Rio put a hand on her shoulder. "Be still, Grace."

The command in his voice froze her in her tracks.

"Can you heal yourself?"

The idle curiosity in his voice baffled her. He was so calm. Unruffled. He spoke of her abilities like they were the most natural things in the world. She glanced nervously between the two men, wondering if this was some kind of trap, though she couldn't imagine what it could be.

The people who'd kept her captive knew well her abilities. They wouldn't have to ask questions. Was this yet another faction who wanted to use her?

Panic was rising swiftly when Rio simply put his hand on her cheek and softly caressed. "Take deep breaths, okay? We're going to help you. This is Terrence. He's my second in command. That's Diego right behind him. Diego acts as our medic when Donovan Kelly isn't around to patch us up, but Terrence is going to set the break for you."

Her brow wrinkled in confusion. She had no idea who any of these people were, but Rio continued a steady stream of conversation, ignoring her befuddlement.

"This is going to hurt like a son of a bitch. I won't lie to you. But I need you to be strong. If you scream, you'll draw attention and that's the last thing we need. I'm going to knot one of my shirts, and I want you to bite down on it as hard as you like. But don't let out a sound. Can you do that?"

If he only knew how much she'd silently endured, he'd never ask that question. But she simply nodded, knowing that whatever they did wouldn't touch what she'd already gone through.

He took out a T-shirt from his pack and began folding and knotting it into a long rope. "You didn't answer my question. Can you heal yourself as you do others?"

"Yes," she whispered. "I mean it's different, but I do

heal faster. But there's been so much . . ." She closed her eyes, holding back more tears. "I don't know . . ."

Rio spoke in low, soothing tones. "It's okay, Grace. I'm going to make sure you get out of this."

Something in his voice settled her. Maybe it was the calm promise or the absolute conviction. Some of the fear faded and she relaxed, letting out her breath in a whispery rush.

"That's my girl," Rio murmured.

He carefully placed the shirt between her teeth, feathered his hand over her jaw and then eased her mouth shut over the material.

"Be strong."

She closed her eyes and nodded, not wanting to see what was coming.

Strong hands gripped her arm in a surprisingly gentle manner. She could instantly tell the difference, knew that it was Terrence who held her hand.

And then he simply pulled and twisted, all at the same time. His strength took her completely by surprise. Her eyes flew open and her teeth bit savagely into the shirt. Her body bowed with the instant flash of pain. As she lay panting, her nostrils flaring with the ragged breaths she tried to suck in, a sense of relief settled over her.

Her arm ached from the manipulation, but the constant red-hot pain had subsided. Diego stepped in and quickly bound her arm, using two sturdy saplings one of the other men had fetched. He wound strips of cloth tightly around the sticks so it was impossible for her to move her arm.

Rio pulled the knotted shirt from her mouth. "Better?"

She nodded, still not trusting herself to speak.

"Okay, this is what's going to happen. We have to move and I can't spare the manpower necessary to keep you immobile. We don't have a stretcher, which means I'm going to carry you out while my men surround us and provide cover. With a broken arm and ribs plus God only knows what else you've got going on, there's no easy way to do this. It's going to suck."

She tried to smile at the blunt way he put it, but her lips trembled and she gave up with a sigh.

"I'll need at least one hand free so I can hold a gun and protect us both. Terrence will secure you to my back. We once carried a teammate's wife out of the jungle just like I'm going to carry you, so it'll work. I don't want you to worry. If you don't trust in anything else, you trust in the fact that we're going to get you out of these mountains."

The unwavering conviction in his voice gave her the first hope she'd experienced in many weeks.

"I won't let you give up," Rio continued. "I know you hurt. I can only imagine what those bastards did to you. But you aren't giving up, Grace. You're a fighter. Your sister's a fighter."

Tears shimmered in her vision again, making Rio grow hazy. "I can't talk to her. I'm not sure I can talk to anyone . . . like before I mean."

Rio leaned over, his face close to hers. "You'll get it back. I heard you last night. It's there. You just have to heal both in body and spirit."

"Who are you?" she whispered around the knot in her throat.

He smiled then, white teeth flashing against dark skin. "I'm the man who's going to get you the hell out of here, and then I'm going to hunt down those sons of bitches who hurt you and gut every last one of them."

She shivered at the menace in his voice but was oddly comforted by the savage vow.

"We need to roll, Rio," Terrence said, startling her. She'd forgotten his presence. Had forgotten all of the men standing in close proximity.

Rio nodded and then stood, towering over her. She suddenly felt very small and insignificant and extremely vulnerable as she lay huddled on the ground, surrounded by the warriors with death in their eyes.

This time Terrence knelt by her side, his voice quiet and she suspected purposely gentle so as not to scare the bejesus out of her. It was a little late for that . . .

"All right, Miss Grace. This is what's going to happen. The men are going to fashion a sling of sorts that will secure you to Rio's back. I'm going to lift you very carefully. I'll try not to hurt you."

She nodded her understanding.

He smiled at her, and she decided he was an extremely handsome man despite his fierce appearance. Moreover, she believed him when he said he'd try not to hurt her.

He slid his arms underneath her body. "Deep breath."

She sucked in, closed her eyes, and he lifted upward. She was amazed at the ease with which he picked her up. She opened her eyes and watched him. There was no evident strain. Just calm focus.

Diego appeared on her other side.

"Diego's going to hook his arm underneath your leg," Terrence explained. "I'm going to take the other."

She appreciated the patience he demonstrated and how he explained every step so she wouldn't be frightened. At this point, she was ready to be done with it all. The sooner they left this place where she was hunted, the better she'd feel. Maybe then she could begin healing.

She nodded her acceptance, and as soon as she did, Diego stepped forward and slid his arm underneath her legs. He hooked his other arm behind her, and he and Terrence held her up to Rio's back.

The other two men quickly wound the long strips of cloth they'd secured together underneath her bottom and underneath her legs. They did a series of figure eights, coiling rope and material up and over Rio's shoulders then under and around her legs and behind until she was solidly supported and attached to his back.

Diego positioned her splinted arm at Rio's side just underneath his armpit and then secured it to Rio's body as well.

She had no idea how on earth Rio was going to be able to move with her plastered to his body the way she was, much less carry a gun, but he didn't seem at all bothered by the prospect.

"How are the ribs?" Rio asked.

"Okay."

"They'll hurt when he starts walking," Diego warned. "Try to press against him to minimize your movements as much as possible. The more you jostle, the more it's going to cause you pain."

She nodded again and pressed in as close to Rio as she could get. Already she was exhausted and they hadn't even begun the journey out. She didn't even know how far they had to travel and she didn't want to ask because she wasn't sure she could handle the answer.

Instead she was going to put herself in their hands because she had no other choice. She had no idea who these men were—only that they knew her sister and they professed to want to help her.

She'd been prepared to die. It shamed her that she'd been so ready to give in. At her absolute lowest point, these men had appeared, refusing to let her give up. Rio had promised to take her home, though she had no inkling of what home meant. She'd spent too much time on the run, separated from her only family.

The idea that she was finally safe and could see her sister after so long was more than she could comprehend.

"Ready, Grace?" Rio called over his shoulder.

She took a deep breath, realizing that she was venturing into the unknown once again. Only this time she wasn't alone, and that bolstered her flagging resolve like nothing else could.

"Ready."

CHAPTER 3

RIO'S admiration for Grace grew with every passing hour. He knew she had to be in excruciating pain and yet she bore it stoically, never uttering a sound as he carried her over the uneven terrain.

His team had set a grueling pace that would have most people reduced to begging. But she hadn't uttered a sound. But he felt her. She wasn't a strong presence in his mind. He thought she was probably tightly protecting herself. But he could still sense the remains of the mental pathway that had been briefly forged between them, and he knew she was suffering.

"Bad news," Terrence said grimly.

Rio looked up to get the report from the man he'd sent ahead to scout the area where they'd left the vehicles. Terrence's lips were set into a fine line, and he kept looking to where Grace's head rested on Rio's shoulder as if he hated having to say what he was about to.

Diego pulled up, standing to the side of Terrence and Rio. He too glanced at Grace, but his gaze was seeking, trying to discern her condition.

"Tell me," Rio said impatiently.

He couldn't be concerned with Grace hearing bad news. Hell, how much worse could it get anyway? She'd already been to hell and back.

"We've got company. Hard to tell from the distance I was doing recon, but our hiding spot has been made and they've set up an ambush."

Rio bit out a string of swear words that had Grace stirring against him. He went still, not wanting to cause her greater discomfort.

"Rio?"

Hearing his name on her lips did odd things to him. His heart turned over at the way she tried to mask her fear. She obviously had no idea how much she was broadcasting. Her fear was a tangible, living thing. He could smell it. He could feel it. He could damn near taste it as it vibrated through the air.

"What will we do?" she whispered.

Terrence and Diego both put a hand out to her, each seeking to comfort her.

"Don't you worry, Miss Grace," Terrence said gruffly. "We've faced a lot worse. We aren't going down to a bunch of good ole boys with peashooters."

Rio felt her lift her head and he grimaced at the effort it took her. She trembled against him and his gut clenched. She wasn't doing well at all. He knew it like he knew nothing else. They had to get her somewhere she could have medical attention or she wasn't going to make it.

"Where will we go?" she asked.

Her head rested on his shoulder again as if she no longer had the strength to hold it up. He could feel her breaths huff out in tiny little bursts against his neck.

It was then he felt the desolation and . . . the acceptance. Her acceptance. She'd resigned herself to death. Embraced it even. Sorrow surrounded him, pulled at him. She knew she was dying but she didn't want to die out here in the cold. In the unknown. Afraid. She didn't want to die afraid.

Rage blew through him. Helpless rage. He wanted to hit

something but he remained still, not wanting to add to her pain. He met the gazes of Diego and Terrence.

"We don't have much time," he said in a low voice. "We need a backup plan yesterday." He stared hard at his teammates, his lips curled up in a snarl. "She's not dying on my watch. Split up. Find us a place we can hunker down and give her some time to heal. We'll figure out a plan after she's taken care of."

"We need to find a place for you to stay with Grace while we scout," Diego said. "That's our first priority."

Terrence nodded his agreement.

Rio glanced over his shoulder but he sensed that Grace had slipped under again, no longer aware or maybe no longer caring of her surroundings. He knew he had to move fast. He didn't have much time because she was fading more rapidly by the minute.

"You hang in there, Grace," he said fiercely. "Don't you dare give up."

She didn't even stir. Rio's men gathered in a tight perimeter and they struck out again, this time heading back up in elevation and away from where the SUVs were parked.

Terrence fell in beside Rio and murmured in a low voice, "I can radio Sam. Tell him what's up. Ask for backup. He could send a helo in. Might take the better part of a day but we'd be out of here."

Rio knew the best thing, the right thing, was to report back to his boss. If he had such a thing. True, he worked for KGI. His men technically worked for KGI. But Rio was his own man and his men were loyal to him. They went where he went. Followed his orders.

His gut told him he didn't entirely trust the situation at the KGI compound. Resnick was involved. Their CIA contact was up to his ears in the mess with Grace and her sister, Shea, only Rio didn't know to what extent.

But he had a bad feeling, a very bad feeling, and it was why he hadn't yet reported in to Sam about their progress or that they'd been close to recovering Grace. Part of his reasoning was that he hadn't wanted to get Shea Peterson's hopes up. She was desperate to locate her sister, and Rio had made her a promise. Her. Not Sam. Not KGI. He'd promised Shea that he'd keep her sister safe.

He blew out his breath. If he called in KGI, they'd most assuredly come. But he couldn't rid himself of the feeling that it wasn't what was best for Grace. Each time he started to agree and tell Terrence to check in with Sam, get the ball rolling, his stomach coiled into a knot and his instincts screamed at him to stand down.

"I'll make the call," Rio finally said. He had to talk to Sam himself. Had to know what was going on and why he was so reluctant to relinquish Grace into someone else's care.

Right now he only wanted a place he could make Grace more comfortable and hopefully start the healing process. She wasn't going to give in. He'd bully her mercilessly if that's what it took, but over his dead body was he going to lose her now that he'd finally taken her from the people who'd done so much damage to her body and mind.

For the next hour, they climbed higher. The sun was starting its slow descent and the air grew cooler the higher they went.

"There," Diego called, holding his hand up to halt the others.

Diego pointed to a series of large boulders jutting upward from the ground. Resting against the side of a steep cliff, the boulders provided a natural shelter. The cliff wall provided cover from behind with no possible access. The only way in or out was the front and Rio could easily pick off anyone coming hundreds of yards away.

"Help me get her down," Rio said, crisp urgency in his voice.

Browning and Alton hurried to unwind the bonds securing Grace to his back. Decker and Terrence lifted her weight and eased her away. Rio stretched his aching shoulders and then hurried into the natural enclosure.

Diego tossed him his pack holding medical supplies and two canteens of water. Terrence pulled the sat phone from his pack and laid it on the ground beside the sleeping bag Browning tossed down.

Rio quickly arranged the bedroll, and Decker and Terrence eased Grace down on it.

"We'll do recon and find a place we can squat for as long as we need it," Terrence said. "Be back soon."

Rio nodded and his men melted back into the trees, leaving him and Grace alone.

His first order of business was to make sure she was protected. Then he'd see to her comfort. Dead was pretty uncomfortable by his standards.

He took his rifle and made a slow sweep of his surroundings through the scope. He took his time, noting the locations of markers and memorizing the landscape.

After positioning himself so he had a prime view down the incline, he propped his rifle so it would be in easy reach, and then he took out several grenades and lined them meticulously against the base of one of the boulders.

Both the knives he carried came out and were placed beside the grenades, and his handgun came last and he put it on his opposite side. Satisfied that everything was close enough for him to grasp in an instant, he turned his attention back to Grace.

She shivered and chill bumps were predominant on her skin. Her lips were set into a fine line, even in her unconscious state. He wondered if she dreamed, if she was reliving her treatment at the hands of her captors.

Her muscles twitched and she moaned softly. Her fingers flexed spasmodically and she tried to curl into a fetal position, drawing her knees up toward her chest.

Knowing she'd only hurt herself further, he straightened her and pulled the top of the sleeping bag over her body. He zipped it up, securing her firmly inside. For now he wanted her immobile and warm.

He slid his hand over her cheek, trying to offer what comfort her could. It seemed to work because she quieted and went still. He left his hand there a long moment before finally pulling it regretfully away.

He glanced at the sat phone and blew out his breath. It was time to check in with Sam.

When he received no answer, Rio methodically went down his list of contacts by command. It wasn't unusual not to be able to contact one or more of the Kellys but all of them?

With a grimace, he punched in Steele's number. Steele was the team leader for the other KGI team, and while they all worked well enough together, Rio would rather eat nails than have to rely on Steele for anything. The other team leader was an ice-cold bastard, more of a machine than a man, and he had an uncanny instinct for nosing out trouble, which meant no one ever got the upper hand on him.

Yeah, well, Rio was waiting for the day that changed. No one was blessed for long. Sooner or later, he'd fall on his face, and Rio would try not to laugh too hard when it happened.

When he couldn't reach Steele, his gut started screaming again. Rio had left the Kelly compound just as Grace's sister, Shea, had been rescued and brought in for safety. But Rio hadn't hung around to get details other than what he needed to track Grace.

Something was wrong, which meant Rio and his men were on their own and it was up to him to make sure Grace got the care she needed. Which was fine with him. He'd much rather rely on himself and his team. KGI always had his back, but he had theirs just as many times, and when it came to something important to him, he'd rather have sole control.

He left a message with the resident tech guru, Donovan, but was purposely vague. An idea—his idea—had already started forming in his head.

He'd been called stubborn. Rebellious even. He'd had a career in breaking all the rules. No one had ever been able to contain him, and his respect and position at KGI had been the closest he'd ever come to being a subordinate in any matter.

Sam trusted him, though, and just as often was content

to let Rio go his own way. He didn't push his team leader. If he had, perhaps Rio would even now be solo. But for now he was comfortable within the confines of KGI, because it suited him.

After so long living and breathing those shades of gray, it was a nice change to be on the Captain America side. He'd lived outside the lines. He'd been the very thing he now loathed. People who'd stolen young women like Shea and Grace Peterson. Used them. Discarded them. All for the greater good. As if there was such a thing. In this world, the struggle was never about good or evil. It was about money and power.

Grace would bring money and power to the men who managed to capture her and bend her to their will. If Rio had anything at all to say about it, they'd never get their hands on her again.

His resolve to protect this resilient woman had nothing to do with penance or guilt. He was pragmatic enough to know that he'd done what was necessary in his life. He had few regrets, but it didn't mean he wanted to remain a ghost. Nobody. Not real. Not existing. Having no life except to serve the next great ambition.

He was his own master, his own God now. He had only himself to answer to. As long as he could wake up every morning and look at himself in the mirror, he was content. As content as someone could be who'd lurked in the shadows for so long that he dared not step too fully into the sun.

He glanced at Grace's still form and was compelled to touch the soft side of her neck. Her pulse pattered softly against his fingers and some of the tension eased in his chest.

It was difficult to explain, even to himself, his compulsion when it came to Grace. The first time he'd laid eyes on Shea Peterson, something inside him had twisted. He'd seen the torment in her eyes. Knew that she'd experienced more than most warriors had faced in their lifetime.

And then he'd been confronted by the video footage of Grace standing in the living room of her parents' house.

Frightened. Skittish and prepared to bolt like a spooked deer.

It had taken him back to years before. The image of Rosalina, his precious younger sister, had burned bright in his memory. Her belly softly rounded. The fear in her eyes. The knowledge of her own mortality. The knowledge that she wasn't long for this world.

It was the same look and the same feeling that he got from Grace. It spurred his determination not to let her slip away. Not like Rosalina had. She'd died in his arms, never once condemning the asshole who'd done so much harm to her.

It had taken Rio an entire year to track the bastard down and another twenty-four hours before Rosalina's former lover had died an excruciating death, begging for mercy the entire last two hours.

Killing was something Rio was no stranger to, but he'd never before taken pleasure in it. Neither did he regret the task. He'd learned early on to have no emotions. It made him a better soldier and assassin. But he'd taken savage satisfaction in making his sister's murderer suffer. And when death was imminent, Rio had stared into his eyes and whispered Rosalina's name so that the bastard would take the knowledge to hell with him that Rosalina had been avenged.

Grace stirred and moaned softly, her forehead wrinkling as if she were in pain. He moved closer, laying his hand against her cheek so she would know he was nearby.

Dusk had blanketed the mountains and the chill had deepened. His men would need to return soon so they could move Grace to a safer, less exposed area. She needed time to rest and to heal before he took her thousands of miles away. To his world. His turf. The one place where he answered only to himself and he could be assured of keeping her safe.

CHAPTER 4

THE ghosts invaded her mind. Her very soul. They murmured. Shared their sorrows, their pain, their insanity. The remnants of so much death and illness weighted her down, mixing with her own pain.

Grace wondered if her own sanity had been sacrificed, if she'd done too much, been broken by the repeated healings. Exhaustion and despair were every bit as prevalent as the pain, and she had no idea how to compartmentalize any of it.

She was an open book, broadcasting to the universe. No barriers. No shields. She was as vulnerable as she'd ever been in her life.

It was cold again, and she shivered but even so slight a movement sent more pain through her body.

There was a man nearby, speaking in low tones. Fear was her first instinct, but there was something familiar and soothing about his voice.

She searched her fractured consciousness for clues, something to tell her he wasn't a danger to her. Then she remembered bits and pieces, it all coming back like some jigsaw puzzle that had been tossed into the air.

Rio. He'd said his name was Rio and he knew Shea.

He'd carried her a great distance, with her slipping in and out of consciousness the entire way. His men had disappeared, and Rio had placed her into a sleeping bag in an effort to keep her warm and motionless.

He had no worries on that count. She hadn't the strength or desire to move.

She blinked some of the fuzz from her vision and stared up at the star-filled sky. Fairy dust against black velvet. Carelessly tossed across the sky like someone throwing jacks.

How many times had she stared up at the stars, silently wishing she was normal, that she and Shea could live a normal life. That they could have their parents back.

She closed her eyes again. No, they weren't even her parents. She wasn't sure who they were. She hadn't had time to fully read Andrea Peterson's diary. All she knew was that she and Shea were some lab experiments and that Andrea and Brandon Peterson were scientists who'd stolen Grace and Shea as very young children and raised them as their own.

"Grace, are you awake?"

Rio's voice was quiet in the dark, barely a discernible whisper.

She nodded and then thought how ridiculous it was because he wouldn't see the small movement.

She inhaled through her nose and then whispered back, "Yes."

He moved closer, and when he did, she could see he held an automatic rifle, and though he shifted so he was against her, his gaze was still trained on the distance, watching, observing, never once looking down at her.

"We've got a problem," he murmured. "We've been cut off from my men. I don't want to engage. It's too dangerous. You could be hurt or killed. I've told my men to stay put where they are. You and I will find an alternate route to where they are."

"Cut off how?"

"There are men looking for you and they're in between our position and where my men found cover for us. I sent them ahead to find a place where you could rest and hopefully heal enough that we could make it out."

Some of the haze surrounding her lifted and she fought through the ghosts battling for control. She turned, searching out his profile in the darkness. Maybe he felt her gaze or it could be a coincidence that he looked down at the same moment.

"I can make it," she said.

He shook his head. "You're not in a good way, Grace. I won't risk you."

She pushed herself up to her elbow, ignoring the pain the movement caused. "I want out of here. You say you're not one of them. Okay, I believe you. So I want as far away from here as possible. Nothing you can do to me can be worse than what's already been done. I can make it."

"I can't carry you," he said softly. "If it weren't just you and me, I could take you like I did before. But I have to have my hands free to protect you, which means you have to walk."

"I can do it."

There was a fierce edge to her voice that reflected strength she didn't have. It didn't matter. She would find the strength. The will. If her choices were staying here and risking capture or crawling off the damn mountain, she'd do it on her hands and knees the entire way.

"Then we leave now and go through the night. It's not going to be easy."

She reached up and put her hand on his arm. He tensed beneath her touch and the muscles went rigid, giving her just a sample of the raw strength he possessed.

"I won't die here and I won't let them take me back."

Rio put his hand over hers and curled her small fingers

around his before squeezing. "You aren't going to die at all."

A tiny beacon of hope warmed her insides. There was such conviction in his voice. It sounded like more of a vow than a statement, and she grabbed hold of that promise.

"Do you feel any change yet?" he asked.

She glanced down at her arm, which was still splinted. She flexed her fingers, waiting for the pain to shoot up to her elbow. Her fingers were stiff, but the pain had subsided to a dull ache. She wouldn't know about her ribs until she attempted to get up.

"It's better," she said, not caring if it was a lie. It was her turn to give him a little hope.

"Okay then, this is how it's going to go down. We're going to move out together. You stay on my six no matter what."

"Your six?"

"My back. You stay behind me. I want you to put your finger through the belt loop of my fatigues, and when I move, you move. I won't go too fast and I'll be careful. If I tell you to get down, you drop. No hesitation. If I tell you to run, you haul ass. *Whatever* I tell you to do, you are to do without question and without hesitation. Understood?"

"Yes."

"We'll rendezvous with my men but it's going to take us longer than it will them because we'll be moving so much slower. They're going to have to cover more ground than us and do it double time so they can provide cover for us as soon as possible."

She had a thousand questions but she knew the only thing that mattered was that they get as far away from here as possible. So she bit her lip and began preparing herself mentally for the ordeal ahead.

First she took stock of her most recent injuries. Breathing was easier even if still painful. Her arm was bruised, tender and still swollen, but it felt stronger, as if the break was already mending.

She knew it would take longer because she was so weakened, but she was gratified that even the few hours of rest had begun the healing process. If only her mind worked like her body.

She forced the weariness from her clouded mind and carefully pushed herself upward. Rio didn't help her, and perhaps he wanted to see how she would do on her own. Or perhaps he just wanted to prepare her for how difficult the upcoming task was going to be.

While he eradicated all signs of their presence from the campsite, she pulled herself to her feet and sucked in deep breaths of the crisp air.

Her legs trembled and the weakness in her pissed her off. She curled her unbound hand into a tight fist and planted her feet firmly, refusing to allow her knees to buckle.

She could do this. She *would* do this.

"Ready?"

His voice was low and husky next to her ear. She turned to see that he'd secured his pack to his back and stood a foot away from her, studying her as if judging her ability to make it.

"I'm ready."

He reached for her hand and pressed the stock of a pistol into her palm. "It's loaded. Here's the safety. If worse comes to worst, just point, fire and keep on firing."

Her hand shook as she pulled the gun back. She looked down, not having any clue where to put it. Rio gently took it from her, turned around and slipped it into a leather holster attached to his pants a mere inch from where he'd instructed her to slide her finger through his belt loop. Then he moved in front of her.

She slid two fingers through the loop and took a step forward, wanting to be as close as possible without hindering his forward progress. There were no words for how much she didn't want to be doing this.

Her body screamed at her for mercy. She needed rest. She was at her limit—beyond her limit. She had been for some time. But she couldn't stop now. She had no choice. It was do or die, and she didn't want to die no matter that she'd come so close to giving in.

"I can do this, Rio," she said in a low voice.

He surprised her by reaching back, closing his hand briefly over hers in a gesture of support. "I know."

CHAPTER 5

RIO'S goal was to get them to the plateau. His men would do their jobs and have transport there waiting. Rio's job was to avoid engaging the enemy and get Grace safely under their radar.

It was a painstaking journey, one that Rio himself could make in a tenth of the time it was taking him to traverse the terrain with Grace slowly at his back. But she didn't offer complaint and she hadn't gone down even once. For that alone, she earned his respect.

He halted in his tracks when Grace yanked on his belt loop to stop him. She pressed in close to his back, her body flush against his as she strained upward so her mouth was close to his ear.

"There's someone out there," she whispered. "I know you probably think I'm crazy, but I can hear him. Just ahead. He's cold and angry and he's thinking that he'd just like to kill the little bitch and be done with it."

Rio stiffened. He didn't think she was crazy. He wasn't sure what her abilities were. From what he'd gathered, Shea's were random and not controlled by her at all. Her telepathy wasn't something she could aim or even use at will. But was Grace more stable? How the hell was she picking up on someone in the distance?

"How do you know?" he asked. It wasn't that he doubted her, but he needed all the information at his disposal.

She leaned her forehead tiredly against his back. "I can't pick up on everyone, but this particular guy is broadcasting loudly. He's an open book. No shields. No natural barriers. He's pissed off, and the angrier he becomes, the more I pick up on his brain waves."

"What else? I need to know how many are with him. If he's armed. I need to know exactly what you see."

She went quiet, resting against him. One hand curled against his shoulder and she seemed to be concentrating hard.

"He's on post," she said quietly. "He's pissed because it's just him and one other guy who he thinks is inferior. They were told to take position. Their goal is to form a triangle and pin us in. I don't know how many, but there must be enough to stagger men over a wide area."

"That's good," Rio said approvingly. He reached behind him to squeeze the hand that had dropped down his back. "That's information we can use. I can take two out before they ever know what hit them. We punch a hole in their line and slip through."

He felt her sudden surge of excitement. She straightened against him, her hand squeezing his. It was as if his matter-of-fact way of laying out his plan had infused her with confidence and renewed hope.

"I'm ready."

The quiet tone was far different from the defeat he'd heard earlier in her voice. This time there was fierce determination.

"How far, do you know?"

"No. I'm sorry. Not far, though. He's very loud in my mind."

He turned and eased her into a sitting position against a large aspen. "Stay here. Don't move." He took the pistol from his holster and handed it to her. "Use this if you have to. I'm going ahead to take care of the two men. I'll be back, ten minutes tops."

She nodded and accepted the gun. Her hands no longer shook and she gripped it like she was well acquainted with how to use the weapon.

He turned then, not wasting another moment. He melted into the darkness, heading in the direction that Grace had pointed him. Stealthily, he moved through the trees, able to move faster and more quietly now that he didn't have Grace behind him.

Slinging his rifle over his shoulder, Rio quickly shimmied up an aspen that was sturdy enough to bear his weight. More than midway up, he paused, locked his legs around the trunk and pulled his rifle over his shoulder to do a quick scan of the area.

He was quickly rewarded when he found the first target in his sites. Before disposing of him, he found the second, made sure there were no others in the immediate area and then squeezed off the first shot.

It was easily a three-hundred-yard shot, but he was deadly accurate. The first victim dropped like a stone. Within two seconds, Rio had the second man in the cross-hairs and dispatched him just as swiftly.

He slid down the tree and hurried back to where he'd left Grace. She looked up when he approached and he was pleased that she leveled the pistol in his direction.

"It's me," he called softly.

She lowered the gun and shot to her feet. "Are they dead?"

There was no regret, no anxiety in her voice. Nothing but hope that he'd accomplished what he'd set out to do.

"They're dead. Let's get moving. We'll only have a short time to get beyond them before they're discovered."

As soon as he turned, she grasped his belt loop and all but pushed him forward. He picked up his pace, trusting that she'd keep up. She didn't disappoint him. They hurried through the trees, descending the mountain once more.

He took her directly by the downed men, not to horrify her or cause her distress, but because he dared not take a wider circumference. He didn't want to engage with Grace at his back.

She didn't flinch. She didn't react. She didn't even slow her pace. He began to wonder just how much she'd endured. He knew it was bad, but he was beginning to think he had no grasp at all of the horrors she'd suffered.

They didn't slow, and in fact, once past the dead men, Rio put on more speed, pushing Grace relentlessly. She stumbled more frequently and he knew she was tiring, but he pressed on. He'd push her to her limits and then he'd carry her the rest of the way if he had to.

He slowed to check his GPS when suddenly Grace shoved him hard. A shot sounded as they both went down, and the handheld unit went flying. Before he could react, another shot sounded in his ear and he realized Grace had yanked the pistol from his holster and had fired.

Instantly, he rolled, taking her underneath him even as he positioned his rifle to pick off any threat. Only silence greeted him and then the soft groan in the distance.

Holy fuck. She'd shot someone.

He scrambled up, keeping his rifle trained as he crept forward. He barked a command for Grace to stay down as he headed away from her.

Fifty yards away, a man lay sprawled on the ground, his rifle just inches from his fingers. Rio bent and did a quick assessment in the dark, but the man was no longer breathing. Grace had nailed him right in the neck.

He glanced back in Grace's direction, stunned that she'd just saved his life. He hadn't heard the man, and with Grace holding on to him, his reflexes wouldn't have been as quick. He would have likely gotten shot before he'd have had time to react.

Instead, Grace had shoved him down and taken out the target with a single pistol shot.

He hurried back to Grace, kneeling to help her up.

"Are you all right?" he whispered.

"Fine. You?" Her voice sounded strained and he knew it had to have hurt her when he shoved her to the ground.

"I'm great, thanks to you. How the hell did you do that?"

"I don't know," she admitted. "I just reacted."

"Well, you saved both our asses," Rio said grimly. "Let's get moving. They'll have our location pegged now."

He very nearly grasped her splinted arm. It was easy to forget just how injured she was when she was keeping up his grueling pace and saving his ass in the process.

"How much farther?" she asked.

Her tone suggested just how much she hated asking, and he also sensed just how close she was to her limit.

He retrieved the GPS that he'd been consulting and studied the path they were taking. His lips pressed into a thin line and he stared into the night.

"We have to keep moving. We're making better time than I counted on, which is good. If we can keep this pace, we should meet up with my team at dawn. If we slow or you can't make it, we'll have to bed down, wait for daylight and hope to hell we don't have to engage."

He could feel the quiet despair emanating from her. It was like watching a balloon deflate. But then she squared her shoulders, her chin came up and she chambered another bullet before setting the safety on the pistol once more.

"Let's go," she said in a quiet, firm voice.

CHAPTER 6

ONE foot in front of the other. Block the pain. Focus.

Over and over, Grace repeated the same instructions to herself. She'd long since lost count of the many times she'd stumbled and righted herself, determined not to slow Rio. By now she was performing by rote, and only sheer grit was keeping her upright and moving forward.

She played this ridiculous game with herself. Each time they topped a rise, she told herself she only had to get over the next one. Finally she stopped pretending at all and she clenched her jaw and blanked her mind to everything but taking that next step.

She retreated deep inside herself, where there was no pain, no exhaustion and no fear. Only the knowledge that if she stopped, she died. They died. And this man was risking everything because of a promise he'd made to her sister. She wouldn't let him die because she was too weak to keep moving.

Finally Rio stopped, pulled out another handheld device and studied it a moment before raising his head to stare into the distance. Her knees locked. Cramps rippled through her calves. Rio started forward and her finger slid from the belt loop that she'd clung to for the last few hours.

He pulled up and turned, coming back to her instantly. He put his hands on her shoulders and tilted her face to look into her eyes.

"Grace?"

She made a grab for his arms just as her knees buckled. She would have fallen hard if he hadn't held her up. She bit her lip to keep from crying out as cramps knotted viciously, spreading into her feet and toes. Both legs were one gigantic cramp.

"I can't," she whispered brokenly. "I'm sorry. I can't. Go on without me. Please."

"Tell me what's wrong," Rio demanded.

"Cramps. Oh God, they're everywhere."

He eased her down onto the ground and then took both her legs, bending them at the knees and putting both her feet against his legs. He pushed forward, stretching her calves. Warm hands massaged and rubbed, easing the tense muscles.

At his side, he fumbled for a canteen and handed it down to her. "Drink," he ordered. "You're not hydrated enough. I should have had you drinking all along. Stupid of me not to have seen this coming."

She drank thirstily, but the longer he stood there, open, exposed and vulnerable as he massaged the cramps from her legs, the more she panicked.

"You can't stay here like this," she said desperately. "Go, Rio. You can't be far. Go find your team. Leave me here and come back."

"Bullshit," he said tersely. "You go where I go. I'm not leaving you so shut up."

Even the words so rudely said slid over her like the best kind of comfort. His tone told her that she was safe with him and that he'd die before leaving her. Even as she knew it was what he should do, she was relieved that he had no intention of doing so.

He retrieved the canteen and then bent down to grip her free hand. "On your feet, Grace. Get off your ass and let's get moving. You can do this. Put the pain behind you, just like you've been doing. We have an hour at most until dawn. Don't quit on me now."

His words should have infuriated her. She should have dissolved into tears and refused. She should have rolled over and given up. She did none of those things. The harsh resolve in his tone didn't fool her for a moment. There was worry and respect in his eyes, and she knew in that instant that if she didn't get up, he would simply pick her up and carry her the rest of the way.

She wrapped her hand around his and allowed him to haul her to her feet. Her legs screamed. More cramps rippled down her calves, paralyzing her feet. The strips binding the splint on her broken arm had unraveled and one of the sticks slipped out. The sudden mobility sent pain streaking through her wrist and into her fingers, but she ignored it, ripped away the rest of the splint and tossed it aside.

Later, she'd never know how she made it that last hour. She didn't remember trekking through the aspen forest or forging a cold stream that went as high as her thighs at one point. She only remembered when she realized that the sky had lightened in the east and that dawn was imminent.

Dawn had become her talisman. The end goal.

The sky was a soft lavender and the morning star shone like a ten-carat diamond against velvet. The trees took shape around her and she could make out the terrain.

She'd survived the night.

She staggered along, tripping and then righting herself before Rio could reach back. It had become important to her not to distract him. He slowed and it irritated her because she knew it was for her he had decreased his pace.

Not now. Not when they were so close. She could taste it. Could feel the sweetness of freedom and safety. Rio had promised to take her away. He'd promised he'd keep her safe. For that, she could fly.

She pushed at him, trying to force him to walk faster,

but he halted and slowly turned, his hands framing her arms. His eyes were gentle, his touch even more so.

"It's okay now, Grace," he said softly. "We've made it. My men are here."

She stared dumbly at him for a long moment, not comprehending what he'd said. Then she saw movement over his shoulder, saw Terrence step from behind an aspen. And then the others. The one named Diego and she couldn't bring to mind the names of the others.

As they neared, it was as if the last of her mental defenses crumbled. Pain screamed through her body, making her gasp as the full shock of it hit her with ferocity she was unprepared for.

She heard Rio bite out a curse as her knees buckled. She went down hard, blackness wrapping itself around her like a warm, welcoming blanket.

CHAPTER 7

"SHE'S a mess," Diego said grimly. "I've reset her arm. Her respirations are shallow and her breath sounds aren't good over her right lung. She's dehydrated, run down, and there's no way in hell she's going to make it off this mountain unless we carry her. She's done."

"I can't believe she made it this far," Terrence muttered.

The two men hunched over Grace as she lay on the ground. Diego had given her a thorough examination and his face said it all. She was in a bad way.

"I don't know how the hell she's survived," Diego said as he rose. "She's a walking corpse."

Rio scowled fiercely at his medic and third in command. He didn't want to hear anything derogatory about Grace. She had more resilience and fight in her than most of the men he'd served with in his years in black ops. His money would be on her any damn day of the week.

"What are our transport options?" Rio demanded.

"I commandeered an old Chevy work truck," Terrence said.

Rio blew out his breath. "That's it?"

Diego shrugged. "We've had worse."

Yeah, they had. Only they hadn't been carrying a woman who was more dead than alive. A woman who needed gentleness and caring, not a bumpy-ass ride down switchbacks in the bed of a farm truck.

"I can make a bed in the back," Browning offered. "It won't be the Ritz, but it'll do."

"How the fuck would you know anything about the Ritz?" Alton grumbled. "Fucking pretty boy."

Browning snorted. "You've got me mixed up with Diego here. He's Mr. Suave and shit."

Rio held up his hands. "We've left bodies all over this goddamn mountain. We've got to pony up and get the hell out of here. I'm going to try and raise Sam again."

Terrence slapped his hand to his pocket as if remembering something. "You have a message from Steele. Must be important. It came in code."

Rio frowned and reached for the handheld unit Terrence pulled from his pocket. He punched in his access code and scanned the tersely worded message.

Resnick involved. Watch your six. Don't know
extent. Don't trust him. Unsure of KGI status
with him. Took Shea. Has history with both
Peterson sisters.

Jesus H. Christ. If this didn't complicate matters. Steele was a cryptic bastard on his best day. What the hell was Rio supposed to do with this?

Rio wasn't one to give his trust to anyone. He respected Sam and the other Kellys. He wouldn't work for them unless there was a level of trust there. But he never went so far as to make himself vulnerable to anyone. KGI included.

Now, if Steele's message was interpreted correctly, Steele was effectively giving the other team leader a heads-up that all may not be well within the KGI ranks and that Resnick was a snake in the grass.

It didn't change that Rio still had to contact Sam, but it

made him a whole lot more leery of handing over information on a woman helpless to defend herself.

He'd already decided his course of action anyway, and it didn't include hauling Grace back to Tennessee. Especially now that Steele had warned him. His gut had already given him a heads-up, and now he knew it was legit.

"Let's roll," Rio said in a grim voice. "Where's this chariot you arranged for us, T?"

Terrence's teeth flashed and he tossed his head to the west. "Quarter mile. Stashed in an aspen grove."

Rio knelt beside Grace and put his hand on her cheek. She didn't even stir. His gaze moved down her body, taking in her tattered clothing, the mix of blood and bruises, the makeshift splint on her bruised and swollen arm.

"One more time, Grace," Rio whispered. "One more trip. We'll get you out of here. I swear it."

"She needs to remain as flat as possible," Diego said. "I'm worried she's already punctured a lung. I don't like her color and I don't like her respirations. They're becoming more labored all the time. If we aren't careful, we could end up doing her more harm."

"If we don't move her, she's going to be dead," Rio said bluntly.

Diego nodded his acknowledgment.

They didn't have time to secure her as they'd done before to Rio's back. They didn't have time to do anything more than hoist her up and hope for the best.

Rio waved off his men. He was taking responsibility for Grace. It was he who'd promised her he'd get her out of this alive. It was he who'd pushed her, bullied her and demanded that she give what she couldn't spare. He alone would carry her.

As gently as possible, he slid his arms underneath her body and lifted, rising to his full height, bearing her weight with him. He cradled her against his chest and then fixed his gaze on Terrence.

"I'm depending on you to get us out of here."

Terrence nodded and then motioned for the men to take

position around Rio and Grace. Guns up and ready, they moved as one, taking a fast clip in the direction of the waiting truck.

The sun had just peeked over the horizon, a burnt orange glow lighting a pink sky, when they reached the grove of aspens where the truck was parked.

Rio grimaced. Terrence hadn't lied when he said it was a work truck. But as long as it got them the hell down the road, it would do.

As they neared the vehicle, movement caught Rio's attention. He dropped like a rock, instinctively positioning himself over Grace. His men reacted, forming a barrier between Rio and the potential danger.

"Don't shoot. I have business with Rio."

The words reached Rio's ears, and every hair on his nape prickled with apprehension. He eased Grace onto the ground and then jerked a thumb at Diego. Diego dropped to hover over Grace while Rio rose, his gun up, pointed at the man in the distance.

"What the fuck are you doing here, Hancock?"

This was bad. Worse than bad. Hancock being here in these mountains could only mean one thing. Titan was after Grace or at the very least had been sent to recover her.

Fuck.

CHAPTER 8

EVEN though Hancock didn't so much as twitch, Rio kept his gun up as he circled warily to get a full view of the other man. Hancock watched coolly, his arms loose at his sides as if sending Rio a clear message that he wasn't a threat.

Which was pretty damn funny because anyone who ever thought someone from Titan wasn't a threat was deluding themselves. Rio should know. He'd been one of them for ten years.

He'd lived and breathed those shadows. He knew what Titan was, what they were capable of. What their purpose was. They weren't black or white. They were so gray that it was easy to get lost in the different world they lived in. A world where there were no rules and the law didn't apply.

He and Hancock had served together. Rio had saved Hancock's life in what would be Rio's last mission with Titan. Rio had walked away, never looked back. He hadn't wanted to look back. Only now his past was staring him right in the face, and he had the sinking feeling that past and present were on one hell of a collision course.

"What are you doing here, Hancock?"

But he knew. He knew exactly why Hancock was here, but he wanted to hear it from the man himself. And then he was going to let Hancock know that it would be a cold day in hell before he ever touched Grace.

"Put down the gun, Rio. I'm armed but you'd have me before I could ever draw. I'm packaged up. See?" He held up his arms so Rio could see the strap of the rifle and the pistol that was holstered just below his armpit.

"I like my gun just where I have it. Now talk."

"I'm repaying a debt. You get a free pass. This time. My job is to bring Grace Peterson in regardless of how. My team is at least two miles away. They'll stay there until you've had time to move out."

He lifted his head a notch so he stared Rio in the eye.

"Next time? All bets are off. I'll bring her in even if I have to go through you."

A growl rose from Rio's throat, and it took everything he had not to lunge at the man he'd once called friend.

Then he turned sideways to look at where Grace lay on the ground, broken and so very fragile. Then he stared back at Hancock. "Take a good look, Hancock. See what you've done. Is this what it's come to now? Preying on innocent women?"

Hancock didn't so much as flinch. "It's a job. Just like all the other jobs. You know the drill, Rio. Don't act like a fucking choir boy. You may have joined up with Captain America and crew, but it doesn't change a goddamn thing about who you were and where you came from. Your hands are just as stained as mine, and you'll never wipe them clean. I owe you. You saved my life. That's the only reason why you're walking out of these mountains. Don't make the mistake of underestimating me or of ever thinking I'll look the other way again."

Rio took a step forward. Then another. Until he was nose to nose with Hancock and could feel the other man's breath on his chin. His voice was cold, so chilled that it made the air around them seem warm. "You don't need to underestimate *me*. You stay the hell away from Grace

Peterson. I'll take you out, Hancock, and I won't have a single regret."

"Guess we know where we stand. I'm coming after you, Rio. This'll be your only warning."

Hancock took a step back, turned and then melted into the trees, gone before Rio could say or do anything further. As questionable as Titan may be, they had a code and they lived by it. It would have been easy for Hancock to take a stand. Make a grab for Grace. He could have pinned Rio and his men in the mountains. With an injured Grace, it would have been next to impossible for Rio and his men to escape, at least not without getting themselves or her killed.

But Hancock was a hard-ass bastard who had a code of honor even if it was a twisted sense of justice. Rio had saved his life once and now the debt was paid. Not only had Hancock looked the other way, but he'd tipped his hand and let Rio know who was after Grace.

He only wished to God the information made him feel better.

He turned back and hurried to Grace, his jaw clenched.

"What the fuck was all that about?" Terrence demanded.

"Not now, T," Rio said in a clipped voice. "We need to get the fuck out of here before Hancock decides he's been charitable enough for the day."

Alton and Browning quickly set to work padding the bed of the truck with a bedroll. They even took their shirts off and laid them across the sleeping bag in an effort to give Grace as much padding as possible.

Terrence and Diego lifted Grace from the ground, and Rio hopped into the back of the truck, leaning against the cracked window. Next, Grace was carefully laid on the bedroll and Rio covered as much of her as possible. Her hair was an issue. Long, black as night but dirty and tangled from her ordeal. He tucked as much of it as he could behind her neck and arranged one of the shirts over her head so she wasn't visible. Not that it mattered, really. Hancock and Titan knew where she was and they sure as hell knew what she looked like. There was little need in concealing her. They just needed to get the hell out.

Diego climbed into the back with him while Browning and Alton piled into the front with Terrence. Diego positioned himself against the back window just as Rio had so that Grace was between them. With their legs stretched out, they provided stability, or as much as they could, so Grace didn't move from side to side.

Rio slid his hand underneath the T-shirt covering Grace's face and rubbed his thumb gently over her cheek.

Stay with me, Grace. Hang in there. You're not a quitter, so don't fucking quit on me now. Not when I'm getting you the hell out of here. You'll like it where I'm taking you. You'll do nothing but rest, eat good food and get better.

There was no response. No stirring in his mind. He hadn't expected one. Grace was beyond her endurance. He wasn't convinced she'd survive this no matter how much he willed it to happen. And now that he knew Titan was involved, he knew they would be relentless. There would be no stopping them. It was a kill-or-be-killed situation.

No longer were they taking on some nameless, faceless, shadowy organization. Titan was government. Buried so deep that only a few even knew of their existence. Highly trained. The best of the best. Funding. Backing. They were invincible.

And they'd been given orders to bring Grace in.

"Who is he, Rio?" Diego asked. "You haven't said a word. We need to know the sitch and you're sitting like a stone. I get that it's bad, but we need to know how bad."

"As bad as it gets," Rio said grimly. "Fuck."

He wiped a hand through his hair. Some of the strands had pulled free of the thong that secured it into a ponytail at his nape. He shoved a piece behind his ear and stared down at the slight bump in the bedroll.

Grace Peterson wasn't just another mission. She wasn't just another victim. He had a very personal stake in this and he couldn't even explain why. He'd volunteered for this job. Sam had been ready to send Steele and his team after

Shea's sister, but after seeing the footage of Grace on the video surveillance just before she disappeared, he'd demanded the assignment. Hell, he hadn't given Sam a choice. He'd told Sam he and his team were going after Grace and bugged out shortly after.

There was no way in hell he was going to let Titan get their hands on Grace. Not that they'd hurt her. In fact, he was certain they had strict instructions not to damage her in any way. But once charged with an assignment, they were relentless. Failure wasn't an option, and in all the years Rio had worked with them, they hadn't ever botched a job.

It wasn't their job to judge. Hell, they didn't have a conscience. It wasn't for them to decide right or wrong. They just followed orders. A conscience was for the weak. They operated as an emotionless machine, and that was what made them so fucking dangerous.

Rio rubbed a hand tiredly over his face. He knew Hancock would come after him with both barrels. It only made him gladder that he'd covered his tracks so well when he'd finally left. Rio had lived his entire life in the shadows. He didn't know any other way. He had a damn fortress in Belize, and until recently, no one but he knew of its existence.

Now KGI knew of it. The wildcard was Resnick. Steele's warning ran through his mind all over again. What was Resnick's involvement and could he be trusted?

He had to get in touch with Sam and warn him. If Titan was after Grace, they'd sure as hell have pegged Shea too. Rio needed information and he needed it yesterday.

"Okay, so it's bad. Give me more to work with, boss man. Will I need lube for this ass fucking?"

Rio grimaced at Diego's dry humor.

"It's a long damn story and I'm not telling it more than once. When we get the fuck out of here, I'll give you all a full report. End result is we're going to have to watch our asses, and if Grace survives to see tomorrow, we're going to have to work damn hard to keep her safe."

CHAPTER 9

AS soon as they reached a town large enough, they ditched the truck and Diego hot-wired an SUV. Driving a stolen vehicle was the very last thing Rio wanted—having Titan breathing down their necks was bad enough. They didn't need local police interference.

When they reached Texas, Rio would have connections. He had people he could count on. Until then, they had to hope like hell they could get there in one piece.

The first call he made after making sure Grace was as comfortable as he could make her was to his buddy Lazaro to let him know he was coming in hot and he needed a plane to Belize.

Then he placed the call to Sam.

"Talk to me, Rio," Sam said by way of greeting.

"No, I need you to fucking talk to me," Rio said. "What's going on with Resnick and how is he involved in all of this?"

There was a long pause and Rio could picture well the deep frown on Sam's face. He wouldn't have liked the two team leaders communicating behind his back but oh well. Steele may not be Rio's favorite person in the world, but the man had his back and he had Steele's.

"Do you have Grace yet?" Sam asked tersely.

"I need you to tell me what the fuck is going on."

"There is some question as to Resnick's involvement," Sam finally said. "Involved, definitely. He nabbed Shea from the KGI compound because the stupid bastard was trying to protect her and Grace. What he did was get her abducted by the assholes who want to use her and Grace as their experimental projects. It's a long, involved story, but Resnick has a connection to the lab where Grace and Shea were born. Or rather they were created by pairing egg and sperm from donors with special gifts or abilities. Resnick was one such failed experiment."

"What the fuck?"

"Bear with me here. Grace and Shea were taken from the lab by the Petersons. They ran and kept running for most of the girls' lives. Resnick later funded them, but then the Petersons were killed and Grace and Shea went on the run. So not only was Resnick hunting them down, but so were the assholes who wanted to harness their powers."

"So what side does Resnick line up on then?" Rio demanded.

Sam sighed. "Who the hell knows? He says he wants to protect them. He went to bat when we rescued Shea from a compound in New Mexico. He swears he'll go public before he allows any harm to come to them."

"Do you trust him?"

Sam snorted. "Do I trust anyone who works for Uncle Sam?"

Relief lightened some of Rio's edginess. He didn't want to question any of the Kelly brothers' motives, but he wasn't a fool either. They may sign his paychecks, and he gave them a lot of loyalty, but nobody got blind faith from him.

"Now you give me some info," Sam said in an impatient tone.

"I have Grace," Rio said in a low voice. "She's not good. Not good at all."

Sam swore softly. "This is going to kill Shea and she's still struggling with her own recovery."

"Look, Sam. We're dealing with some heavy-duty shit. There are things you don't know. About me. My past."

There was heavy silence. "I know you did a lot off the record," Sam said quietly.

"Titan. Ask your man Resnick about it. He probably knows what it is. I don't have the time to explain. But Titan is involved. Black ops. Off the books. These guys are legit. They don't fuck around. They damn sure aren't amateurs. They're some of the most highly trained operatives you'll ever encounter. And they've been called up to bring Grace in."

"Fuck."

"Yeah, fuck. Look, if they want Grace, chances are they aren't giving Shea a pass. You need to look out for you and yours. Think about moving Shea and then you need to watch your six. These men will do anything to accomplish their mission. The mission *is* everything. It's the *only* thing. Get in their way and they'll take you down. I'm taking Grace with me. Let Shea know . . . Hell, lie to her for now. Just tell her Grace is safe and is with me. Tell her whatever you have to. Between you and me, I don't know how much Grace has left, but Shea doesn't need to know that."

"Christ," Sam muttered. "Steele and his team are on a mission. Simple in and out. Hostage retrieval. Something they can do in their sleep. I expect them back in two days."

"You may not have two days."

"Then we'll do whatever needs to be done," Sam said in a grim, determined voice. "I'll let my brothers know and then we'll get Nathan and Shea the hell out of here."

"Good call. I'm doing the same with Grace."

There was another distinct pause. "Safe journey, Rio. If you need backup, you got it. Steele will be available in forty-eight hours or so. I'll send Joe and Swanny with Nathan and Shea so they aren't unprotected, but you know Van, Garrett or Ethan will come to you at a moment's notice."

"If it's all the same, we'll be going to ground. Radio silent. I'll check in when I think it's safe to do so and not before."

"You don't fully trust me," Sam said mildly.

"I trust you as much as I trust anyone."

Sam laughed. "That doesn't say a whole lot, you bastard. Just don't get yourself killed."

"You just protect your family," Rio said in a quiet voice. "And I'll protect what's mine."

GRACE opened her eyes and blinked at the stab of sunlight that shone through a dirty window. Her brow furrowed and she squinted, trying to bring her surroundings into focus. The last thing she remembered was reaching Rio's teammates and having the last of her strength flee.

Where was she now?

She lifted her head, shocked at the effort it took. She was in the backseat of an SUV. Looking forward, Rio and his team were crammed into the middle row and the front two seats. She struggled to sit up, and Rio turned in his seat, his gaze freezing her in her tracks.

"How are you feeling?" he asked.

She eased back down, her breath leaving her in a hard whoosh. "I don't know. Let me get back to you on that."

He smiled, warmth flooding those dark eyes.

"Where are we?" she asked weakly.

"We rolled into New Mexico a couple of hours ago. Making good time. If we keep pace, we'll get into El Paso by sundown."

"What's in El Paso?"

She shifted and tried to sit up again, but Rio reached over the seat and put his hand on her shoulder. "Don't. Just take it easy. Lie there and be as still as possible so you'll heal."

She turned slightly so that she was more on her side then sighed when she was comfortable again.

"As for what's in El Paso, I have a friend there who's getting us on a plane to Belize."

Her eyes went wide and she stared up at him, mouth drooping open. "Belize? Why Belize?"

"My home is there," he said. "It's safe. For now. We can at least have a place where you can recover until we figure out our next move."

"I don't have any ID. I mean no passport. No driver's license. Nothing."

Terrence turned, a wide grin on his face. "The kind of transportation we're taking isn't exactly American Airlines, if you know what I mean. They won't be asking you for a ticket to board."

"Oh."

Rio slid his fingers over her arm. "I don't want you to worry. All I want you to focus on is healing. Let us do the rest."

She nodded, realizing she had no other choice. She was at these men's mercy. She'd already made her choice to trust them. She certainly knew what the other alternative was, and it wasn't an option. At least Rio hadn't locked her up in some cold, sterile room and forced her to heal like a trained puppet. At least not yet.

She lowered her head to the seat and closed her eyes. Belize. It scared her to death to think of going outside the United States. It seemed so permanent, like the final nail in a coffin. She had no recourse in a foreign country. No passport. No proof of citizenship. What could she possibly do if these men did turn out to be her enemies?

No, she couldn't dwell on that because her panic was rising with every minute that passed. These were the good guys. She had to believe that. Because if they turned out to be of the same caliber as those who'd kept her prisoner for so many days, it was over for her.

Rio shook her awake sometime later. She rubbed her hand over her eyes, not having realized that she'd fallen back under. The vehicle was cloaked in darkness. It was also slowing to a stop.

"Just stay down, Grace," Rio murmured. "Stay low until

I tell you to get up, okay? I just want to check things out here first."

Rio got out of the back of the SUV then motioned for Terrence and Diego to keep watch over Grace while Alton and Browning took up posts on either side of the truck.

Then he walked toward the rickety storage shed that doubled as the "office" for Lazaro's transport business. As soon as he neared, he heard the betraying click of a gun being put off safety.

He drew his own weapon and then called out, "It's me, you stupid paranoid bastard. Put your damn gun up before you get yourself killed."

There was a moment of silence followed by a scuffling sound. Then the door creaked open and a tall, lanky man stuck a shotgun through the crack.

"Rio? That you?"

Rio sighed. "Who the fuck else would it be? I called you an hour ago and told you we were close."

Lazaro slipped out, still clutching the shotgun, but he pointed it upward instead of at Rio, a fact Rio was grateful for. Lazaro was as jumpy as a frog. It wouldn't take much for him to accidentally discharge his weapon.

"The plane ready?" Rio asked.

Lazaro nodded and jerked a thumb over his shoulder. "It's around back. Pilot will be here in five minutes. You'll make an unscheduled, off-the-books stopover in Belize and then the plane will continue on to Peru on a delivery route. I've already done the paperwork and made it all official like. As long as you don't make a splash when you get to Belize, no one should ever know. Buddy of mine there is willing to keep it all hush-hush. No record of any plane landing there, if you know what I mean."

Rio clapped Lazaro on the back. "Good man. I knew I could count on you."

"Get loaded," Lazaro returned. "You don't have a whole lot of time."

CHAPTER 10

"**WHAT** the fuck do you mean, they escaped the mountains?" Gordon Farnsworth bellowed. "I called you in because you're the best. This isn't acceptable. Not on any level."

"Keep your underwear on," Hancock said in a cool voice Farnsworth didn't like. It was too collected. It was too "I don't give a fuck what you think or say." On some level, Farnsworth knew he needed to tread lightly. Titan wasn't a force to be fucked around with. But desperation made a man do and say stupid things.

"The idiots who were hired to bring her in the first time made a clusterfuck of the entire situation. The mountains are littered with their dumbasses. We're stuck cleaning up their damn messes. Grace Peterson escaped because she's not acting alone. She has help. Good help."

Farnsworth swore. "Who? Tell me who. I'll take care of it."

"Doesn't matter who," Hancock said calmly. "I'll find Grace Peterson and I'll bring her in. You'd be best served to stay out of it and let us handle the situation."

It was the closest that anyone had ever come to telling Gordon Farnsworth what to do. No one else dared. But there was something in this man's voice that gave him pause. Farnsworth tasted fear for the first time in his life and he didn't like it a bit.

"See that you do," he clipped out. "I don't have any time to waste. I don't have weeks or days. I may only have hours, and each hour that rolls by and she's not here is one hour I can't afford to lose."

There was silence in his ear and he was stunned to realize that he'd been hung up on. Swearing viciously, he shoved the phone into his pocket and strode down the hall to his daughter's room.

At her door, he paused, breathing in heavily, ridding himself of the rage and the awful taste of fear in his mouth. Elizabeth needed him to be strong.

He pushed inside and saw the nurse he'd hired to remain by Elizabeth's bedside day and night checking Elizabeth's vital signs.

"How is she?" he whispered, afraid of the answer.

The nurse shook her head. "No change. She's resting easily. Breathing is good for now. No temperature."

Farnsworth waved her away and then settled into the chair beside his daughter's bed. He collected her tiny, frail hand in his and bowed his head, staring down at his feet. He closed his eyes as cold fury laced with paralyzing fear gripped him.

He couldn't lose her. She was the only good thing in his life.

"Daddy?" she whispered.

He yanked up his head, surprised to see her awake and staring at him.

"What are you doing?"

He put his other hand to her cheek and rubbed his thumb up and down, the knot growing in his throat. "Just checking on you and saying good night. How are you feeling?"

"I'm good."

It was her standard answer no matter how she really felt.

It enraged him that she sought to protect him. She never wanted him to know when she was tired or hurting. It should be him protecting her. Him finding a way to make her well again.

"That's good," he said, moving his hand to her forehead to stroke away the golden hair. "I need you to hang in there. I have someone coming who can help you."

Elizabeth cast him a doubtful look. It was what he'd said a hundred times before when he'd brought in a new doctor. And always the result had been the same. Nothing could be done.

"This time will be different," he promised. He leaned forward to kiss her forehead. "This person is going to make you all better, and then think of all the wonderful, fun things we can do together. I want you to make a list. We'll do every single thing on it."

And he would. He'd spend any amount of money in the world to make her happy.

"I'll do it tomorrow, Daddy. I'm tired tonight."

He squeezed her hand. "Of course you will. We'll make a list together. How's that sound? Maybe we can order pizza and have a party right here."

Elizabeth closed her eyes. "That would be awesome. Maybe I'll feel better by then."

Tears burned Farnsworth's eyelids and he furiously blinked them away. "Go to sleep, baby. Daddy's right here. I won't leave until you're asleep."

CHAPTER 11

THEY landed in Belize in the dead of night. Rio helped Grace from the plane after wrapping her in a dark, hooded coat. The warm, humid air was a welcome change to the chill of the Rocky Mountains. She embraced it, breathed it in to alleviate some of the cold that had settled into her bones.

Some of her shock had worn off and her mind wasn't as fuzzy as it had been for so long. But with the new awareness came consequences. Fear that she'd trusted the wrong men. Memories of the horrors she'd endured. Phantom pain mixed with the very real pain of her current injuries. It all mixed and swirled in her mind and body, overwhelming her.

Lucidity sucked.

Rio ushered her into a pitch-black battered van and instructed her to lie down in the cargo area. Truth be told, she'd done nothing by lie flat on her back for the last umpteen hours. She crawled inside but sat up with her back resting on the side of the van.

Her rib cage was still sore as hell, but her breathing felt

normal to her. Perhaps not quite as strong or as deep. She could tell her respirations were shallower than usual. But she was at least in the early stages of healing and already she could tell the difference.

She glanced down at her arm and slid her fingers over the area where the break had occurred. She flexed the affected fingers, satisfied that there was no lingering numbness. Terrence setting the break had helped enormously even if it had hurt like hell. If he hadn't done it, she might have lost the hand before her body began the healing process.

There was still some swelling, and definite tenderness and bruising, but there was no crepitus to denote weakness in the fracture.

In a day's time, provided she had ample time to rest, she should demonstrate marked improvement.

Rio hopped into the back a moment later, and the doors shut behind him. When one of the front doors opened, the overhead light came on and Rio's eyes narrowed.

"I thought I told you to lie down. I don't want you to make your injuries worse."

"I'll be fine," she said quietly.

"How is your breathing?"

"Good," she huffed out. She was still a little short of breath, but nothing that was going to kill her. She'd already survived unimaginable events.

The light went off as all the doors closed and the van pulled away. She and Rio rocked and swayed as they went over a series of bumps.

"Is your house far?" she asked.

"Up the river," he said shortly. "It's a short drive to where we'll put in."

"The river?"

"Yeah, we'll take a boat the rest of the way."

She was gripped by a sudden chill and she wrapped her arms around her waist, ignoring the slight protest offered by the arm she'd broken.

She couldn't shake her unease. So far Rio had proven to

her that he was a man of his word. But the farther he took her from civilization and all she knew, the more her panic increased.

She'd learned the hard way that she could trust no one. Her entire life had been spent on the run, moving from town to town, house to house, always shrouded in secrecy. And then when her parents had been murdered, she and Shea had split up and running had become their reality.

Had she traded one hell for another? How did she know Rio wasn't working for people who wanted to cash in on her gift just as the others had? Was he even now taking her to some isolated laboratory, hidden so deeply that she'd never be found?

She began to shake, and she hunched forward, pulling her knees to her chest and ignoring the pain the movement caused.

"Grace?"

She ignored the question in his voice and laid her forehead on the tops of her knees, sucking in breaths.

His hand slid through her hair, gentle and comforting. "Hey, what's going on? You're shaking like a leaf."

She lifted her head and stared through the darkness. "I'm scared."

He scooted closer until his leg touched her feet and she could feel his warmth wrapping around her. "Of?"

She took another breath and opened herself to him, hoping that she'd get something from him, some hint of his true intentions or at least if he was genuine or not. He'd claimed that he'd heard her, mentally, and she remembered his voice in her head but she couldn't be sure she hadn't imagined it.

"Of you. Them. All of this. I'm scared that I've traded one kind of hell for another. Same prison. Same horror. Just different jailors."

At first she thought she'd angered him. Then she assumed he'd rush to reassure her. But he did nothing. For a long moment he was silent.

"You're smart to be wary," he finally said. His statement

took her by surprise. She hadn't expected this. "You've been through a lot. There's nothing I can say that's going to make you think any differently. You're just going to have to see for yourself and make up your own mind whether you trust me."

He wasn't saying anything she didn't already know, but it seemed different coming from him. And she supposed it didn't matter to him one way or another whether she trusted him or not. She assumed he was getting paid to do this and not acting out of the goodness of his heart. For that matter, she wasn't entirely certain what he was, who he was or what his connection to her sister was.

She opened her mouth, intending to get clarification on just that, when the van ground to a halt.

Seconds later, the back opened and Diego stood there motioning for them to get down. Rio went first and she crawled after him. When she reached the edge, he and Diego both reached to lift her down.

She landed softly on her feet.

"Can you make it?" Rio asked.

"Yeah."

She stared at her surroundings and saw the inky black water of a river that snaked through the landscape. The moon was high overhead but covered by a thin layer of clouds, moving rapidly through the sky.

"Let's go," Rio murmured, taking her arm.

He led her to the water's edge and into an aluminum boat with an outboard motor operated by a hand-held lever. She stepped down and wobbled when the boat swayed. Terrence, who was already in the boat, quickly steadied her and held on to her hand while she made her way toward the front.

Diego motioned for her to take the bench directly in the middle. Rio came to sit beside her. Diego and Terrence took the front while Alton and Browning settled in the back. Alton took position to pilot the boat and a moment later they eased away from the bank and slipped down-river.

It was eerie traveling through the dark waters. The only light was from the sliver of moon visible through the hazy cloud cover. Unease gripped her and she warily stared from side to side but she couldn't even see the shoreline. Only the dim shape of passing trees and what looked to be thick, junglelike terrain.

Fear knotted in her throat. Heavy silence was thick like fog. Only the gentle purr of the motor as they pushed farther down the river echoed through the still night.

Her heart thudded and adrenaline surged through her veins when she saw a burst of light to her right. She whipped around to see a flaming torch make two circles in the dark before quickly being extinguished. Rio uttered what sounded like an animal call, though she sure as hell didn't know what kind of animal made such a sound and she wasn't in any hurry to find out.

There was an answering call from the shore and then the sound faded as they continued on their way.

"What was that?" she whispered.

"Shhh," Rio said. "Not now. Remain quiet."

Chastened, she hunkered down and stared straight ahead. This whole scene was something straight out of a horror movie or some terrible remake of *Anaconda* or something. She half expected something to explode out of the water and rip their boat to shreds then swallow them all whole.

She hated the dark. Hated being scared shitless and hated the thought of what was in the water below them.

She only hoped that wherever the hell they were going, they'd get there soon.

Moments later, her prayers were answered when the boat turned and glided into a dark inlet off the main stretch of the river. Alton beached the boat, and Diego and Terrence quickly hopped out to pull it farther onto the shore.

"Let's go," Rio said shortly.

He urged her forward and Diego was waiting to lift her out of the front. Rio came next, followed by Alton and Browning.

She paused a moment to gather her bearings and stop the endless shaking of her knees and legs. Rio bumped into her then put his hand on her shoulder to steady her.

"It's not far," he said quietly. "Just a hike through the jungle about a quarter mile. I didn't want to hit the inlet closest to the house. We'll circle around back and go in through one of the escape routes."

She arched an eyebrow. "Sounds like you've got a place like my parents did."

"You could say that. I don't much believe in paranoia. In my line of work, expecting the worst saves your ass."

She couldn't argue with that.

He urged her forward once more, but he kept his hand at her elbow, while Terrence and Diego led the way. Every once in a while they'd stop and hold back a tangle of vines and branches so Grace could pass and then they resumed their journey through the dark. It was so dark, she could barely make out Terrence's hulking figure in front of her.

A few minutes later, they stopped and Terrence and Diego bent, pulled aside what appeared to be camouflage netting and then pulled open a wooden door from the ground. It reminded Grace of a storm cellar, only this was flush to the ground and not readily visible.

Diego dropped down and Terrence stood guard at the entrance, motioning for the others to precede him. Rio held on to Grace's hand until she found her footing and Diego was waiting, his hands around her legs as she descended.

The smell of dirt and mud was heavy. The ceiling was low and she had to duck, even at her height, so she didn't bump her head. This was no high-tech escape tunnel like her father had constructed. It was a tunnel carved into the earth, with no lighting, no support.

She ran her hand along the side of the tunnel and felt dirt and a tangle of roots.

Then Rio flipped on a flashlight, blinding her momentarily. He handed it ahead to Diego, who shined it down the tunnel to light their way. Rio then moved in front of Grace to follow Diego, but he reached back to take her hand.

She found comfort in the gesture as he pulled her along behind him. He held her hand tightly, his fingers laced with hers as they plunged ahead.

They came to a halt a few minutes later and Rio pushed in front of Diego and entered a code into the electronic keypad. The barricade that looked like a solid wall of steel suddenly parted.

Once again, Rio reached back for Grace's hand and pulled her inside the door. They were in what looked like an ordinary mudroom.

"Shoes off," Rio said, a slight quirk at the corner of his mouth. "I'm kind of picky about getting my floors dirty."

She wasn't entirely certain he was serious until the others started shucking their boots. She toed off her worn sneakers and then he unlocked yet another door.

This time, when they entered, it was into a spacious room that looked precisely like a normal residence. It was a living room, with couches, a coffee table, and a huge fireplace, although she noticed it wasn't a traditional wood-burning hearth. It looked like a gas log.

There was a multitude of comfortable-looking leather chairs and a huge big-screen TV mounted above the fireplace. It looked like a veritable man cave. The perfect bachelor's den.

Rio flipped a series of switches, and more lights came on until Grace was blinking rapidly to adjust.

"Welcome to my home," he said in a somber tone. He extended his arm with a slight flourish. *"Mi casa es su casa."*

CHAPTER 12

SAM Kelly stood on the deck overlooking an expanse of Kentucky Lake, gripping the railing as he leaned forward. He was waiting for Resnick to call him back, and he found he had little patience to play a waiting game.

When it came to his family and the members of his KGI teams, he was fiercely protective. With Rio's cryptic call, he now knew that both were in danger and they all had to be careful of every step.

Already he'd sent Nathan and Shea away. Shea was still vulnerable and fragile, though she was improving with each day. Sam worried, though, that this would set her progress back. Hers and Nathan's both.

He sighed wearily. Sometimes the weight of so much worry wore him down. It was a burden shared by his brothers, but it didn't make it any easier for Sam to bear.

The door leading out to the deck slid open. Light footsteps and then a warm, soothing hand slid over his back. Sophie. His wife. The mother of his child. How could it be possible that she meant more to him with each passing day?

He turned, seeking the comfort of the hug he knew was coming. And sure enough, her slim arms wrapped around his waist and she went into his arms, burying her face in his chest.

He tucked her head underneath his chin and savored the sweet scent of her hair. Of her. Nothing ever felt as right as Sophie did in his arms.

She pulled away and tilted her chin up so she stared into his eyes. "What are you out here fretting over?"

His mouth formed a grim line. "I hate this, Soph. I hate it all. I wonder sometimes if this family will ever find true peace. When does it end?"

She reached up to touch his jaw, tracing a line with her fingers before stopping at his chin. "I know you're worried about Nathan and Shea and now Rio and not knowing where he is. But Nathan will be fine. Joe and Swanny are with him."

He caught her hand and kissed the soft skin of her palm. "I love you, you know."

She smiled. "I do know. I hate to see you like this. Always taking on the burden of responsibility by yourself. You have so many others willing to share it with you. Garrett. Donovan. Even Ethan. Your parents. We're a team, you know? We're family. And family supports family."

He trapped her in his arms and hung his arms loosely around her waist. Then he leaned in to kiss her. "How did you get so damn smart, Mrs. Kelly?"

Her eyes sparkled mischievously. "I've been told ever since I came back into your life what family is for and what it's all about. Maybe it's time I started dishing back what I've been served."

He lowered his head until their foreheads touched. "You're a pretty special woman, Sophie. My woman. My wife. My love. I don't want you to ever forget that."

"And you're mine, Sam Kelly. You damn well better never forget that fact, mister."

He chuckled and then kissed her again. He was about to

suggest they go inside and find some extracurricular activities to indulge in when the sat phone beeped an incoming transmission.

He grimaced. "I have to take this. I've been expecting a call from Resnick. I need to tell him what all Rio had to say."

Sophie retreated a few steps but held on to his hand for a bit longer. "I'll be waiting inside."

He watched her walk away, his heart in his throat. It happened every time he watched her. Love was an ever-changing emotion. Strengthening every day.

Halfheartedly, he reached for the phone. He'd rather be inside making love to his wife than on the phone with a man he was no longer certain he could trust. Resnick had been solid in the past. He'd brought many of KGI's missions to them. He was largely responsible for the success of Sam's brainchild. Uncle Sam had certainly pushed enough money KGI's way over the years.

But they'd damn sure earned every penny.

"I need information," Sam said bluntly as he put the phone to his ear. He was in no mood for pleasantries, not that there would be any.

Resnick had been responsible for Shea falling into the hands of the bastards pursuing her, and as a result, she'd been all but tortured, hooked to a machine that monitored brain activity so that every time she tried to reach out to Nathan with her mind, she'd received an electrical charge.

While KGI may have helped Resnick in the days following Shea's rescue, they damn sure hadn't forgiven him. Nor could they be certain how well intentioned he'd claimed to be.

"What is it you need?" Resnick asked.

Sam could perfectly picture the nervous, agitated bastard lighting a cigarette and sucking on it like a whore giving a blow job.

"Titan," Sam said.

There was a long silence. Too long. Resnick's breathing filtered over the line.

"What about them?" Resnick finally asked.

"I need to know everything you know about them and I need it all yesterday."

"What the fuck is going on, Sam? Level with me here. Titan is or rather *was* some heavy-duty shit. Deep. Like as deep as it goes. But they aren't anymore."

"What do you mean anymore?"

"Tell me why first," Resnick persisted.

Sam's nostrils flared. "Listen to me, you little prick. You owe me. You owe KGI. More than you could possibly ever repay. If it weren't for me pulling Nathan off you, he would have killed your sorry ass. Hell, he'd be there kicking your teeth in now if I'd let him. I'm not playing games with you here. I need to know who and what Titan is and why they'd be after Grace and possibly Shea."

"Fuck," Resnick breathed. His voice came out all shaky. Sam could hear the forceful exhale as he puffed on his cigarette. "Look, Sam, back in the day, Titan was the badass. They were who you called in when no one else could get the job done. They cleaned up messes. They created them. They did whatever the hell the military or government needed done. No questions asked. Their fingerprints are all over some of the world's biggest shake-ups. But they never existed."

"Yeah, I know how that goes," Sam said dryly.

"They never officially existed, but here's the thing, Sam. As of two years ago they no longer unofficially existed either. They were disbanded, retired, whatever the fuck you want to call it. A few politicians out to make names for themselves got a little too close for comfort so they shut Titan down."

Sam frowned. "I got a call from Rio who says differently. He told me that Titan was after Grace and that Shea could be a target too. He told me to make sure Shea was safe and that he would take care of Grace."

"Wait a minute," Resnick said eagerly. "He has Grace? He found her? Is she okay? When is he bringing her in?"

"He's not."

"What?"

"Rio isn't taking any chances with her safety. He thinks, and I agree, that it would be stupid to put the girls together right now. He warned me about Titan. Said a lot of the same things you told me, which tells me he has firsthand knowledge of this group. If he says they're after her, then I believe him."

"Fuck, Sam. Fuck, fuck, fuck. This isn't good. If he's right, then it means that Titan has gone rogue or for hire. Which means we have no idea who they work for or what their goal is. They could be working for anyone in the world."

"Exactly. My first priority is the safety of my family and my teams. I've taken steps to ensure their well-being. Rio has Grace. I believe he'd die before allowing anything to happen to her."

"I hope you're willing to bet that on her life," Resnick said. "Because your man, Rio? Was Titan's front man from its inception until he walked away several years ago. Maybe you should think about that and whether you should trust him with the woman that he claims Titan is after."

CHAPTER 13

WHAT was she supposed to do now? Flop onto the couch? Catch some television? She stood stiffly as the others came in behind her, shedding backpacks, setting rifles aside and conversing among themselves.

She knew what she wanted, but somehow it seemed . . . rude. She nearly laughed at the notion that after all she'd been through, she was concerned with not being Miss Manners.

She wanted a bed. Any bed. Hell, even the floor. She just wanted to be able to relax, let go of some of the awful tension and fear. She wanted to sleep where she felt safe and protected.

Rio took a step toward her and put a gentle hand on her shoulder. "Diego is going to take a look at you. I thought you might like a shower first. I have a shower and a tub. Will you be okay on your own or do you need help?"

Heat singed her cheeks and for a moment her lips went numb. What the hell was she supposed to say to that? Even if she couldn't bloody well get herself into and out of the shower, she sure as hell wasn't going to ask him to come in with her.

"I can manage," she said in a low voice.

"Okay, then I'll show you to the bedroom where you'll sleep. After you get out of the shower, Diego will check you over and by then I'll have you something to eat. You have to be starving."

She blinked in confusion. It had been so long since she'd eaten a normal meal that she'd forgotten what it was like. She'd lost weight and she could feel her ribs protruding against her skin. She probably looked like a damn gaunt scarecrow.

She rubbed over her slim abdomen as she stared down, almost as if expecting some sign of life from her belly. Truthfully the idea of food didn't appeal to her at all, but she knew she should at least make the effort.

"Come on," Rio said gently.

She let him guide her through the living room and down the hall past a series of rooms. At the end, he opened a door, flipped on the light and gestured her inside.

It was a large room. Huge, in fact. And it looked masculine. It was then she realized that this must be his room. She shook her head and took a step back.

"I can't take your room. Surely there's another one I can have."

Rio smiled and shook his head. "Nope. Taken by the other guys unless you want to bunk with one of them."

Her forehead crinkled and he laughed, making her realize her expression had reflected her horror over that idea.

"I'll take the couch. I just need a blanket. Not even that really. The couch will feel like heaven."

"Grace," he said, lightly touching his finger to her lips. "Shut up. You're staying here with me."

Her eyes widened and her legs started to tremble.

"Don't look so afraid. I'm going to be camping on the floor next to the bed. The others will be just down the hall. I want you to feel safe and you will be. We're going to do all we can to make sure you're protected."

"You can't sleep on the floor," she fretted. She pulled up her hands to wring them. Somehow the image of him lying on the floor while she slept in such wonderful comfort made her feel guilty. He was already doing so much for her.

Rio smiled again. "Honey, the floor of my house is far superior to a lot of the places I've slept in the past. I have some pretty damn fine linens. A down comforter and a few down pillows and I'll think I'm staying at a five-star hotel. Now stop arguing with me and get into the shower. I'm sending Diego in after half an hour, so if you don't want him seeing what he shouldn't, you need to hurry it up. I'll be in right behind him with food."

Her eyes watered suspiciously and she swiped at one with the back of her hand. A hand that was dirty and shaking.

"And don't you dare cry on me either," he warned. "A woman who's survived all you've survived doesn't cry. She holds her head up and dares the world around her to fuck with her."

Her lips trembled upward into a smile, but his gentle reproach just made her want to cry all the more.

To her surprise, he gently gathered her in his arms and hugged her. His big arms surrounded her and his chest was a solid wall of support. He held her there, smoothing a hand up and down her back to comfort her.

"It's going to be okay, Grace."

Such simple words and yet so powerful. Full of promise and encouragement. She hadn't realized just how badly she needed them. She closed her eyes and rested her head just below his chin. Then she carefully slid her arms around his waist and pressed herself more fully against him, enjoying the comfort of another's touch.

"Thank you," she whispered.

He ran his fingers through her hair and then gently pulled away, his hand still stroking her hair away from her face. "Go on now. Get cleaned up and feeling human again. I'll put out something for you to wear."

What she wanted to do most was to lean back into his

arms and wallow in the warmth and comfort of his embrace. She was starved for touch. Affection. Human contact that wasn't *forced* on her.

She missed her sister, and here, standing in front of this man who'd hugged her, she felt the loss of her sibling more keenly than ever before.

"You say you promised Shea," she said huskily. "So you know her. You've seen her and talked to her. How is she? Is she safe?"

Rio's eyes softened and he once again touched her as if he knew just how much she craved it. "How about I promise to tell you all about it once you've been tended to and had something to eat. Better yet, we'll talk over dinner."

Grace nodded and slowly turned toward the bathroom. She fumbled for the light switch and trudged inside. She barely took in the gorgeous bathroom. All she wanted was a shower and bed. She spared a glance at the huge tub but decided it would take too long.

She leaned into the large shower stall, turned on the water as hot as she could stand it and then stepped back to strip out of her tattered clothing.

She looked like something out of the zombie apocalypse.

As she stepped into the shower, she clipped the door with her side. Pain shot through her rib cage, and wincing, she pushed herself under the spray, standing there a long moment, her chest heaving as she sucked in deep breaths.

Finally the pain subsided and she began the arduous task of soaping her hair and body. By the time she was done, she was exhausted by the effort it had taken her to do something so simple.

She was careful as she rubbed the towel over her body. There wasn't a part of her that didn't hurt in some way or another. Her arm was still weak but she was relieved to note that the swelling had gone down and the bruising was already fading. It only bothered her when she flexed and extended her fingers.

After wrapping a towel around her hair, she then pulled

another of the big, soft towels around her body and went back into the bedroom.

She saw clothing laid out on the bed and headed toward it. She was halfway there when she abruptly pulled up, realizing she wasn't alone in the room.

Clutching the towel tighter around her, she cast a wary glance in Diego's direction.

"I'm sorry if I frightened you," he said softly, almost like he was trying to calm a wild animal. "I thought Rio had let you know that I was going to examine you."

"H-He did, but . . ." She clamped her lips shut to prevent the warbling and then tried again. "I'm not dressed. I mean he said he'd leave clothing out for me."

"I need to check you over before you dress," he said.

She took an instinctive step back.

He put his hand up. "Hey, it's okay. I'll get Rio. He should have been here by now with your food. It wasn't my intention to frighten you. He was supposed to be here when I looked you over. Tell you what. I'll go see what's keeping him. There's a robe in the closet you can put on until we get all this sorted out."

He opened the closet door, and a moment later came back with a thick, white robe. He laid it beside her clothing on the bed, flashed her a reassuring smile, and then went for the door.

Grace's shoulders sagged. Then she grabbed for the robe and hurried back to the bathroom before anyone else came into the bedroom while she was wearing nothing better than a towel.

RIO was heading down the hall when he met up with Diego. He stopped and frowned. "I thought you were going to take a look at Grace?"

"Yeah and I thought you'd have your ass back before she got out of the shower. I scared the piss out of her. She came out of the bathroom in just a towel because you left her clothes on the bed. She wasn't expecting me to be there, and when I mentioned that I'd need her not to be dressed when I looked her over, she went into meltdown mode."

Rio cursed under his breath. The last thing he'd wanted to do was frighten her.

He turned sideways and slipped past Diego and entered the bedroom, only to find it empty. The clothes were still on the bed.

"I gave her a robe," Diego said from behind him. "She was just wearing that towel, and she looked cold and extremely nervous. I thought the robe would make her feel not quite so vulnerable and it's possible that we can work it so that she stays mostly covered except for each part I check out in turn."

Rio thrust the tray at Diego. "Here, you take this. I'll get Grace out of the bathroom."

Diego took the tray and Rio hurried toward the bathroom door. He knocked softly. "Grace? Honey, you can come out now. I brought you some food. If you'll let Diego check you over, then I'll get rid of him so you can relax and eat and then we'll talk about Shea."

Rio turned to see Diego throw him a sour look. "Gee thanks," Diego mouthed.

The door cracked open and Rio turned back around to see Grace peering out, her eyes wide and wary.

"Hey," he said softly. "You ready to do this? We just need to make sure you're okay and don't need more medical attention than what we can provide you. He'll be quick."

"I want you here," she said in barely above a whisper.

His chest kind of caved in at the vulnerability in her voice. Already, whether she realized it or acknowledged it, there was a thread of trust between them. She felt safe with him. It was a start.

"I'm not going anywhere," he promised. "Come on out so we can get this over with before your food gets cold. I had gumbo in the freezer and I nuked it. It'll cure what ails you for sure. The ultimate comfort food."

He held out his hand, holding it just outside the crack in

the door where she could see it. Slowly, she opened the door wider and then slid her hand into his.

It was soft against the roughness of his. Velvety. An electric sensation shivered up his arm, prickling the hair all the way to his nape. Then she wrapped her slender fingers more firmly around his.

She was enveloped in his robe. It dragged the floor at her feet and the sleeves fell to her knuckles. She had it wrapped almost double around her and he smiled at the image she presented, all damp and shiny and wearing his clothing. He liked it and felt rather stupid about that fact.

He shook himself out of his stupor and tugged her into the bedroom. Diego had put her tray on the nightstand and stood away as if not wanting to overwhelm Grace more than she already was.

He led her to the bed and then paused. He put one hand on her shoulder and turned her so she looked directly into his eyes.

"Now you tell me how you want to do this, okay? I can leave, I can stay, I can sit beside you and not look. I'll hold your hand. You'll know I'm here but I won't do anything to make you uncomfortable."

"Just stay next to me. I mean unless you aren't comfortable with it," she added hastily. Then she closed her eyes. "I'm being stupid. I'm sorry. I can do this."

Rio tucked his fingers underneath her chin and nudged upward. "Grace, you've been brutalized by ruthless men over and over. I'd be a little worried if this didn't freak you out on some level. You're not stupid."

She sucked in a deep breath and then glanced nervously in Diego's direction. Then her shoulders sagged and she started to untie the robe. "Let's just get it over with."

Diego stepped forward and put his hand gently on Grace's hand to stop her. "Go to the side of the bed. Undo your robe. Rio and I will turn our backs while you get on the bed. Once you're there, cover yourself with the robe. I'll only uncover what I need as I examine you, okay?"

She gave him a tremulous smile. "Okay."

Rio dutifully turned his back while Grace walked around to the side. A moment later, he heard her move onto the bed.

"You can turn around now," she said softly.

Rio and Diego turned, though Diego didn't spend any time staring. He swiftly moved around to the side, brisk and all business. Rio stood for a moment, staring down at the woman with a robe pulled up to her chin. Only her bare feet and a portion of her legs poked out from underneath.

She looked . . . She looked scared and nervous and he wanted more than anything to make it all go away. He went around to the opposite side and then climbed onto the bed. He plumped the pillows behind his back so he could prop up beside her and then he reached for her hand and squeezed.

She smiled and it did funny things to his throat and his chest.

On her other side, Diego examined her injured arm, holding it up, asking her to flex and extend her fingers and then her wrist and then to bend at the elbow. She did all without complaint, though he saw a slight grimace when she made a fist.

Diego gently laid her arm back down and then pushed the robe up just enough that he bared a portion of her rib cage. He examined a small area, stopping to ask her if it hurt, then continued over the rest of her abdomen.

"Did most of this happen when you fell?" Diego asked. "Or were you injured before that as well?"

She sighed. "It's difficult to explain."

"Try me. Take your time."

She glanced over at Rio and he squeezed her hand again just to let her know that it was okay. She turned her head so that she stared up at the ceiling and then she took a deep breath.

"Before the fall, I was sick, injured, ill, whatever you want to call it because I'd healed so many people in a very short period of time. I never got a break. It was one after another, a never-ending litany of pain and madness. I was weak and I was sure I was going to die.

"When I fell, those injuries were . . . real time. Not that the others weren't. They were just different. They happened directly to me, not because I absorbed them from someone else. So to answer your question, the injuries from the fall were just more in a line of injuries, but the others had already started to heal, or as much as they could, given the circumstances."

Rio and Diego exchanged glances. She gave a very cut-and-dried explanation, but the underlying despair and anguish in her voice came through loud and clear. She'd suffered greatly. And even though the physical wounds would heal, the emotional wounds cut deep and would remain with her forever.

"All right, Grace, almost done. But I need you to tell me what all you hurt when you fell. You were a little out of it before. You said ribs and your arm. What about your head? Do you hurt anywhere else?"

She pursed her lips and wrinkled her brow in thought. Then she slowly shook her head.

"And how does it feel to you now? Does it feel like you're healing? Is it taking longer than usual?"

"It's slower. Hurts more. I feel more . . . fragile. Like I'm still broken somehow," she whispered.

Rio put his arm around her shoulders and then leaned into her. She immediately tucked her head underneath his chin.

Hell, she *was* broken. In spirit and body. How she was still so determined and hanging on was beyond him. He'd sensed her acceptance of her fate and yet it was like she simply didn't know how to give up. Even as she was thinking of death, she was pushing herself with superhuman strength. Past all endurance. A point when most everyone else would have just given up.

Diego carefully arranged the robe back over her. "I'd say you're doing remarkably well given that you most certainly broke ribs and punctured a lung. Your breath sounds had decreased markedly on one side and yet they sound almost normal now. You have a full range of motion with your arm, and I can't even tell where it was broken. That's pretty damn amazing."

"I guess I just don't know how to die," she said wanly.

Rio frowned. Diego's expression wasn't any better.

"How about we don't talk about dying and instead focus on getting you strong again," Rio said. "Starting with a good meal. Diego, are you finished?"

Diego nodded and started for the door.

"Diego?" Grace called.

He paused and turned around.

"Thank you."

He smiled. "My pleasure. You're an amazing woman, Grace. I'll never know how you made it out of those mountains in the condition you were in, but I'm damn proud of you for doing it."

Grace's cheeks colored under the praise and her lips held a glimmer of a smile as Diego turned and exited the room.

"I'm going to turn away and get your tray ready," Rio said. "Why don't you go get into the sweats and T-shirt I put out for you and then come climb into bed. I'll fix pillows for you to prop up on so you can eat off your tray."

She sat up, clutching the robe to her chest. "Then we'll talk about Shea?"

Rio nodded. "Yeah, I'll tell you all about Shea."

CHAPTER 14

GRACE hurriedly dressed, nervous that Rio was so close and she was completely naked. Not that she should be worried in the least that he'd be tempted or overtaken by lust. The last year had been hard on her and the last months especially harsh.

It was when she was yanking the oversized sweatshirt over her head that she realized she was self-conscious about the way she looked . . . to Rio. Not the others. Just Rio.

Embarrassment tightened her cheeks. Of all the things she could be thinking or should be contemplating, how she looked to this man shouldn't be one of them.

"You finished yet?"

She flinched and then realized that she'd been standing there, hands fisted around the hem of her sweatshirt at her sides for God only knew how long.

She turned and hastily crawled back onto the bed. "I'm done."

Rio turned and she could barely meet his gaze for feeling so stupid. She was a grown woman acting like an irresponsible twit. She was more than embarrassed. She was pissed at herself for deciding to give her girly side even a brief moment of freedom.

If and when she ever got out of this alive, she'd go book a day in a spa and get her fingers and toes done and indulge in pure girly delight. Then maybe she'd find some hunky replica of Rio and let her imagination run wild.

Until then, she needed to focus on actually being alive long enough to worry over what color she wanted her toes.

He helped her sit up against the headboard and positioned several pillows behind her. Then he put one across her lap and reached back for the tray on the nightstand. He set it up across the pillow and the aroma of the gumbo wafted through her nostrils.

Finally her stomach came to life and it was like it suddenly caved in and began kicking and screaming. Sweat broke out on her forehead and her stomach knotted viciously. Her hands shook as she reached for the spoon.

Rio's hand closed over hers, halting her motion. Gently he pried the spoon from her tight grip and then he stirred the gumbo. He lifted a spoonful to his mouth and tested it on his lips.

Then he put it to her lips.

She was too surprised to protest, and the warm liquid slid into her mouth. It was heaven in a spoon. Heat traveled down her throat all the way to her stomach.

When he went to repeat the process, she finally found her tongue. "Rio, don't. I can feed myself. God, I feel ridiculous. This is so embarrassing."

"Your hands are shaking so bad it'll be a wonder if you get any of the gumbo in your mouth. It'll be all over you and the bed. Now shut up and eat," he said mildly.

To reinforce his point, he put another spoonful to her lips and she sucked it in, savoring the burst of flavor.

After that one, he shifted position so that he was angled toward her instead of side by side.

"You need to drink plenty of water," he said in a gruff

voice. "You haven't been hydrated and I don't want you getting cramps again."

Automatically, she reached for one of the opened bottles of water on the tray and took a long series of swallows. Once she started, it was as if she couldn't stop. She was starved for water. Nothing had ever tasted so good.

Rio carefully pulled the bottle down until she held it to the side. "Careful. You'll make yourself sick. I want to get some nourishment in you as well."

As he continued to slowly feed her spoonful by spoonful, his other hand crept over her free hand. His thumb rubbed over the tops of her fingers. Just his touch soothed her, made her relax, and some of the terrible tension knotting her neck muscles began to disappear.

"Good?" he asked.

"Wonderful," she breathed. "I don't think anything has ever tasted so good."

"Tell me when you start to get full or if you start feeling sick. I don't want you to overdo it."

She was already at that point, but she ate a few more bites because it was too damn good not to. Finally she leaned back with a sigh. "I'm good. No more."

Rio scooted back on the bed, slid off and then reached back for the tray. Wordlessly, he ambled out of the room, leaving Grace alone in the silence. She strained to hear any other sounds in the house. The other men. But it was completely quiet.

They'd probably all gone to bed. She felt a surge of guilt thinking back on just all they'd sacrificed to get her here safely. Were they for real? She had so many questions to ask, more than her tired mind could even process.

She glanced back up when Rio reentered the room. He hesitated a moment and then said, "I promised you we'd talk and we will, but I'd like to jump in the shower if that doesn't bother you. I'll be out in five. Think you'll be awake that long?"

Again, she felt guilt that he'd put her before everything

else, even his comfort. He was still wearing the same clothes he'd been in for as long as she'd been with him.

"Please do," she said quietly. "Take your time. I'll be awake. It's important to me to know what's happened to Shea and how she's doing."

Rio nodded. "Okay, give me five and I'll be back."

He went to his chest of drawers, pulled out a change of clothes and then disappeared into the bathroom. She heard the shower come on through the closed door and she sank farther down into the bed, hoping she hadn't been lying about being able to stay awake.

WHEN Rio came out of the bathroom, exactly four minutes later, he was still toweling his hair. He hadn't wanted to stay gone long because Grace had looked like she was about to fall over at any second.

He smiled when he glanced toward the bed and saw that she was indeed asleep, her head and body tilted precariously to the side of the mound of pillows propping her up.

Tossing the towel aside, he walked silently to the side of the bed, eased onto the edge and gently shook her awake.

"Grace," he murmured. "Wake up, honey. Just long enough to get you under the covers and comfortable, okay?"

Her eyes flew open and her breath ended on a gasp. He could feel her pulse racing against his fingers resting on her wrist.

"Sorry. I didn't mean to startle you."

She righted herself, pushing back against the pillows so she sat farther up. "No, it's okay. I didn't mean to fall asleep anyway."

"It's probably a good idea if you get some rest. You're dead on your feet."

Her face fell. "You said we'd talk."

"I did," he said gently. "And I will. Just maybe not tonight. You're exhausted, Grace. I don't know how you're even conscious right now. Any normal person would be damn near in a coma."

Her lips tightened into a stubborn line. "I'm okay. I want to know about my sister. I'll go to sleep after we talk."

"Okay, but I want you to get comfortable first."

He held out his hand to help her off the bed and then he turned down the covers, arranged her pillows and motioned for her to crawl back in. Once she was settled, he walked around to the other side and sat at the opposite end of the bed on top of the covers so they faced each other catty-corner.

"How do you know my sister?" she asked before he could open his mouth.

"She helped an American soldier escape captivity several months ago."

Grace nodded. "Yes, I know. I was sort of there when things got bad. I was worried that Shea was going to get hurt. Using telepathy for any prolonged period of time weakens her, and then there was the fact that she was absorbing all his pain."

Rio cocked his head. "Shea swears she's very different from you. She says she can only temporarily take away a person's suffering but she can't truly heal anyone."

"It's true," Grace said quietly. "We're different in some ways. But the same in others. Shea's abilities are random, a fact that has always frustrated her. She never knows who she'll connect with. Who she'll hear. Who will be able to hear her."

"And you? You have the ability to focus your telepathy?"

Grace looked down at her hands, and Rio very much wanted to touch her. To somehow make contact. Pull her into his arms and just hold on to her until she knew she was safe.

"I could. I'm not sure about now. It's all a mess really. I'm not sure how what they did to me will affect me in the long run. I severed my link to Shea because I wanted to protect her. But when I tried to reach out to her again, I couldn't. It feels random to me now. I heard the man in the mountains. He was broadcasting so much anger, I could literally feel him as well as hear him. But everything is silent around me now. I learned to focus my talent better than Shea did. But I don't have the same control now that I've always had. Maybe I never will."

Her lips were turned down into an unhappy frown that made his chest ache. There was so much despair and fatigue in her voice.

"So this soldier Shea saved . . . You know him?"

Rio nodded. "I work with his brothers. They're all ex-military. They run a special ops group that takes on dangerous jobs no one else can or is willing to do. Sometimes we contract with the government and take military assignments that the government can't officially get involved in. Other times we do private sector jobs, like hostage retrieval, tracking kidnap victims, protection, basically anything that takes a lot of muscle and stealth."

Grace's eyes widened. Her hands twisted nervously in front of her, and he could tell her unease had just shot through the roof. It didn't take a rocket scientist or being telepathic to figure out what was going on in her head.

"Grace, listen to me. The people after you may well be backed by a government group. We may all be on the same team on paper, but there are any number of shadow groups with their own agenda and each serves a different master. We don't work for the government. We aren't government owned. We contract with Uncle Sam on certain assignments. We don't prey on innocent civilians."

"Where is Shea now?" she asked nervously.

Rio smiled. "If I had to guess, she's with Nathan and he's keeping very close watch over her. She couldn't be in safer hands. He loves her. They've been through hell together."

"But she's all right?" Grace demanded.

"Yes, she's safe with Nathan and the rest of KGI."

"KGI? Is that the name of your . . . organization?"

Again he nodded.

"Do you know who's after me and Shea?"

Rio's lips tightened. "That's the thing. I'm not convinced that there isn't more than one faction after you. I saw the video surveillance when you went to your parents' house. Shea saw it too. She went there looking for you with Nathan. I promised her then that I'd bring you home."

Grace closed her eyes and leaned her head onto her upturned palm for support. "How are we supposed to live when every moment of our lives someone is after us, wants to destroy us for their own purposes."

When she reopened her eyes, to Rio's dismay, they were glossy with tears. Oh hell. If she started crying, he was so fucked.

"What happened after you went to your parents' house, Grace?" he asked, hoping to distract her. "Were you taken then? Did you manage to escape?"

She sighed. "Shea was right. It was probably stupid of me to try to look for answers. I was just so frustrated with our lives. Or lack of one. We'd been running for an entire year. Never seeing each other. Always scared out of our minds that whoever killed our parents would catch up to us. Jumping at my own shadow. Never trusting anyone. Someone smiled at me, I was immediately suspicious and couldn't get away fast enough. Someone says hello, I freeze up. Someone looks at me too long and I'm convinced that they're following me. It was no way to live. I missed my sister. I wanted a normal life for both of us. So I went looking for answers. I found my mother's journal, or rather who I always thought was my mother," she said bitterly.

"She was just a scientist who created me and Shea in a lab and then felt sorry for us and took us away to raise as her own."

"Shea told us," Rio said quietly. "She found the journal you dropped in the escape tunnel."

Grace's mouth drooped. "So she knows the truth now."

He nodded. "What happened when you left? Did you manage to escape?"

"I did, that time. But they were close and I was panicked and stupid. I didn't cover my trail as well as I should have and they picked me off a few weeks later. I can't even tell you where I was. I was drugged for most of the time. Until they started bringing in their test subjects for me to heal. Then they wanted me alert and able to do their bidding."

Rio felt sick. He could only imagine what she'd been forced to do and experience. The toll it had taken on her was something she may never fully recover from. The stupid bastards didn't even realize the precious gift they had. They were too busy trying to destroy her without even knowing what they were doing.

She frowned. "You said there could be more than one group after me."

Rio nodded. "I don't know for sure, but it's possible from what I know."

"The day I escaped, the facility I was being held at was bombed. I remember hearing gunshots. It was chaos. The cell I was in collapsed and I was able to crawl out and escape, but many of the researchers were dead and I don't think it was from the explosions I heard. There was blood everywhere, like they'd been slaughtered."

She broke off and put a hand to her head, closing her eyes as she swayed back and forth. Alarmed, he reached forward to touch her arm but she pulled back.

"Just give me a minute. I had something for a moment. It was a brief memory of that day. I picked up something from a man close by. I remember how cold I felt and how frightened he made me feel. I could sense his determination to find me and to destroy those who had any knowledge of me." She glanced back up at Rio. "What does that mean? Why would he do that?"

Rio blew out his breath. "Titan."

"Titan?"

This was the part he hated the most. He didn't want to frighten her. He didn't want to appall her. But he wouldn't be anything but honest with her because deception would only cause more problems down the road. The very last thing he needed was for her to bolt unexpectedly because it looked like he was trying to deceive her.

No longer able to sit still, he pushed off the bed and paced back and forth at the end.

"Titan is a highly classified specialized military black ops group. Doesn't officially exist. These are the last-resort guys. The guys you call in to clean up messes, the guys you call in because you have no other options."

Her brow wrinkled in confusion. "Then how do you know so much about them?"

"Because I used to be one of them."

For a moment she was completely still, as if she hadn't really processed what he'd said. Then alarm flared in her eyes and she shrank back against her pillow. But to her credit, she didn't freak out.

"You said used to be," she said in a steady voice. "Why aren't you any longer?"

He stopped his pacing and looked at her. She was asking, not judging. His admiration grew for her by the hour. She was rock solid. Someone who didn't crack under pressure or fold in a crisis. He didn't think he'd ever met a woman quite like her and he'd met all the Kelly women. They were certainly remarkable women. Survivors. Fighters. More courageous than most men.

But there was something about Grace that made him stop and take notice.

He eased down on the edge of the bed. "I decided that unwavering, unquestioning loyalty wasn't for me."

She cocked her head to the side. "Some would say those aren't bad traits."

"Blind faith is never a good thing. Being a unit of automatons trained to do as ordered without conscience, without question . . . I couldn't do it anymore. I lost a lot of my soul during my time with Titan. I'm hoping I haven't lost all of it."

"That bad?" she asked quietly.

He ran a hand through his still damp hair. "Not all. Depends on what side you're on. There's always a good and a bad depending on perspective. Are there things I regret? Yeah. But there are also things I don't regret. It was time for me to move on or lose myself completely."

"And KGI is better?"

"Different," Rio said. "We decide what missions to take. We decide what side we line up on. The Kellys . . . they're righteous. Upstanding. They have integrity and principles. It's why I work for them. It's why my team works for them."

She looked relieved by that.

"Shea is in very good hands, Grace. Nathan loves her a hell of a lot. He'll protect her with his dying breath."

She gave a wistful-sounding sigh. "I'm glad she's found happiness and that she's safe. It's what I always wanted for her—for us—just a normal life."

Rio reached across the comforter and gathered her hand in his. "You'll get there. KGI isn't walking away from this."

"Thank you. I don't know what I would have done if you hadn't found me when you did. I . . ." She closed her eyes and bowed her head. "I was ready to die. I think I even wanted to. I was just so tired. I can't even explain to you how I felt."

Rio brought his hand up to touch her hair, letting one of the damp strands slide over his fingers. "There's no shame in admitting you were at your lowest point. We've all been there."

She lifted her head and met his gaze. "What was your lowest point?"

He swallowed because the pain of Rosalina's death still lived inside him. She'd been all he had left. And he'd failed to protect her as he should. In a lot of ways she'd been the impetus for him to walk away from Titan.

"My baby sister died," he said quietly. "She was pregnant with a child. She was beaten by her lover, the father of her baby. All because she spoke to another man."

Grace's face twisted in sympathy. "I'm so sorry. What happened? Was he punished?"

"He's dead," Rio said bluntly.

Grace's eyes widened. She bit her lip and stared hard at him, almost like she knew and wanted to ask but hesitated.

He took the decision from her. She should know the kind of man she'd trusted with her safety. She should have all the facts.

"I tracked him down and killed him."

"Good," Grace said fiercely. "I hope it wasn't quick either."

Rio blinked in surprise and then burst out laughing. Her face was drawn into a scowl and her nose was scrunched up making her look . . . cute.

"It wasn't quick."

"Any man who abuses those who are weaker and defenseless deserves to have his balls cut off."

Rio smiled. "Indeed they do. I'll spare you the details but he was repaid in kind."

His heart felt a little lighter. Not as heavy as it always did when he spoke of his sister. Grace looked like she wanted to go track the bastard down and kill him all over again. He found that ferocity very attractive in a woman.

"I'm glad," she said. She rubbed her hands up and down her arms as if she'd gotten a chill. "It's the most helpless feeling in the world not to be able to fight back."

"You're not helpless anymore, Grace. You've got me."

She squeezed his hand, curling her fingers tightly around his. "They took something from me, Rio. Something I may never get back. I hate them for it."

He scooted even closer, pulling her hand until it rested on the top of his thigh. "What's that?"

Her face creased in anguish. "My sister. They took my link to her. I never realized how much I depended on it and her until it was gone. I hate the silence. I feel so . . . alone."

Rio carefully pulled her into his arms and laid her cheek against his chest. "You'll get it back. I have some exercises for the mind that may help. You've been through hell, Grace. You can't expect to come out unscathed. You have to heal. Not just physically but mentally as well. Especially mentally. Your body will take care of itself, but your mind has been deeply bruised by all you've endured. It's likely shut down to protect you. It's in survival mode just as you are."

"You make me feel hope," she whispered against his chest. "I've been without hope for so long, but with you, I can remember what it feels like to believe and have faith."

He held her for a moment longer and then finally pulled away. "We've talked enough for one night, I think. I'm sure you'll have more questions when you're not falling-down tired. You need to rest and completely heal. I'm not going anywhere. We can continue this conversation tomorrow."

She nodded and he tucked her back underneath the covers. Then he went to the closet, pulled out several blankets and some extra pillows. After arranging a comfortable spot on the floor, he turned back to her. "Ready for lights out?"

"Yeah," she murmured.

Already she'd snuggled into the pillows and was lying on her side facing his direction. She looked tired. Worn down. Like she'd been through hell. And yet he'd never seen a woman who looked more beautiful to him. Maybe it was because he'd seen the heart of her. Her spirit and resilience.

Grace had made a huge impact on his life in the very short time he'd known her, and he knew he'd never forget her.

He reached for the light switch and doused the room in darkness. Then he crawled beneath the covers he'd arranged and closed his eyes. His muscles screamed their protest, and fatigue beat relentlessly in his head.

He had almost drifted off when he heard her soft whisper.

"Rio?"

He opened his eyes and half turned in her direction so he could hear her.

"Are you awake?"

It was said so softly he almost didn't hear her.

"Yeah. You okay?"

There was a long pause.

"Grace?"

"Would you . . ." She trailed off like she was having difficulty asking what it was she wanted. "Would you sleep with me? On the bed, I mean? I feel . . . safer . . . when you're near."

His chest did funny things. His heart turned over at the fear and hesitancy in her voice. Hell, he'd move a damn mountain for her.

He pushed himself upward and then flipped on the lamp. She blinked and then peered anxiously up at him.

Then he pulled the covers back and crawled into the bed. He reached back to turn off the light. Once again darkness settled over the room, and he turned back so they were facing each other, though he could barely make out her features.

They lay there silently, so still he couldn't hear her breathe. She was stiff and completely immobile, but he could tell she hadn't relaxed or gone to sleep.

"Come here," he said quietly.

He lifted his arm and she immediately snuggled into his embrace. Her body was a warm shock to his, flush against his chest, her legs touching his.

He remained still, waiting to see if she'd react or if she seemed uncomfortable with his proximity, but to his surprise, she burrowed farther into his embrace, emitted a sweet-sounding sigh and then settled limply against him.

"This better?" he asked.

She nodded against him, her head bobbing just underneath his chin.

For several long moments, he lay there, unsure of what to do next. Finally he lowered his arm, curling it around her midsection and anchoring her to him. She didn't even stir. She'd already fallen asleep.

He relaxed, letting his head and hers sink farther into

the pillows. She felt small and slight next to him, and he was further reminded of just how fragile she was and yet how much inner strength she possessed.

He turned his mouth down until his lips brushed over her hair. "Good night, Grace," he whispered.

CHAPTER 15

GRACE awoke with a throbbing headache. Her brow wrinkled at the effort it took to open her eyes. She lay there a moment as she evaluated her body and her injuries. Then she lifted her arm, examining the place where the bone had broken. She flexed and extended her fingers, but other than a little stiffness, all seemed well.

Her dreams had been fractured, a mixture of reality and a product of her fears. She'd tried repeatedly to reach out to her sister, and at this point she hoped she hadn't been successful because Shea would have been terrified for Grace, and the very last thing Grace wanted to do was upset her sister. Especially now that Rio had told her she was happy.

In love.

Protected.

Envy bit hard and guilt crowded swiftly in for thinking even for a moment that she was jealous of what her sister had.

She sat up, realizing that Rio had likely long vacated the bed. Sunlight streamed through the one window at the very top of the wall. She thought it odd that all the windows in the house were positioned that way. There was no view to the outside. Nor were they large enough for a person to fit through. She wondered if Rio had given thought to being able to escape in a fire.

She shook her head. Somehow she didn't think such a thing would ever escape Rio's planning. He seemed too focused and calculating to miss something so simple.

She moved slowly, though she did feel better and not as broken. She didn't want to take anything for granted, however. She wanted—needed—to be whole again and not just physically. There was a need that transcended simple desire for the woman she'd been before this whole nightmare began.

She found a pair of jeans and a T-shirt on top of the dresser. Frowning, she let her fingers run over the worn softness of the material. She was struck by a longing sensation so keen that she yanked her hand away, palming her fingers with the other hand.

Tears stung her eyelids as she stared down at the clothing. Shea's clothing. When had she been here? How had Rio gotten these things?

Her heartbeat thundered against her chest until she was dizzy and swaying. She hated the anxiety that gripped her every time she considered that she'd been too trusting of Rio and his men. What if they were the ones she should fear the most? Here she was in Belize, God knows where on some river way out in the middle of nowhere.

She closed her eyes and reached for Shea's clothes again, pulling them to her chest for comfort. For a brief moment it was like holding her sister again.

She'd spent the night in Rio's arms because she'd been lonely, afraid, and she'd trusted him. Now she wondered if she hadn't been incredibly stupid, but then this was an argument she'd waged with herself since they'd been in the mountains.

More than anything, she was afraid of making the wrong choice and trusting the wrong people. For so long, she'd refused to trust anyone else. Only Shea. And now that link was gone.

She pulled Shea's T-shirt over her head and down her body. Normally Shea's clothing wouldn't fit her. Shea was smaller, shorter, not as muscled as Grace, but Grace had suffered in the last months. Now Shea's shirt hung loosely on her.

Next she put on the pants, and other than being a bit short in the length, they fit her fine. Grace had lost a lot of weight. She was afraid to know how much.

She closed her eyes and inhaled. She could smell Shea. Could feel her wrapped around her just like her clothing was. If Rio worked for the organization that was currently protecting Shea, then Grace should be able to talk to her, right?

Then she could put at least one worry to rest. Whether she should be wary of Rio and his team or whether they were really the good guys here.

For the time being, if they weren't the good guys, she was at least being treated far better than she'd been with the last people who'd held her captive. So far . . .

She poked around in the bathroom until she found deodorant, a toothbrush and a brush for her hair. It was bedraggled from the night before when she'd washed it and gone straight to bed.

She settled on the bed and set to work on detangling the mass of hair. Cross-legged on the mattress, she didn't overlook the normalcy of doing something so mundane as brushing her hair. Any other time she would have overlooked it, been in a hurry, not dwelled on something so everyday. Now, she was grateful for it.

Closing her eyes, she stroked the brush through the strands and tried to center her scattered emotions. She thought of Shea, focused intensely on the familiar path, but each time she reached for it, blackness swelled in her mind. Her despair heightened with each failed attempt to reconnect to her sister.

I'm so sorry, Shea. This is my fault. I shut you out. But I need you now.

Her hand slowed in its downward progression through her hair, and tears were hot at the edges of her eyes. She inhaled sharply through her nose and blinked them back. After several steadying breaths, she lifted her head, only to find Rio standing in the doorway, his gaze trained on her.

"Feeling better?" he asked.

She nodded slowly and retraced the same path with the brush, enjoying the soothing rhythm against her scalp.

"You seem upset."

She sighed, put the brush down and flipped her hair back over her shoulder. She let her hands rest on her crossed ankles and threaded her fingers nervously.

"I need to talk to Shea. I can't connect mentally with her, so I need for you to call her. You said she's with people you work with, right? I want to talk to her."

Rio leaned against the doorframe, cocked his head to the side and studied her a long moment. Then he smiled slightly, his eyes gleaming with amusement. That smile made her uncomfortable. Like he had secret knowledge she wasn't aware of. She fidgeted under his scrutiny but refused to back down.

"You don't trust me, do you?"

It was on the tip of her tongue to hurriedly deny any such thing, but she wasn't going to lie. Instead she leveled a stare at him. "I haven't made up my mind yet. The jury's still out. But being able to speak to my sister would go a long way in allaying my concerns."

The crooked grin got bigger. "Some might say you're in no position to be bargaining."

Her cheeks grew warm but she wouldn't allow herself to lose this silent war of wills with the stare-down. She wouldn't beg. She'd begged until she was hoarse. Had begged for mercy. For freedom. Her pleas had fallen on deaf ears. Never would she do it again.

"I need to speak to her," she said in a controlled voice.

"If I'm not a prisoner, surely I rate this simple consideration."

Rio arched a brow. "Prisoner? Honey, I carried you all over the Rocky Mountains on my back. If you were a prisoner, I'd have made you walk it your damn self."

"I did walk!" she said indignantly. "I made it by myself. Without your help. Maybe not at first, but I made it in the end."

Rio's face softened but his eyes were still bright with amusement. "That you did, Grace." He ambled forward then perched on the corner of the bed, turning so he could look at her. "I can't guarantee that I can get you Shea. I can try. You have to understand that she is in as much danger as you are."

Grace frowned as worry slid down her spine. "I have to talk to her, Rio. She won't understand why I haven't reached out to her. She's probably frantic. I need to know she's okay but I also need to let her know *I'm* okay."

Rio glanced at her, his expression mild but his eyes sharp. He seemed to be contemplating the matter, and she hadn't realized how close she was to doing what she'd sworn she wouldn't. She bit her lips to call back the plea. Damned if she'd beg for anything ever again.

"I can try," he finally said. "I'm not at all certain where Shea is. But I can place a call to Sam to see what I can do. There are conditions, however."

She raised an eyebrow. "What conditions?"

"I have to have your agreement to my conditions before I'll consider placing the call."

Frustration simmered and it took everything she had not to lash out and instead remain calm and centered as she stared back at him.

"What conditions?" she said from behind clenched teeth.

He shook his head. "I'm holding all the cards here, Grace. I'm not trying to be an asshole, but it's imperative if I'm going to keep you safe that you agree to my conditions regardless of whether you find them unreasonable or not."

She honest to God wanted to hit him. Her fingers curled into a tight fist, and she had to clamp her other hand around it to keep from flying into a rage. She was tired of feeling helpless. Tired of being subjected to the whims and subjugation of others.

As if he knew exactly what she battled, he reached over and gently picked up her tightly coiled fist. He rubbed his thumb over the white knuckles and gazed into her eyes.

"Would it make you feel better to hit me? You can, you know. Go ahead, Grace. Give it your best shot."

She stared at him like he was nuts. He wasn't angry. In fact, he was extremely calm. She couldn't wrap her mind around what on earth he was doing. Was he mocking her?

"Hit me," he said again. "Take back control, Grace. Assert yourself. Did you feel weak and powerless when they had you? Did you wish you had more power? That you could fight back? Or maybe you were too scared to. Did you cower in a corner waiting for someone to save you?"

Rage was red-hot, blinding. She swung, connecting with his chin. His head popped back and pain flashed through her knuckles. For a moment she was too stunned to comprehend what she'd done.

He lowered his head, holding his chin. He grinned crookedly as he rubbed at his jaw. "Nice shot. We'll work more on getting more power into your jab but not bad at all."

Her mouth popped open. "Are you insane?"

Rio cocked his head to the side. "I've been accused of that a time or two. Depends on your definition of sanity."

"I just *hit* you. Aren't you angry?"

"Did it make you feel better?"

She frowned. She wanted to hit him again. He was so damn calm. Did anything ruffle him? She flexed her fingers then glanced at his jaw, where a slight red spot marked his dark skin.

"Yeah, it did."

And she did feel marginally better. Some of her intense rage and anger had slid away as soon as she'd exploded into action.

He smiled then. "Mission accomplished."

She shook her head. "You're nuts."

He put her hand down and leaned back. "We can work on a few self-defense moves. You've got a lot of power considering how low your reserves are."

"I just want to talk to my sister," she burst out.

"As long as you agree to my conditions, I'll do my best to make it happen."

"What conditions?" she asked in exasperation. "I can't agree to anything until you tell me what they are."

He lifted an eyebrow. "On the contrary, until I have your absolute agreement, you don't talk to Shea."

Hurt crowded in. For a moment she couldn't even muster a response. How could he use her sister as a bargaining tool?

"You're a bastard."

He shrugged. "I've been called worse. And I'm the bastard who's going to keep you safe."

He was immovable as a mountain. Somehow she didn't think tears or feminine distress would make a dent in his resolve. Not that she'd reduce herself to that level of manipulation. She had pride. She'd been stripped of everything, her dignity, her will to live. At times she was convinced that her very soul had been forfeit. But she refused to let go of her pride.

"All right, I agree," she said in defeat. "To whatever it is." She braced herself for what those conditions would be and hoped she hadn't just agreed to a deal with the devil.

Rio nodded but he didn't appear smug over his victory. His expression became serious. "I know she's your sister and that your inclination is to share everything with her. However, I do not want our current location compromised."

Grace's brow furrowed. "But wouldn't they know where you lived? I mean, this is your house, right?" Then remembering the clothes she hadn't mentioned, she said, "For that matter, Shea has been here. These are her clothes. How did you get them?"

He held up his hands. "One thing at a time. Yes, they're

Shea's clothes. No, she hasn't been here. I saw her last when she and Nathan returned from your parents' house just after you contacted her last. We had video surveillance of you in the house. Shea asked KGI for our help in finding you. I volunteered to go."

She glanced up in surprise. "Why?"

He cocked his eyebrow. "Why what?"

"Why would you volunteer? What could you possibly care about a woman you didn't know?"

The corner of Rio's mouth curled upward. "I get that a lot of your life has been spent dealing with people without honor. But not everyone is an asshole. I wanted to help Shea. I wanted to help you. It's as simple as that."

Ashamed, Grace glanced down, only to have Rio nudge her chin upward again.

"As for your other questions, yes, KGI knows of this location. They only recently acquired knowledge of it. But knowing I own it doesn't mean they know where we are. I'd rather keep it that way."

"Don't you trust them? You work for them, right?"

"I don't trust anyone," he said bluntly. "Not when it comes to something as important as your safety. Which is why if you speak to your sister, the extent of your conversation has to be that you're okay and whatever pleasantries you exchange. She's going to want you to come home. She's going to want you right there with her."

"Why can't I be?" Grace asked quietly. "Didn't you say when you first came to me that you were there to bring me home?"

Rio nodded. "Eventually. When it's safe. When we know for certain it's safe. Until then the very last thing you and Shea need is to be together. Makes the enemy's job that much easier."

"So all I have to do is agree not to tell her where I am and you'll let me talk to her?"

Rio nodded. "I, of course, will sit in on the conversation. If at any time you venture into forbidden territory, I'll shut it down immediately."

She opened her mouth to argue but remembered that this was a take-it-or-leave-it situation. Rio showed no sign whatsoever of being able to be talked into anything.

"All right," she finally conceded. "I agree."

Rio rose from the bed and stood at the end. "Okay then. Why don't you come out, get something to eat and then we'll make the call."

CHAPTER 16

GRACE walked down the hall shoeless, flexing her toes into the plush carpet. When she reached the living area, polished wood replaced the carpet and was cooler on the soles of her feet.

She paused just a few steps in, staring at the array of men slouched in chairs and on the couches across the room. They were watching a football game on the big screen and arguing about point spreads and fantasy football picks.

It all looked so . . . normal. Like she'd stumbled into some bachelor pad. Not like she was surrounded by mercenaries hired to protect her.

Terrence looked up and saw her first. He raised a beefy hand—one that was nearly as big as her head—and waved her over.

"Come on, Miss Grace. You don't want to miss the big game."

She glanced around, automatically looking for Rio. She found him behind the island bar in the kitchen, obviously preparing something to eat.

He dipped his head in Terrence's direction. "Go on over. They don't bite."

Wiping her hand down her jeans, she walked hesitantly toward the mass of testosterone. There was a mad scramble as they sat up straight and made room for her on the couch next to Terrence.

She took the corner, grateful to have a guy on only one side of her, and leaned into the arm.

"How you feeling?" Terrence asked.

Grace nodded. "Better. Thank you."

Diego cast her a sideways glance, studying her for a long moment until she was ready to fidget right off the couch.

"Your color is better," he finally said. "Still a little pale but you're getting there."

"Thanks, I think," she mumbled.

"You care if I ask you something?" Browning called out.

She blinked and looked in his direction. He was sitting sideways in an armchair with one leg dangling over the arm, beer in one hand, his other propped on the back of the chair.

"Uhm, I don't guess so."

"That healing thing you do. How do you do it?"

She was so used to being highly guarded when it came to any mention of her abilities that she immediately tensed and became wary.

Terrence frowned in Browning's direction. "Don't be an ass."

Diego shrugged. "He's only asking what the rest of us are wondering. We've all met Shea. We know what she did for Nathan. According to Shea, Grace here is the one who helped Swanny when he and Nathan were escaping in Afghanistan. I'd say that makes us curious."

Grace turned almost in panic, her gaze seeking Rio. He stood in the same spot as before, tending to something on the stove. But he was looking at her, his gaze steady and unreadable. Almost as if he was telling her that she was on her own. Fight her own battles.

For a moment, it irritated her that he wouldn't come to her rescue, but then realization was swift that he saw what she didn't want to. That she needed to toughen up. She needed to regain her confidence and spirit. How could she do any of that if she was always leaning on him?

She glanced back at Rio's men and forced herself to relax. Of course they'd be curious. Any normal person would be. And they likely thought she owed them some sort of explanation given they'd risked their lives to save her ass.

They'd probably be right.

She took a deep breath. "I don't know how I do it. I just always . . . have. The first memory I have of healing is when I was very young and I found a bird fluttering on the ground with a broken wing. I picked it up and I can remember wishing with all my heart that I could make it better."

The rest of the men tuned in, leaning forward in their seats.

"Did you? Heal it?" Browning asked.

She nodded. "For a long moment it remained completely still, cupped in my palms. Then it started flapping and struggling, trying to get away, so I opened my hands and it flew off. But the next thing I knew, I felt this awful pain in my arm. I could literally feel my own bone breaking. I was terrified. I went running to my mother, who told me I was never to do such a thing again.

"Shea was with her and she took my pain. I can remember being on my mother's lap and having Shea put her hands around my arm. Her face was so solemn. I can still remember what she said. 'I'll make it better, Grace.' And she did. At least temporarily."

"Wow, that's heavy," Decker said. "It's incredible what the two of you can do."

"As I got older, I was able to focus my ability more. Direct it. I don't know how to explain it, really. I could be a great distance from someone, but if I had a connection to them, I could still heal them. As I did with the man you called Swanny through Shea's connection to Nathan."

"It's no damn wonder there are people so eager to get

their hands on you," Terrence said in a somber voice. "The possibilities are endless. You'd be of vital interest to the military or any radical group."

"An unstoppable fighting force," Diego interjected. "Someone goes down, Grace heals them through a psychic link. Boom, up they go again."

Grace was shaking her head before he even finished. "I'm not psychic. I mean I can't predict events, tell the future. I'm not a mind reader in the sense that I can pick out your thoughts. It's . . . different. I'm telepathic, which just means I can communicate mentally. I can heal remotely, telepathically I suppose you'd say."

"So you can't read our thoughts?" Browning asked.

Of everyone, he seemed to have the keenest interest in her abilities. He'd remained thoughtful throughout the conversation, his brow etched in concentration.

"Not unless I connect to you."

"Can you connect to just anyone?" Decker asked. "Shea said her abilities were random."

"I could at one time," she said softly. "I'm not sure I can anymore."

They all looked inquisitively at her. An uncomfortable silence fell.

"You'll get it back."

Grace turned to see Rio standing behind the couch just over her shoulder.

"With the proper care and reconditioning, you'll get it back."

"I hope you're right." She sighed and her shoulders slumped as she turned back around. She remained sideways just a bit so she could still see Rio while including the others in her sight. "I used to think that I didn't want my gift. That it would be easier—my life would be easier—if my head was silent. If I couldn't hear other people. If I couldn't heal."

"And now?" Diego prompted.

"I miss my sister," Grace said, an ache building in her chest as she thought of losing that link to Shea. "This past year has been difficult. She's tried to keep communication to a minimum because she always feared knowing too much about me and where I was. She didn't want to be used against me or to draw me out."

"How did you lose it?" Decker asked. "I don't understand. What happened?"

Grace went numb as memories of all she'd endured came hard and fast. Residual pain echoed through her joints and muscles. The voices in her head screamed. Before she realized what she was doing, she'd lifted her palms to her temples and closed her eyes in an effort to make it all go away.

"That's enough," Rio said in a terse voice. "It's time to eat, Grace. You need to keep your strength up."

She swallowed, realizing that Rio had just bailed her out where before he hadn't and she'd recognized the importance of standing on her own, of not being so damn weak all the time. The past couldn't hurt her. Memories couldn't hurt her. Only the present and the future had that ability. She had to stop fearing the ghosts.

They were all still staring at her. She cleared her throat and pushed away the lingering shadows.

"When they . . ." She took another deep breath. *Pull it together, Grace. This isn't a big deal.* "When they made me heal all those test subjects, it hurt me. Not just physically but mentally. When I heal someone, I take on their injury or illness. It becomes mine. As if I lift it straight from them and absorb it. They go away free, recovered. I have to then recover myself.

"Some of the subjects were hard. With each one I grew weaker until I was sure I would die. I severed the link to my sister because I didn't want to become so weak that I called out to her without realizing it. I never wanted her to see me as I was and I didn't want to endanger her."

Terrence scowled fiercely. Diego was frowning as well while Decker and the others still wore puzzled looks.

"You just severed it? You can do that?" Decker asked.

Grace nodded, tears crowding her eyes. "It was the hardest thing I've ever done in my life. She was . . . she was a part of me. Always with me and suddenly I was alone and frightened. And slowly dying."

"Ungoddamnbelievable," Diego muttered. "What the fuck were they hoping to prove? That they could kill you? How would your death benefit them at all? If they wanted to use your powers, why the hell wouldn't they take better care with you?"

Grace wiped at her cheek in an offhand manner, relieved to find no trace of tears there. "I don't think they understood. How could they? I think they thought I was acting because I didn't want to perform to their expectations. It wasn't until . . ."

She shook her head and clamped her lips shut. She didn't want to go there. It still shamed her even though she knew it wasn't her, that she hadn't had any control.

Rio cleared his throat. "That's enough. Come eat now, Grace."

She glanced gratefully over, this time allowing him to rescue her. She pushed herself from the couch and slid her shaking hands into the pockets of her jeans to disguise how traumatized she still was by the past weeks.

To her utter shock, Terrence stood, towering over her briefly before he pulled her into a huge bear hug. She stood there plastered against the big man's chest, mouth open as he squeezed the breath from her.

Touched by the show of support, she slowly put her arms around him and returned the hug. He swiped a big hand down her back and then patted her awkwardly on the shoulder as he pulled away.

"You're a tough nut, Miss Grace," he said gruffly. "Don't ever let anyone tell you different."

She smiled up at him. "Thank you, Terrence. You're very kind."

"Let's go eat. Rio cooks some good stuff when he's home in his kitchen."

She allowed Terrence to lead her into the kitchen and up to the large island with barstool seating. She glanced

around, having just given everything a cursory once-over
last night. It was indeed a dream kitchen. A chef's kitchen,
she believed they were called. Top-of-the-line appliances.
A huge, six-burner gas stove. Double oven. Stainless everything.

It didn't compute.

She'd spent time in the mountains under the worst conditions possible with these men. Rio was a badass. A dark,
brooding type that looked like no one ever dared cross
him. But here? He was relaxed. Obviously a fan of creature
comforts, judging by the custom home, the appliances and
all the luxury items.

The bedding alone was simply to die for. She hadn't
stayed in hotels that had better linens.

Rio was obviously someone who liked to live well when
he wasn't out saving the world and getting shot at. It was
hard to reconcile this man standing before her with the
man who'd carried her all over a mountain tied to his back.

Terrence seated her on a stool close to the end and then
took the one next to her. There was only one left on the
other side of her, which she assumed was for Rio, since the
others were all claimed by his team members.

Rio put a plate in front of her and the scent wafted
through her nostrils. Her stomach immediately growled
and she closed her eyes, savoring just being able to sit down
and enjoy a meal in the comfort of a home.

Rio slid onto the stool beside her after serving the others and glanced over.

"Eat up," he said gently. "As soon as you're done, I'll try
to get Shea on the phone for you."

CHAPTER 17

THE meal was rather simple. Baked chicken, vegetables and rice, with hot rolls straight out of the oven. But for Grace it was the closest she'd come to having a normal meal in longer than she could remember.

She savored the sheer mundaneness of sitting there, cutting into her chicken, the burst of warmth and flavor on her tongue. She purposely took her time, not wanting to hurry the moment. It was probably a sign that she really had lost her mind that she was taking such pleasure in drawing out a meal.

But for her, it was like Christmas and Thanksgiving all rolled into one. All that it lacked was Shea.

Remembering what Rio had promised her, she dug into her food more rapidly, not wanting to waste a single bite. She was already full, but she was compelled to eat it all. Going for so long without food made a person not take a meal for granted when they finally got one.

When the last bite was consumed, she looked up to see that the men had already finished and were staring oddly at her. It made her self-conscious and she pushed the plate away, her cheeks warm under their scrutiny.

"That was really good, Rio. Thank you."

He continued to look at her, his lips set firm. He inclined his head to the side, motioning for the others to leave. When they were gone, he took her plate and the others and stacked them in the sink. Then he glanced up, catching her gaze and holding it for a long moment.

"How long has it been since you ate?" he asked bluntly. "I mean really ate, Grace. I watched you last night and now today and you never once looked away from your food. It was as if you were afraid it was going to get up and walk off your plate."

She bit into her bottom lip and ducked her head to avoid his scrutiny.

"You've lost weight. Even since I saw you in that surveillance footage. You were lean and toned. You had more muscle mass. You look like they damn near starved you."

His words stung even though she knew he hadn't meant them to be demeaning. He was angry. Not at her. She knew what she looked like. Like someone who'd been as close to death as one could be without sliding all the way into the grave. There were times when she swore she felt the cool earth cover her and darkness surround her. It was all in her mind. Her mind had become hell instead of a refuge.

"They mostly gave me IV fluids," she said in a low voice. "I'm not sure what all they gave me, to be honest. Those weeks are—were—a blur. But they certainly didn't bring me regular meals that I ate on my own if that's what you're asking."

Rio's expression grew stormier. His eyes darkened until they were nearly black.

"I'll make you special meals for as long as you're here. You won't go hungry again, Grace."

She blinked in surprise and then smiled, some of the shadows lifting at the fierce vow. Being plied with yummy food and luxurious surroundings wasn't exactly a hardship.

"Can . . . Will you call Shea for me now?" she asked anxiously.

His expression grew more serious. "You need to understand that I may not be able to make this happen."

Her lips turned down and she was unable to call back the unhappy frown.

"I'll do what I can. I know this is important to you."

He walked around the island and held out his hand to her. She slid her fingers over his palm, tangling with his fingers, and allowed him to pull her from the stool. He led her beyond the kitchen and into a small enclosed space that resembled a patio except it was cut off from the outside. The windows were dark and seemed thick, and there was almost a distortion of the view.

But beyond was a lush garden, well attended. A small pond sporting Japanese koi had a cascading waterfall that slid over a series of rocks before splashing into where the fish swam in lazy circles.

"What is this?" she asked as she stared around at the enclosure.

"It's a safe room. A place to enjoy the outdoors without actually being outdoors. There's an indoor pool just around the corner and behind the same bulletproof glass that currently surrounds us."

Her eyes widened. "Do you have that many enemies?"

"Yes."

She hadn't quite expected his terse, blunt response, and if she'd thought he'd go into further detail or perhaps elaborate, she was completely wrong. He said nothing more and instead drew out a phone and began punching a series of numbers.

Rio waited while the call connected, capturing Grace from the corner of his eye. She'd turned away but her body posture was stiff. Agitation rolled from her, almost tangible in the quiet. Then she paced a few steps, turned, and he could see her hands clenched tightly together.

When the line opened, Rio uttered the password and then Sam was there, immediately brisk and all business.

"Rio, what the fuck is going on? Where are you and is Grace okay?"

Rio lifted a brow. "Is there any reason she shouldn't be? She's with me and recovering well."

"I got a call from Resnick. It would appear you have a problem that isn't entirely exclusive to Grace."

Rio almost laughed. Like that was anything new?

"Cut the bullshit, Sam. Just tell me what he said. I assume you mentioned Titan to him."

"Yeah. He said that as of two years ago they no longer unofficially existed. They were disbanded and retired."

Rio snorted. "That's a pretty damn naïve assessment from someone who should damn well know better. Does he think just because the government no longer had a use for them that they'd just go away quietly, take up normal jobs, buy houses with picket fences and raise a brood of children?"

There was a long silence. "He said you were one of the original members of Titan."

Yeah, Rio had figured that would come out. It wasn't a shock. He'd be damned if he spent even a minute apologizing or explaining his past.

"What's your point?" Rio asked.

Sam blew out his breath. "There is no point. Look, I know you're a secretive bastard, but do you think at any time this would have been a good thing for me to know? If everything you and Resnick say about Titan is true, then you've put KGI in a dangerous situation. Groups like that don't just let people walk away, as Resnick so eloquently put it. Which means they've probably been hunting your ass all along."

"If they wanted me dead, I have no doubt I'd already be six feet under. Or in pieces somewhere."

"You give them that much credit?"

"They're the real deal, Sam. They aren't amateurs or a bunch of boys playing at being G.I. Joe. I'm sure I've remained on their radar, but the man who took over after

I left owed me. I saved his life. That and that alone is the reason I'm still breathing."

"Just as long as I know where your loyalties lie," Sam said quietly.

Rio was silent for a moment. He didn't like being questioned even as he knew why Sam had to do it. "I'm here, Sam. I'm doing the job. That should be enough loyalty for you."

"You should bring Grace in."

"I don't agree."

Sam sighed. "You can't keep her forever, Rio."

"No, but I can damn well make sure I don't put her in any more danger by exposing her and doing the very thing they expect me to do, which is reunite her with her sister."

"I'll agree to go along. For now," Sam said. "I want frequent updates. We made a promise to Shea, one I'm not willing to back down on. Not after all she did for Nathan and Swanny."

"Grace helped them too," Rio said evenly. "They wouldn't have made it out if not for her."

"I'm not arguing that. I just want to make sure we make it right for both of them," Sam said.

"For now she stays with me. Now, Grace wants to talk to Shea."

Rio could all but hear the wheels turning in Sam's head.

"She can't use her telepathy," Rio said quietly, hoping Grace couldn't hear. "She's too damaged. But she's desperate to talk to Shea and I promised her I'd try to make it happen."

Sam swore. "I can't do it. Not yet."

"What do you mean you can't do it?" Rio snapped.

"It's not that I don't want to. I sent Nathan and Shea away. At your suggestion, I might add. They haven't checked in with me yet. They're still traveling. As soon as I hear from them, I'll make the call happen. You have my word."

Rio cursed under his breath and stole another glance in

Grace's direction. She was staring at him with hope in her eyes. Hope he had to now crush.

"I need this fast," Rio said in a low voice.

"You'll get it. Just give me time."

"I don't have it."

"Nothing I can do, man. I'll let Shea know what's going on the minute I hear and then I'll arrange the call."

Rio muttered his agreement then ended the call. Even before he turned fully to Grace, he could feel her disappointment.

"What happened?" Grace demanded, her voice quivering. "Is she all right? Why can't I talk to her?"

Rio framed her shoulders in his hands and squeezed. "Nathan has taken her somewhere safe. Sam's going to let her know you want to talk to her as soon as they check in. I know you want to talk to her, Grace, but your safety—the safety of both of you—is the priority here."

She swallowed back bravely but he could see the grief and devastation in her eyes. Then she turned away and went to stand by the glass looking out to the garden. She leaned her forehead against it, closed her eyes, and then he could see the strain ripple across her forehead.

An uneasy sensation prickled his nape. His gaze narrowed as he watched Grace. Her hands pressed against the glass and then curled into balls.

She squeezed her eyes shut, and her entire body tensed and bowed inward. She let out a small cry and then she went limp. Tears slipped down her cheeks in silver trails. She turned and slid down the glass until she sat on the floor, her legs tugged up to her chest, and she buried her face against her knees as quiet sobs shook her shoulders.

CHAPTER 18

PAIN echoed through Grace's head, pain she was responsible for because she'd kept pushing, refusing to believe that she couldn't carve out that path to her sister again.

"Grace."

Her name came softly. So gentle and quiet that she almost didn't hear it. But she *felt* it. Like a warm brush, soothing away some of the darkness in her mind. Calming the wild, chaotic buzzing in her head.

She barely managed to lift her head and saw Rio crouched on the floor in front of her, concern creasing his brow.

"What is it? What happened?" he asked.

She lowered her forehead to her knees once more and took in long, steadying breaths. "I can't do it. I tried so hard but it's just not there. Oh God, Rio, what will I do?"

"What's not there?" he asked quietly.

"The link," she said in frustration. She raised her head and stared fully into his eyes, despair overwhelming her. "The link I destroyed to my sister. It's gone. All of it's gone. I can't focus. I can't reach out to anyone. It's like there's this yawning black hole in my mind and it's consuming me."

Instead of saying anything further, Rio rose and then reached down to pry her hand away from her legs. He tugged upward until she gave in and let him pull her to her feet.

"You need shoes," he said as he pulled her back toward the main living area.

She stared after him, utterly baffled. "Where are we going?"

He remained silent as he walked through the kitchen and then to a closet off the living room. He let go of her hand to rummage around a moment and then came out with a pair of shoes that looked like they'd fit her.

He dropped them on the floor beside her feet. "Put them on."

She stood there a long moment wondering what she'd missed, but seeing his determined look, she sighed and did as he said. When she was done, he went to the gun rack just inside the back entrance and pulled a pistol off the shelf. He shoved in a clip, pocketed two others and then reached for yet another gun. After giving it equal treatment, he donned a shoulder holster and tucked away both pistols.

He glanced her way and then crossed the room, took her hand and started toward another section of the house.

She shook her head to rid herself of the cobwebs that seemed to cling to her brain. She couldn't imagine what on earth had spawned this reaction. "Rio, where are we going?"

"You'll see."

They took a short flight of stairs down into what appeared to be the basement. To her surprise, he stopped and pushed a button and elevator doors opened. Her mouth gaped as Rio ushered her inside. He hit another button and the elevator started down.

She tried not to think of down, because down was below the ground. Like way below. She had the sudden hysterical thought that he was taking her somewhere to execute her.

When they stepped off, they were surrounded by complete darkness. As her eyes adjusted, she could make out dim lighting ahead. Rio tucked her hand in his and guided her toward the distant glow.

It took a moment for her to figure out that the light was coming down from a long tubelike opening in the ceiling of a tunnel.

It was cool and kind of damp, like a cave, and she supposed that was indeed what they were in. Man-made but a cave nonetheless. She shivered, though she wasn't at all cold, and Rio automatically pulled her in close to his side as if to share his warmth with her.

Men who did those kinds of things for a woman didn't turn around and shoot them, right? What would he care if she was cold? If she were dead, she'd be plenty cold. She coughed to cover the hysterical laughter that threatened to bubble out. She'd well and truly lost her mind.

Rio wasn't going to kill her. He'd had ample opportunity. Moreover, it was uncharitable of her to think it, given how good he'd been to her. Hell, he'd risked his life. His team had risked their lives. And here she was being a complete wuss because he was taking her down some dark tunnel God knows how many feet underground.

They continued a ways down until she was certain they were away from the house. She also honed in on the fact that they were gradually working up in elevation.

In the distance a faint noise made her brow wrinkle in concentration. She couldn't quite make out what it was. It was a dull roar that got a little louder with every step they took.

Then she saw a small sliver of light from behind a boulder. There was a marked difference in the air. Mist. The sound was water. A lot of water.

Rio pulled her toward the light, and she realized it was an opening in the rock, well hidden from view. As she looked out, she saw that they were coming out behind a waterfall.

Transfixed, she followed Rio, her stare riveted to the

beautiful water cascading from the rock above and plummeting to the pool below. They were standing in a large hollow behind the falls, and there was a small footpath leading around the edge and away from the falling water.

"Wow," she breathed.

Rio smiled and then directed her toward the path. She put her back to the rock and inched her way out so she didn't get soaked by the spray. Once outside, she gazed around at the tranquil paradise that surrounded them.

"This is amazing!"

"It is, isn't it? It's my own private getaway. I come here often when I need to pull myself back together."

Pull himself together? This was a man who looked permanently cemented together. He wasn't someone who had so much as a crack, certainly not any she'd seen. He was solid. Dependable. Calculating and . . . confident. That was the word escaping her. He was confident but not in an arrogant asshole kind of way. He clearly knew he was competent— no, not competent. That made him seem merely adequate. He was certainly beyond simple competency and adequacy. He was . . .

Her gaze stroked over him, taking in every detail. His demeanor, his silent strength and his composure. There was something magnetizing about him and she couldn't even put her finger on what made it so.

Her gaze fell to the guns at his sides and then she frowned as she turned in a circle, surveying the jungle canopy that seemed a barrier to the rest of the world. A world that suddenly didn't seem so idyllic. Not when she knew that evil was out there. Stalking her.

"Are we safe here?"

Rio tugged her farther down the path, spiraling down to the ground level, where the pool rippled and then led out to a small river cutting through the terrain.

"I like to be prepared. The tunnel leads to the back of the waterfall. I'm not saying that the falls and the pool aren't accessible, but it would be damn hard and I'd certainly know if anyone was near. The jungle is thick here, never touched. It's overgrown and surrounds the rock face where the water comes over the edge. It's not even visible from the air because the canopy is so thick in this area. So are we one hundred percent safe? I'm never that naïve. But I'd say we're pretty close to ninety-nine."

She cut a glance at him to see the corner of his mouth twitching. His eyes twinkled and then his smile broadened. She was transfixed by the transformation from the serious, hard-as-nails guy surveying the terrain to the sudden teasing, lighthearted exchange.

He gestured for her. "Come on. I have the perfect place to sit and enjoy the falls."

She followed him down to the water's edge and saw that he had a bench fashioned from a tree trunk. It utterly charmed her. She sank down onto the smooth wood and inhaled deeply, soaking in the beauty and peace around her.

He took the seat beside her, their legs nearly touching. For a long moment he stared, as did she, at the spellbinding sight of the water pouring down into the pool.

"I want you to do something for me," he said.

She glanced over to see him looking at her with those intense, dark eyes, almost like he was peeling back every layer of her soul.

"Close your eyes and focus inwardly. Picture where you're at. Take a good look but then close your eyes and reach out with your senses. Smell the air. Listen to not only the water but the other sounds around you. Feel the mist on your skin and the warmth of the air.

"Push the pain and the fear and the anxiety out of your mind. Focus on your sister and on that path that you've used for so many years. It's still there, Grace. You just have to find it again."

Her eyes became gritty and hot. She was tempted to rub them but didn't want to express more emotion than she already had.

Rio touched her face as if he understood. "I don't claim to know much about telepathy. Hell, I didn't even know it existed outside of movies until I met Shea. But I do understand mind over matter. I understand that to be strong, your mind has to be strong and focused. It has to heal just like your body had to heal. The mind is a very peculiar thing. Your brain has a way of protecting itself and you from complete devastation. You were at your limit, so it shut down as a protective measure. Now you just have to give it time to heal and for those pathways to your sister to reopen."

"Do you really think it will work?" she whispered, afraid to hope, but already feeling the stirring deep in her heart. That little burst of excitement that she couldn't control.

Hope was such a gift and a curse all rolled into one.

"There are many who would sneer at things like meditation. But the strongest warrior knows that his body is only as strong as his mind. A physically weaker person can defeat a much stronger opponent if he's stronger mentally."

She reached up to tentatively touch his cheek as he'd done with her. "How do you know so much? It makes so much sense when you explain it. I don't feel so . . . crazy."

He smiled. "You aren't crazy, Grace. You're just damaged. But you're a survivor and you'll get through this."

She turned to face the falls again, feeling more . . . confident. A little lighter and, yes, optimistic. When was the last time she'd felt hope?

She gazed around, memorizing every detail of the little slice of heaven, and then she did as Rio had told her and she closed her eyes, channeling all of her focus inward.

"Control your breathing," he murmured. "In, out, deep. Hold it. Relax and let it out. Focus on each part of your body relaxing and then make it happen."

His voice dimmed and became distant. She held on to the image of her beautiful surroundings and then she inhaled, sucking in the scent of the water, the plants, even the dirt and then a faint sweet smell, like an exotic flower.

Gradually she was able to separate the roar of the water from the other sounds and she concentrated on those. Birds. Insects. Even what sounded like a monkey in the distance. Lots of birds. She began to differentiate the calls, picking out at least half a dozen different bird sounds.

She turned her face upward, feeling the light mist blow over her skin, cooling and refreshing her.

And finally she reached inside her mind, tentatively pushing out, searching for that pathway to her sister. The blackness was intimidating, but she didn't give up.

For several long minutes she forced herself to remain calm. She floated in that darkness that enveloped her mind and tried to make peace with it.

The longer she sat there, the less overpowering the darkness and silence became. Instead of feeling powerless and terrified, peace settled over her like the sun on a warm summer afternoon.

She grabbed on to it. Held tight. Refused to let go and reimmerse herself in the horrors of the last months.

To be free even for a moment of the choking fear, despair and frustration was to spend a few seconds in heaven.

She had no knowledge of how long she sat there. It could have been hours or just a few minutes. When she reopened her eyes, she found Rio still sitting where he'd been, staring into the distance. Patient. Waiting for her.

As if feeling her gaze, he turned his head and then lifted one eyebrow in question. "Feel a little better?"

"You're amazing, Rio. You would have made a terrific therapist or maybe a yoga instructor or someone specializing in meditation. Or something. Heck, I don't even know myself. I'm having the hardest time reconciling this man here with me now with the warrior who rescued me from hell. I can't fit the two together in my mind."

"We're human too," he said, though there was no censure in his voice. "All of my men. They're the best of the best. No better anywhere. I'd stake my life and yours on that. But they also have a very human side, one that has nothing to do with blood and death and fear."

"I didn't mean to imply otherwise," she said regretfully.

"How is your head now? Still hurt? Are you tense?"

She took a moment to evaluate and then slowly shook her head. "I'm fine. Truly. I feel . . . sorta empty. It's nice. Like nothing weighing down on me."

"That's good. The next step is to talk about it."

Startled, she yanked her gaze back up to him. "Talk about it? You really are starting to sound like some arm-chair psychologist."

He ignored the defensive reaction and tilted his head to the side, staring until she fidgeted on the makeshift bench.

"What were you going to say earlier? When the guys were asking you about everything that happened. You implied that they didn't really take care with you until . . . Until what, Grace? What happened to make them realize they were slowly killing you?"

She dropped her head, shame immediately crowding into her mind. She closed her eyes tight as if she could push away the memories. But they clung tenaciously, a cruel reminder of the person she'd become for that short time.

"What are you afraid of?" he asked. "They can't hurt you now. You survived. They didn't break you."

"But they did!" she burst out.

Tears burned until she no longer had the strength to fight them. They were like trails of acid down her cheeks, and she choked back the urge to scream. God, she wanted to just yell.

Rio took her hand, softly turned it over until her palm was up, and she instantly tried to yank it back. He held firm, his grip not painful, but neither was it relenting.

He traced a path across the thin, fading line over her wrist. It had taken a long time to heal, so savage the wound had been. She curled her fingers into a tight fist, her wrist flexing in his grasp. She closed her eyes as if she would simply will him to drop the subject.

"What happened here, Grace?" he asked quietly. "You have a nearly identical mark on the other wrist. Given your ability to heal, these must have been terrible wounds."

"They broke me," she said again, her voice defeated and small. "Oh God, Rio, it was so terrible. I tried to kill myself. I'm so shamed by what I did. They nearly didn't save me. If they'd been a few minutes later getting to me, I would have lost too much blood, and what shames me the most is when I was myself again, my first thought was that I was sorry that I hadn't succeeded. But oh God, it wasn't me. I swear to you it wasn't me, but I still couldn't keep from wishing that I'd been successful."

He curled his entire hand around hers and rubbed his thumb over the still healing scar.

"What happened?"

"It was a test," she said bitterly. "I'd already gone through so much. I was exhausted mentally and physically. I was in constant pain. I was sick from a dozen different ailments. It hurt to even *breathe*."

"What kind of test?" he gently prompted.

"They brought in a woman who'd been institutionalized because of the danger she was to herself. She was mentally ill and suicidal. She'd already tried to kill herself multiple times, and she was under constant supervision and heavily medicated. They brought her to me and forced me to heal her."

"Oh, Grace."

His tone was heavy with sorrow. He continued to stroke her wrist, and she found she didn't mind quite as much as she had a moment ago.

"It was hell," she whispered. "I've never felt such despair. It was overwhelming, coming at me wave after wave. The voices all telling me I was worthless, that I was nothing and that I'd be doing the world a favor by killing myself. I wasn't worthy to be alive.

"I fought it at first. I knew that it was her who'd taken over. I knew it wasn't me. But after a while I could no longer distinguish between where I began and she ended. All I heard was that I needed to die, that I *had* to die."

"I'm sorry," Rio said, his voice husky with emotion. "Oh, honey, I'm so sorry."

"I managed to pry off one of the parts of the bed frame. It had a point on it, and I plunged it into my wrists and started tearing at the skin. It was a compulsion I was no longer able to ignore. I couldn't fight it. It took over until I was a puppet being jerked by the ghosts in my head.

"When they found me, I was nearly unconscious and I begged them, I *begged* them to just let me die."

Rio reached for her, carefully pulling her into his arms. He smoothed her hair through his fingers and simply held her as she recounted the horrors she'd endured.

"What shames me is that even though I knew it wasn't me, I still wanted to die. I gave up. I just gave up and tried to take the coward's way out."

She turned her face into his shoulder and then wrapped her arms around him, holding him tight. He adjusted his position so that he could anchor her more firmly against his chest.

After a moment, he pulled her away, moved his hands up to frame her face and then leaned in, his mouth closing in on hers. She blinked and then held her breath, shocked by what was about to happen. Shocked that she wanted it so much.

His lips touched hers. Warm, sensual. Electric. A full body shiver overtook her as he pressed farther, melding their mouths as he exerted gentle pressure.

His hands were like a brand on her skin, holding her for the loving assault on her senses.

Then he deepened the kiss, his tongue running over the seam of her mouth. Once, twice, the hot brush coaxing and seeking entrance to her mouth.

With a breathy sigh, she surrendered, leaning into him.

It was the closest bond she'd established with anyone outside of a telepathic connection to her sister. She craved this. Simple intimacy. A gesture of caring. Knowing that for at least a moment she mattered.

Their breaths were sporadic. Staccato, uneven and jerky.

No longer was she content with sitting there still, an inactive participant. She wanted to touch him. She wanted to taste him. She wanted to absorb him into her senses until he was all she could see, smell or feel.

When he finally pulled away, she was dazed. Unbalanced. Like she'd been knocked over by a wave and hadn't yet regained her footing.

He gently stroked her hair, smoothing both hands down the sides of her head as he stared tenderly into her eyes.

"You're an exceptional woman, Grace. You didn't just survive. You overcame. You've been through unimaginable hell and yet you've fought your way back."

She leaned into him, closing her eyes at the pleasure of his touch.

He pressed his lips against her forehead in the gentlest of kisses. "I'm going to make love to you, Grace. Not right this minute. I'm not going to pressure you or rush this. But from the moment I saw you on that video surveillance tape, you were mine. I have no explanation for it. I don't even entirely understand the connection. But it's there, and I think you feel it too. I'm willing to wait until the moment is right, but you're mine."

Her brain sizzled and nearly short-circuited. She stared back at him openmouthed as the shock of his words fully hit her.

She was utterly bewildered by his bold statement. It hadn't been a question or even a hint of wishful thinking. He'd stated it as matter-of-factly as he gave orders to his men.

And the way he was staring at her . . . If she had any doubt as to the truth in his statement, the look in his eyes convinced her that he meant every single word.

An ache began deep in her heart. Deeper, to her very soul. Longing rose swift and piercing. How long had she dreamed of having such closeness with a man? Someone whom she didn't have to worry about knowing her secrets.

Rio already knew. He accepted.

He'd said she was his.

She'd never truly belonged to anyone. Not even to the

people who'd claimed they were her parents and had raised her most of her life. She'd only ever had Shea. No one else had ever gotten close to her.

"I don't know what to say," she finally managed to get out.

Rio's smile was gentle but assured. "There's nothing at all to say, Grace. You're mine. You've been mine from the beginning. You never stood a chance once I decided that I was going to be the man who brought you home."

CHAPTER 19

GRACE was light-headed, unsteady on her feet, and gone was any lingering pain or sorrow over her failed connection to her sister. Her mind buzzed with Rio's bold statement.

What did it mean?

What exactly did it mean?

She couldn't even begin to grasp the ramifications or the reasons why. Before the last year, she would have said she was an attractive enough woman. Did any woman truly consider herself beautiful? But Grace hadn't had any serious esteem issues. She was just shy and awkward when it came to any sort of personal relationship.

Growing up as she and Shea had done, there'd never been any opportunity for Grace to have friendships or an eventual boyfriend, much less an involved relationship.

But in the last year, she'd lost a lot of her strength. Her tone. The fitness regimen she'd always adhered to had no doubt saved her because had she not been as strong as she was going in, she wouldn't have been strong enough to survive the unimaginable.

She was thinner now. Worn. Fear and fatigue seemed to surround her. Men weren't attracted to timid little mice, were they? They at least wanted someone who was stable and not a complete head case who'd tried to kill herself and was sorry she hadn't been able to.

Besides all that, how could she or he even entertain the thought of any sort of . . . well, anything!

Rio caressed the sides of her face. "I didn't say all that to frighten you, Grace. Subtle and tactful are two things I've never been accused of. I'm blunt and I don't like or play games. This is the only way I know how to be, so I'm sorry if that makes you uneasy."

She didn't even have a response for that. What could she possibly say anyway?

He feathered another kiss over her lips and then solved the issue of what the hell she was supposed to say back to him by turning her toward the path leading to the falls.

"We should get back. While it's safe here, I still don't want to leave you exposed for long periods of time. I want you to work on the things we talked about, though. Try meditation and the mental exercises I gave you. Keep working at reestablishing the path between you and your sister. It'll come in time."

She tugged on his hand to make him stop his progress around the back of the falls. When he turned with an inquisitive look on his face, she leaned up on tiptoe and initiated her own kiss.

It was shy, awkward and not nearly as toe curling as Rio's had been. In fact, she couldn't back up fast enough once she'd brushed her lips across his.

But he didn't seem to mind her obvious inexperience at all. His expression went from surprise to utter satisfaction.

"Thank you," she said in a grave tone.

He lifted a brow in question.

"For everything." She swept her arm out toward the falls and the surrounding area. "For this. For understanding. For risking so much to save me. For wanting to help me and not believing the worst or judging me for the things

I've done. I don't even know how to express the gratitude I feel, but it's more than that and I don't have the words to explain to you *what* all I feel. I just want—*need*—you to know that."

"Do you know what I need you to know?" Rio asked solemnly.

She wrinkled up her brow and cocked her head to the side. "What?"

He touched her nose with the tip of his finger. "I need you to know how special you are, Grace Peterson. I think you haven't believed that in a long time. Maybe you never believed it. But I see it, and now I want you to see it too."

It was simply too much. How he could reach inside her and see what it was she needed the most? Someone to believe in her. Someone who wasn't trying to use her. Someone who thought she was special, not because of her powers, but because . . . because she was simply Grace Peterson.

"I'm going to kiss you again," she whispered.

His eyes darkened and he went still. He reached for her hand, twining his fingers with hers. "By all means, I'm at your mercy."

Tentatively, she leaned into him until her breasts brushed against his chest as she rose up on tiptoe. But then his hands closed around her waist, slipped down over the curve of her behind, and he leaned down to meet her.

She kissed him once, but was unsatisfied with the brief contact. She wanted more. She wanted to explore this time. Before, he'd done it all and she'd stood there, stunned and overwhelmed by the intensity.

This time she wanted it slow, lingering. She wanted to taste him. Take her time and enjoy the intimacy of being so close, his hands on her body.

She kissed him again, this time leaving her lips pressed to his. Nervously she ran the tip of her tongue over the seam of his mouth. His lips immediately parted, coaxing her inward.

He kept still, seemingly content to allow her to take the lead. He held her steady, his hands still resting possessively on her bottom, but he didn't move. Not even a muscle as she continued her gentle exploration of his mouth.

Gaining confidence and feeling a little bolder, she reached up, wanting to run her fingers through his hair. It was loose today and not tied back in a ponytail at his nape.

It was long and silky, just brushing the tops of his shoulders. There was a slight wave to it, only enough to make it unruly, but it was far from being actually curly.

She let the strands slide through her fingers and then she finally got the courage to let her hands drop to his chest. The skin rippled beneath her fingers as his muscles flexed and rolled. His broad shoulders seemed to quiver, and his breathing changed from the even calm to a more sporadic, rapid staccato.

Slowly, she pulled away but he didn't relinquish his hold on her. He kept his hands molded to her behind, and he reclaimed the step she'd taken back.

"I like when you take advantage of me," he said with a slight grin. "Feel free to do it again anytime you get the urge."

Her cheeks went instantly hot and she ducked her head.

He chuckled and released his hold, his fingers gliding over her hips before finally dropping to his sides. Then he lifted one hand again, tipping a finger under her chin and gently forcing her head upward again.

"You're mine," he repeated again. "We're going to get there, Grace. Where 'there' is, I'm not altogether sure yet, but we're going to get there together."

Gathering every ounce of the courage she'd thought was long gone, she slowly nodded, feeling like she'd just taken on the world.

His eyes glowed with a savage light. They gleamed in triumph, and his smile was one of complete satisfaction. It was the look of the victor in a hard-fought battle. Only she hadn't been a difficult conquest.

Whatever this was between them. Whatever the dangers

they faced. Whatever happened tomorrow. Today, they were bound by a nearly silent agreement. A bond that perhaps had formed even before they'd met and most assuredly had been cemented when he'd pulled her back from the brink of death.

What mattered was that right now she wasn't alone. She was no longer running blindly and scared out of her mind. It was time to take a stand, and this man would be there beside her.

How could she lose?

CHAPTER 20

"**WHAT** do we do, Rio?" Grace asked from her perch on the couch.

She was settled in the corner, sitting cross-legged and surrounded by plump pillows. It was her nest, one she'd burrowed into and had no desire to leave anytime soon.

The others filtered through periodically. Diego had gone for a swim and Grace had gotten quite a view of the man in swim trunks. From the looks of him, he maintained a tight fitness regimen. Not that the other men could ever be considered lacking in the physique department, but Diego was . . . He was beautiful to look at.

Terrence had ambled through after Diego, wearing a muscle shirt and gym shorts. Her eyes had bugged at the huge tree trunks he had for arms. Hell, his muscles had muscles. He didn't walk so much as he swaggered and not from innate cockiness. No, the man was simply so big that he just sort of swayed when he moved.

Decker, Alton and Browning were on patrol, or so Diego had thrown out when he'd passed through the kitchen.

Rio looked up from where he stood in the kitchen chopping vegetables on a cutting board. It was amazing how this badass warrior looked so comfortable doing such domestic things like puttering around the kitchen. And one thing she'd quickly noticed was that he was meticulous in his care of all of his things. Whether it was a towel hanging correctly in the bathroom or fingerprints being wiped from the refrigerator.

He never let anything just sit out. Furthermore, it was as if he had his men trained according to his expectations because they carried their weight. The team reminded her of a well-oiled machine. Smooth. Seamless. Almost as if they read one another's minds.

The thought made her smile. Maybe they were the ones with telepathy. Wouldn't that be a kick?

"Grace?"

She blinked and refocused on Rio, who was staring expectantly at her. It was obviously not the first time he'd said her name, judging by the look on his face. While she'd been analyzing him and his men, he'd been trying to get her attention.

"There you are," he said when she found his gaze.

She flushed. "Sorry. What did you say?"

He shook his head in amusement. "You asked me what we were going to do. I merely asked what you were referring to."

She frowned a moment, not really remembering what her point had been. But then as she reflected on all she'd observed with his men and the fact that everything seemed so ordinary and everyday, she realized *that* was the point.

She waved a hand, gesturing around the room as if somehow that would signify her thoughts. "I was asking what we do. Now, I mean. We left the U.S. We came here. What now? When do I see Shea? You mentioned safe, but will I ever be safe? As much as I appreciate what you and your team have done—I'll never forget—you can't keep me here forever in some bubble. You have a life. I don't have much of one, but one day I'd like to."

Rio walked around the counter. She thought he was

going to come over to where she sat, but he simply leaned his back against the bar, thumbs tucked into his jeans pockets as he studied her.

"It's a good question. I'm not entirely certain yet."

Her brow furrowed. That hadn't been what she thought he would say. But then he hadn't lied to her. Not once. He hadn't shielded her from the truth no matter how harsh it may be. He didn't offer false hope and he didn't talk around issues.

She hugged one of the pillows to her chest and leaned forward until her chin rested atop the harder edge of the cushion. "Are we leaving again?"

Somehow the thought of leaving this place made her anxiety level rise sharply. Which was stupid considering she'd been there less than twenty-four hours. But she felt safe here. And *safe* hadn't been a word she could use to describe her feelings in a long damn time. She'd forgotten what it felt like to be able to relax her guard for five minutes.

Rio shook his head. "No. At least not yet. I have some feelers out. I'm calling in a few favors. Right now what I know is that Titan is after you. I warned Sam so he could make sure that Shea is safe and they're prepared for anything."

Her brows came together in a scrunch. "Sam. He's your boss, right? The one who kind of runs KGI? Isn't he Nathan's older brother?" And then a completely unrelated thought occurred to her. It blindsided her and momentarily paralyzed her.

She glanced up at Rio, her fingers knotted into tight balls. "Is Shea married already? You said she and Nathan were together. That he loved her."

The idea of having missed her sister's wedding was more than she could bear. It took everything she had not to break down into a torrent of tears. The only thing holding her back was the knowledge that if she started, there would be no stopping. It would be the last straw. Further proof that she and Shea led completely separate lives now.

This time Rio did move to the couch where Grace sat. He eased down, brushing her knees with his thigh. He took one of her hands and gently uncurled her fingers. Then he reached over, slid his hand up her cheek and brushed his thumb across the corner of her eye as if checking for tears. The movement forced her to look up again and meet his gaze.

"She wouldn't get married without you," he said in a low voice. "You're all she's thought about. She went back to that damn house you had no business going back to because she knew you'd been there, knew you were in trouble, and she would have done anything to save you.

"She felt guilty because she was in a safe place, surrounded by people who cared about her, and she had no idea where you were. If you were scared and alone. Hurting or in danger. She reached for you constantly. When I volunteered to lead my team to find you, she begged me to keep you safe. All she wants is you home. With her."

Tears burned but she smiled through the anguish, knowing too well how fierce Shea was when it came to people she loved. Shea had been so protective, though Grace was the older by a year. But in a lot of ways Shea was more . . . Grace wasn't sure what word she was searching for. The events of the last year had changed Shea dramatically. She was no longer the sweet, naïve, soft woman who wouldn't hurt a fly. She was harder and more cynical, and Grace had worried endlessly over those changes.

"Tell me about Nathan and his family," she said, the ache still in her voice. In her very soul. "Are they good to her? Is she happy? I just want the best for her. She deserves so much. I said some unforgivable things to her when our parents were killed. But if it hadn't been for her, I doubt we would have made it out of that house alive. I just want her to be happy. And loved."

Rio extended his arm over the back of the couch, wrapped it around her shoulders and pulled her toward him until she was settled underneath his shoulder.

"Nathan adores her. I don't know a whole lot. I left soon

after he returned with her to Tennessee. Her first concern and priority was you. She didn't want to leave Oregon because she was so sure you were somewhere close. But Nathan got her the hell out of there, as he should have, and took her to a place where he could keep her safe.

"Nathan, and by extension, Sam, made her a promise. A promise fulfilled by KGI, that we would do whatever necessary to bring you home. That we wouldn't quit until you were safe. I asked for the assignment."

"Why?" she whispered.

"Because when I looked at the surveillance footage, I saw a vulnerable woman with fear in her eyes. But I also saw a strong woman who was a fighter. I saw someone I wanted to know better. I saw someone I considered mine from the first moment I laid eyes on her."

Grace held her breath until she was dizzy and then let it out in a long whoosh that weakened her to her knees.

"As for Nathan, he's had a rough time. A time that Shea got him through. She saved him. He was held captive in Afghanistan for two months and was finally able to escape with her help. KGI was able to get to him because Shea helped get us information. But he's solid. He and Shea both have a lot of healing to do, but they'll do it together. I don't think you could pry them apart with a crowbar. The concept of soul mates is kind of cheesy when said aloud, but there's no other word for the bond that exists between them."

"It doesn't sound cheesy," she said softly. "It sounds wonderful."

"She's in good hands, Grace. I swear it. Nathan will never let anything happen to her. He'd die for her. He has five older brothers who are more than willing to go to the wall for him, and then there is Steele's team and my team. I'm pretty damn picky about who I trust and who I call family, but if I ever call anyone family, it would be the Kellys."

"They sound so awesome," she said wistfully.

"You'll love them and they'll love you."

She frowned a moment because they didn't seem real. Just a topic of conversation, but one day . . . One day she'd see her sister again and they would be by extension her own family of sorts if Shea married Nathan. The idea of having this huge, protective family wasn't something she could wrap her head around.

But it sounded so nice, it made her chest ache.

They weren't hers, though. They were Shea's. Shea had Nathan. Grace was savagely happy for her sister. And relieved. But she was also envious because she wanted so badly to have those things Shea now enjoyed.

Love. Comfort. Stability. A normal life. Laughter. Children. A big family. Being able to breathe. Smile. Life without fear.

She closed her eyes, reaching out again, her longing for her sister a tangible, breathing entity.

Shea. Please be there.

For a brief moment, she swore she heard an echo in her mind. Just a faint call. So much like Shea. As if Shea was saying her name. And just as quickly it was gone.

But the sensation lingered, and Grace could feel the comfort as it seeped into her mind, soothing some of the sadness away.

She opened her eyes to see Rio staring at her, his gaze so soft and understanding.

"She was there," Grace said, her voice cracking. "For just a moment, I swear I heard her. Maybe I imagined it but I swear I felt her."

She rubbed her hands up her arms and then wrapped her arms around herself as if by hugging tightly she could prevent the lingering aura of her sister from fading.

Rio pulled her farther into his embrace, holding her firmly against his chest. She rested her cheek on the faded T-shirt, soaking up the warmth and comfort he offered. He laid his cheek against the top of her head.

"You'll get there, Grace. You're already making such improvement. You bear no resemblance to the defeated, broken woman who begged me to let her die just a few days

ago. You walked out of those damn mountains under your
own power with a broken arm, broken ribs and unimaginable mental and physical strain. I've served with men who
couldn't have done what you did, so cut yourself some
slack."

She smiled, absorbing the gruff reprimand as though it
were a gentle stroke to her back. She liked Rio when he got
growly and bossy.

"So what do we do for now?" she asked, taking the conversation full circle.

Rio stroked his hand through her hair, toying with the
strands. "We wait."

She pushed up so she could meet his gaze. "For what?"

He eyed her seriously, his words as blunt as always.

"We wait until it's safe to leave or they show their hand.
We'll either bring the fight to them or we'll let them bring
it to us. One way or another, the battle is coming. It's just a
matter of when and where."

Grace sucked in her breath and tried not to shake but
she knew she failed miserably.

"Titan is that dangerous?"

"Titan doesn't play by the rules," Rio said matter-
of-factly. "In their world the only rules are the ones they
make. Failure isn't an option. They only know how to
achieve their objective. In this case their objective is you."

Helplessness gripped her, squeezing the very breath
from her lungs. "Then what is there to do? How can we
fight them if they're so damn undefeatable?"

"I didn't say they weren't able to be defeated. I'm just
telling you that they're a serious threat. I want you to
understand it. Know it. Live it. Breathe it. Never let your
guard down even for a moment."

"So we can beat them?"

She tried to keep the hope out of her voice because
she didn't want to sound desperate—even if that's what she
was feeling.

"We have no other choice," Rio said in a grave tone.
"KGI has the resources but we're divided. We can't leave

Shea, and I'm damn sure not leaving you. Which means that half of us will be pitted against all of Titan. But the other thing you need to know is that KGI doesn't lose. There's not another group of men who have more heart, determination and courage. Anywhere. We fight because we believe in what we do. Titan fights because it's what they're paid to do."

The tension that had coiled and pitted in her belly loosened and gradually slid away. She reached up to touch the hard lines of his face.

"You know what I think?"

He lifted an eyebrow. "What's that?"

"I think you're pretty damn special yourself."

He looked discomfited, as if he had no idea how to respond. And she didn't really give him a chance to. She leaned up, cupped his cheek and turned him so she could kiss him.

Somehow with him, she was bolder. More confident. She believed all the things he said about her. He made her believe them. He made her feel . . . worthy.

Nowhere in her life had she really given thought to being with a man beyond simple girlish fantasies and giggly conversations with Shea, who'd been a little more daring in her forays into sex.

Grace had been too timid. Too afraid to get close, only to be yanked up by her parents when it was time to move again. She longed for roots and a relationship but was deathly afraid to try to have one for fear it would be taken away.

Now probably wasn't the time either, but when had she ever felt as safe as she did now? Rio didn't just make her feel physically safe and secure. It was more than physical protection. Somehow he made her feel whole. Alive. Vibrant.

He made her feel . . . cherished.

She inched upward, pressing her mouth more fully over his. It was exhilarating to be the one making the moves. It was freeing after being captive for so long. She was making the decisions. She had control of her destiny. And right now, what she wanted, more than anything in the world, was to be loved by this man.

She wanted to get lost in his arms for a few hours. Hide from the world. Explore his body and let those wonderful rough hands glide over hers.

The fantasy was so vivid that she nearly moaned at the sheer pleasure coursing through her veins.

Rio pulled away, abruptly dimming some of her euphoria. His eyes blazed and his fingers were tight—painfully so—around her chin as he held her in place so their gazes were locked.

"Grace," he said hoarsely. "This has to stop. Unless . . . Unless you don't want it to. But I need you to know where this is headed. Because unless you tell me right here and now that a kiss is all you wanted, I'm taking you into my bedroom and I'm going to make love to you until neither of us can walk."

"I want more," she whispered.

The minute she said it, she was swamped by varying emotions. Fear. Terror. Nervousness. But also the satisfaction that she was speaking up, being courageous. Taking that chance and risking rejection.

Her whole life had been one of uncertainty and holding back. Never taking chances. Not wanting to step, for just a moment, into the sun and reach for what she wanted.

"How much more, Grace?" Rio asked, his gaze so intense that it blistered over her skin like a blowtorch.

"Everything. Anything. Whatever you can give me. Please, Rio. Don't make me beg. This is hard enough as it is."

He uttered what sounded like a curse under his breath and then he crushed his mouth to hers in a kiss so intense that she was consumed. His mouth took hers. It was no gentle inquiry. It was a stamp of possession. It was a promise of what was to come.

He dragged his mouth away, his chest heaving for breath. His eyes glittered and his hand shook against her face.

"You'll never beg. Not me. Not anyone. I'll give you what you want, Grace. I just want to make damn sure you know what you're getting into."

Her lips trembled and her knees wobbled precariously. Her skin was flush with heat. Achy and alive.

"Tell me what you want," he said in a near growl. "I want to hear you say it."

It was quite possibly the boldest, hardest thing she'd ever done, but the words came with no hesitation. "I want you to make love to me, Rio."

CHAPTER 21

IT took every bit of restraint not to haul her over his shoulder and run toward the bedroom. The very last thing he wanted to do was scare the shit out of her.

Beg? She honestly thought she'd have to beg him to make love to her?

Hell, he hadn't been far from being on his knees begging her to just let him touch her. Let him show her tenderness she'd long been denied.

He didn't even know where to start, so overwhelmed was he over this beautiful, brave woman who stood before him looking as though she was afraid he was going to tell her no.

He kissed her again, just because he couldn't resist. She was sweet and warm and so very soft. He loved the way her lips went pliant against his, like she was soaking up every bit of the moment.

He lowered his hands down her body until his fingers tangled with hers. Then he took a step back, tugging her along with him. He dropped one hand but kept firm hold on the other as he turned and headed toward the bedroom.

She hesitated a moment and he nearly cursed. Damn it, he'd lost her. She'd changed her mind, and it was nothing more than an impulsive declaration made in the heat of the moment.

"What about the others?"

Relief was instant. She wasn't backing out.

"They know better than to disturb me. They'll do their own thing until such time as I tell them differently."

He touched her face, softly stroking the line of her cheekbone. "Trust me, Grace."

Her eyes warmed and the blue became darker.

"I do trust you."

He squeezed her hand and then continued the rest of the way to the bedroom.

The awkwardness once they were behind the closed door was unfamiliar. Most of his liaisons, if you could call them that, were fast. Night out, ending in a hotel room. He usually bugged out the next day on assignment.

He liked to blow off steam as well as the next guy but he'd never let sex or a woman interfere with his job. What the hell was he supposed to do when the woman *was* the job?

And she wasn't just any woman. She wasn't someone he wanted to fuck to quick orgasm and then roll out of bed and into his combat boots.

He wanted to take his time, lavish her with the attention she deserved. He wanted to touch and taste every single inch of her beautiful body. But more than that, he wanted to slide into her mind and fill it with beautiful things to replace all the evil she'd been exposed to.

She tugged her hand from his and looked away, her bottom lip tucked between her teeth. She looked hesitant and adorably shy, and it made him want to pull her into his arms and promise her the world.

"Grace."

She glanced up, her chin wobbling just a bit.

"I'm going to undress you, but you need to tell me if that's okay. If you want me out of my clothes first so you don't feel at a disadvantage, I can do that. You tell me what you need and I'll make sure it's done."

Her brow furrowed and she looked genuinely perplexed. It was then he realized that the thing he could do most for her was to simply take control so she felt secure at all times.

Without waiting for an answer, he moved in and slid his hands underneath the hem of her shirt. His palms skimmed over her lean belly and upward, dragging the shirt with him.

"Lift your arms."

Slowly she raised her arms and he pulled the shirt over her head. His gaze was riveted to the soft swells of her breasts. So plump and delectable. Perfectly feminine. She was thin from weight loss, which made her breasts seem even plumper on her small frame. They were a perfect size, just enough to fill his hand.

And her nipples were a delicious pink. Soft around the nipple and then hard and erect, puckered and just begging for his mouth.

She started to cover herself self-consciously, but he put out a hand to stop her.

"Don't. You're beautiful, Grace. So very beautiful. You have nothing to hide. Certainly not from me."

Her smile was wavering but her eyes lit up. She stared at him like he was the only man in the world. Like he was somebody damn special.

He fumbled with her pants and pushed downward until they bunched at her ankles.

"Sit down on the edge of the bed," he directed.

He held on to her hand so she didn't trip as she took the few steps back. Once she was perched on the edge, he pulled the pants off.

She was only in a simple pair of white cotton panties, but she rocked them like they were Victoria's Secret's sexiest lingerie.

"Lie back," he said in a husky voice.

Slowly she reclined until she was on her back, her hair

splayed out around her. Her legs still dangled from the bed, her toes just grazing the floor.

He slid his hands up her legs, starting at her knees and working up to her hips. Then when his thumbs slipped under the band of her underwear, he leaned down and kissed the shallow indention of her navel.

She shivered and chill bumps dusted a fine layer over her skin.

Slowly, he eased the panties over her hips, uncovering the dark curls at the apex of her thighs. He continued sliding them down until they were free and he dropped them onto the floor.

He found her gaze again, read the stark vulnerability shining back at him.

"I'm going to love you, Grace. I'm going to taste you and touch you and I'm going to make you feel so very good. But you have to tell me if I ever do anything that makes you uncomfortable. Promise me that."

"I promise," she whispered.

He kissed one knee and then the other. Then he slid his hand between them and nudged them apart. He enjoyed the silky expanse of skin on the insides of her thighs. So satiny. His palms glided toward the juncture, spreading her wider as he went until her soft woman's flesh lay open and glistening before him.

Reverently, he lowered his mouth, dying to have his lips on her. Just wanting her taste on his tongue.

Gently, he opened her farther, using the pads of his thumbs. She shivered uncontrollably, her legs tightening. He stroked her a moment, content to explore the soft folds.

He touched her clitoris, just a simple touch, and then followed it with a firmer caress. This time, her hips lifted and her hands balled into fists at her sides.

After he teased the flesh into a taut bud, he swept his tongue over it. She cried out but he didn't lift his head to check her reaction. He could tell by the instant tension that rolled through her body that she'd found pleasure.

He sucked tenderly, flicking the tip of his tongue repeatedly over the bundle of nerves, stroking and teasing.

"Rio!"

It came out more as a breathy sigh. It was the kind of sound that boosted a man's ego. It told him he was pleasing his woman. That there wasn't another man she was thinking of at this moment.

He worked downward, savoring her taste and the way she arched into him. He licked over her opening then reached down to slide one finger inside.

He nearly groaned. She was so damn tight and all he had was his finger inside her. How much more glorious would she feel all snug around his cock?

Even though his body screamed at him to get his damn pants down and thrust inside her warmth, he knew he couldn't blow this. Grace deserved better than a quick lay. He wanted to give her more. He wanted this to be . . . Well, hell. He wanted it to be special.

Nothing like performance anxiety at the two-minute warning. Right now his dick was warning him that if he didn't get inside the end zone soon, it was going to be all over.

He sucked in a deep breath, inhaled her scent and nearly came in his pants right there. He needed out of his damn clothes. He was about to crawl right out of his skin.

He kissed her again, withdrew his finger and glanced up to see her staring down at him, her expression dazed and eyes burning with desire.

"Don't move a muscle," he managed to grind out.

He hastily stripped, or he started to. He'd ripped his shirt upward when her husky voice reached his ears.

"No, don't hurry. Please. I want to watch."

He had to close his eyes and collect himself. Everything she did and said just did it for him. He couldn't ever remember a woman being so curious and eager to see and enjoy him. His body. They were usually in as every bit of a hurry as he was. It was sex. Hot, sweaty, *quick* sex.

If he had his way, he was going to stretch this out the entire damn night.

He slowed down and eased the shirt up his chest, baring himself inch by inch to her avid gaze. And she was staring hard at him. He lost her a moment when he finally pulled it over his head, but when his gaze settled back on her, she was caressing him with her eyes.

Her enjoyment of him was there for the world to see. Shining in her eyes. Clear, unapologetic appreciation. It made him want to bow up and flex or do some other equally immature male posturing.

"Now your pants," she whispered.

As she made the request, she rose up to one elbow then pushed back with her other hand so she could fully see him. Just to make sure she was completely satisfied, he backed up a step so she could see all of him.

When his hands went to his fly, he heard her breath do a little fast hiccup. Getting into the spirit of the striptease, he took his time undoing the fly and easing the zipper down. He locked on to her gaze, enjoying watching her every reaction. He wondered if she even realized how expressive she was, how every thought seemed to be reflected in her eyes.

With the fly open, he slid his thumbs around the waistband, paused a moment and then began to ease his pants down. As soon as his dick popped free, her eyes widened. Her gaze went up to his, then back down, then back up again.

He couldn't help himself. He let out what might be the cockiest grin ever.

"Like what you see?" he drawled.

"Somehow I didn't see you as going commando."

He lifted an eyebrow. "That's all you have to say? You little tease."

She smiled and then blushed. "I'm just glad you can't read my mind."

His eyes narrowed and he advanced, his cock surging

upward even more. It was so damn tight and swollen that even moving was painful. He felt like he was going to split apart at the seams. He'd never been so goddamn hard in his life.

He placed his hands down on the bed on either side of her hips and leaned in until their mouths were close and he could feel her breath on his lips.

"Tell me what you were thinking, Grace."

Her eyes widened again and she blushed even harder.

"Tell me. I want to hear every little dirty thought that went through that mind of yours."

Her pupils widened, darkening her eyes to midnight blue.

"I was wondering how we'd ever fit," she whispered as if imparting a secret.

He smiled and then kissed her. Hard. When he pulled away, he was still smiling. "We'll fit, Grace. I'll make damn sure of that."

CHAPTER 22

GRACE'S eyes widened once more and she glanced down as if seeking confirmation herself. He curled his hand around his length and stroked up and down, allowing her to see for herself his size.

"See? Not so bad," he said in amusement.

She still didn't look convinced, but he figured if she was still worrying about the size of his cock when he got inside her, then he was doing it all wrong anyway.

After a gentle squeeze to the head and a moment to ward off impending orgasm, he put his hands on her shoulders and once more guided her down. This time he wanted to feast on those perfect breasts.

He wanted to lick down one side of her body and back up the other. And although he loved breasts as well as the next man, he was dying to fondle her ass and spend time exploring every curve and swell of that delectable backside. A curvy behind did it for him every time, and while Grace may be slender from her ordeal, she still had an ass to die for. He'd done his share of fantasizing about cupping it as he plunged into her.

Or of palming it as he took her from behind.

Hell, he'd even imagined taking her anally, which caused him to call himself all sorts of foul names. She was so damn sweet and gentle and beautiful and he was playing out scenes in his head from some skanky porn movie.

He positioned himself between her legs and lowered his body down so he could finally have his mouth on her taut nipples. His cock brushed over her pussy and lay sandwiched between their bodies, the tip touching the soft skin of her belly.

He angled himself so he could reach her breasts without having to move. He loved the feel of her surrounding his cock. She twisted restlessly beneath him, and he knew she was growing impatient. That made two of them.

He licked over one hard point, licked again and then sucked gently. Her fingers dove into his hair, surprising him with the ferocity of her grip. Her fingers were clenched tight around the long strands, her hand balled into a fist at his scalp.

Hell, she'd probably pull him bald, and he didn't really give a damn. She could pull it all out as long as she was screaming his name while she did it.

"I like that," she breathed.

He smiled against her breast then lifted his head to meet her gaze. "I like it too. You have beautiful breasts, Grace. The entire package is beautiful inside and out."

Moisture gleamed in her eyes and he leaned up to kiss her full on the mouth. "I didn't say it to make you cry. It's the God-given truth."

She caressed his cheek, rubbing soft fingers over the roughness of his jaw. "Thank you for that. For giving me back some of what I've lost."

"If I have my way, you'll get it all back."

He kissed her lips once more and then angled himself toward her other breast. He cupped it in his palm, plumping it upward so the nipple protruded even farther. He grazed his teeth over it ever so carefully, giving it a gentle nip before sucking it fully into his mouth.

She gripped his hair again, directing his movements. He quickly discovered she liked the light touches followed by hard sucking motions.

He rubbed his cock up and down the seam of her pussy and then onto her belly, mimicking movements their bodies would be doing soon. Each time he suckled at her breast, she grew wetter and slicker around his dick. He'd definitely found her sweet spot. She responded more avidly to having her breasts touched and kissed than she had when his tongue was inside her pussy, though she hadn't exactly *not* liked that.

"You're driving me crazy," she said as she pulled him back down to her breast.

He chuckled, wincing as she gripped his hair tighter. She may be timid and shy about the whole lovemaking experience, but when it came to what she liked, she wasn't hesitant whatsoever.

He kept his mouth on her breasts, but he slipped one hand down between them. He slid his fingers through her wetness to her opening, testing her readiness.

She was hot and wet, and as soon as he breached her entrance with just the tip of his finger, she arched up and moaned.

Oh hell yeah, she was ready.

He kissed her one more time for good measure and then pulled her down the bed so that her behind was perched just on the edge and was at just the right height and angle for him to take her.

"Hook your legs around me," he directed. He didn't want her uncomfortable, and being so close to the edge of the bed, if he didn't support her legs, it was going to be a hell of an uncomfortable ride for her.

She readily looped her legs around his waist and he slipped his hands underneath her behind, loving the feel of those lush cheeks in his palms.

He withdrew one hand, slid a finger inside to better prepare her and then he grasped his cock and fit it to her opening.

He pushed forward the barest of inches and her heat immediately enveloped him. Her swollen tissues hugged him tightly, making it difficult for him to gain entrance.

It was the single fucking most incredible sensation he'd ever experienced.

But she looked uncertain, and she was tense, her eyes wide.

He withdrew, though he'd barely gotten the head inside her opening. He reached down and stroked over her flesh, teasing, wanting to make her relax. She was slick against his fingers and she began to arch upward, responding to the gentle caress.

Once more, he found her opening and pressed forward, and she immediately went tense again. Her brow furrowed and creased in consternation and it was then realization struck him. He pulled away from her instantly, making no attempt to hide the shock he was feeling.

"Grace?"

She stared up at him, her blue eyes glossy with a sheen of tears. He felt sick. He'd hurt her. He'd hurt her and it was the very last thing he'd ever intended to do.

She was a virgin and he hadn't known. He'd almost taken things too far, had almost pushed inside her with one thrust because he'd been so eager to be balls deep in her sweet heat. He would have torn her in his haste.

"Why didn't you tell me?" he asked hoarsely. "This is definitely a conversation we should have had before now."

She flushed and started to look away as shame crowded into her eyes. But he leaned over her, his body pressed to hers as he framed her face, forcing her to look at him.

"Don't misunderstand me," he said fiercely. "This isn't about disgust or the fact that I don't want you. It's about me making this the best possible experience for you. You've had nothing but pain and abuse heaped upon you. This isn't just your first time, Grace. It's my first time too. It's my first time with *you*, and I don't want us both to remember this experience as anything but something beautiful."

"You *are* making it beautiful," she whispered. "You make me feel beautiful. Wanted. Nobody has ever made me feel the way you do, Rio. Please don't stop. I'm sorry I didn't tell you. I should have trusted you enough to have been honest from the start. I just wanted you so much and I didn't want my virginity to cause any weirdness between us. And maybe . . . maybe I thought you wouldn't want me quite so much if you knew I didn't have any experience," she added with a grimace.

Not want her? Hell, right now the primitive caveman inside him was roaring in triumph and beating his chest like a damn Neanderthal. It was a stupid fact that he was damn glad she hadn't had another lover. That she hadn't ever wanted someone enough to give herself to another.

"It was a stupid thought," he said with a scowl.

Her lips quirked upward in a grin and her eyes sparkled. She raised her hands to his face, framing it as he'd done hers, and then she lifted her mouth to his. "Then make love to me," she murmured against his mouth. "Please."

He slid his body down hers, pausing to tongue her nipples. "Just as soon as I make you crazy with lust again."

"Already there," she gasped.

But he patiently wooed her, with his mouth, with sweet words, with gentle caresses. He kissed a line down her belly and then knelt at the end of the bed so that his mouth hovered just between her thighs. One kiss. Just a simple kiss that he pressed to her quivering flesh, and it was like being hit by lightning. She arched upward, gasping as his tongue circled her clit and teased it mercilessly.

Her knees shook. Her entire body trembled as he continued to make love to her with his mouth. He kissed the mouth of her opening. Sweet, gentle kisses of apology as if to say he was sorry for hurting her. Then he pulled away and slid his finger into her opening, testing the resistance. He stretched experimentally, watching her face the entire time. When she grimaced, he withdrew immediately and then lowered his mouth to soothe away the hurt.

"Rio, please!"

He rose up and over her, his eyes serious. "I told you that you'd never have to beg me, Grace. Not for anything."

He slid his palms over her belly and up to her breasts, cupping them both. Then he stared down into her beautiful eyes as he reached down to position himself between her thighs once more.

He slid his thumb over her clit and then began to push inside her with steady pressure. He didn't want to just rip into her, but neither did he want to delay the inevitable and cause her more pain by drawing it out. She gave way underneath the relentless pressure and he heard her soft gasp.

She went tense all around him. Her eyes widened and her lips parted in a silent cry but then she bit down hard, as if to stifle any outburst. He swallowed and clenched his jaw as he sought valiantly to get himself under control.

He was about to crawl right out of his skin. She was hot and swollen around him, gripping him so tight that he was nearly senseless with pleasure. He'd never felt anything so damn good in his entire life.

But when he looked into her eyes and saw the tears she was valiantly trying to hold back, the ache in his chest grew until it was painful to breathe.

"I'm so sorry, baby," he whispered.

He kissed her forehead, her cheeks, her nose and then each eyelid. He kissed the corner of her eye, where a single tear had escaped, and he licked it away.

"I won't hurt you anymore, I swear it."

She turned her chin up, hungrily finding his mouth. "Please, just don't stop. Don't . . . leave. You didn't hurt me. It was just a shock and then it was so overwhelming. I just got emotional."

"Shhh, honey," he soothed. "I'm not going anywhere." He thumbed a tendril of hair from her cheek and then kissed her again, lingering, so tender it made him ache.

As if he would leave her. He wasn't going anywhere until she was more than satisfied. Over his dead body would he leave things as they were right now.

There were so many questions running through his mind that he was dizzy with them. Uppermost was how in the hell did this woman ever get to here and now without having had a man make love to her? Were they all brainless idiots or had she purposely kept her distance? And if she had, why him and why now?

It was stupid and pointless to try to read too much into the fact that she'd given her virginity to him. Not to anyone else. Him. It was a precious gift that he felt savage satisfaction over receiving. No one would ever have what she'd given him. It was his alone.

"Look at me," he said. When she complied, he kissed her once more and remained completely still. He was afraid of moving too soon, too fast, of hurting her more than he already had. "We're going to take this nice and slow and easy."

She nodded and he saw relief flash in her eyes.

"I'm going to rise up just enough that I can get my mouth on those gorgeous breasts of yours again. I want you to try to relax as much as possible. I want you to enjoy this. You liked it when I touched your breasts and your nipples."

She blushed hard but nodded her agreement.

"When I did it before, you got wet. So we're going to do that again and then I'm going to take it really slow and be extra gentle until we get the hang of this, okay?"

She teared up again, nearly ripping his heart out of his damn chest. Then she reached up with both hands and framed his face. She pulled him down into a ferocious kiss that left him breathless. It also had the unfortunate result of making him even harder inside her.

She twitched and fidgeted underneath him as if trying to find just the right spot while she adjusted to his size and just having a man where no one had ever been.

"Thank you for making this so perfect," she said in a choked voice.

Her statement robbed him of speech. His mouth opened but just stayed there. Perfect? He stared down at her like she'd lost her mind, but she just smiled and then kissed him again.

"I can't imagine anyone else being so sweet and gentle. You're an enigma, Rio. So hard on the outside, but you know what? I think you're a giant fluffball inside."

"Fluffball?"

He was horrified. Fluffball? Hell, if his men ever heard that, he'd be fucking toast. They would never, ever in a million years let him live it down.

And then if the other team, Steele's team, got wind of it . . . It didn't even bear thinking about. Steele would ride his ass hard for the next ten years.

Her smile grew bigger. "Yes, a fluffball. A sweet, wonderful fluffball."

"Ah hell."

She laughed and he supposed he could take her laughing at him over the tears she'd shown just moments ago.

"Now as I recall, you said something about my breasts," she murmured.

He lifted a brow. "Oh yes, ma'am. I like it when you get kind of bossy on me."

"Kiss them," she begged softly. "I love your tongue and your mouth and when you suck on them. I can't even explain how good it feels."

Her words hummed like sweet music over his ears and down his body, eliciting a bone-deep shiver. His cock surged forward and he was about to apologize but she moaned softly, closed her eyes and tilted her breasts upward in silent invitation.

Relieved that the worst seemed to be over, he was more than happy to oblige her. He licked over one nipple then went for the other, giving it equal treatment.

He nibbled, sucked and licked, going back and forth until she was writhing beneath him. He doubted she even realized that she was doing all the work around his cock and he let her do it at her own pace even though it was killing him not to go at her and go hard.

She was arching her hips up, taking him deeper, her

ankles crossed at the small of his back. She was wrapped so tight around him that he swore he'd wear the indentions from her heels in his ass for days to come.

"Rio, please."

"Please what, baby?"

"I don't know!" she wailed. "I need . . ." She closed her eyes and arched her hips again. "Please."

She was wet around him. Slick and hot and she wasn't quite as snug before. She was close to her orgasm and he wanted to make it pretty damn awesome for her.

"Hold on to me, honey, okay? And trust me to take you where you want to go."

Her hands instantly went to his shoulders. Her nails dug into his flesh and her gaze locked with his. Trust was shining, a light on the darkest night. It hit him in the gut. It humbled him that she was giving him so much.

He gathered her tightly in his arms and began a slow, measured thrusting pattern. She sighed and then she moaned. She let out little gasps and whimpers. She was noisy and fidgety and he loved every damn minute of it.

"More," she demanded.

He grinned, kissed that luscious mouth of hers and then began driving into her, deep, hard, showing her that she was his.

"Oh yeah," she breathed out. "Oh, I like this too."

"So do I, honey, so do I."

His muscles flexed and bulged. He gritted his teeth together, determined that she would be satisfied first. Her eyes widened, her body tightened, and her pussy fluttered around his cock, driving him to further insanity.

"Let go, honey. Go with it. Don't fight it. Just let it happen."

She went slick, like liquid silk, surrounding him, bathing him in her sweetness. And then he felt her spasm around him.

"Oh hell. I'm coming too. Don't let me hurt you."

She roared at him not to stop. He roared her name as he came in wave after wave. He was still coming several long moments later when she went limp beneath him. He pounded into her over and over as he poured himself into her.

He leaned down, his hips still jerking as he settled over her. God, she felt good. He didn't ever want to pull out. His cock was still twitching and leaking semen, but he was deep inside her and he'd never felt so goddamn content in his life.

He pulled her close until he wasn't certain she could breathe, but she was against him, around him, skin to skin, and that was all that mattered.

After a moment, he rolled them to the side, ignoring her sleepy protest. The movement caused him to slide out of her warmth, and they both moaned, though he suspected for different reasons.

She had to be tender after that epic lovemaking session. He'd never spent so much time inside a woman for one sexual encounter in his life. And she'd been a virgin.

He glanced down as he came free, frowning at the smear of blood on his cock. He didn't like to think of hurting her at all. She'd had enough hurt in her life.

"Stay on your side," he murmured next to her ear. "I'll go get a cloth so we can clean up and then you can sleep if you want."

"Mmm-hmm," she mumbled.

Smiling, he got out of the bed and went into the bathroom to clean himself off with a damp washcloth. Then he ran the water until it got hot, wet another cloth and wrung it out.

When he returned, her eyes were closed, but as soon as he slid onto the bed, her gaze found him.

"Open your legs for me," he said softly.

Shyly, she parted her legs, lifting one upward and then bending her knee so she could prop her foot against her other leg.

She sighed when he pressed the warm cloth to her skin. There was something decidedly intimate about him wiping away the proof of his possession. The rag came away sticky with her blood and his semen. He stared at it for a long moment, realizing the significance.

She'd been a virgin and he'd been her first. He also hadn't thought to use a condom. Perhaps more irresponsible than not using a condom was the fact that he didn't give a shit that he hadn't.

In his mind, she was his. Whatever happened as a result of their lovemaking, they'd face together. Just like they'd meet head-on the dangers that pursued them.

He tossed aside the washcloth and then pulled back the covers so he could get her underneath. After she was settled, he climbed in beside her and pulled her flush against his body, tucking her head beneath his chin.

There was a lot to think about. A lot to decide. But some decisions had already been made. Such as the first time he'd ever seen Grace Peterson and decided that she was his.

He'd tracked her down. He'd sworn to protect her. She was here in his arms, in his personal sanctuary.

For him, that was akin to a freaking marriage proposal.

CHAPTER 23

GRACE dozed lightly, snuggled tightly in Rio's arms. She never slept fully but instead existed in a dreamlike state. She was limp, drained of energy, but in an oh my God good way.

He felt good against her. Strong. Hard as a brick. Warm. And so comforting. She felt cherished and that was her weakness.

She wanted someone to demonstrate the kind of caring that went beyond an impersonal relationship.

She rubbed her cheek over his chest and sighed.

"What's the sigh for?"

She lifted her head to see that he was very much awake and staring inquisitively down at her. She propped her head up in her palm and nudged her elbow up under her pillow so she could see him while still remaining as close to him as possible.

"Just seemed like the thing to do," she said simply.

He touched her cheek and then her hair, stroking lightly as he continued to study her. Then he cocked his head to the side. "Why me?"

Warmth seeped into her cheeks. She didn't deliberately try to misunderstand his question. She wasn't entirely certain just how honest she should be with him. How she answered could change a lot between them. Or change nothing at all.

"You have to know what my life's been like," she said in a low voice. "Always moving. Never having friends. Never trusting anyone. It was so ingrained in me and Shea that after a while being loners was just natural.

"Shea . . . Shea was a little better at it than I was. I mean she tried more. She wanted a normal life and I think in the beginning she was more naïve in thinking she could actually have that normalcy. We both were in denial of our circumstances, but she more than I ignored the reality of who and what we were. I think Shea thought if she didn't acknowledge it, then it didn't exist.

"For me, it was an everyday battle. Always seeing people hurting. In need. Knowing of sick children. I lived with the knowledge that I could help them. That I could make a difference and yet I could tell no one, and if I reached out to one of them, it would mean discovery not only for me but for my sister."

"That's a hell of a lot of responsibility to take on your shoulders," Rio muttered.

"I hated myself."

Rio slid his hand over her face, cupping her cheek as his eyes bored into hers. "No. Don't hate yourself." He kissed her, leaving his lips pressed against hers as he stroked her hair. "You can't be responsible for the world. You can't help everyone. You know what it does to you. How does it help anyone if you die?"

"It frustrates me, you know? I feel like I've been given this really awesome gift but, oh wait, I can't use it because it may be too much and I may die. What kind of deal is that? What's the point? Not using it seems so irresponsible and selfish. And yet if I use it, it endangers me and my sister. No matter what I do, the outcome sucks."

She was near tears again, and instead of showing her utter weakness once more, she turned her face into the pillow and then burrowed closer to him so that her head was wedged between his chin and the pillow.

Rio continued to run his hand over her hair, pulling through the strands with his fingers. For a long moment, he was silent. Only the sounds of his breathing filled the room.

When he spoke, it was a low rumble, serious and yet calm.

"I don't have the answer to that, Grace. Maybe your purpose hasn't yet been revealed. Maybe what you're supposed to do is survive until the day when you know why you've been given this gift."

His words sank in and she went still. Slowly she raised her head and stared into his eyes. "You think so?"

Rio shrugged. "I'm a big believer in everything having a purpose. *To everything there is a season, and a time to every purpose under heaven.*"

Her eyes widened as he quoted a passage from the Bible.

He gave her a mocking look. "What? Don't think I'm the religious type?"

She had no idea what to say to that so she remained silent.

"My point is that even in olden times, the wisest of men believed that everyone had a purpose and that there is a time for everything under the sun. This is your time to heal. To grow stronger. And then one day the time will come when your purpose will be revealed. It may not be today or tomorrow or even next year. But I don't believe in accidents of nature. You were given this gift. Your sister was given her ability. For a reason."

Her mouth turned down. "But we weren't born. We weren't God's creation at all. We were conceived in some petri dish in some cold, sterile lab where they wanted to replicate instances of special abilities occurring in the human populace. They hoped by mixing the right genes together that they'd create something extraordinary."

He smiled and touched his finger to her lips. "You don't

think He had any hand in it whatsoever? Just because you weren't conceived the old-fashioned way doesn't mean your purpose isn't any greater. What if He decided to take something bad and make it good? Look at what Shea did for Nathan. And for Swanny. They're alive because of her. Never underestimate your value, Grace. Or your purpose. You were put on this earth for a reason. You're here with me now for a reason."

He curled a thick strand of her hair around his finger and tugged slightly. "Has it ever occurred to you that you're here for me?"

Her eyebrows went up. What could she say to that? So she turned it back instead. "And maybe your purpose was to save me."

He smiled. "Maybe so. Maybe we'll end up saving each other."

"Why do you need saving, Rio? Who are you? Is Rio your real name?"

Some of the light dimmed in his eyes and his lips flat-lined. He went silent and his fingers slowly drifted from her hair. Then he grimaced. "My real name is Eduardo Bezerra. There, I've told you something that most other living people don't know."

Her brow wrinkled. "You don't look like an Eduardo. Rio suits you. But how did you get the name?"

"Everyone usually ends up with a nickname in the mili-tary. My father was American. My mother was Brazilian. I was born in Rio de Janeiro, but we moved with him back to the U.S. when I was very young. I joined the military right out of high school. When I entered Black Ops, I ceased to exist as Eduardo Bezerra anyway, and anyone who knew him was told he'd died in combat."

The implication of what he said hit her hard. She frowned and stared up at him for confirmation. "But what about your family? Your parents? You said you had a sister. Surely they weren't told you died."

Pain swamped his eyes and then he simply turned away,

rolling to the edge of the bed. He sat up, pulling the sheet with him, and he sat there on the edge, leaning forward, head down.

She got awkwardly to her knees, feeling exposed and vulnerable. But there was something about the look in his eyes that struck a chord deep within her. She'd felt his pain. For a moment it was as if her mind had opened up that path again and she'd gotten a glimpse inside his mind.

Tortured. Guilt. So much guilt and sorrow.

Tentatively, she touched his shoulder. He flinched and the muscles jumped and coiled underneath her fingers, but she didn't remove her hand.

Then she wrapped her arms around him, laid her head on his shoulder and hugged him tightly, her breasts pressed to his back. She kissed the ball of his shoulder and simply knelt there holding him.

"Did you see it all? I felt you in my head for just a moment," he said bitterly.

She kissed him again and ignored the sharpness in his tone. "No. Even if I could, I wouldn't have. I don't establish links with people I'm not close to. It's a breach in privacy and I'd never encroach on yours."

He slid his hand up to cover one of her hands that lay over his chest. "Well, that put me in my place, I suppose. I snap because you're in my head and yet I don't like you saying that you wouldn't because you don't establish links with people you aren't close to. Guess I can't have it both ways, can I?"

She rested her chin on his shoulder and sighed. "Tell me what's wrong, Rio. It doesn't have to be so difficult that I have to read your mind or see your thoughts. All you have to do is tell me what it is. They told your parents that you'd died?"

He gripped her hand tighter and then carefully loosened his hold. "Yes. At the time I was young and idealistic. It was all for the greater good. In order to serve my country, I had to die. I couldn't have ties. They needed the ultimate soldier. No family. No baggage. Nothing to hold me back.

Nothing that would take a higher priority than my mission. My parents had Rosalina, and I thought everything would be fine."

He sighed deeply and wiped a hand over his face, pushing it back into his hair and holding it there at his nape, his knuckles white from his grip.

"I was a selfish, glory-seeking fool."

Grace winced at the self-condemnation in his voice. "And now? Do they know you're alive?"

"They do," Rio said, so soft she almost didn't hear. "And yet I am dead to them still."

Grace blinked, not sure she'd heard him correctly. "I don't understand."

"You know this part. My sister got involved with a man who was all wrong for her. He was older, controlling. He was a bastard of the first order. He killed her."

Even though he'd already told her as much earlier, she still winced at how casually violence had been meted out.

"I should have been there. It would have never happened. My father had suffered a heart attack. I never knew. I was too busy out saving the world, or so I thought. In truth, I was drowning in shades of gray so murky that I was treading water you couldn't see through. My mother was afraid of Rosalina's husband and there was little my father could do in his failing health.

"I was between missions and having doubts about my purpose. Having doubts that I'd done the right thing. I no longer believed in what we were doing. I wasn't even sure what master we served. I went to my sister's house, intending only to see her. I didn't even know if she had children. I just wanted to look. To make sure she was happy and healthy. What I found was a pregnant woman beaten so badly that she died in my arms, thinking I was a fucking ghost."

He choked off and covered part of his face with his hand. "I swore vengeance. It was all I could think to do. I felt so damn guilty. I felt responsible. It became my sole mission in life to make the bastard pay for what he'd done.

I tracked him down and I killed him. I don't regret it. He suffered just as Rosalina suffered. And when I was done, I went to my mother and my father and I told them what I'd done. All of it."

Grace caught her breath and went still against him. She hugged him tighter because she sensed that this was where it had gotten bad. She held her breath, dreading what he would say next.

"I'll never forget the way my mother looked at me. With such grief and disappointment. My father just looked weary and gray. She said that no son of hers would have ever let his family grieve for his death and that no son of hers would come to her house with blood on his hands, stinking of revenge. She then said that in her eyes I was no better than the man who'd killed her daughter and that *her* son died years before."

"Oh, Rio," she whispered. "I'm so sorry."

"I deserved it," he said bleakly.

"No one deserves to be denied forgiveness."

"I turned my back on my family."

She didn't argue. There was a lot she could say, but in the end, it wouldn't make any difference. And he didn't need meaningless platitudes. Some pain just had to be healed over time. And some wounds took much longer than others to mend.

But she could offer him comfort. The same comfort he'd given to her. She slid off the bed and then climbed onto his lap, straddling his legs as she wrapped her arms around his neck.

He stared into her eyes, his own gaze serious and intense. "You have to understand, Grace. I'll never turn my back on you. I'm not walking away. I swore I'd protect you and I'll die before going back on my word. I'll never let what happened to my sister and to my family happen to you."

She ran her hand over his brow, pushing at his hair. She stroked softly, hoping her touch was as comforting to him as his was to her. "Had you already walked away from Titan before you went to Rosalina?"

"I hadn't decided fully yet. As I said, I was between missions. When she died, I quit and spent the next year hunting the bastard. And then after the confrontation with my family, I knew I couldn't do it anymore. Couldn't go back. It felt like a betrayal even though they didn't acknowledge that I was alive. But even then, I didn't join KGI for them. I did it for me. Because I wanted to be able to look at myself in the mirror each morning and recognize the person looking back at me. And be at peace with him."

"Is that why you took the mission to come after me?" she asked curiously. "Was it penance? Did you feel like you had to make up for the past?"

Rio frowned and his expression grew fierce. He caught her chin in his hand and held her firmly in place as his stare blazed over her face.

"Fuck no. You're not some object to assuage my guilt. Is that what you think? Because you couldn't be more wrong. I volunteered to find you because when I looked at you, I saw my future. It was like a flashbang grenade in the face. It all came together in my head. I couldn't have walked away if I wanted to."

She stared at him in utter bewilderment.

He rubbed his thumb over her bottom lip and then leaned forward to kiss it. "I don't expect you to understand it. Hell, I don't understand it myself. But I do expect you to accept it. And me. Because, honey, whether you realize it or not, I'm going to be a steady presence in your life from now on. It's just a matter of how and where I fit in when all of this is over with, but I'm telling you right now, I'm not going away."

CHAPTER 24

IT amused Rio to see Grace so befuddled over his claim. He'd all but told her she was his and she had no choice in the matter. Not that she didn't. He wasn't good enough for her, and he damn well knew that. She needed someone far better than him. She deserved better. And if she told him to take a hike . . . Well, he'd be lying if he said he'd give in gracefully.

Some things were worth fighting for. Grace Peterson was one of them.

But he also knew they had a very long road ahead of them. Hurdles both visible and not yet visible. It wouldn't be easy and it wouldn't be overnight.

As much as it amused him, however, it also pissed him off that she'd be so bewildered that someone would be so adamant about wanting her. She acted like she'd never really had anyone but her sister care for her.

Just the idea of her having those kinds of thoughts made his chest ache. It was high time someone appreciated what an amazing woman she was.

She touched his face again with those soft fingers and

he couldn't help it. He just reacted to her. His dick stirred and hardened. Since she was sitting on his lap, he couldn't very well hide that fact from her. Hell, he was prodding her ass with the goddamn thing.

"I never know quite what to say around you, Rio. I keep thinking that none of this is real. That it's some bizarre figment of my imagination and that I'll wake up in captivity and all of this will have been a wonderful dream. Stuff like this just doesn't happen."

He laughed. "Honey, listen to what you're saying. You're being all skeptical and saying that stuff like this doesn't happen. Do you have any idea how absurd that sounds coming from a woman with extraordinary abilities? It's me who should be screaming shit like this doesn't happen in real life. But the fact of the matter is that it does happen. To me. To you. I go on missions all the time. That's nothing new. What's different is being knocked on my ass by simply seeing a woman on surveillance footage and knowing that somehow her life is irrevocably entwined with mine. Now that's the kind of stuff that doesn't happen every day. Everything else? Completely normal."

She kissed him. One minute he was talking to her and the next she slammed her mouth down over his and took him hungrily. He nearly lost his balance and fell backward, so fierce was she. She wrapped her arms around his neck, thrust her hands in his hair and balled up one fist, holding him in place. As if he'd actually move a damn muscle.

He'd sit here all night if she wanted to keep kissing him this way.

He almost whimpered when she pulled away. She continued to stroke his face and he felt like purring. He was such a goner. He wondered if she had any idea that all she'd have to do is pet him a little, look at him a certain way, and he'd lay the damn world at her feet.

It was insane. All of it. He'd never fallen for a woman. Certainly not in the span of a few days. Certainly not before meeting her.

But fuck it all, he had fallen hard for Grace Peterson.

She eased from his lap, and before he could protest, she lowered herself to her knees right between his thighs. She wrapped her fingers around his erection and slid gently up and down, staring avidly as he hardened further.

Oh hell, this was going to be torture. She looked for the world like she wanted to explore. Like she was checking things out and doing a little experimenting. Not that he had any objections whatsoever, but this would be a test of his endurance. If he got through this without embarrassing himself, he was going to deserve a medal.

"Rio?"

His name came out all breathy and hesitant but a little excited, which made him a lot excited. But he forced himself under control and tried not to think about the fact that his cock was wrapped up in her hand and she was driving him crazy with her every movement.

"Yes, honey."

"I don't really know how to do this. But I'd like to. I mean . . ."

She broke off, blushing madly, and ducked her head.

"Can you show me how to do it?"

Unless he was completely off by a mile, she was kneeling in front of him, hand around his cock, asking him to show her how to give him a blow job.

One side told him not to be an asshole and to pick her up, spread her out like a feast and show her how good his mouth could feel on her. No way he was going to get inside her when she'd been a virgin just an hour ago and was likely tender from the experience.

The other side, the side screaming at him inside his head, was telling him to show her exactly how he liked it in great detail.

What decided it for him was when she looked back up at him, those gorgeous blue eyes wide and imploring, and said, "I want to taste you, Rio. Like you were doing with me. I know guys like it but I have no idea what I should do or how I should do it."

He groaned. "Oh yeah, baby, we like it all right."

She smiled. "Then show me."

He slid his hand over the top of her head and then dove his fingers into her hair. With his other hand, he gently took his dick from her grasp and pumped a few times until he was rigid.

"Up higher on your knees," he directed.

She braced both palms on the tops of his thighs and pushed herself upward.

He rubbed his hand over her nape, gently squeezing and caressing to put her at ease. He positioned his cock so it was in line with her mouth.

"Now open," he said gently. "Lick the head. Don't take it in just yet. Tease me. I love to be teased. Think of it like flirting. Give me just a taste of how good it can be."

Her pink tongue slid over her lip and tentatively touched the tip of his cock. He sucked in his breath harshly and called back the groan of agony. Goddamn it felt so good and she'd barely touched him.

"A little more," he encouraged.

She circled the head with her tongue and then gave him a little extra stroke to the underside. Ah shit but he loved that. It was his favorite place.

He grasped his dick with a firmer hand and pulled back. She frowned and looked so dismayed that he was kicking himself.

"Was I doing it wrong?"

"Oh, hell no. I was going to tell you how right you were doing it."

He lifted and ran his fingers up the length to the tightly stretched underside right below the angled tip of the crown. "You're sweet spot is your breasts. This is my sweet spot. I love to be touched there. Sucked, licked, whatever you want to do, I guarantee I'll love it."

"Oh," she said with a smile.

He clutched at her hair and guided her back. "Open again."

This time she took more initiative. She licked teasingly over the top and then around, pausing to give extra attention to the area he'd pointed out. He closed his eyes and let her play for a moment.

"Now take me deeper. Real slow. Watch your teeth and make it tight. Suck lightly as you take me in but not too hard."

He eased his length deeper into her mouth. All the while, her gaze was locked with his. She watched him closely as if gauging his reaction to each touch, each suck, and each time she moved her tongue sensuously over his length.

"We'll take it nice and slow. I don't want to overwhelm you," he said. "As you get used to it, I'll show you more. For now, find your rhythm and find a way to breathe. Suck in through your nose when I'm deep. As I slide back out, you can breathe around me. In a minute, I'll want to go as deep as you can take me. I don't want you to panic. You're in the driver's seat. You'll take as much or as little as you feel comfortable doing, okay?"

She nodded, the motion sliding her tongue up the underside of his erection.

"Get a little higher on your knees so you're above me. Then I'm going to move my hand and you take me. I'm just going to lean back and let you do what you want for a little while."

She cast him an anxious glance but he smiled reassuringly at her. Hell, she didn't need any instruction, but he had to admit, it was a hell of a turn-on to have an almost virgin between his thighs, listening to his every instruction on how to please him.

She was pulling fantasies out of his head that he hadn't realized he had.

As soon as her hand slid over his, he loosened his hold and allowed her to take over. He leaned back, bracing himself with his palms on the mattress while she rose up and over him.

"Move your hand in time with your mouth," he said. "When you suck in and take me inside, work your hand down to the base. As you let out, work your hand back up and make it tight."

"Like this?" she asked innocently.

She tightened her grip around his cock and then slowly sucked the crown inside her mouth, but she didn't stop. She rolled her hand down and followed with her mouth, taking him deep while exerting pressure with both her hand and her mouth.

Holy shit.

"Exactly like that," he rasped.

He felt her smile around his erection and then she let back up, gliding her warm, moist mouth over his length. At the top, she stopped and held the head on her tongue and then swirled it around, laving the bottom and teasing the area with a series of licks and swipes.

"You're an awful quick study," he said from behind clenched teeth. His entire jaw was set tight, bulging outward as he struggled not to orgasm.

She pulled her mouth away but continued to stroke him with her hand. She looked up, her lips swollen from the attention she was giving him.

"I like the way you taste," she said in a sweet, shy voice that had him groaning all over again. "You're so hard but yet completely soft. It's so interesting."

"Interesting?" he croaked.

"What does it taste like when you come?"

He coughed and leaned upward again. "Uh, as I've never tasted it, I can't really answer that one for you."

She laughed. "Do you mind coming, in my mouth, I mean? Or is it too soon? I've heard that it takes a long time for guys to . . . you know . . . rebound after having sex. I've read that women can orgasm much more quickly and don't require as much recovery time between."

"What the hell have you been doing, checking out library books on the subject?"

"You can find anything on Google," she said with a grin. "Do you mind?"

An anxious note had crept into her voice, and he nearly shouted hell no but he managed to control himself. Barely.

Mind? She had to be kidding. He'd shock the hell out of her if she could see into his mind at the moment because he was holding on to a particularly vivid image of him being so deep inside her mouth that his balls rested on her chin while he came.

He even managed to sound calm when he finally responded.

"I don't mind at all. I just want to make sure this is what you want."

She nodded as she continued to stroke him. "I do. I like the idea . . . I mean I guess it sounds stupid, but there's something so . . . intimate about it, don't you think?"

He closed his eyes and merely nodded because, at this point, if she kept this up, he'd never make it to her mouth before he started coming.

And to think she was worried about recovery time. He didn't know whether to be insulted or amused. It was obvious she really didn't know that much about sex but had tried to remedy it and have as much foreknowledge as possible for when she made love the first time.

This time she uncurled her fingers so she wasn't fisting him and held him by her fingertips. Then she licked from the very base, her tongue glancing over his balls, all the way up the underside to the very tip. Before he had any chance to imagine what she'd do next, she sucked him in deep and hard.

He landed at the back of her throat, and he automatically bucked upward, unable to control his response.

She gripped him again, steadying herself, and then she slowly worked back up. This time she didn't tease but rather set a steady rhythm with her hand and mouth, growing tighter with each stroke.

"Use your other hand to cup my balls," he said in a tight voice. "Squeeze but not too hard. Work them while you suck me."

The raw, coarse language had the same effect on them both. Grace trembled. Her nipples tightened and became rigid, erect points as they bobbed in front of him. Precum leaked into her mouth, and he worried at first that she'd decide this wasn't what she'd imagined and bail.

Instead she slowed and seemed to savor it, almost like she was deciding how she liked it. She rolled her tongue around, catching every bit of the liquid before resuming the slow, sucking motions.

She had both hands wrapped around him, one around his balls, squeezing and massaging gently, and the other stretched around the base, working up and down in time with her mouth.

"Deeper," he urged. "Take me deep, baby. Hold me there. See how deep you can take me."

He didn't want to take over and force her to do anything. He'd rather let her set her own pace, explore at her leisure and do what came naturally to her. It was sexy as hell to discover a blow job with her.

In a lot of ways it felt like he was getting his first ever. He could also say he'd never had anything better than right here, right now, with a woman who wanted nothing more than to please him.

She sucked down until her chin brushed over his balls and her nose rested against his groin. Then she swallowed, her throat closing around him, and he lost the last vestiges of his control.

He arched into her, barely able to utter a harsh warning that he was coming. He began to spill into her mouth but she kept sucking and moving, seemingly unfazed by the sudden, forceful ejaculation into her mouth.

He reached out to run his fingers through her hair, his touch gentle and loving as she slowed in her movements. He felt her swallow against him and groaned, knowing she'd just taken everything he'd had to give.

She seemed to instinctively know he was a lot more sensitive now, and she loosened her grip and suction until she very gently released him. His erection sagged to the side, still semierect, and she looked up at him, her lips still glistening with his release.

"That was incredible," he said hoarsely. "Thank you."

She blushed but smiled big, her blue eyes shining.

"Come here," he said, finding her hands and pulling her toward him.

He wrapped his arms around her and lay back so she was atop him on the bed. Then he rolled so she was tucked into his side, their legs all tangled up.

"Thank you. That was very sweet of you. I don't think I've ever had a woman who wanted to please me as much as you."

She tilted her chin up so that her mouth was close to his ear and she whispered as if imparting something top secret. "I love the way you taste. Can I do it again sometime?"

He groaned again. Did she honestly think he was going to tell her no?

CHAPTER 25

GRACE was shaken awake to see Rio looming above her, a tight frown marring his face. She came instantly to awareness, blinking away the layers of sleep. Sunlight shone in from the high window, softly illuminating the room in morning sunshine.

"I have to do some recon," he said tersely.

She scrambled to a sitting position. "What does that mean? Do I need to go?"

He held out a hand. "No, no. You stay here. Browning's going to be here with you. I'm going out with Terrence while Decker, Diego and Alton are going to post a perimeter to make sure no one gets in."

"Is someone here?" she demanded. "What's going on, Rio?"

"Maybe nothing, but I'm not taking any chances. Browning just came off his watch and he reported movement in the southern sector bordering the river. Said they didn't look like locals. As I said, it could be nothing, but I'm sure as hell going to check it out."

She bit her lip but nodded.

"Listen to me. I want you up and dressed and prepared for anything. But I want you to stay in this room until I come back. Unless Browning tells you to move out. If for some reason I can't return to get you and we need to move, he'll bring you to meet me through one of the escape tunnels."

Her pulse raced out of control until she could feel it at her temples. She scrambled out of bed, staring left and right, unsure of what she was even looking for.

Rio put his hands on her shoulders and then turned her around to meet his gaze. He lowered his head and kissed her hard and quick.

"Don't freak. I need you calm. There are clothes in the closet. Get what you need. I'll be back as soon as I can."

He kissed her one last time and then was gone before she could even tell him to be careful.

There was no hope of her actually relaxing after that kind of wake-up call. She rummaged through the closet until she found a shirt and a pair of shorts with a drawstring waist. Perfect.

She frowned as she considered whether or not to take a quick shower. He hadn't really had time to leave yet. If he found trouble, he wouldn't find it this quickly, would he?

Finally deciding to risk it, she set a record for getting hair and body washed and clean. She toweled off, pulled her clothing on and then began drying her hair. She combed it out, left it mostly damp and pulled it back into one of the rubber bands she found in the bathroom drawer.

She wouldn't win any beauty contests but she was ready for anything.

Knowing her morning was shot to hell and she needed to find a way to relax, she climbed onto the bed and went through the exercises Rio had shown her the day before.

Gradually the anxiety melted away and she found her focus. Calm descended. It was as if her mind was a knotted rope that was uncoiling and loosening and finding its way free.

Tentatively she reached for her sister, trying to find her

way back to that familiar path she'd used for so many years. She was changed, though. Her mind was different. *She* was different. Nothing was as it was before, and she had to find her way again.

She brought the image of Shea's face to the center of her focus and let everything else fall away. She brought to mind the sound of her sister's voice. How it echoed in her memory. The way it sounded through the telepathic link.

Warmth spread over her, soothing and comforting. She could literally feel her sister's smile. And then the faintest echo, so faint she thought she'd imagined it.

Grace.

Her name. Shea was calling to her.

She was about to respond when her door burst open and Browning flew inside, his expression grave.

"Let's go. We have to meet Rio."

Her heart pounding out of her chest, she scrambled off the bed, thrust her feet into the pair of shoes on the floor and hurried after Browning, who was already on his way down the hall.

"What is it? What's happened?" she asked.

"I don't have all the details. Rio said to get you out and that's what I'm doing. He'll meet us in the northwest corner."

Grace frowned. That was away from the river. Had they come for her? Had she been found this quickly?

Browning led her through a tunnel she hadn't been in. It came out in a small cave, really more of a carved-out hole a few feet up a cliff overgrown with vines and thick moss.

He dropped down first and then motioned for her to jump to him. He broke her fall and then took her hand, tugging her farther into the dense foliage.

Limbs and brush slapped at her face, chest and legs. Several times she got tangled up in the undergrowth and nearly fell. She stumbled into Browning, who seemed impatient with how slowly she was moving.

Several times he looked as though he would say something, but he clamped his lips shut and urged her on.

After what seemed like an hour of him all but dragging her through the jungle, they stepped into a clearing. Ahead, there was what looked like a village right on the banks of the river. Browning had said northwest, but northwest from the house wasn't the river.

She struggled to catch up then pulled at his arm when several people stepped from the small huts that were erected a distance from the banks.

"Browning, what's going on? What are we doing here?"

He grimaced and then caught hold of her wrist. He held it so firmly that it hurt, but when she tried to twist away, he only tightened his hold.

"I'm sorry, Grace," he said in a low voice. "This is something I had to do. Rio's going to be pissed that I gave him false information so he and the others would go out, but I had to do it because he would have never let you come otherwise."

Fear burned through her stomach. "What the hell are you talking about?"

She tried to take a step back, but he wouldn't release her hand. She started to struggle, but he pulled out his pistol. She went still, unbelieving what she was seeing. What was happening? Browning pointed the gun at *her*.

"Don't, Grace. Please. I'm not going to hurt you unless you make it necessary. Just listen to me, okay? We don't have a lot of time."

Just then a young woman ran up to Browning, babbling a stream that Grace didn't understand. Browning held up the hand holding the pistol to silence the other woman but then pulled her into his side and held her, even as he gripped Grace's wrist with his other hand.

Grace's blood ran cold and panic gripped her throat. She hadn't questioned Browning. Rio himself had told her to go with Browning if he told her to. She'd trusted Rio's men because they were an extension of him. What was she supposed to have done, though, when Rio told her to do just as she'd done?

Browning had set Rio and the others up so he could get Grace out of the house. But why?

Browning said something to the woman and then gestured her away. He then turned his attention back to Grace. "I need your help."

His tone was pleading but Grace was just pissed. "Lying to me, dragging me through a jungle and pointing a gun at me isn't the way to go about asking for my help." She looked pointedly down at her wrist. "You're hurting me."

He loosened his grip slightly but wouldn't let her go. He kept looking in the direction that the woman had run, and a moment later, relief flooded his eyes. Grace followed the direction of his gaze to see the woman hurrying toward them with a baby in her arms.

Several of the villagers had formed a loose perimeter, and still more gathered, murmuring in low voices. Several shot the young woman holding the baby looks of sympathy. Others shook their heads and made gestures to suggest she was crazy.

The woman slowed as she approached Grace. Her expression was pleading and she spoke to Grace in broken English. "Please do not be angry with Mitch. I begged him to do this. It's the only way. You're our only hope."

Grace looked at Browning in confusion.

"Mitch is my first name," he muttered.

"What the hell is going on?" she asked for what seemed like the hundredth time. "Why am I here?"

Finally he let go of her wrist but then she noticed that several of the villagers were behind her as well. She had nowhere to go even if she decided to run. She cupped her arm, rubbing absently at the red marks as she waited for someone to tell her what the hell was happening.

Browning pulled the young woman into his side, his arm wrapped possessively around her waist. There was a fierceness in his expression, one she recognized because it was the way Rio looked at her.

"This is Sumathi, my woman, and our child, Ana. Ana

is . . ." He broke off, his voice thick with emotion. "She's sick. She's dying."

Sumathi interjected again. "Please, you must help her. There is nothing else to do. She's so weak. I'm afraid she will die today if nothing is done to help her."

Some of Grace's anger slipped away as she stared at the infant in Sumathi's arms. She was a thin baby, not at all like the chubby, rosy-looking babies that signified good health. The baby lay listlessly in the blanket.

"What's wrong with her?" Grace asked Browning.

"The doctors call it failure to thrive. No one really knows. She just won't eat. She has no strength. She's wasting away and I don't know what to do. I wanted to take her to the U.S. so she could be hospitalized. I was going to ask Rio for help. I know he would have given it to me. But I didn't know until just a short time ago and now I don't think she would be able to make the trip. Sumathi has taken her to see doctors here, but they tell her to feed her. Give her special formulas. She's tried everything, even asking another woman to nurse her. But she's dying."

The despair in his voice softened her anger. She looked helplessly at the baby, knowing that she had to try. Knowing what it would do to her and that she might not be able to sustain another healing.

She wasn't even sure she *could* do it.

Her voice cracked. Emotion and dread knotted in her throat. "You should know that I'm not certain I can do this. I haven't been able to connect to my sister since . . . all this happened. I haven't tried to heal. I don't know if I can do it anymore."

"All I ask is that you try," Browning said in a soft voice. "All *we* ask is that you try."

Grace glanced around at all the curious spectators. Unease crawled over her. Did they all know what it was Browning was asking her to do? She glanced sharply at him.

He shook his head. "I've only told them you were a physician and that you specialized in matters like this. They don't know what you can do. I may be a selfish, lying bastard, but I wouldn't have exposed you like that."

"I'll want privacy," she said.

"Then you'll do it?"

The instant hope in his voice was crushing. Sumathi's eyes lit up and tears swamped her vision.

"Thank you," Sumathi whispered. "May God bless you for the rest of your days."

How to tell this woman that the end of her days might well be here and that she could well be trading her life for this child's? But as she stared down at that tiny life, so weak and barely fighting, Grace knew she couldn't turn her back. She couldn't walk away no matter what it did to her. This child was innocent. She deserved a chance to grow up and be someone extraordinary.

Maybe her purpose was to save *this* child.

"Come this way," Browning said, guiding her toward a distant hut.

"Why are they here?" Grace demanded. "Why aren't they with you in the U.S., where they can be taken care of?"

Browning sighed. "I didn't know of Sumathi's pregnancy. We met between missions, when I was here with Rio. The next time I was able to see her was for just a few moments because we were involved in another mission, using Rio's place as a safe house. I came to see her this time because I wanted her to come back with me to the U.S. I wanted to buy her a house so we could be a family. I've missed so much of Ana's childhood already and she's just an infant. Maybe . . . Maybe if I'd been here sooner, I could have done something. Taken her to doctors in the U.S. But now we're out of time and you're our only hope."

Grace closed her eyes. It was a familiar story. She was someone's only hope. Who was supposed to be hers?

When they reached the hut, Grace stepped inside and Browning came in behind her, closing the door. Sumathi stood anxiously to the side, cradling Ana as she stared hopefully at Grace.

"You know what this does to me," Grace said in a low

voice. "You can't just leave me here. I'll be completely help-less."

"Whatever you may think of me, I would never just leave you. Rio will know where to find you."

It was only a small consolation. She was still riddled with fear and uncertainty. She warred with the consequences. Before she wouldn't have hesitated. She'd been so depleted, so broken, she would have chosen to give this baby her life at the expense of her own in a heartbeat.

But things were different now. Weren't they?

Someone cared about her. Rio said he was going to be part of her life.

But then she stared at Sumathi's tearstained face and saw a mother's love and desperation shining in the nearly black depths. How could she live with herself if she sentenced this baby to die in her mother's arms?

She would be no better than the man who'd murdered Rio's sister.

"Bring her to me," she said in resignation.

Sumathi hurried over and readily relinquished the baby into Grace's arms. Grace sank to the floor on her knees and then positioned the baby so she'd be warm and comfortable.

She was so listless. As if she'd already given up the fight.

Grace reached out to her, hoping to find a connection. She made the contact as warm and as soothing as she knew how. Closing her eyes, she narrowed her focus to nothing but this baby in front of her. She blocked out her surroundings, the distant noises, even the worried parents who loomed over her.

The pathway was so feeble that Grace almost missed it. There was only the faintest sign of life, and she knew that indeed it was nearly too late for this little one.

As soon as she was able to feel the pathway, she then concentrated on drawing away the weakness, the faint darkness that seemed to surround the baby's soul. Death had come for her and it was up to Grace to deny it.

Even the smell of death hovered close by. Grace drew it

into herself, pulling all the blackness away from the baby, replacing it with gentle warmth, encouragement and the goodness that had seemed so distant to Grace until the last few days.

She drew on the strength that Rio had given her. The will to live that he'd inspired. And she gave it to this child.

Weakness invaded her body. She moaned with the weight of it. It was suffocating, pressing down relentlessly. Despair tugged at her, sucking her into a black hole she'd sworn she'd never return to.

She wobbled and felt Browning hold her up, supporting her as she slumped. But it was useless. Grace lacked the strength even to hold up her head.

She was no longer herself, but this tiny baby barely clinging to life. She was cognizant of the need to break away and summoned the last of her strength to sever the connection between woman and child.

A lusty cry split the air and Sumathi gasped in wonder. Grace stared dully down at the baby, who now kicked and threw her arms about as if demanding to be fed that instant. Her color was better and she no longer looked as if death was winning the battle.

But as she glanced up at Browning and saw the paleness of his face and the horror in his eyes, she knew that death had found a new victim.

CHAPTER 26

RAGE was a terrible, black thing, swelling out of control as Rio cut a path through the jungle. Terrence was barely able to keep up, and Decker, Alton and Diego followed close behind but no one was able to keep pace with their team leader.

The message had been simple. Browning had Grace and now Grace needed Rio. Browning had sounded bleak and resigned through the com. Fear as Rio had never experienced had struck him and then black rage that he'd been betrayed by a man he trusted. One of his *team*.

They weren't just a team. They lived, breathed the same air, they had a bond unexplainable by most. And yet Browning had taken Grace. Had put her in unimaginable danger. He'd lied to Rio. Lied to his teammates.

For that alone he deserved to die.

But Browning had messed with Grace. The one thing Rio considered his own. A woman he'd die protecting.

He'd put his hands on Grace. He'd frightened her and God knows what else. He'd touched what belonged to Rio.

"Rio, man, you have to slow down," Terrence called. "You'll kill him before we get the full story."

Rio paused only long enough to stare coldly back at his first, a man he trusted implicitly, but then he was fast learning that trust could be broken as easily as a bone.

"He's going to die. There is no doubt about that. The question is how long he suffers before I kill the son of a bitch."

Diego let out a curse and surged forward, trying to overtake Rio. But Rio resumed his ruthless pace through the jungle toward the southeastern bank of the river. His pulse was like a hammer, pounding furiously through his veins.

What had Browning done? And why?

He'd entertained countless scenarios. That Browning had turned traitor and delivered Grace into Hancock's hands. But then why would he tell Rio where to find Grace and that she needed him?

He charged through the last of the thick overgrowth separating him from the village that was just down the river from his compound. His gaze swept the perimeter, his rifle raised and ready to lay waste to any threat.

Villagers scattered. Sounds of distress and fear rose, and children were quickly herded away toward the cover of the jungle. But Rio wasn't focused on them. His gaze found Browning, standing outside one of the huts, unarmed, stiff and straight as if awaiting judgment.

Rio charged toward him, but Browning didn't flinch away. Didn't even try to defend himself when Rio drove him to the ground.

"Where is she?" Rio growled.

His voice was of someone possessed. A product of his demonic rage and overwhelming fear for Grace.

He grasped Browning's shirt, yanked him upward until their faces were close.

"Inside," Browning said, sorrow thick in his voice.

Rio dropped him and then got up, running for the door. He yanked it open and saw Grace lying on the floor, a young woman hovering over her. Across from Grace on a tiny pallet lay an infant swaddled in a blanket.

"Get away from her," he snarled.

He dropped to his knees, nearly shoving the frightened woman out of the way. Grace lay completely still, pale, her breathing so shallow he could barely see her chest rise and fall. He felt for a pulse and it fluttered ever so lightly, erratic and weak.

Oh God. What had she done?

He picked his head up as the door opened and he locked on to the guilt in Browning's eyes. Terrence stood behind Browning, his face a mask of rage.

Terrence shoved Browning through the opening. "Tell him what you did."

The woman scrambled up and ran toward Browning. She threw herself between him and Rio and clung tenaciously as if trying to protect him.

Gently, Browning disentangled the woman and pushed her away. "No, Sumathi. You knew this would happen. A trade. My life for my daughter's. You knew he would kill me for this betrayal." He cast a look filled with regret and sorrow toward where Grace lay. "I didn't want to hurt her. I didn't know what else to do."

Rio rose, his hands trembling. "You did this to her? After seeing what it did, you made her do this?"

Sumathi thrust her chin up. "No! He didn't make her. It was her choice. He brought her here, but it was her choice!"

"Sumathi, be quiet," Browning said in a low, firm voice. "Take our daughter and leave. Go to your parents' hut and stay there until this is over."

She started to protest, but Browning quieted her with a look and an upheld hand.

Sumathi flew toward where the baby lay, gathered the sleeping infant in her arms, and with a last sorrowful look in Browning's direction, left the hut.

Rio couldn't wrap his head around any of it. There was a lot he didn't know but all he could think of was the fact that Grace lay a few feet away and she was in a bad, bad way. And his teammate was at the heart of it all.

"You have thirty seconds to explain yourself," Rio gritted out.

Browning gestured in the direction Sumathi had fled. "She's my woman and she had my child. Ana. But she's been sick since birth. She's never gained weight. She grows weaker by the day. The doctors say it's failure to thrive and that we should do this and that but nothing has worked and she was dying."

The frustration in Browning's voice mounted and echoed through the small room.

"When we pulled the mission to retrieve Grace, it gave me hope. After hearing of what she could *do*, I thought, my God, she's a miracle. She could save my daughter. And I knew then, that I'd do anything at all, even betray you, to save her."

A sick knot formed in Rio's stomach. "Did you force her to do this? What did you threaten her with?"

Browning's head snapped up and his eyes blazed. "I didn't threaten her. I gave you false information so I could set it up to get her out of the compound without raising suspicion. I brought her here and then explained why. She was frightened and confused at first. Then she seemed resigned. Once she saw Ana, she couldn't refuse. I knew she shouldn't have done it. God, I knew it, but I didn't care because I also knew she was my daughter's only chance."

There was a mixture of emotions on the rest of Rio's men's faces. Anger. Betrayal. But also understanding. And indecision. As if they couldn't make up their mind to be judge and jury over a man desperate to save his daughter.

But Rio couldn't give him a pass. Not when it meant Grace could die. May even be dying now. Browning had broken the trust of the team. He'd betrayed them all. How could they ever trust him again? How could he possibly trust Grace to Browning's protection now that he'd shown he would sacrifice her to achieve his ends?

Rio wanted to rage at him. Wanted to kill him. But he couldn't bring himself to give in to the urge when there was so much resignation in Browning's eyes. A man would do a lot to protect what belonged to him. Rio didn't fault the intent, but he sure as hell took issue with the method.

Knowing he had to see to Grace, he turned away from Browning, his action significant in that he no longer looked at or acknowledged his former teammate. His heart was heavy as he bent and gently picked up Grace's limp body from the mat.

As he walked toward the door of the hut, Diego, Alton, Decker and Terrence all stood to the side to let him pass. Browning stood, unmoving, and Rio walked by him without a word or a glance.

Browning had made his choice. It was a choice that he was right to make, but Rio couldn't forgive it all the same. Not when what he loved had been sacrificed for what Browning loved and valued.

Now Browning would live with the consequences. As would Rio.

Silently, Terrence, Decker, Diego and Alton followed Rio from the hut, leaving Browning inside. Rio stepped into the sunlight and then waited for Terrence to catch up.

"See if there is a boat that will take us back. I want the journey to be as smooth as possible for Grace instead of us making a rough trek through the jungle the way we came."

An older man, his skin worn and leathery from a lifetime in the sun, stepped forward. He wore baggy, torn pants and a dirty T-shirt. He was missing at least two of his front teeth but he regarded Rio somberly.

"I have a boat."

"My woman has great need," Rio said in a quiet voice. "I'll pay you well for the use of your boat."

The old man shook his head and then stepped forward. He placed his palm down over Grace's forehead and murmured a quiet incantation. Then he stepped away and motioned for Rio to follow.

"T, you're with me," Rio said. To the others he said, "Meet us back at the house. I want the perimeter secure."

The boat was small, one guided with poles, though there were other motorboats pulled up on shore. Rio stepped carefully into the boat, keeping his weight in the center as he gently eased down with Grace held tightly in his arms. Terrence came aboard, followed by the old man, who then gestured for a young boy to come. The boy clambered on, moving swiftly to the back.

The old man and the young boy worked in unison, positioning the poles and pulling the boat into the current. They kept close to shore, in the shallower water, poles moving swiftly.

"How is she?" Terrence asked in a low voice.

Rio stared down at Grace's still face. She was unmoving against him. She wasn't moving enough air for him to even notice the rise of her chest. "I don't know. She wasn't strong enough for this, Terrence. I could kill Browning for this. She's already been through so much. How could he ask her to do more? To risk her life this way?"

Terrence sighed and looked away. The big man was struggling. Rio knew him too well to be fooled.

"Say whatever it is that's on your mind," Rio said grimly.

Terrence looked back. "There's no doubt what he did was wrong. I've gotten attached to this little lady. She's strong. She's a fighter. I like her style. Part of me wanted to stomp Browning's miserable ass into a paste and feed him to the crocs."

"And the other part?"

"Understood why he did what he did."

Rio nodded. "That's fair. If it were only that, I could overlook it. But he betrayed the team. He went against us. He chose dishonor over unity. That I can't forgive."

"Yeah, I don't disagree. I guess I just get why he did it."

"I let him live," Rio said simply. "He's free to make his life with his woman and child. But he'll never work for me again."

"That's fair," Terrence said. "Some wouldn't have been as understanding as you."

Rio's lip curled into a snarl. "I wanted to kill him for daring to touch her. For frightening her and for one minute making her doubt me. Because he led her away on my order. I told her to go with him if he told her to. I told her to do it. And now she has to believe I fed her to the wolves. He's lucky that my concern for Grace overshadowed my rage because I wanted to shed his blood."

"She wouldn't have believed that," Terrence said in a quiet voice. "No matter what line of bullshit he fed her, once she was there, she knew you would have never sent her to do that."

Rio returned his gaze to Grace and then leaned down to press his lips to her forehead. "I hope you're right, T."

As soon as the boat neared the dock in the alcove off the river that led to Rio's compound, the old man leaned forward, waited until the boat got close enough and then jumped onto the aged wood and held the boat against the dock with his pole so the others could get off.

Terrence went first and reached down to collect Grace from Rio. Rio then hauled himself out of the boat and stopped beside the old man.

"Thank you. I appreciate your help."

The old man nodded formally. "Ana is my granddaughter. This woman gave her back to me. My debt is still great. May the Great One be with her on her journey."

"She's not going anywhere," Rio snarled.

The old man studied him for a long moment and then flashed a toothless smile. "No, I don't suppose she will."

He hopped down into the boat, and he and the boy maneuvered back into the main river channel to return to the village upriver.

Rio strode toward Terrence, who waited on the dock on the bank of the alcove, Grace still in his arms. Rio took her carefully from Terrence and cradled her close. He tucked his chin over her dark hair and began the climb up the stone walkway leading to the first security gate.

Fifteen minutes later, Rio stepped inside his house, some of the anxiety evaporating away. He was home. This was where he felt the safest. He had Grace back where she belonged. Now he had to make sure she got well again.

He laid Grace down in the bed where he'd made love to her just a day ago and tucked the covers around her chilled skin. He had no idea what to do for her. He had no idea to what extent she'd be ill.

Judging by what she'd said of the other illnesses and injuries she'd healed, she'd taken the baby's ailment and made it her own. If the baby had been failing to thrive, for the next while, Grace would also struggle to thrive and survive. He just had to hope to hell she had the strength to fight long enough not to succumb to a losing battle.

CHAPTER 27

RIO never left her bedside over the next two days. He sat with her, not sleeping except in fits and spurts. He tried to get her to eat, to drink, but as with the baby, it did no good. She lacked the strength and will to survive.

Rio knew that it wasn't her. It wasn't her wanting to give up. But she was having to battle not only the weakness and the illness itself but the child's will. He could only imagine the hell she was enduring.

And so he stayed with her through it all, never once leaving her side. He held her through the night. Sat with her during the day. He spoke to her, mostly nonsense, but he was determined that she not think he left her even for a moment. If he could somehow lend her strength by allowing her to know that he was fighting with her, then he'd damn well do it.

He called Sam the morning after he'd retrieved Grace. In terse tones, he informed Sam they were short a man. When Sam asked, Rio would only say that it wasn't because they'd engaged the enemy.

Sam was wise enough to leave the running of Rio's

team to him. He trained his men. He trusted them. He dealt with any issues that arose. Rio's men followed him and him alone. They didn't take orders from Sam or KGI. They came from Rio.

"I'll send someone to you," Sam said.

"No," Rio said shortly. "I need a few days here and then we're going to move out. That gives Steele time to be back from his assignment unless you have him scheduled for something else."

"No, we're clear right now. I can provide all the backup you need."

"I'll need it when we bug out. I don't want to draw attention by having you guys swarm in here. We'll move out and then meet up with the teams at a different location."

"Name it and I'll make damn sure we have the manpower there," Sam said.

"What's the word on Shea? I'd like to be able to give Grace good news when she comes out of this."

There was a long pause.

"What the hell happened, Rio? When we spoke last, Grace was doing better, or so you said."

"She will be better," Rio said, determination resonating from deep within. "I won't let her be anything else."

There were several more moments of silence and then Rio said grimly, "We're going to have to fight, Sam. There's no way around it. Titan's not going to give up and we can't run forever. I'm buying as much time as possible because I need Grace as close to a hundred percent as I can get her before the shit hits the fan. But it's coming and there's not a damn thing I can do about it."

"No pissant special ops wannabe group is going to get one over on us," Sam growled.

Rio laughed at Sam's arrogance. Titan was far from a special ops wannabe, but Rio liked the insult that Sam hurled out.

"Now tell me about Shea so I can give Grace something when she comes around."

"She's not happy with you or me at the moment," Sam

said dryly. "When I told her that you'd called, she immediately wanted to talk to her sister. Telling her it wasn't possible because I didn't exactly know where you were wasn't one of my more favorite moments in my leadership capacity."

Rio chuckled. "No, I don't imagine it was."

"But she's fine. Tell Grace she's doing far better than Grace herself is from the sound of it. Nathan is taking very good care of her. She's desperate to reconnect with Grace, and she asked me to pass along that she's felt close to the path more than once. She wanted Grace to keep trying."

"I will," Rio said in a somber voice. "Grace has been trying. It hurts her that she's been unable to forge that path again. If you could talk to Shea again, tell her . . . Look, I know Grace hadn't wanted Shea to see what all she's endured. But Grace needs her help. She wouldn't want me to say it. She wouldn't want me to involve Shea, but right now I'll take whatever I can get. She's not doing well, Sam," he said bluntly. "If Shea can somehow break through to her, I think it would make a world of difference. I need . . . I'll do whatever it takes to get her back."

"What the hell happened out there, Rio?"

Rio hesitated a moment and then said, "Someone I trusted took advantage of what Grace is able to do. He put her in a position where she couldn't say no, and she was in no condition to be healing another. She nearly died when I found her, and now she lies here hovering between life and death, fighting a battle that I can't help her with."

"You care for her. More than just in a capacity of the mission."

Rio went silent, refusing to acknowledge Sam's realization.

"I should have seen it when you jumped on this mission the way you did," Sam murmured. "I'm sorry things aren't good, man. I'll talk to Shea immediately. She'd want to know. Nathan won't be happy about it but he can't very well tell Shea she can't help her sister out. Particularly when

Grace helped Nathan and Swanny when Swanny was injured during their escape."

"I appreciate it, Sam," Rio said in a low voice. He hated asking for anything, but for Grace, he'd set aside his pride. He'd do anything to get her back. "I'll be in touch."

"Tell me when, Rio. I'll have everyone in position on your go."

"I'll contact you in forty-eight hours. Hopefully the situation here will have changed for the better by then."

"I'll be waiting," Sam said. "We all will be."

Rio ended the call, and then returned to where Grace lay so quiet and still on the bed. He sat on the edge, angling his body so that he could see her face. He reached out to touch her, flinching at the chill of her skin and how pale and translucent her face was.

She looked so vulnerable and defenseless even though Rio knew her to be far from it. She had the courage and resiliency of the strongest of warriors. He'd never witnessed anything like it.

"Come back to me, Grace," he whispered. "I won't let anything hurt you. You're safe here. Just come back to me. Fight this, baby. Fight one more time. Come back to the people who love you."

GRACE knew she was dying and it pissed her off. Her body just sort of accepted it, lying there like it was already dead and her brain just hadn't gotten the message.

It was as if it had endured enough and finally just shut down. Her natural ability to heal wasn't responding as it normally did.

The dark shadows of death clung to her, enveloping her in their uncomfortable embrace. The longer she drifted as she did, the more the darkness crept in until she existed in that dark place. A world with no lights. It was the ultimate dark room, the bedroom with no night light. It was scary and overwhelming, and the longer it went on, the more she seemed to drift farther away from where she knew she wanted to be.

It was hard to separate herself from the child she'd saved. She no longer knew where one began and the other left off.

She was so tired. It would be so easy to just let go and drift away to a much more comfortable place. The shadows whispered to her. Beckoned her gently, a soft lullaby that soothed her soul.

But each time she thought that she would give in, she was pulled back by an unseen force. A will much stronger than her own in its current state.

It was uncomfortable. Stark. Unyielding. And yet she gravitated toward it because she sensed that it was where she needed to be. Not this other dark, quiet place.

And then, in the dark, a gentle presence. A sliver of sunshine. Warmth stole over her, replacing some of the bone-deep cold that had invaded her body.

Grace.

She stirred, hearing her name. She tried to respond but lacked the knowledge of how to. She waited, wanting to hear her name again, but silence settled around her and the cold crept back in.

No! She wanted to weep. For just a moment, she'd known true comfort. She'd felt warmth and gentleness. She'd felt love and known it was for her, aimed at her, that someone was fighting for her.

Grace, goddamn it. Don't you fucking give up. I have no idea if you can hear me. I don't know if I'm doing this right, but don't you dare leave me.

She frowned because that was someone entirely different. It confused her, being pulled in two directions and yet they both beckoned from the same place. There were two distinct people fighting . . . For her.

Grace. I know you're out there and that you need me right now. I'm here. I love you. Please fight.

Shea.

Hearing her sister's voice after so long devastated Grace.

Crumbled her heart to pieces. Stripped her down to her very soul. Tears were wet on her cheeks. Warm tears against cold skin.

Can you hear her, Grace? Is Shea talking to you? You're crying, baby. I know you can hear at least one of us. Fight this. We want you back. Fight, Grace. Don't you dare give up. You're stronger than this. There is nothing that can beat you down. Do you hear me? Nothing can defeat you except your own will.

Rio.

Grace, please talk to me. Let me know how to help you. You've always been so strong for both of us. Let me be the strong one now. Let me help you.

Shea?

She put everything she had into reaching out to her sister. Fear paralyzed her because if she couldn't reconnect, if she couldn't respond, it would devastate her.

Grace! I hear you. I hear you, Grace. Barely. You sound so weak, but you'll get stronger. Talk to me. Don't let go. Tell me what you need.

Didn't want you to see me like this.

The tears were strong in the message she sent back to her sister. Her best friend in the whole world. The one person she loved and who loved her unconditionally.

Oh, Grace. Don't you know how much I love you? How much you are loved? We've both been so intent on protecting the other that we've forgotten that we're best when we're strong. Together. Side by side. No more shutting each other out. Do you hear me? From now on, it's you and me against the world.

Grace smiled at the ferocity in her younger sister's words. Warmth was spreading through her mind and heart. Sunshine replaced the darkness, chasing away the shadows that stubbornly clung, unwilling to relinquish their hold just yet.

I'm just so tired, Shea. So cold. I've never felt this weak. I don't want to give up, but I don't know if I have the strength left to fight.

And then she felt another presence. Warm but different. So strong and overpowering. It surrounded her from every angle. Lifting her up, lending her the strength she so desperately needed.

I'm here. We're here. I can feel him there with you. Can you feel him? I can sense him through you, and he's strong, Grace. He's strong enough for both of you. Lean on him. Lean on us.

Rio.

She sent out the one word, releasing it from the deepest part of her soul. It was a cry in the night, chased by the promise of dawn.

I'm here, Grace. Right here, baby. I won't let you go. Take what you need. You've been alone for so long. Never leaning on anyone else. This time be strong enough to ask for help.

She soaked up every bit of comfort. Absorbed the light, embracing it to ward off the dark. She grabbed hold of the hope and the love so readily offered by the two people who loved her.

Warmth spread to every part of her body. It was an electric current arcing through every muscle, ridding her body of the lingering effects of illness, madness and the loss of hope.

I'm so glad you're here.

She sent out the message to both Rio and Shea, bridging the gap, forming an irrevocable pathway between the three of them.

Don't let me go. I don't want to go.

This time, the voices were stronger. Louder in her mind. So very close.

No one's letting you go, honey.

I'm here, Grace. I'm always here. Always with you, Shea said fiercely.

And then some of the pain and despair simply began fading away. Absorbed by Shea, who had the ability to take people's pain and emotions and absorb them into her own body. Just as she'd done for Nathan when he'd been tortured.

Just as she'd done so many times since. This was why she hadn't wanted Shea to know. Hadn't wanted her to see the depths of Grace's pain and despair.

No! Shea, stop it! Don't you dare take this. It's enough that you're here. Don't do this. Do you hear me? Don't suffer this for me. You've been through enough.

Tears of frustration burned her eyes. This wasn't what she wanted.

Let her help you, Grace.

Rio's command was strong. Compelling. He was firm and unyielding. He had a tight hold on her and he wasn't letting go, almost as if he had a part of her captive.

I don't want her to ever feel this, Grace choked out.

She has people to support her. She has Nathan there. She isn't alone. And now neither are you. Don't be so stubborn. Lean on us. Allow us in. Allow us to take it for you until you're strong enough to bear it yourself.

More warmth and love poured into her through the connection to Shea. Grace felt herself enfolded by her sister, held tight and rocked back and forth as if she were a child in need of comfort.

She clung to her sister, hugging her back, afraid to let go for fear the connection would be broken. Shea pressed a gentle kiss to her forehead and smoothed away the hair from her face.

Sleep now, Grace. Rest so your body can heal, so that when you awake, you'll be stronger and yourself once more.

Then she felt the kiss of another. More intimate. Loving. The kiss of a lover. A warm caress. A gentle touch. His arms replaced Shea's, pulled her into his embrace. Strong. Protective. A barrier between her and all the darkness.

It's okay now, Grace. I've got you. You're going to be okay. Sleep now and know that I'll be here when you wake.

CHAPTER 28

WHEN Grace opened her eyes, she wasn't entirely certain where she was. The ceiling came into focus and then she saw the high window and the soft light pouring into the bedroom where she and Rio had made love.

She then became aware that she wasn't alone. Not only was she not alone, but Rio was wrapped around her as if he was shielding her from the world. His leg was thrown over hers. His arm lay possessively over her midsection and his other arm was beneath her head so that she was cradled into his side. And she was completely naked.

She smiled. She was back. She was alive. She'd made it through.

There was no doubt she was as weak as a newborn kitten. She felt as limp as a wet noodle and her mind was mush. But she had renewed strength. Strength she hadn't possessed before and an awareness she hadn't felt since before she'd severed the link between her and Shea.

Shea! The awareness was of her sister's presence in her mind. Always there, just as she'd been before. Tears gathered in her eyes and she bit her lip, afraid to call out, afraid that she'd only dreamed that she'd been able to reconnect with Shea.

I'm here, Grace.

The calm sound of her sister's voice sent joy coursing through her soul.

I worried I'd dreamed it all. I'm so glad you're here. I've missed you so much.

I've missed you too, Grace. I love you. It's been too long. We can be together now. Things are different. We can have a . . . life. I don't want to be without you anymore. There's no reason for it. Nathan and his family have promised to keep you safe. And now you have . . . Rio. You know you're going to have to tell me all about him.

Grace smiled through her tears. Happy tears. So like old times when they shared everything.

Deal. Just as soon as you tell me everything about Nathan.

She felt Shea's answering smile.

We'll talk when you're stronger, Grace. Right now I just want you to focus on getting better.

Love you.

Love you too.

Even though the communication ended, Grace could still feel the lingering presence of her sister. She hadn't realized just how much she'd missed having her there until she'd been permanently gone.

"Have a nice chat with Shea?"

She turned, realizing that Rio was awake and had been silently watching her. She smiled. "Yeah. I can't believe she's back. I thought I'd never be able to talk to her telepathically again."

Rio kissed her, his lips gentle and loving over hers. For the longest time he stayed there even when he'd pulled his mouth away. His forehead rested against hers and he cupped her jaw in his palm.

"I'm just glad *you're* back," he said. "You scared me, Grace. I thought I'd lost you."

"I thought I'd lost myself," she said honestly.

Rio pulled slightly away but kept hold on her jaw, tilting so she met his gaze. "Why did you do it?"

She sighed and closed her eyes. "I didn't want to die if that's what you're thinking. I almost refused because I was afraid I *would* die."

Rio's face went hard and his eyes cold. "Browning said he didn't threaten you. Did he? Did he hurt you?"

She could only imagine what Rio had done to his teammate. She wasn't sure she wanted to know. She shook her head, feeling the firm imprint of his fingers on her face. It was comforting. There was strength in his touch. And possession. A clear message that he considered her his.

"I think he was scared. And resigned. It was as if he knew the consequences of what he'd done. Knew you'd be furious. I was pretty pissed too. But I also understood why he'd done it. I can only imagine how I'd feel if it were my child and I couldn't do anything to help her. I'd lie, cheat, steal, threaten or kidnap anyone who could help her, you know?"

"Is that why you did it? Because you understood?"

She leaned her forehead against his lips, liking the warmth of his mouth on her skin. "I did it because once I saw her, I knew she was dying. I knew she wouldn't last much longer. Death surrounded her and I knew that if I didn't help her, I would be responsible for her death and I couldn't look Browning and Sumathi in the eye and tell them I wouldn't help their daughter because I was afraid of dying when I'd finally found a reason to live."

His hand stilled in her hair. He pulled her back so they were looking eye to eye. "What's your reason, Grace?"

There was such a multitude of things in such a simple question. There was hope. Curiosity. A little dread. Didn't he realize? She guessed he didn't. Things had moved so fast. She hadn't really been that forthcoming about her feelings. She hadn't even been sure of what she felt.

Her entire world had been turned upside down. She'd barely existed for the last year, and yet in the midst of it all, her life in ruins, had come this man.

He'd challenged her, bullied her and made her feel more loved than she'd ever felt with another human being. He hadn't allowed her to quit.

Why? What had he seen in her that very first time to make him so determined to track her down?

She touched his face, stroking over the roughness of his jaw. He hadn't shaved and the stubble was bristly over her fingers.

He looked like hell.

"How long have I been asleep?" she whispered.

His eyes narrowed at her avoidance of the question. But she just hadn't quite found the right words yet.

"Three days."

Her mouth popped open in dismay. "Three days?"

He nodded grimly.

"What about the baby?" she asked hesitantly.

His lips thinned. "I don't know. I assume she's fine."

She wanted to ask about Browning and what had been done with him.

Rio sighed. "What are you thinking?"

She nibbled at her bottom lip. "About Browning. And his family. Did you kill him?"

"And if I did? The bastard deserved it."

She frowned unhappily. "He was only protecting his daughter."

"Yeah, by risking what belongs to me and betraying his team."

"I can see why you'd be angry."

"Really, Grace? You can see why I'd be angry? I was fucking *furious*. You don't get it, do you? He took what was mine. He took what was important to me and he used you. He could have killed you. And you see why I'd be angry."

"He betrayed you," she whispered.

Rio rose up on his elbow, his eyes blazing. "It has nothing to do with me, goddamn it! Don't you get it? I *love* you and he tried to suck the life right out of you. Yes, he betrayed me, but I wanted to kill him because he nearly took you away from me."

She swallowed, opened her mouth and then snapped it shut again. He didn't give her another opportunity. He slid his hand around to her nape and pulled her to meet his kiss.

It was fierce and possessive. She felt branded and marked. He kissed her like he was swallowing her whole, devouring her and pulling her into himself.

He turned her fully onto her back and then he was over her, pushing into her, hot and hard. He slid into her body, locking them together, and then he stared down at her, his eyes burning with emotion.

"Do you get it *now*, Grace? You're mine. I've never felt this way about a woman, and I don't like how goddamn crazy it makes me."

She smiled and arched up with a sigh, taking him farther inside.

"I'm glad you find this so damn funny," he growled.

Her smile got bigger. She wrapped her arms around his neck and pulled him down into a kiss.

"Would it make it better if I told you that I'm just as crazy over you?" she whispered.

"Maybe."

"Or that I'm pretty sure I love you just as much?"

"Now we're getting somewhere," he grumbled.

She stroked his cheek. She wrapped her legs around him, wanting him closer still. Wanting to find that warmth that burned from the inside out.

"Or that my reason for finding the will to live after wanting to die is you?"

His eyes darkened and he went still above her. For the longest time he simply stared down at her as if he was trying to collect himself.

He was still deeply embedded inside her. She was tight around him and he seemed to swell larger even though he hadn't yet moved.

"I don't know what to say," he said hoarsely. "I've never mattered to anyone. Not in this way. No one has depended emotionally on me. I'm depended on for leadership and strength. Discipline and determination. No one has ever needed me for *who* I am. Just *what* I am."

"I do," she whispered. "I need you, Rio. You saved me. I've never mattered to another soul besides my sister. No one has ever cared about me or about what happens to me. Not until you. I wasn't just someone with special abilities to you. You saw the real me, and you cared about *her*. Not what I could do for the world or for someone you knew. You looked inside and saw *me*."

He lowered his forehead to hers until they were touching. "Say it. Say the words, Grace. I don't just want to hear them. I *need* to hear them. I need . . . you."

She smiled, tenderness filling her heart. "I love you, Rio."

His nostrils flared and his jaw went tight as if he were fighting to maintain his control and composure. There was such vulnerability in his dark eyes, and she realized in that moment that for all his strength and resolve, for how protective and possessive he was of her, he needed those same things from her.

"I love you too, Grace Peterson."

He withdrew and then pushed forward again, more gently this time and without the urgency he'd displayed when he'd first taken her.

He kissed her lips then moved to her cheeks, giving each a kiss in turn. Then he kissed her nose, her eyelids and each temple. All the while he continued his gentle thrusting, gliding in and out as he restaked his claim all over again.

Slowly he ran his hands down her body, then underneath to cup her behind. He held her in place, positioning her for his thrusts as he worked deeper.

"Don't ever risk yourself like that again," he admonished. "You can't save everyone, and I won't lose you so that you can save one more person. Maybe that's selfish of me, but I don't really give a damn."

She smiled at the gruffness of his tone because underneath

was a layer of fear. Fear for her. Fear that he'd lose her. She kissed him again as the first waves of her orgasm rolled over her.

She held on to him, her anchor, the person who'd taken her from death's grasp more than once. He'd protect her. She had absolute faith in him. How could she not? He'd faced death down for her and *won*.

CHAPTER 29

"**YOU** better have something good to report," Farnsworth growled into the phone. "With what I'm paying you, you should have had Grace Peterson to me weeks ago."

"I don't respond well to threats, Mr. Farnsworth. You'd do well to remember that."

Farnsworth froze at the icy implication in Hancock's voice. He hated that this man intimidated him. And he didn't simply intimidate him. He bloody well terrified him, and that pissed him off because he feared no one. People feared *him*.

Except this man who headed up Titan. Farnsworth was certain there wasn't a man alive that Hancock feared.

"Well? Have you located her yet?"

"I have," Hancock said simply. "Rumor is she healed a child in a village on the Belize River and that it nearly killed her. Nothing is known of her current condition, but I have a lock on her location. My contact there says they're moving her out soon. If I'm patient, they'll come to me."

Farnsworth swore savagely. "I can't afford to wait a minute longer. What if the little fool had killed herself trying to heal this other child? If she's going to die healing someone, it's damn well going to be my daughter."

"I understand your impatience," Hancock said in a mild tone. "But impatience won't get you what you want any faster. You hired me to do a job. I've never failed a mission yet. Think about that when you're issuing idle threats because my next mission will be to come after you if you continue your present line of discussion."

"Just get her here. I'm running out of time. I'll double your price. I don't care what it takes. You can have all I have because if my daughter dies, I'll have nothing anyway."

"Your devotion to your daughter is admirable and I've already said that I would have Grace Peterson delivered to your daughter's bedside in a timely manner. She won't escape. I know the man who protects her far too well. I know how he thinks. I know his next move. I should. He taught me everything I know."

The line went dead and Farnsworth threw it across the room. He hated how this mercenary reduced him to feeling insignificant and powerless. As if Hancock held all the cards and he knew it.

Time was running out. The doctor had seen her again today and had faced Farnsworth with a grim expression and a shake of his head. She didn't have long. She was growing weaker. Her body could no longer fight off the cancer. It was insidious, growing and multiplying at an alarming rate. There was simply nothing to be done.

She had days, maybe weeks, but nothing more. She could die tonight or she could die next week. He was afraid to enter her bedroom for fear that he'd find her already gone.

He slumped into his chair and buried his face in his hands, and for the first time since learning of his daughter's illness, he wept.

CHAPTER 30

"RIO, I'm perfectly capable of walking," Grace protested as he carried her out of the bedroom and into the living room.

He ignored her and she sighed, though she really didn't mind him carrying her. She was still living in the new and shiny revelation of knowing this man cared so much for her. It was a little frightening and yet it made her giddy, like a teenage girl with her first crush.

She was deathly afraid of having that bubble burst. They were not living in a dream world. Not everything was hearts and roses. They'd hollowed out a little niche, a temporary break from reality, but the real world waited like a predator. Teeth gnashing, evil. Those who pursued her hadn't given up. And they wouldn't.

Soon they'd go back into that harsh, cold reality, a place where people died, a place where people gave no thought to humanity. She'd be caged, used, the equivalent of a monkey taken out when it was time to perform and then shoved back into her cold, impersonal prison.

"Grace."

Rio's impatient voice cut through her maudlin thoughts and she realized it wasn't the first time he'd called her name. She blinked, also realizing that he'd already put her on the couch and apparently he'd been trying to get her attention for some time.

"What the hell is going on in that head of yours?"

His frown was deep, his lips set into a firm line. It was clear he had no liking for her expression, or perhaps the darkness of her thoughts had transmitted themselves to him. He looked worried and a little pissed.

She closed her mouth mutinously, not wanting to be a huge damper. It wasn't as if he didn't know all of what she'd been thinking anyway. It was a reality he lived with each and every day. He didn't need her adding to his worry with her whining.

He sighed. "We're seriously going to have to work on communication. This clamming up when I ask you what you're thinking drives me insane. I'm a result-oriented guy. When I ask, I'm not used to being told no."

She grinned. "Guess there's always a first time for everything."

He gave her a dark scowl.

"I'm not one of your men or your underlings," she said with a snort. "I don't take having orders barked at me too well. It's the rebel in me. Shea used to try to boss me around all the time, especially after we split up and went our separate ways for safety reasons. We see how well that worked out."

Rio tipped her chin up so they were eye to eye. "The only time I expect you to obey me without hesitation is when your life is on the line and we're in a combat situation. The rest of the time, you're perfectly free to argue all you like. But I'll tell you now, if I tell you to do something when it counts and you balk, I'll tan your behind. You don't get a free pass from me just because you're gorgeous and I happen to be in love with your ass."

A giggle escaped and she clapped a hand over her mouth.

"Now, you want to tell me what had you looking so worried a minute ago? It has nothing to do with you being submissive to my overbearing arrogant self. I can't exactly reassure you if I don't know what the hell you're worrying over."

Her heart softened and she reached out to touch his cheek. "I love that you don't want me to worry, but until this is over, until I know for certain that I'm safe and can lead a normal life, I'm going to worry. Because now, I don't only have myself and Shea to worry about. I have you and your men. Shea's new family and her loved ones. You're all involved and I hate that I'm responsible for so much danger to so many people."

He started to protest, but she silenced him with a finger to his lips. "You asked and I'm just being honest. I know that we're in this kind of bubble right now where time is standing still and that, all too soon, at any moment, we're going to be thrust back into the harsh reality that is my existence. And I hate it. I dread it. I'm sick with worry. Before, I was ready to die. I had given up. I didn't care what happened to me because I couldn't imagine ever being free and I'd rather have died than to continue to live in captivity being used on a daily basis.

"But now I have people who matter to me. People I care about. And I don't want them to die for me. I don't want them to make sacrifices for me. So I dread losing the temporary reprieve, the fantasy of a normal life with a man who loves me. Because I know tomorrow, it may all come to an end."

Rio framed her face in both hands, his eyes as fierce as his expression. "I'm not going to lie to you, Grace. I don't know what will happen. I'm not going to offer you any guarantees and say that we're going to be able to keep you safe from any threat or that nothing will ever hurt you again. I can't do that. I know what we're up against. But what I can promise you is that, as long as I'm breathing, I will do *anything* I can to protect you. With my dying breath, I'll always be between you and whatever is threatening you. And if,

God forbid, you're ever taken from me, I will go to hell to get you back."

She pulled him to her, kissing him fiercely, allowing the depth of her feelings to pour out physically and emotionally. She opened the path between them, showing him not only with her body but with her mind what his declaration meant to her. To have this proud warrior pledge his very life to keeping her safe was more than she could even process.

She wasn't deserving. She wasn't brave like he was. She didn't have a fourth of his courage. She had no idea why of all the women in the world, he'd chosen her. But she was savagely happy that he had, and by God, she'd never let him go.

Rio yanked away, his eyes sparking with fury. "Bullshit."

She blinked and then her eyes widened.

"Deserving? You aren't worthy of me? You don't have my courage or bravery? That's the biggest bunch of bullshit I've ever heard in my life."

Her mouth fell open. Yeah, she'd opened the link but hadn't considered the consequences of him knowing her *every* thought.

"Let me tell you something, Grace. I'm not worthy of you. Do you even know the things I've done? What's your worst sin? Wanting to give up rather than face a lifetime of pain and misery and of having the misery of others foisted onto you in an endless cycle? Look at the things you've done, willingly or not. You've given people a new lease on life. You saved a child who would otherwise be dead right now and you risked your own life to do it because your heart is too soft for you to say no even though it might have meant your own death.

"You have no idea of the things I've done, the choices I've made. Most of my life has been spent in areas so gray that light had long since fled. Always in the shadows. Questionable causes. Hell, I'm a mercenary, Grace. Which means that if someone pays me enough money, I'll do the job.

"You don't even want to know some of the jobs I've taken. Your soft heart would weep over some of the things I've done and the choices I've made. All in the name of the greater good. Fuck that. Good for who? That's always the question. Someone always benefits and someone always suffers. There's no way for everyone to be happy or safe or content. I'm a saint to some, the very devil himself to others. It all depends on which side of the coin you find yourself on. So don't give me this bullshit about how you don't have my courage or bravery because that's just going to piss me off. What you have is something I'll never have. Goodness that goes bone deep. Unwavering convictions and empathy for others. You have a soul, Grace. I lost mine when I allowed myself to die and my parents to be told I no longer existed. I lost my soul when my sister died in my arms because I wasn't there to protect her."

Grace silenced him with a kiss. She grabbed his face and slammed her lips over his, feeding hungrily on his mouth. Tears ran freely down her cheeks until they both tasted the slight salt on their tongues.

"Stop, just stop," she whispered brokenly. "I can't bear that you see yourself that way."

He pulled gently away, his eyes bleak as he stood. He believed everything he'd said so passionately. And she hated it.

She scooted forward on the couch, not willing to let him escape. She tried to stand but he wouldn't let her, and so she pulled him back down until he was on his knees in front of her, their faces just inches apart.

She stroked his face with both hands, smoothing over his jaw and cheekbones, frantic to ease some of the pain and self-condemnation that billowed from his soul.

"Do you want to know what I see when I look at you?" she said around the knot in her throat.

He tried to look away but she held firm, turning his face, refusing to allow him to escape her gaze.

"I see a man who's honorable. Who gave his everything to a cause he believed in. I see a man who, upon realizing that the path he'd chosen was no longer in keeping with the principles he held close, walked away and re-created himself in a role as protector, savior, leader and, yes, hero. You may not like the label, Rio, but you are a hero. You're my hero. You're my savior and protector. Who else would have come for me if not you? Who else would have fought for me, refusing to let me go?

"We all make mistakes, Rio. The mark of a man is how he makes up for those mistakes, and you've more than paid your penance."

He leaned his forehead against hers, and for a moment they sat there in silence, their breathing the only sound in the room.

"I'll make you a deal," she murmured. "I won't think I'm unworthy of you and your love if you never ever question that you're worthy of mine. Deal?"

Rio smiled. He kissed her long and sweet, their tongues dueling and teasing. Light touches. Loving touches. His hands were on her face just as hers were on his. Holding. Touching. Caressing.

"Deal," he said huskily. "Now I want you to sit here while I fix you something to eat. You need to regain your strength for what lies ahead. The others will join us because we have to plan our departure."

She tried not to flinch. She knew it had to come to an end, this idyllic escape from reality. But it didn't stop the regret or the knowledge that her entire world could change and she could lose everything in as little as a day.

CHAPTER 31

GRACE was welcomed by Rio's team members with great enthusiasm. They all gathered to sit at the bar in the kitchen while Rio fried up hamburgers. They spent several minutes grilling her on her condition, how she was feeling and if she was going to be okay.

Smiling, she assured them that she would be fine.

Rio let them fuss over Grace for a period of time and then he effectively put a halt to any lighthearted banter by announcing that they were pulling out.

The men immediately became all business.

"What's the plan?" Terrence asked.

Rio stood over the stove eyeing his team with utter seriousness. "I feel like they're getting close. It's a gut feeling and I don't want to take any chances. My main reason for coming here was to give Grace time to heal. This isn't where I want to engage Titan. There are some advantages. This our home turf. We know the lay of the land. But we don't have the manpower necessary, and if Sam sends in Steele or we have all of KGI pouring in here, if Titan didn't already know where we were, they sure as hell would at that point."

"Makes sense," Diego agreed.

"Plus we're a man short," Alton said grimly.

"Doesn't matter," Decker said. "We'll get the job done."

"We're good," Rio said matter-of-factly. "But not that good. Against a group like Titan, we're going to need all the manpower we can get. You can bet your asses they aren't coming to a fight with only a few good men. They'll come with the best and they'll come to win. Which is why we're going to rendezvous with Sam. He's calling in all we've got on this one."

Grace's brows came together in confusion. She put a hand up to massage her temple because this whole thing was making her crazy. Rio made it sound like they were going to schedule a damn war or something. On the count of three, everyone starts shooting. That sort of thing. It sounded . . . crazy.

"I don't get it," she said. "You make it sound so organized. How do we know when or where this happens. I mean, are you actually going to pick a place and start shooting each other?"

She couldn't keep the horror from her voice. The very last thing she wanted was people to die because of her.

She turned to Rio, her expression pleading, but she used telepathy because she didn't want the others to hear.

Let's go away, Rio. Just you and me. Why couldn't we go someplace where they'd never find us? Why do we have to involve so many people? I don't want them to die for me. I don't want anyone to die.

Rio used the spatula to remove the last burger from the pan, then put it aside and walked around the bar to where Grace sat. He framed her face and stared down at her, his eyes intense and sincere.

"This doesn't just involve you, honey. If it did, then what you suggest might be the best option. But it involves Shea and, by proxy, everyone at KGI because now you and your sister both are part of us. We don't run from a fight.

It's not what KGI is about. KGI is about family. It's about protecting what matters the most to us. It's about never letting anyone take what is ours. You and Shea are ours now, and we'll protect you with our last breaths."

"That's straight-up righteous," Terrence rumbled out.

Diego, Decker and Alton all nodded their agreement.

Grace shook off Rio's hands but kept hold of one, lowering it to her lap. It was comforting. Just being able to touch him calmed her more than she could have imagined.

"I'm scared," she admitted. "Not just scared. Terrified. For the last year, I've lived my life day to day, never looking ahead, never knowing if I had a tomorrow. But now . . . I look to the future. It's a future I want more than I can express in words. And I'm scared to death to trade someone's life for that bright shiny future I now dream about."

Diego stared at her for a long moment. "If you hadn't already won my respect and admiration, you would have just now. It's an unselfish person who can acknowledge that they value someone's life over their own dreams. But here's the thing, and maybe you already know this. Nobody made us take this mission. Rio is our leader, yeah, and we follow him. But we do it because we want to. We can walk away anytime. No one owns us. We don't give our loyalty blindly. It's earned, and he and KGI have earned ours. And now so have you. So while it's admirable that you don't want one of us to sacrifice anything for you, we'd prefer you just shut up and deal with it because we aren't backing down from this."

Decker grinned and Alton slapped Diego on the back. Even Terrence laughed.

"You know, Diego doesn't always have a whole lot to say, but when he does, it's usually something epic," Alton said with a laugh.

Rio was smiling when Grace turned back to him, completely befuddled by their reaction.

"See?" he said. "You're one of us, Grace. We wouldn't leave any one of us to fight alone and we're damn sure not going to bail on you. So get used to it. You're not getting rid of us, and you sure as hell aren't getting rid of me."

Relief, light and bubbly, flooded her heart and soul. She smiled, her smile growing bigger and bigger as she glanced around to all of Rio's men sitting at the bar.

"So when do we leave?" she asked.

RIO made the call to Sam that afternoon. He wanted to give Grace more time to rest, and he put her to bed to ensure she did just that. But his gut was screaming that they needed to move now. They didn't have a few days to wait for Grace to rebound totally.

She'd made it out of the mountains by sheer grit and determination. She'd basically been a walking corpse. If she could do that, then she could handle what was ahead.

"Here's the plan," Sam said. "We'll rendezvous at the airstrip in Virginia. We'll take both jets to Kodiak and then boat over to Afognak Island. If they show, we'll know. We'll fight on our terms, our turf."

"And your family?" Rio asked gruffly.

"I'm stashing them at Fort Campbell under heavy guard. No one in their right mind would stage an attack at a U.S. military base. It's the safest place I can think of for them to be. Shea will be staying behind too. You may want to consider sending Grace to her."

As much as it went against his every principle to trust Grace's safety to anyone but himself, he also knew that it was, in fact, the safest, securest place for her to be. She wouldn't like it, but he wouldn't give her a choice in the matter. Plus, he'd dangle a reunion with her sister in front of her, and she would have a much harder time arguing with him then.

"We have to make this look good then," Rio said. "If we're going to lure Titan to Afognak Island, then we have to make damn sure they think Grace is with us. Otherwise this is a pointless endeavor—they'll sit back and bide their time and strike when we've relaxed our guard."

"Yeah, I know. I've already thought of that. We're going to make P.J. be a stand-in for Grace. She has a similar build, similar coloring. It'll kill her to have to get out of her combat boots and lose her weapons, but she'll do her job."

"And how do you plan to get Grace from Virginia to Fort Campbell safely?" Rio asked.

"I'll call in a favor and have a pilot from Fort Campbell accompany us so he can fly Grace back to the base to meet Shea."

"That's not enough," Rio said bluntly. "This isn't a simple escort. One army pilot won't be enough if they run into Titan."

Sam paused for a moment. "What do you want then?"

"I want at least two other men with her. Not cops either. I'm already down a man, but if Steele's team and the rest of KGI are going, then I can spare two of my team to go with Grace. They're the only ones I'll trust her with apart from myself. Terrence and Diego will go with her. They'd die before allowing anything to happen to her."

"All right," Sam said. "Then that's what we'll do. Can you make it to Virginia by sixteen hundred hours tomorrow?"

"We'll be there," Rio said grimly.

ADAM Resnick never knew anyone was in his house until he felt the cold slide of a knife against his neck. His hands froze on the keyboard of his computer and he went utterly still, not wanting to do anything to make the blade sink farther into his flesh.

Already blood welled and trickled down his skin. He could smell it.

He was disciplined enough not to shake, but that didn't mean his pulse wasn't about to explode inside his head.

"Very good," the man murmured behind his ear. "Most people would panic, then have their throat cut and die as a result of their own stupidity."

"What do you want?" Resnick demanded, his hands still locked in place.

"I understand you have quite the association with KGI.

I need information. They'll be making a move soon and I, of course, want to head them off at the pass."

"Who?"

The knife bit farther into his neck, and Resnick gritted his teeth against the sting.

"Let's not play games. You know who I am. I know who you are. I know you have KGI in your back pocket and I also know you have the information I want."

Resnick's lip curled in disgust, but he held his tongue. Pissing off this faceless man would only get his throat cut.

And then the knife was gone and the hard point of a pistol dug into the back of his head.

"Get up. Slowly. No sudden moves. My friend here is somewhat of a whiz when it comes to computers. They like him, you see. They always tell him what he wants to know. I have a feeling yours will have everything we need to know about KGI."

Resnick closed his eyes, knowing there was no way out. He could die but they'd still have access to his computer, and Titan would have someone who could hack into the best system. The average computer expert wouldn't have a prayer of hacking into Resnick's files, but Titan wouldn't have anyone average on their payroll.

He slowly rose, holding his hands up where they could be seen. A hand curled around his arm and pulled him to the side. He stumbled over the chair leg and then righted himself before he was instructed to stand facing away from the desk.

"Hands behind your head, fingers laced together. I better not even hear you breathe or you're a dead man."

He was a dead man anyway. It was a simple truth, one he accepted with no emotion. He should have already died. He was a marked man, and not by Titan, but by his own government for what he'd done to help Shea and Grace Peterson and, by proxy, KGI.

He'd blown the top off the secret research that had been resumed after years of dormancy. Even now, in the upper echelons of the military and the U.S. government, an investigation was ongoing about who and what was responsible for the group who'd been behind the creation of the two women with extraordinary powers.

And Resnick was waiting to die for the simple fact that he now knew too much.

He closed his eyes and listened to the tapping of fingers on his keyboard. The men didn't talk, didn't communicate verbally, not until the end when the newcomer said, "I have it."

"Thank you, Mr. Resnick, for your service," the one who'd held the knife to his throat said.

A single pop followed, the unmistakable sound of a silencer. Pain sliced through Resnick's back and into his chest. His knees buckled and he pitched forward, agony tearing through his body at supersonic speed.

Blood was warm, the smell sickening, and it pooled underneath him, soaking into the carpet.

After a moment the pain faded, replaced by complete numbness. He couldn't breathe. Every time he tried, a peculiar gurgling sound erupted from his throat and the metallic taste of blood seeped onto his tongue.

He tried to roll over, tried to move, but even sliding his hand along the carpet took unimaginable strength.

The phone. He had to get to the phone. He had to warn Sam.

CHAPTER 32

RIO gently shook Grace awake as the plane touched down on the private airstrip owned and maintained by KGI. He dreaded being separated from Grace, especially when he had no idea if he'd make it back to her. But what mattered was her being safe, and he didn't want her anywhere near when Titan made their eventual appearance.

Grace sat up, sleepily rubbing at her eyes, and then she looked at Rio, sorrow tugging at her features as she realized where they were.

"Don't look like that," he said, forcing a smile. "I'll be back for you before you know it. And you'll get to see Shea."

Grace nodded. "Yes, I can't wait to see her, but I don't want you to go, Rio. I hate that you'll be so far away and I won't know what's happening."

He touched his mouth to hers as the plane came to a stop near the hangar. "You'll know. We have a connection that distance can't break. We'll still be together."

She smiled then and squeezed his hand. "I love you, you know."

"Yeah, I do know. We're going to do this, Grace. Go see

your sister and get better for me, okay? I want you at full strength when I get back."

Rio stood and then motioned for Alton and Decker to follow him. Grace also stood, but Rio put his hand on her shoulder and gently pushed her back down.

"I don't want you to get off," he said. "Terrence and Diego will stay on with you while the plane is refueled and you'll be taking off immediately. You have clearance to land at Fort Campbell. Sam brought along an army pilot who'll fly you to Kentucky."

Panic flared in her eyes as the hatch opened and the steps were pushed to the doorway. Rio leaned in one last time, kissed her hard and then pulled away, not looking back as he disembarked the plane. If he looked back, he wouldn't be able to walk away.

On the tarmac stood the rest of KGI. It was an impressive sight. Sam and his brothers Garrett, Donovan, Ethan, Nathan and Joe, along with Swanny, their newest recruit, stood next to Steele and his team. Dolphin, Renshaw and Baker stood on one side of their team leader, while Cole stood near P.J. Rutherford, the only female member of KGI. P.J. was in civilian clothing, though she didn't look too happy about it. Her hair hung loose, fashioned like Grace's. She wore jeans, a T-shirt and simple tennis shoes.

As soon as she saw him, she walked toward him. When she neared, she bared her teeth in a smile and spoke from behind those teeth.

"Hello, sweetheart. I hear we're off on a lover's retreat to bum fuck Alaska."

Rio chuckled. "And may I say how lovely you look, P.J."

"It's Grace, dumbass. We can't afford any fuckups, so get it right."

Rio looked beyond P.J. to where Sam stood next to Garrett. "We ready to roll?" The longer they stood around, the uneasier Rio grew. His gut was screaming and the hair prickled and stood up on his nape.

There was something decidedly wrong with this picture.

He was about to shout a warning when a gun barrel was shoved against the back of his head. In his periphery, he saw the men who were refueling the jets yank out automatic rifles and train them on the assembled group.

The reaction was instantaneous. Steele and his team dove behind the pile of bags and supplies. Sam and his brothers scattered, some hitting the ground, others diving for cover behind one of the planes. Guns came up in all directions.

Hancock grabbed P.J. by the hair and yanked back. Then he glanced sideways at Rio. "Do you think I'm that dumb, Rio?"

"Do you really want an answer to that?" Rio snarled.

"Don't do anything stupid," Hancock called out. "This can be as bloody or as civil as you choose to make it."

"You aren't getting her," Rio gritted out.

"You'll never make it out of here alive," Sam returned from behind a barrel where he'd crouched.

Dolphin scooted out to the side, rifle up, aiming toward Hancock. A shot rang out, knocking Dolphin back several feet. He hit the ground hard.

"Son of a bitch!" Dolphin yelled. "Fuck, I'm hit! Goddamn it!"

"Get him back," Steele snapped. "Get him out now!"

Cole grabbed him by the back of his shirt and dragged him to cover.

"Sniper at six o'clock!" Garrett yelled.

"And nine and noon and three," Hancock calmly called out. "We have you completely surrounded. Yeah, we can shoot each other all to hell, but in the end, you'll all be dead and I'll still get the girl. If I die, she still gets delivered. Mission accomplished. Maybe Rio hasn't informed you, but Titan never fails to complete their mission."

"Bunch of crazy-ass motherfuckers," Donovan snarled.

"So how do you want this to go down?" Hancock yelled. "Grace, I know you can hear me. Is this what you want? Do you want them all to die for nothing? If you come with me, there'll be no further need for bloodshed. My mission isn't to kill all these men. My mission is to bring you in however

I have to accomplish it. So, it's all up to you. We can do it the easy way. Or we can do it the hard way."

"Fuck you!" Rio snarled. "Grace, don't you goddamn do it, do you hear me? You stay the fuck out of sight."

Inside the plane, Grace shook so hard that she managed to shake Terrence, who covered her. The moment the gunshot sounded, Terrence and Diego had hauled her over the seat and stuffed her underneath them. They were crouched behind a row of seats, using them for cover, their rifles up and trained on the doorway.

The door was wide open. She could hear every single thing that had occurred. She knew that a member of KGI had been shot. He may even now be dead.

She opened her mind, put all her strength and energy to reaching out, casting her net wide to pull in the surroundings. She was instantly bombarded by a myriad of adrenaline, anger, fear, calm assurance. There. She refocused on the calm one. He was the one dictating the action. He was the one who'd issued her the challenge. Come quietly or suffer the consequences. •

She focused intently on him. His mind was a fascinating irregularity. More machine than human. He had an objective and he was single-minded in his determination to achieve that objective. But what she saw, what she knew without doubt, was that he was utterly serious about killing every last person who stood between him and his objective.

He may die doing it, and he was at peace with that outcome. But he'd turn the airfield into a war zone and take out any threat to his success.

She pushed at Terrence, panic rising sharp and furious within her. Diego turned, his face a mask of anger and determination.

"Do you honest to God think Rio would ever let you just walk into the hands of the enemy? Think about what you're doing, Grace. He'll go crazy. He'll get himself killed. Is that what you want?"

"He'll be killed anyway," she said with forced calm. It

was imperative that she convince Terrence and Diego that this was the only choice. This was their only option. "I saw into his head, Diego. You don't understand. I saw him. I know how he thinks. I saw his resolve. He has a sense of honor, as twisted as it may be. His only objective is to take me. However he has to do it. He is absolutely prepared to give the order for every single person out there to be killed."

"You aren't giving us any credit," Terrence snarled.

She shoved at him again, pushing herself up into the seat. "It has nothing to do with credit. What I'm trying to tell you is that he is perfectly willing to die. It doesn't matter to him because he has men behind him who'll complete the mission. He has snipers surrounding us all. They've already shot one of your men. How many more are you willing to sacrifice?

"He's not normal. Threats won't work. He doesn't care if KGI starts shooting back. He doesn't care if they take a stand. He'll mow down anyone who gets in his way. Will we win in the end? Maybe. But at what cost? How many families will lose their husbands, fathers, sons, brothers? Is one person worth that many deaths? No. It's not. And what you're not considering, what you don't realize, is that they have no intention of killing me. They want me for what I can do. And that buys you and Rio and KGI time. This isn't the time or place to take a stand. They have the advantage."

"Son of a bitch," Diego swore. "Goddamn it, Grace. We can't just let you walk into that son of a bitch's clutches. Do you not remember what they did to you before?"

"I survived," she said calmly. "I survived before. I'll do it again. Besides, I have a hell of a lot more to live for now. If you think I'm giving up and rolling over, you have another think coming. I'm going, but I damn well expect you guys to get your asses in gear and come save my ass before it gets too bad. All I'm doing is buying us some time."

Terrence stared hard at her, respect and admiration

bright in his eyes. "I've never known another woman with bigger balls than you, Miss Grace."

She forced a laugh. "Thanks. I think."

Slowly she pushed upward and this time they let her go. Diego caught her hand, and she turned to look at him.

"This is a hell of a brave thing you're doing. I won't ever forget it and I'll make damn sure no one else does either. Go with God, Grace, and fight like the devil himself."

She smiled faintly and then turned her head toward Terrence. "Give me your handgun."

He looked strangely at her but didn't hesitate. He pulled a smaller nine millimeter from his ankle holster and extended it to her. She slid her fingers around the stock, jacked a shell into the chamber and thumbed off the safety.

Then she took a deep breath and stepped onto the platform that had been pushed up to the hatch.

"I'm here," she said calmly.

"Goddamn it, Grace, get the fuck back in the plane!"

Rio's furious voice made her flinch. He stood a short distance away, beside another woman who'd been made to resemble her. The woman's hair was twisted tightly around the fist of the man holding her captive while he held a gun to the back of Rio's head.

She took a step down, her gaze connecting to the man behind Rio. Then she paused, never backing down from his stare.

"I want your word. I go with you, no one else gets hurt. I know much about you, Hancock. I've seen inside your mind. I know how it works. So maybe you'll appreciate the implications of what I'm about to say."

The entire area went quiet, held captive by the strength in her words.

She raised the gun held loosely by her side, but she didn't point it at anyone. There was a mad scramble within the ranks of Hancock's men, and he barked a terse order for them not to shoot her. No, they wouldn't shoot her. A point that worked hugely in her favor. She could take one of them out right now and they still wouldn't shoot her. They'd just slaughter everyone else while she watched.

Instead she continued to raise the gun until she pointed it at her own temple. A series of gasps, curses and what-the-fucks quickly made the rounds from both sides.

"What the hell are you doing?" Rio croaked. "Put the gun down and get your ass back in that plane."

"Here's the deal, Hancock," she said in just as arrogant a voice as he'd used moments earlier. "You're going to let every last person go until it's just you and me."

"And if I don't?"

There was more curiosity in his voice than any real threat. It was apparent that he'd been caught off guard by her approach. Maybe he'd expected her to be crying or screaming or cowering behind Terrence and Diego.

"If you don't, then I shoot myself and you have yourself one fucked-up failure of a mission."

Rio's roar of denial echoed and mixed with all the other shouts and exclamations of surprise.

Hancock smiled. "You're bluffing, and you're insane. No one here believes you. I hold all the cards, Grace. You hold nothing."

Her stare grew colder. She stared until he actually flinched and glanced away for the briefest of moments.

"Really?" she said coolly. "I saw into your mind, Hancock. I know you're telling the truth about slaughtering these people to achieve your aim. I also know that your death is meaningless to you. Your sense of honor, however twisted, is that the mission comes first. Above all else. Above life. Even your own. You don't care if you die because one of the others will deliver me, accomplishing the mission. But guess what? I'm about to let you into my mind so you can see that I'm dead serious too. The very last thing I want to do is go back to the endless torture I was subjected to. But I'll do it if it saves people I care about. If you kill them, I'll have nothing left to live for anyway, and it would give me great pleasure to deny you what you most want."

For the first time, a flash of uncertainty crossed his face. She opened herself to him, focusing intensely on the pathway she'd traced to him just moments earlier. She saw his indecision and oddly his admiration for her. There was grudging respect that she'd stand up and bargain for the lives of the others.

Then she closed her eyes and let him feel her own determination. Let him feel the despair and the helplessness that had long been weighing down on her. She let him see the past and how many times she'd wanted to die. And then she showed him cold resolve. Her decision to die by her own hand before she allowed that evil son of a bitch to win. She felt his shock at the realization that she'd been utterly serious.

She felt the quick change in him, his sudden urgency to acquiesce to her demands. The very last thing he wanted was for her to kill herself because then it made him a failure, and he saw failure as the ultimate dishonor.

She also saw the acknowledgment that he would end his own life before ever facing the shame of that dishonor.

She stared at him, a mocking smile on her lips. "It would seem we're both willing to die but for different reasons."

"Stand down," Hancock shouted. Then he pushed Rio forward, and the rest of the men behind him spread out, training their guns on the members of KGI.

Don't be angry, Rio, she said gently in his mind.

Why? Why did you do it?

His voice was shaken and broken, despair ripping through him. Feelings of failure, his inability to protect her. That she'd sacrifice herself for the rest. It made him furious and yet he was awed by her courage. And finally, finally she felt worthy of that regard. She'd taken a stand. No longer was she a victim.

Because it's the only way. I won't have you all die for nothing. Either way he's going to take me. You can't help me if you're dead. It'll be up to you to find me. Don't keep me waiting, Rio. I don't know how long I'll last this time.

You survive, he demanded harshly. *You do whatever the fuck it takes to survive. You stay alive for me. I'll come for you. There isn't a force on this goddamn earth that can keep me away from you. You just do whatever it takes. You do what they want. And you goddamn stay alive for me. Live for both of us, baby. Because I'm coming for you and I'll go to hell and back if that's what it takes.*

I love you.

God, Grace, I love you too. So damn much.

Make sure they leave. All of them. They will kill you. I saw into his mind, Rio. He doesn't care about you or anyone else. All he cares about is carrying out his orders.

"Stand down," Rio barked, echoing Hancock's order. Then he turned to stare hard at the man who now held Grace's fate in his hands. "How are we going to play this, Hancock?"

"Tell your men to get out of the plane. We'll take that one. It's been refueled already. As long as Grace is in that plane, you won't do anything to bring it down."

Rio gave a terse nod and then called to Terrence and Diego. A moment later they appeared just above Grace and she moved to the side so they could pass.

The gun in Grace's hand never wavered. She kept it firmly to her temple, a sight that would forever be burned into Rio's memory. It scared him to death because he too had seen Grace's resolve. He was so damn in awe of her courage and daring he could barely breathe.

Hancock let go of P.J.'s hair and pushed her forward. She stumbled and went to her knees but then slowly picked herself up and held her hands out from her sides.

"Everyone over in the hangar," Hancock directed. "No surprises or I give the order to start firing. I've always thought playing last man standing would be kind of cool."

Insane son of a bitch. He'd always been a morbid bastard, but he hadn't been this fucking crazy. Maybe Rio would've been this way if he hadn't walked away from Titan when he had. Maybe he would be the one throwing

Grace to the wolves. The knowledge hurt. This was what he used to be. Mission above all else. No conscience. No sense of right or wrong. Only of what his directive was. Right or wrong hadn't been for them to decide.

Sam motioned for his men to fall back. Cole and Steele dragged Dolphin toward the hangar. He was bleeding heavily and Rio's heart sank. He hadn't wanted to lose even one man to this. He'd been a fool.

"Disable the other planes," Hancock called to his men. "Make damn sure they can't take off in them."

Then Hancock turned to face Grace, and it was all Rio could do not to lunge after him.

"Well, Grace? Care to give me the gun now?"

"Fuck you," she snarled.

The corner of Rio's mouth lifted in a half smile. She was fucking fierce.

Hancock held up his hands. "Okay, okay, we'll do it your way. Tell me what you want."

"What I want and what I can have are two different things," she snapped. "You don't really want to know what I want right now."

"Then tell me what the next move is. Ball is in your court."

"I want every one of your men gone. If they're getting on the plane, then get them there now. You have five minutes or I decorate the tarmac with my brains."

Rio winced and closed his eyes. *Calm down, Grace. You're scaring the shit out of me.*

She ignored his reprimand and continued to stare at Hancock like he was the nastiest sort of bug. "Get them moving. We don't have all day. They have an injured man who needs medical attention."

Hancock directed the men on the tarmac to board. Grace quickly stepped down and away so they couldn't get close enough to wrest the gun from her grip. Rio had to admit, she'd thought this through with admirable speed and common sense. She was giving them no opening. No opportunity to back out of the agreement.

When the last of the men was on board, leaving only her and Hancock facing each other, Grace said, "Now you."

"I'm not boarding without you."

Slowly she lowered the gun and then extended it toward Hancock. Rio died a thousand deaths. Terrence wrapped beefy arms around him as if knowing he was about to go after Grace.

"She knows what she's doing," Terrence said quietly. "You've got one hell of a woman, Rio."

Don't make any moves, Rio. He has snipers out there. At least half a dozen. I have no way of knowing if he called them off but I'm betting not. You'll have to figure a way out of the hangar without getting shot at.

You leave that to us. You just do what he says and give them no reason to hurt you.

I love you, Rio. I don't regret any of our time together. I wouldn't change a single thing about what happened to me because it brought us together if only for a little while. Thank you.

It sounded too goddamn much like good-bye and he couldn't stand it. His mind was filled with so much grief and rage that he couldn't even communicate back.

He'll likely make it impossible for me to communicate with you. He knows I'm telepathic and he won't want me to be able to relay information. Don't panic if I go silent. If and when I'm able, I'll tell you what I can.

Rio closed his eyes as Hancock slowly took the gun from Grace's hand and gestured for her to climb the steps leading back into the plane.

The door closed and for a moment Rio felt a surge of fear through the pathway to Grace. And then, as she'd predicted, he sensed a sudden flash of pain and then darkness settled over his mind.

The plane began an immediate taxi and soon it was zipping down the runway, lifting off in the distance until the lights from the wings were barely visible in the overcast sky.

CHAPTER 33

STEELE tossed P.J.'s rifle toward her. She deftly caught it, checked the chamber and then set it aside to yank a camo shirt over the soft yellow T-shirt she'd worn to pose as Grace.

"Never could stand yellow on me," she muttered. "Makes me look washed out."

"P.J. and Cole, I need you to find those goddamn snipers and take them out," Steele barked. "Renshaw and Baker and I will try to draw their fire. When they shoot, take them out."

Rio dove for the hangar just as a shot cracked in the distance. The bullet ricocheted off the concrete a mere foot from where he landed, kicking up shards of rock.

"You okay?" Ethan Kelly yelled in his ear.

He was surrounded by Kellys, all pulling him farther into the hangar and out of danger. He felt gut-shot. He rolled to his back and stared up at the faces looking down at him.

"Grace," he croaked out. "We can't let that bastard get far."

Nathan Kelly knelt beside Rio while Sam, Garrett and Donovan hurried over to tend to Dolphin, who was steadily swearing a blue streak.

"Shea felt her go out too," Nathan said quietly. "Shea's going to try to stay with her, but it takes a lot out of Shea. She isn't like Grace. She doesn't have Grace's control or focus. But she's going to keep trying. She said to tell you to keep trying."

Joe and Nathan reached down to pull Rio to his feet.

"Got one," P.J. called. "Motherfucker is ball-less and singing soprano."

"Jesus, that woman is vicious," Joe muttered.

"That's our girl," Renshaw called back smugly.

"Shut the fuck up and do your job," Steele barked. "We have a man down and I'm not losing him. We have to get him to a hospital yesterday."

"Two down," Cole called from his position in the far corner. He'd settled beside a small hole in the metal building and had the barrel of his rifle inserted through the opening. There was just enough room for his scope without having his vision obscured.

"Like hell you're outdoing me," P.J. muttered. "Number three down. Ah hell, there's four. Seven o'clock, Cole, moving out fast. Nail his ass."

Cole fired and then held up four fingers to signal his man was down.

"On my count," Steele said. "Renshaw, you take right. Baker, you're my left. Make a run for the jet and take cover. P.J., Cole, be ready. Make this count. I'm not getting my ass shot off because of you two."

"Suck it," P.J. snapped. "I haven't missed my mark yet."

Steele uttered the count and he and his men ran, ducking and rolling. Gunfire erupted from the surrounding wooded area, and P.J. and Cole were quick to get off their shots.

"I got two," P.J. called. "Cole?"

"One. I don't see any more."

Swanny edged to the doorway and peered around,

quietly surveying the area. In the distance, Steele and his two men had their backs to the side of the jet, guns up as they awaited word.

Swanny motioned for Ethan and Joe. "Let's go for round two and see if they take the bait. If there are any more out there, P.J. will get them."

"I heard that, asshole," Cole snapped.

Swanny grinned and P.J. blew him a kiss.

"Let's go," Swanny said.

Ethan and Joe exchanged amused glances. "Since when does he give the orders around here? He's the freshman in this operation," Joe complained.

Still, he and Ethan ducked out, running balls to the wall toward the plane. Not a single shot was fired from the woods, which meant the snipers had wised up and weren't giving up their positions, there weren't any left, or they'd just decided to retreat and make a run for it.

Rio stood amid all the chaos, his heart numb. Breaths frozen in his chest. Blackness filling his mind. Grace was gone. Hancock had taken her. How the hell had he gotten to them so fast? How could he have anticipated their move before they ever made it? How could he have known where they were going?

None of it made sense.

Unless they had a goddamn leak. Before Browning, he would have beat the hell out of anyone who suggested anyone in the KGI organization would be capable of selling out a teammate. But now he wasn't so sure.

Sam rose to his feet, his expression grim. "I've got a chopper coming for Dolphin and transport for us to the nearest hospital. Our first priority is getting him help. Then we have to regroup, consider our options and figure out our next move."

"Our first priority is Grace," Rio snarled.

Sam held up his hand. "I get it, man. But I have a man down. They aren't going to kill Grace. At least not yet. They haven't had time. Dolphin's going to die if we don't get him stabilized. He comes first."

Rio closed his eyes because he knew this to be true. Team first. Never leave a man down. It was a motto they clung to as fiercely as they did anything else. But goddamn it, that had all changed for him the minute Grace had entered his life.

Nothing—no one—mattered as much as she did, and if something happened to her, he was done for.

"P.J., Cole, I need you guys to spread out. Do a recon of the area. Make sure it's safe for the incoming chopper. ETA is fifteen minutes, so you have to make this fast. Rio, I need your guys to help," Sam said.

Terrence, Diego and Decker grabbed their rifles, followed quickly by Alton, and then Garrett left Dolphin's side and grabbed his gun. The six men followed P.J. and Cole out the back and into the dark.

Rio hurried over to where Dolphin lay. Blood soaked his entire chest. The bullet had entered at an angle, effectively going under the Kevlar vest. Hell. It was a mess, and he was bleeding like a stuck pig.

"Don't look at me like that," Dolphin snarled.

Rio couldn't even believe he was still conscious.

"And tell your damn woman to get the fuck away from me. I can do this on my own. I won't be responsible for her going down."

Rio stared down at Dolphin, sure he hadn't heard right. "What the fuck? What the hell are you talking about, Dolphin? Are you out of your head? Quit talking shit."

"She's here," Dolphin gasped out. "I can feel her. She's fixing shit. I'm a mess, man. Couldn't breathe for shit. I tried to fight her and she told me to stop being a goddamn baby and take it like a man."

Rio reached out, sharp and probing, like an arrow aimed at the very heart of their connection. *Goddamn it, Grace, you stop it! Do you hear me! We've got this situation under control. You have to save your strength because you have no idea what they're going to make you do.*

Her answer was faint, barely discernible, almost as if she wasn't fully conscious herself.

I couldn't let him die because of me.

Rio swore viciously. He balled his fist, wanting to destroy something.

"Save it, man. She said to tell you to chill out. She's only sticking a Band-Aid on me until they can get me to the hospital. She actually apologized for not being able to do more. Son of a bitch."

Dolphin wasn't any happier about Grace's help than Rio was. But Rio also knew the moment Grace broke away from the other man. He lost color and slumped weakly back onto the concrete. His strength seemed to leach right out of him, but at least he wasn't coughing up blood and his breaths were even and strong.

"I'll be a son of a bitch," Donovan murmured. "Damndest thing I ever saw."

Donovan had been working diligently on a pressure bandage, trying to stop the bleeding. He was up to his elbows in bright red blood. It was all over his shirt. All over the ground. And yet now it had slowed to an ooze.

"I hear the chopper," Steele bellowed from the runway.

The others scrambled, forming a tight line all the way to the landing pad so that Dolphin could be carried behind cover. As soon as the helo touched down, Donovan, Garrett and Sam hoisted Dolphin upward and rushed him toward the waiting stretcher.

Donovan climbed in with the other medic, and the chopper immediately took off, buzzing over the distant trees.

A few moments later, a line of SUVs roared down the runway.

"That'll be the cavalry," Sam said. "Fall in and let's get the hell out of here!"

Rio didn't question who came to get them or how Sam had arranged it so fast, but then Sam had a lot of damn connections, especially with the military. He was just grateful to get away so that they could regroup and figure out where to find Grace.

He reached out to her again, needing reassurance that she was okay.

Are you okay, honey? Do you know where they're taking you?

There was only a faint whisper back. *They drugged me, but I have to pretend it's stronger than what it is because I don't want them to know I can still function. I was out for a while because he hit me over the head. I don't know anything yet. Don't contact me. I don't want to betray our link. I'll reach out to you when it's time.*

I love you, he said fiercely. *I'll come for you, Grace. I'll never leave you. Rest now and know that we're going to get you out of this.*

He felt her answering smile, so full of love and trust. Trust. It hit him like a hammer. She had absolute faith that he would indeed come for her, and like hell he was going to let her down.

CHAPTER 34

"RIO, you're going to want to hear this," Sam said in a grim voice.

Rio turned where he'd taken position in the hospital waiting room with the others. Dolphin had been taken to surgery a half hour before and they were likely in for a long wait.

Garrett stood next to his brother, and Steele was on Sam's other side.

"Resnick was shot earlier today in his home."

Rio's brows went up. "Dead?"

Sam shook his head. "Critical. He was found by Kyle Phillips. He was the one who notified me. He and his team are on constant guard because they fear Resnick is still a target and someone will want to finish the job while he's vulnerable."

"So what's this have to do with what's going on here?" Rio asked impatiently.

"Because I was the last person Resnick tried to contact, and when Phillips found Resnick, his computer files were open to everything he had on KGI. Including the airfield we flew into and the locations of the majority of our safe houses. Phillips lifted fingerprints not belonging to Resnick from the keyboard, and when he ran them, they came back to a deceased former member of the Army Special Forces. Pretty coincidental, isn't it?"

"Fuck," Rio swore. "They got to him. Titan fucking got to him and that's how they knew where to find us. Son of a bitch, Sam, why the hell does Resnick have that kind of information?"

Sam's eyes narrowed. "I know you're pissed, but you need to back the fuck off, Rio. We do a lot of damn jobs for Resnick. Hell, he's paid for half of those facilities, from the safe houses to the airstrip we used today. In the past we've never had a reason not to trust him. It wasn't until recently that he gave us a reason to second-guess that decision."

Rio shoved the strands of hair that had come loose from his ponytail behind his ears and blew out a breath.

"I think we should go see Resnick and Phillips," Garrett said in a low voice. "If Resnick comes around, he may be able to tell us something that helps us locate Grace."

Rio's nostrils flared. "How far? Where is he?"

"An hour away. We can get there quicker," Sam said. "Let me tell the others what's up. I want protection for Dolphin but I also want them on standby for orders if we get information that helps us from Resnick."

"Thank you," Rio said quietly. "I know I've made this personal. She's not just a mission, Sam. She's my fucking life."

Sam smiled faintly. "Every mission is personal, Rio. Some are just more personal than others."

Sam slapped him on the shoulder and then walked away to talk to Steele. Nathan came up behind Rio and nudged him over to the side.

"What's up? Has Shea heard anything from Grace?" Rio asked anxiously.

Nathan shook his head. "Look, I just wanted to tell you or rather explain something. When Shea was taken, it was hard. A lot harder because she can't focus her ability like Grace can. Plus they'd drugged her with something that made trying to communicate telepathically unbearable and caused her unimaginable agony. We have an advantage here because Grace is smart. She's tough as nails. She's a fighter. And she can talk to you. She can talk to Shea. She can pretty much damn well talk to whomever she needs to talk to, so that gives us more to go on.

"She took charge of the situation and in a lot of ways she's calling the shots because she knows they want her alive. As soon as she has information to pass on to us, I know you'll hear from her. Shea has a hard time maintaining a link for a long period of time. It makes her weak, and she's still recovering from what she went through at the hands of these bastards. But she's ready and willing to do whatever Grace needs even if it means making herself vulnerable."

Rio put his hand on Nathan's arm. "Thanks, man. I appreciate that. Tell Shea that I appreciate her. I also want you to tell her that I'm going to get her sister back. I don't give a fuck what it takes. And if she hears from Grace before I do, I want to know about it. I'm going with Sam and Garrett to run down a lead, but let me know the minute you hear anything and tell Shea I'll do the same."

Nathan nodded. "They're special, Rio, but then you know that. Shea and Grace are very special and they don't deserve what's happened to them. They just want to have a normal life and I'm going to make that happen for Shea if it takes the rest of my life."

"Sounds like we're on the same page." Rio murmured.

He caught Sam's eye from across the room and Sam flung his thumb over his shoulder to let Rio know it was time to bug out.

"I'll catch you later, Nathan."

Nathan slapped Rio on the back as he walked away. "Good luck, man. You know we have your back."

RIO hated hospitals. He hated the cold, sterile smell. He always thought that hospitals reeked of the stench of death.

Sam took care of getting them into the ICU wing and whatever he said must have impressed the hell out of someone, because they let all three men pass with no argument.

When they got to the end where Resnick's room was, Kyle Phillips was standing guard outside the door.

"Any change?" Sam asked the young Marine.

"Yes, sir. Some. He came around briefly. Kept saying your name. He was extremely agitated. Wanted to warn you."

"I need to get in there to see him," Sam said. "A woman's life depends on it."

Phillips hesitated only a moment and then opened the door, calling to one of his men who was stationed at Resnick's bedside.

Once the other Marine took Phillips's post, Phillips then motioned Sam, Garrett and Rio inside, following close behind.

The mechanical sounds of so much hospital equipment were loud in the otherwise silent room. It creeped Rio out. He wanted to get the hell out as soon as possible. He wanted to get to Grace. He wanted this over with.

Sam stopped at the head of the bed and lowered himself so he could speak close to Resnick's ear. "Adam, it's me, Sam. I'm here. I need to talk to you. Grace's life is on the line."

For a moment there was no response from Resnick, and then he stirred lightly. His eyes fluttered open and he gave Sam a groggy look of half recognition.

"Titan," he rasped.

Rio simmered with impatience. "We know it's Titan."

Sam shot Rio a scowl to silence him and then returned his attention to Resnick.

Resnick tried to raise his hand to grasp Sam's shirt. Sam caught Resnick's hand and held on so he wouldn't overexert himself.

"Was looking up a lead I had when I was shot. Take a look at Gordon Farnsworth. He's dirty but pays a lot of damn money for legitimacy. He's got his fingers into damn near everything under the sun. Politics. Military. Funds other countries. Drugs. Gun running. There isn't much he hasn't done. He's on everyone's list but he's slick as snot and no one's been able to nail him on shit yet. He's someone who would have had access to Titan and also the means to purchase their services."

Sam frowned. "Why would he want Grace? Money? Sell her to the highest bidder?"

Resnick slowly shook his head then made a choking sound. He went gray, and for a minute, Rio thought they'd lost him. He leaned forward, desperate to know what Resnick could tell them.

"Has a daughter," Resnick rasped out. "Rumor is she's very ill and he's desperate to save her. All the money in the world can't buy her a cure. He's tried. She's the only thing he loves. The only thing that makes him halfway human. She is his one weakness. The one thing that can be used against him."

Rio straightened, his face going tight, his nostrils flaring. The bastard didn't want Grace for any research program. He didn't want her for the military and what she would mean for soldiers in battle. He wanted her to save his daughter.

"Find him," Resnick whispered. "If he's after Grace, I'd bet all I own that he wants her because she's the only person who can save his daughter."

Garrett pushed forward. "Do you know where he is, Adam? Do you have any information at all?"

Resnick sank into the pillow, and for a long moment was silent, his chest barely moving with air exchange. Phillips shot them a nervous look.

"Maybe you should go now. The nurse would have a fit if she knew we were pushing him this far."

Rio leaned down, so he was just inches from Resnick's face. "You care about her. You care about her and Shea both. You tried to protect them. Shea has Nathan, but now Grace has me. I'm going to get her back, Resnick. If I have to turn the whole goddamn world over, I'm going to get her back. Now help us, damn it. Anything. Give us a starting point. You have to know something. You're a goddamn library of classified information."

Resnick's eyes opened to narrow slits, like he didn't have the strength to open them farther.

"It's rumored he has an island in the Mediterranean, just off the coast of Greece. He's generous to the local economy, and with Greece in the economic state it's currently in, his money has bought a lot of loyalty. Even if they do know who and what he is, they'll never give him up because he provides jobs for the entire island and keeps the economy afloat.

"He's flown in doctors from all over the world, and the word is, they've all told him the same thing. That there is no hope and that she doesn't have long. Such news would have made him desperate enough to do whatever it took to save her."

Resnick paused and labored to catch his breath. His face was strained and it was evident he was in a great deal of pain. Again, Phillips stepped forward as if to put an end to the inquisition, but Resnick stopped him with a barely raised hand.

"Most notable is that CIA surveillance tapped into a phone conversation between Farnsworth and the man they believe led Titan when it was still in existence."

"Hancock," Rio muttered. "Goddamn Hancock."

Sam put a hand on Resnick's arm. "Thank you, Adam."

Resnick stared up at Rio. "You just get her back. I very much want to meet the woman I consider a sister."

Rio swallowed and nodded. "Failure isn't an option."

"Unfortunately that is also Titan's motto," Resnick said quietly.

"Yes, I know," Rio said calmly. "I'm the one who coined it for them."

CHAPTER 35

"**YOU** realize if you try to communicate with your boyfriend, Rio, that you'll just get him killed."

"Fuck off," Grace said rudely from her perch on the couch in the airplane. They'd flown from the airstrip in the small jet that Hancock had appropriated from Rio's group, but they'd landed an hour later and boarded a larger jet, taking off immediately. She still had no idea where they were going and she was pissed enough not to feel fear. Yet.

Hancock laughed. "I can see what he sees in you. You're well matched, I think. I can't ever imagine Rio with a dainty little mouse. He'd eat her alive."

Grace faked a yawn. "I'm not interested in your analysis of Rio's love life. I want to know where the hell you're taking me and why."

Hancock ignored her and looked out the window before checking one of his handheld devices. "We'll be landing soon."

"Soon? Soon would have been six hours ago. We've been on this plane forever."

"Such a complainer. Don't bite the hand that will have

to keep you alive once you've served your purpose," he said in a dangerously soft voice.

The subtle threat sent chills dancing up her spine.

She glanced toward the window, but Hancock snapped it shut, blocking her view. All she knew was it was daylight and they were over a large body of water.

She wouldn't panic yet. There was plenty of time to glean information to pass on to Rio. Shea had been a quiet presence in her mind. As was Rio. It was the only reason she hadn't lost her composure yet.

Neither had tried to talk to her. She'd been very specific in asking them not to use the pathway until she initiated contact. Knowing Rio, he'd wait only so long before his impatience got the better of him and he would be yelling in her head, asking her if she was okay.

Strangely, that thought brought her comfort. It was nice to have someone who cared.

The plane continued its sharp descent and then she heard the sound of the landing gear lowering. She instinctively braced herself, tensing until they touched down.

Now fear began a steady thrum in her chest. She tried to swallow it back, but it choked her, cutting off her air.

This was it. Wherever it was that Hancock was taking her, they were here and hell awaited.

Grace, goddamn it, I can feel your fear. Tell me what the hell is going on. Where are you? Can you tell me anything about your location?

Rio's voice blew into her mind, taking away some of the fear that threatened to overwhelm her.

We just landed. I don't know anything more yet.

She forced calm into her message and made sure to include Shea. Neither of them needed her to be hysterical. They felt helpless enough not knowing her fate, not knowing what lay in store for her or where she was.

I'll tell you more when I'm able. Please be patient. He watches me and he knows when I'm communicating with you. I have to remain conscious or I'll never be able to give you any information.

I'm going to kill that son of a bitch for hurting you, Rio seethed.

But Grace shut him out, forcing a bland expression to her face. Emotionless. Untouchable. She wouldn't show this man her fear. She wouldn't show anyone how terrified she was. She was finished being a victim, and by God, she was through wishing to die. She wanted to live. She was *going* to live. She'd promised Rio she'd do whatever it damn well took to survive, and it was one promise she wasn't going to break.

To her dismay, Hancock jerked her upward, twisted her arms behind her back and handcuffed her wrists. Then he hastily tied a blindfold around her eyes before the hatch opened so they could disembark.

She was careful to keep her emotions in check because they would only set Rio off again and Shea would worry more than she already was.

Hancock's men filed off the plane and then Hancock took her arm in a surprisingly gentle grip and guided her toward the steps.

"Watch your step," he ordered. "First one coming up. Stay beside me and take your time."

"It wouldn't do to have the lab rat break her neck before she can perform," Grace said nastily.

"If you break your neck, I don't get paid."

"I hope you choke on your damn blood money."

He chuckled. "In another situation, I just might like you, Grace. But quite frankly you've been nothing but a pain in my ass since I took this mission and I'll be happy to see the back of you."

"The feeling is entirely mutual," she snarled.

She found herself shoved into the back of a car. It was comfortable. Expensive leather. It even smelled expensive. The ride was smooth too. Unlike the various vehicles she'd been hauled around in when she'd been captured before.

"Who do you work for?" she asked softly.

"You'll meet him soon enough."

Him. Not them. One person. She didn't know what to make of that revelation.

I don't think this is the government or some lab like last time, Rio. She tried to keep the worry out of her message. *It has a different feel. Not much has been said but I just got off a plane and I've been on one since we left you in Virginia. Hancock just said "him" when I asked who he worked for. Not "them." Not some faceless group. He said "him." But I'm blindfolded so I can't see anything!*

We're on our way, honey. I don't want you to worry, okay? I want you to stall for time. Do what you need to do but do not make them angry. If your choices are to submit or for them to hurt you, then you damn well do what they want you to do. Do you understand? No matter what happens, baby, you and I will deal with it together. I'll always be here for you. You'll never be alone again.

She closed her eyes, knowing Hancock wouldn't be able to see through the blindfold. She knew exactly what Rio was telling her. No matter how bad it got. No matter what she was asked to do. No matter what was done to her. He didn't want her to give up and choose to die. He wanted her to live.

I'll be here waiting. I know you'll come for me, Rio.

She poured every ounce of her trust, her faith, her absolute belief in this man. He loved her. She had no doubt. He was an honorable man no matter what he thought of himself or his past choices. She knew without doubt that he'd move heaven and earth to bring her home again. Home to him.

What seemed an eternity later, the car ground to a halt and the doors opened. There was urgency to everyone's movements. Orders were issued in stilted English, with an accent she didn't recognize.

Hancock yanked her roughly from the car and shoved her forward. Her tennis shoes crunched the gravel beneath them and then she nearly stumbled when it turned to smooth pavement. Hancock righted her and continued forward past the sound of bubbling water. A fountain?

The air was warm. Hot even. She could feel the sun's direct rays on her arms. The smell of salt was heavy in the air and a breeze blew over her, bringing with it the feel of the sea. They were close to the water.

As soon as they stepped inside the building or house or whatever the hell it was, the air was much cooler. She went through a series of hallways before Hancock finally stopped.

She heard the door in front of her fly open and she took an instinctive step back, bumping into Hancock.

"Is this her? Is she the one?" a man demanded in a voice that sent fear snaking down her spine once more. There was something about his voice. It reeked of desperation. It was cold, hard and determined. *Evil.*

Her pulse sped up and her hands began to shake in the cuffs that still circled her wrists.

"This is her," Hancock said in an even tone.

She found herself yanked forward and then the door slammed behind her. Suddenly the blindfold was torn from her eyes, and she rapidly blinked to adjust to her surroundings.

She was in a large study or office. It had the look of a library but there was a large executive desk at the back. To the right was a large fireplace, which despite the warmth of the day, was burning.

She took in as much as she possibly could as quickly as she could. She glanced left, hoping for a window, hoping for some sign of where she was, but was frustrated as she realized there were no windows. It was more like a dark cave where a beast skulked about.

Then she focused on the man in front of her who was staring every bit as hard at her as she was at him. For someone who'd frightened her so much with his voice alone, his appearance was deceptively mild.

He was average height. Maybe late forties. He was obviously a bit prideful because there wasn't a hair on his head that was out of place, thanks largely to the amount of styling products evident.

He wore expensive clothing. Diamond cufflinks. A gaudy gold chain hung around his neck, and in one ear he wore a diamond stud earring.

He would probably appear arrogant on most days, but there was so much relief in his expression that it took Grace aback. He looked . . . *happy* . . . to see her.

"Get the cuffs off her," the man ordered. "We don't have any time to lose. I need her upstairs right now."

Hancock quickly unlocked the cuffs and Grace pulled her hands around to her front, rubbing her wrists as she stared warily at the man in front of her.

"Who are you and why am I here?" she demanded.

"Who I am isn't important. What's important is that my daughter is very ill, and you're going to heal her."

CHAPTER 36 •

GRACE was taken aback by the utter despair that choked his voice. It wasn't that she hadn't expected to be used for her abilities. She just hadn't expected . . . this. A man on a mission. A single mission.

She reached into his mind, wanting confirmation or perhaps to know what else he intended to use her for. Was she some sort of experiment once again? Was his daughter a guinea pig, and if Grace was successful, would she then be turned over to some government agency? Sold to the highest bidder?

What she found shocked her. Gordon Farnsworth wasn't a good man. She saw things that made her blood run cold. He'd led a life filled with atrocities, bloodshed, selling out whomever he needed to, to achieve his ends. He was unapologetic and completely unremorseful over his choices.

But she also saw a grieving father whose only daughter was dying, and he was frustrated by his inability to buy her health and happiness. It was a harsh realization for him, that given his immense wealth, he couldn't have the one thing he most wanted.

His daughter's life.

Though she knew the answer to her question, she posed it anyway in an effort to buy time, to plan her next move and to somehow maneuver herself out of an impossible situation.

"What's wrong with her?"

"Cancer," he bit out. "It's a particularly invasive, aggressive form of cancer. Supposedly rare. The doctors all have names for it. I just know that it's slowly sucking my daughter's life from her. It began in an innocuous enough place, but before she could be treated, it had already spread to her liver and then into her bones. She's riddled with cancer. There isn't a part of her body that hasn't been besieged by the disease. It's in her lungs, and at times she has to be put on a respirator so she can survive. It's spread to her brain and at times she'll lie in a coma, unaware of her surroundings."

He advanced on Grace, his face ugly, and she got her first look at what this man was to the rest of the world. Cold, evil, the very devil.

"You'll cure her. I know of your abilities. I made damn sure that you were able to do what was said could be done before I had you brought here. I wouldn't trust my daughter to someone who would cause her harm."

Grace swallowed, sent a simple message to Rio.

Gordon Farnsworth.

Rio was silent but then he had to know how precarious Grace's current position was. Shea stirred in her mind but also remained silent, a steady support.

"It would seem, Mr. Farnsworth, that *I* hold all the cards," Grace said coolly.

"You hold nothing!"

He yanked her toward him, his hands wrapped in her shirt until their faces were inches apart. Spittle hit her cheek from the explosion of his outburst.

"You'll heal my daughter or I'll make you wish you were never born."

She reached for his wrists with renewed strength and

yanked them downward, separating herself from his touch. It repulsed her. His entire being vibrated with the stench of evil and death. It nearly overwhelmed her.

"You're too late for that," she said in a low voice. "I've wished for my death many times. Threats have no meaning to me. How much is your daughter's life worth to you?"

Clearly he hadn't expected this. He took a step back, eyes narrowed in rage and surprise. He seemed at a loss for words and then he slammed his gaze back into hers and made a visible effort to collect himself.

"Money? Is money what you want? You'd sell your ability to save a child's life?"

The judgment and condemnation in his words pissed her off. Dangerously so. She had to remain calm. She couldn't allow her own volcanic rage to erupt.

"After everything you've done to ensure that I was brought to you, after the countless days of agony and pain that were brought on me as a result of your experiments to make sure I was qualified to touch your daughter, you dare to come at me with this holier-than-thou put-down because I would bargain with you?"

She gave a derisive laugh.

"You hold none of the cards, Mr. Farnsworth, and if you think you do, you're as deluded as your ego is. Kill me. Go ahead. I dare you. Then who will save your daughter? Torture me. Spend days trying to make me desperate enough to give in to anything. Your daughter doesn't have those days. But I don't care. You can't do anything to me that hasn't already been done. It's not possible to endure more than what I've already endured. While your conceit and arrogance tell you that you are all mighty and powerful, just remember that your daughter could be dead in the next hour or the next day. And then you stand there like a pompous jackass and presume to call my ethics into question. Do you think I give a shit what you think of me, you worthless, dirt-eating worm?"

Hancock chuckled, which only served to enrage Farnsworth further.

"She's right, Farnsworth," Hancock said in amusement. "Did I tell you she threatened to kill herself if I didn't co-operate with her demands? I saw into her mind. I assure you she isn't bluffing. She's just crazy enough to blow her own brains out to spite you."

Farnsworth looked between Grace and Hancock, sucking in air through extended nostrils. Then he visibly collected himself and turned away, walking toward his desk. He turned back, calmer now, and he stared at Grace with a calculated gleam.

"All right, Miss Peterson. What do you want? Money? You can have all that I own in exchange for my daughter's life. I'll make you wealthy beyond your wildest dreams."

"You have no idea what I dream about," she said bitterly.

"Then tell me. What do you want?"

"Peace."

Farnsworth's brows drew together in confusion.

"I want a life. I want to be free. I want to be able to have what your kind takes for granted. Freedom from looking over my shoulder every damn minute because some fuck-wad wants to use me like a lab rat. I want my freedom, and I want your guarantee that when I heal your daughter, you will cease to pursue me. You'll call off Titan, and more-over, you'd do well to make damn sure I stay safe, because if I don't?"

His eyes narrowed in fury. "You dare to threaten me?"

Grace eyed him calmly. She needed him to believe what she was about to say. And honestly who was to say she couldn't do it? She'd certainly never tried. Given what she could do, it wasn't out of the realm of possibility that she could do the complete opposite.

"You'll grant me everything I want, or I'll suck the life right out of your daughter."

He whitened. His jaw clenched and he seemed speechless.

"Let me just explain how my ability works," Grace said in a quiet tone. "I absorb an illness or an injury from the affected person. I take it from them and make it my own. They leave happy and healed. I'm crippled by their affliction, and then I have to take the time to heal myself. But just as I take the illness or injury, just as I give life, my life, to the person I'm linked with? So too can I take their spirit, their life, their very soul. And I don't have to be standing next to her, so if you think you can hide from me, if you think you can take her some place I'll never find her, you're dead wrong. Once I link to her, I'll be able to locate her anywhere and I'll take what it is you treasure so much."

Farnsworth stared her down, almost like he was trying to see into her mind. Evaluating whether she was telling the truth. She met his gaze unflinching. Then Farnsworth looked to Hancock as if for guidance. Hancock shrugged and the corner of his mouth turned up in a smirk.

"I'd say you have yourself a standoff, Farnsworth. In some circles, this might be called checkmate. I believe she has you by the balls."

"And while you stand here being outraged that I would actually give a damn about my own life and my own future, your daughter is upstairs dying," she said. "So I'd suggest we come to an agreement pretty damn fast. Or maybe your ego is worth more than your daughter's life."

Farnsworth whitened and he leaned over, slapping his hands on the polished surface of his desk. For the first time, she absolutely believed the conviction in his voice.

"There is nothing. *Nothing* more important to me than Elizabeth. You think me an evil man, Miss Peterson. You're right. I'm a bastard of the first order. But I love my daughter and I'll do anything at all to save her. So give me your conditions. I'll do whatever it takes to gain your cooperation."

"I want Rio here," she said calmly. She opened her mind, that pathway to Rio so he would see and hear what it was she was saying. "I am defenseless once I've healed. It would be easy for you to go back on your word. I would have no recourse."

"You think I'm going to just turn myself over to some

mercenary? Do you realize how many government and
nongovernment agencies are after me? You're out of your
damn mind."

"I don't give a fuck about you," she said in an even tone.
"What I care about is my ability to walk out of here. You'll
excuse my lack of trust in you, but your promise doesn't
mean shit to me. I've told you I can kill your daughter at
any time, so that gives you more incentive to kill me once
you've gotten what you want."

She felt Rio stir, felt his anger and his fear for her. His
anger that she'd provoke him and that she'd bargain so
ruthlessly and risk the very thing she'd just accused Farnsworth of being able to do.

"We both want the same things, Mr. Farnsworth. I have
no desire to ever see you again. Call me self-centered but
I'm more interested in having a normal life than I am in
seeing you punished for your crimes. I want Rio here. I want
his team to be allowed here. They are my protection. My
guarantee that you uphold your end of the bargain. And
once I've completed the healing, he'll walk out of here with
me because I swear to you by all that's holy, if you kill me,
if you *try* to kill me, I'll take your daughter with me."

Farnsworth went pale. He shoved a hand through his
hair, mussing the immaculately styled strands. Then he
yanked his hand away. "It will take too damn long to get
them here!"

She smiled. "Oh, I think they're probably closer than
you think. Shall I find out for you?"

*Rio, I need you. I've been buying time, but I don't have
it to spare. If his daughter dies before you get here, he'll be
out of control. He'll kill me. He'll kill you. The one thing
keeping him in check right now is his utter terror that his
daughter will die. If that happens, nothing will matter to
him any longer.*

*We're on our way, Grace. You did good, baby. You
scare the shit out of me, but you did good. You're so damn
fierce. You even have me convinced you'll take his daughter down with you if it comes to that.*

We got a lead even before you told me who he was. We're in the air now. Tell him we'll land on the mainland and then take a chopper to the island. The others will boat in, but he doesn't need to know that. Three hours, Grace. Buy us three more hours and we'll be there.

She looked back up at Farnsworth. "Three hours. Rio and his team will land a helicopter here. Until he arrives, I won't do a thing."

Farnsworth closed his eyes. "Will you . . . Will you at least go see her? Will you stay with her? I need her to have a reason to hold on. A reason to hope. I'll give the order for my men to stand down. Your Rio and his team will have clearance to land and will be escorted to you the moment they arrive."

"And after?" she asked softly.

"You can leave the same way they came. You have my word."

She reached into his mind but only found sincerity. No hint of deception. He was too focused on having his daughter well and healthy. He'd gladly let her go if it meant having Elizabeth be a normal little girl again.

"Then take me to her," Grace said quietly.

Hancock automatically took Grace's arm and she tried to yank it away, but he held firm.

She glared pointedly at Farnsworth. "Does he have to come?"

"You have your conditions. I have mine. He's there to make sure you uphold your end of the deal."

"He doesn't have to touch me in order to do that," she snapped.

Farnsworth gestured for Hancock to let her go. Hancock's gaze was cool and unreadable. Like his mind. He had admirable control over his thoughts. Every time Grace tried to get a read on him again, she saw blankness. Like he was so focused and disciplined that he could shut out everything but what was his primary goal. She'd thought it before and she hadn't seen anything to the contrary—he was more machine than man and it creeped her the hell out.

She thought she saw annoyance in his gaze, and irritation, as if he loathed taking orders from Farnsworth. But his thoughts didn't reflect his expression whatsoever.

He let go of her arm but not fast enough for her liking. She ached to put her knee right in his balls and see if the bastard was more machine than man then.

Farnsworth walked ahead of Grace, leaving her sandwiched between him and Hancock. They mounted a winding staircase and then traveled to the end of the hallway once on the second floor.

When Farnsworth opened the door, she could see the immediate fear that leapt into his eyes. His entire body went tense, as if he was afraid to hear the worst.

From the bedside of the little girl Grace still couldn't see, a man looked up, a stethoscope in his ears. On the other side was what appeared to be a nurse or at least someone who sat with the girl.

"Get out," Farnsworth said in a low voice that carried for its sheer determination.

"But she needs care," the doctor protested as he took down the stethoscope and let it hang from his neck. "She shouldn't be left alone right now."

"Get. Out." Farnsworth enunciated each word, so much menace in them that the doctor paled and backed away from the bed. "There is a helicopter waiting to take you back to the mainland. You're dismissed." He motioned for the woman. "You too."

They hurriedly left the room, the doctor muttering about the "poor girl" as he passed Grace.

Farnsworth immediately went to Elizabeth's bedside and knelt beside it. He cupped his hand over her forehead and gently stroked away her hair.

"Elizabeth, sweetheart, I have someone I'd like you to meet. She's here to help you."

Curious, Grace moved in closer until finally she could see the tiny, fragile girl lying on the bed. She looked as delicate as a porcelain doll. She looked nothing like her father. While he was all dark and sinister—he had that smarmy used car salesman look—Elizabeth was blond and pale.

Elizabeth struggled to open her eyes and then she dimly focused on her father. "Daddy," she whispered.

"I'm here, baby," Farnsworth said in a choked voice.

"You always say that. That someone will help me. But they never do."

"This time is different. She's special. Her name is Grace. She's promised to help you."

Elizabeth pursed her lips as if she was giving the matter serious consideration. "Grace. I like that name. Maybe God sent her. Everyone needs grace."

Grace's heart clutched. It went against everything she was and who she was to have threatened this child as coldly as she'd done, but she'd known that it was the only way she'd save herself. Even now, she steeled her features, trying to be as impassive as she could because she didn't want Farnsworth to know she'd already lost her heart to this beautiful, brave little girl.

She moved forward, not waiting for permission. She pulled the chair from the opposite side of the bed and positioned it right next to Elizabeth's head.

"Hello, Elizabeth," she said in a low, soothing voice. "My name is Grace and I fix people."

Elizabeth turned slowly, her eyes weak and dull as she focused her stare on Grace. "You mean like God does?"

Grace smiled. "No. Not like God. I believe He gave me the ability and I don't always know what to do with it. Someone wise once told me that perhaps my purpose hadn't yet been revealed. But I'm learning and I'm going to do my absolute best to take away your sickness."

Elizabeth nodded solemnly. "I want to make Daddy smile again. He's been sad. I don't want to die and leave him alone. He needs me."

Farnsworth made a choking sound and abruptly rose, turning his back to face the other way.

Grace slipped her hand into Elizabeth's and squeezed lightly. "Can you hold on for just a little while longer? I'm waiting for some people to get here. Healing someone takes a lot of energy and I need them to help me afterward."

Elizabeth frowned. "Will you be all right? Daddy can help you, can't you, Daddy?" She turned in her father's direction.

Farnsworth slowly turned, struggling to smile through his obvious distress. "Of course I will, sweetheart. I've given my word to her that all will be taken care of. All I want you to concern yourself with is getting better."

Grace slid into Elizabeth's weakened mind, nearly weeping as she witnessed firsthand all that the child had endured in her very short life. But she was also awed by Elizabeth's sheer determination. Her strength of will. It was the only reason she was still alive, because her body had long since given up.

She pushed as much hope and warmth through the pathway, hoping to bolster the child's spirits.

Elizabeth's eyes widened as she stared at Grace in wonder. "How did you do that? I felt you. Inside my head, I mean. It was wonderful. Like magic."

Grace smiled. "I suppose it is magic in a way. No one really knows why or how I can do it."

"You should eat," Farnsworth said gruffly.

At first Grace thought he was talking to his daughter, but he was staring directly at Grace.

"You'll need your strength. I don't imagine you've eaten for hours."

Grace turned to Elizabeth. "What do you say? Are you up for something to eat? Maybe we both need to keep our strength up for what is to come."

Grace felt a stirring in Elizabeth's mind. A tiny beacon of hope. The child was afraid to hope. She'd been disappointed so many times so she'd resigned herself to her fate long ago. She kept up the act for her father because she knew how devastated he'd be, but she'd long since stopped believing in miracles.

Don't ever give up hope. Sometimes it's all we have.

Elizabeth's smile broadened, her eyes widening in wonder as she nodded wordlessly in response to Grace's silent communication. Then she turned to her dad. "I'd like some soup. Could I have some?"

"Of course you can," Farnsworth said in a shaken voice. "I'll have something brought up for the both of you. I need you to hold on, baby. Just a little bit longer, and then I promise everything will be all right."

CHAPTER 37

HANCOCK put his hand to his ear for a moment and then said, "The helicopter is landing."

Grace looked up, her heart leaping into her throat. She was suddenly grateful she'd merely picked at the food, because her stomach rolled up into a tight ball.

Elizabeth glanced up, her fingers curling tightly around the spoon she'd used to eat her soup. There was so much hope and fear reflected in her gaze that it made Grace want to wrap her arms around her and hug her.

Farnsworth leapt to his feet, agitated, pacing toward the door until Hancock put his hand out to halt the other man.

"My men will handle the situation."

"You tell your men to get them up here at once," Farnsworth snarled. "My daughter has waited long enough."

Hancock gave Farnsworth a chilling stare that immediately took some of the belligerence from Farnsworth's stance.

Grace rose, her fingers fisted at her sides. She stared expectantly at the doorway, and after what seemed an interminable wait, Rio appeared.

His gaze immediately found Grace and he would have started forward but she reached out to him.

Don't. Don't give him any reason to believe I'm anything more than a mission to you. Just as Hancock's is to Farnsworth. Don't give him anything to use against you or me.

Are you all right?

Even as he murmured the words in her mind, he relaxed, glancing around the room, his gaze cool as he seemed to take in any potential threat. He finally settled on Hancock and his lip curled in distaste.

"Is that any way to greet an old friend?" Hancock mocked.

Farnsworth's gaze narrowed suspiciously. "You know each other? What's going on here?"

"Nothing you need concern yourself with. Merely renewing an old acquaintance," Hancock said mildly.

One by one, Rio's team filed into the room. Elizabeth shrank into her pillow, and Grace reached down to take her hand.

"It's all right," she soothed. "No one here will hurt you."

Soon the room was filled with men. Hard warriors. Armed. Expressions harsh as they seemed to weigh the opposition.

"This is how it's going to play out," Hancock began.

But Grace slipped her hand from Elizabeth's and boldly stepped forward, staring Hancock in the eye.

"No, you aren't calling the shots here. *This* is the way it's going to happen. I want everyone out."

She felt Rio's immediate protest, but she shut him down with a quick mental rebuke.

"I won't have this little girl intimidated by a bunch of hulking Neanderthals. You can all wait in the hall."

"I'm not leaving my daughter," Farnsworth said tightly.

"Of course not," Grace murmured.

Then she looked to Rio. "Make sure he isn't armed. He only stays if he has nothing on him that threatens me."

"How the hell could you defend yourself against anything at all?" Rio ground out. "You're going to be defense-less. He could kill you with nothing more than his bare hands."

Elizabeth made a sound of alarm and then stared ques-tioningly at her father.

"He and I have an understanding," Grace said calmly. "He's well aware of the consequences of him trying to kill me."

Farnsworth whitened but he nodded. "All I want is for my daughter to be well again. What happens after is of little consequence to me. I've given her my guarantee that she and whoever accompanies her will leave the island unharmed."

Rio looked like he wanted to say more, but instead he looked at Grace.

I love you. The fierceness in the declaration gave Grace the strength she needed for what was to come. *Don't you dare leave me. You hang on.*

I love you too. Trust me.

I do, honey. I do. If I didn't, I'd be tearing this fucking place apart from the top down. I don't want you to worry. The entire KGI team is here. We're not going to go down without a fight if that's what it comes to.

Grace looked pointedly at Farnsworth. "We're wasting valuable time."

Farnsworth jerked in reaction and then barked the order. "Everyone out."

Hancock waited until Rio made the first move, and when Rio and his team retreated from the room flanked by Hancock's men, Hancock left last, turning one last time. But it wasn't Farnsworth he looked at. It was Grace. His gaze was intense, and she was sure it held some meaning she wasn't able to pick up on.

When everyone had left, Farnsworth closed the door and then turned back to Grace, hurrying to the bed. "Hurry, please. Whatever it is you need, just tell me."

"What I need is for you to take a seat over there," she said, pointing calmly to a chair by the window. "And don't interfere. I don't care what you see, what you hear, what happens. Do not interfere."

Farnsworth leaned over the bed, gathered his frail daughter into his arms and pressed a kiss to her forehead. "I love you, little one. Daddy loves you. I want you to always know that."

Elizabeth smiled faintly. "I love you too. Now go so Grace can help me. She promised she would and I trust her."

He looked startled by his daughter's words, but he backed away, taking position on the very edge of the seat.

Grace took a deep breath and then she settled onto the bed next to Elizabeth, took both hands in hers and tried to infuse as much confidence into her smile as she could. She dreaded what she was about to do. She knew it could well be too much. The child was too far gone. So much cancer. Maybe they'd both die. But at least Grace would try. She had so very much to live for, and she knew if she failed, Rio and all his men's lives would be forfeit.

"Close your eyes," Grace said softly. "And I want you to concentrate hard. You're going to feel me. Don't fight it. But what I need you to do for me is to focus on being better, on fighting this illness and on getting better. The stronger you are, the stronger I can be."

Elizabeth nodded and squeezed Grace's hands. Grace smiled at the child's obvious effort to give Grace reassurance.

Grace sucked in another breath, closed her eyes and then focused all her mental energy into the pathway between her and Elizabeth.

She nearly recoiled from the sheer magnitude of the cancer eating away at Elizabeth's body. It was everywhere. There was no medical explanation for why this child had lived as long as she had. She'd hung on by sheer force of will.

Grace drew it away, absorbing it in her own body, and felt herself weakening with every passing second. But then she was joined by Elizabeth's own iron will.

It was a light in the darkest tunnel. Dawn breaking after

a stormy night. Strength. Hope. Love. Only the resilience offered by the young. Elizabeth's spirit was as strong as her will. Her soul hadn't given up. Nothing about this girl had signaled defeat.

Fused together, their wills strengthened, the light became stronger. The warmth and power of their combined determination infused Grace with much-needed support.

Grace sagged, struggled to keep herself upright, to keep her focus and not lose the battle for Elizabeth's life. And then tiny arms wrapped around her, holding and supporting her.

A whisper in her ear. "You can do it. I know you can. Thank you."

Grace reached for the last of the darkness, those ugly shadows that hung tenaciously, and with the last of her strength, she yanked them away, taking them into her own body. She fell forward into the pillows, heard Elizabeth's cry of alarm. Her plea for her father to help.

Farnsworth's hands gripped her shoulders, turned her until she was on her side. His face was grim, but full of hope as he looked between her and his daughter.

Elizabeth scrambled up to her knees, looking worriedly down at Grace.

"Help her, Daddy. She needs help!"

Farnsworth's eyes filled with tears as he stared at his daughter, pink, healthy looking, her eyes full of vibrancy that had been lacking for so long.

"Elizabeth," he whispered.

For a moment, he left Grace and enfolded his daughter into his arms. Muffled sobs erupted as he crushed her to him.

"My baby. My baby."

Elizabeth pried herself away and again looked down at Grace, who tried to offer her a reassuring smile. She was weak, yes, but she wasn't incapacitated. She had Elizabeth to thank for that. Elizabeth, who was strong, whose will to live had been so strong that it had aided Grace in the healing process.

She'd lent her strength to Grace so that Grace hadn't shouldered it all alone.

"Daddy, she needs help. Go get them. They can help her. You promised they could go."

Farnsworth looked reluctant to leave her even for a moment, but he edged away from the bed and then walked toward the door.

RIO paced outside the doorway. The hall was filled with soldiers. Mercenaries. It was tense. Titan had their guns on Rio's team as if daring them to make a move. Any move. They looked way too damned trigger-happy.

Rio just hoped to hell that the rest of KGI had made it ashore after the helo drop and were in position. This could all go to hell at a moment's notice, and he damn sure didn't want to be without backup.

The door opened and the tension soared in the hallway. Farnsworth stepped out, his back to Rio as he faced Hancock.

"It's done. She needs help, though. She's weak. Let them take her and go. I promised them safe passage off the island."

Hancock pulled his gun, pointed it at Farnsworth, and shot.

Rio leapt instinctively to the side, drawing his own weapon. The hallway became instant chaos. Another shot fired and pain screamed through Rio's chest.

"Cease fire!" Hancock roared. "Goddamn it! I did not give the order to fire!" He turned in rage and squeezed off another shot, downing the man who'd taken the shot at Rio.

Then he held his gun up high while every one of his team members covered Rio's team, effectively preventing them from acting.

Rio slid to the floor, blood running like a damn river from his chest and onto the floor. "Son of a bitch! Hancock, you stupid fuck! What the hell are you trying to pull here?"

Hancock nudged Farnsworth's body as if making sure

the man was dead, and then he crouched down beside Rio. His expression was grim.

"Fuck it all, Rio. This wasn't supposed to happen. This was a planned maneuver and one of my goddamn men panicked and got trigger-happy."

"Daddy!"

The shrill, high-pitched scream echoed through the hallway. Elizabeth ran, trying to get to her father, but Terrence scooped her up, hugging her to his broad chest and shielding her from the gruesome sight.

"Get the fuck out," Hancock bellowed. "Clear this goddamn area." Then to Rio, "I know goddamn well you have the rest of your team here. Unless you want this to become a goddamn bloodbath, you better get a handle on them quick. We have no interest in KGI. You were just collateral damage."

"Diego," Rio called, his voice fading with every breath. Son of a bitch, it hurt. "Get word out. Stand down. Meet with Sam. Tell him what's happened. For God's sake, tell them not to fire unless fired upon."

He looked up at Hancock with glassy eyes. "You better be telling me the goddamn truth about this. If not, I can guarantee not a goddamn one of you will leave this island alive."

Hancock nodded.

"Tell Grace . . ." He gasped, pissed that he couldn't seem to get air into his lungs. "Tell Grace I love her."

"Rio!"

Grace tried to push Hancock aside, but nearly fell over with the effort. Hancock reached up to steady her with a gentle grasp.

"It's too late," Hancock said gruffly.

Fear and panic slammed into Grace. She collapsed to her knees, wobbling precariously. "No!"

She reached down, putting her hands over the wound just below Rio's neck. Blood was everywhere. Soaking his clothing, her hands, seeping onto the floor.

Hancock tried to pull her away and she rounded furiously

on him. "You know what I can do. Damn it, let me go. I have to save him. I won't leave him like this!"

Hancock stared hard into her eyes. "You can't do this, Grace. You're too weak and this is a mortal wound. There's no saving him. You need to leave."

"Fuck you!" she yelled. "You have no idea what I can do."

"It will kill you," he growled.

"Do you think I care? Do you think I could live with myself knowing I did nothing to save him? Do you think I want to live knowing he died for me? Get out of my way. If you won't help me, then go. Go with the others. But get out of my way."

Hancock sighed and then slowly relinquished his grip on Grace's arm. She fell over Rio's chest, hugging him tightly to her.

Don't leave me, Rio.

The broken words poured from the very depths of her soul.

Grace.

There was a faint stirring as if he was barely hanging on.

Don't you dare do this. Get out. Go to Terrence. He'll get you out safely. You're too weak, baby. Don't do this. I'm begging you.

She ignored his pleading. She slammed into his mind with the last remaining strength she had. She overpowered his objections, held her ground when he would have fought her off. Nothing, no one, would keep her from saving him.

He was hers, goddamn it, and he'd damn well live even if it killed her.

She reached deep, found reserves she never knew she had. Desperation and her love for this man gave her power she would have never dreamed she possessed.

She pulled, absorbed, and the more she did, the more pain cracked through her, splintering, cutting into her like a thousand knives.

She gasped, flinched. She thought she cried out, but she

couldn't be sure. Her focus was solely on him. On stopping the flow of blood. On healing the terrible wound that would most certainly kill him if she couldn't save him in time.

The smell of blood was strong. So strong she gagged. It was then she realized it wasn't his blood. It was hers. On her tongue. Seeping down her neck.

As his wound closed beneath her hands, hers opened, tearing a hole in her flesh.

Her vision went dim. It was hard to breathe. So very hard to breathe.

Never had she felt this kind of pain.

Her body, already so weak and embattled by absorbing Elizabeth's illness, had reached its limit. Not even she could help herself anymore.

She was dimly aware of footsteps pounding down the hallway. Distant gunshots. Yells. Barked orders.

With the last of her waning strength, she sealed the wound in Rio's chest. And then she gave one last, stuttered breath and slid soundlessly to the floor beside him.

CHAPTER 38

RIO took a huge, gulping breath, jerking to awareness as if someone had just defibrillated his heart and he'd come back from the dead. His hand automatically went to his upper chest, to the terrible wound so near his throat. Only he found nothing. No gaping hole.

His hand came away bloodstained. He hadn't imagined it. And yet the pain was gone. He could breathe. It was as if it had never happened.

And then he remembered Grace's broken pleas. Her desperation to save him. And him begging her not to try to save him.

He rolled, immediately coming into contact with her limp body lying next to his. The wound—his wound—was there in her chest. The flesh lay open, and blood ran in a seemingly never-ending stream.

"Grace."

It came out as barely a whisper.

"Grace!"

He went to his knees, his hands covering the wound,

trying desperately to stop the flow of blood. He looked around, panicked. No idea what to do, how to save her.

Hancock shoved in beside him and Rio went for him, not wanting him to so much as touch Grace. Hancock knocked him back and then pressed a thick towel to Grace's wound, holding firm pressure.

"Terrence!" Rio yelled. "Diego! Somebody! Goddamn it, I need help! We have to get her out of here!"

He returned to Grace, noting the pallor of her face and her complete lack of movement.

"Oh God, Grace," he said, his voice completely cracking. "No, no, baby. Why. Oh God, why?"

The rest came out in a tortured moan. With Hancock still holding firm pressure to Grace's wound, Rio gathered her in his arms, rocking back and forth as tears ran freely down his cheeks.

He knew. He knew what this had cost her. He could feel no air exchange. Could feel no breath from her nose or mouth. He buried his face in her hair and wept because he'd lost the one thing in this world that mattered the most to him.

She hadn't been strong enough to heal him. Not a mortal wound. And so she'd taken it in his stead, knowing the sacrifice she was making.

He kissed her temple, his tears wetting her hair. He gently pushed the strands back away from her beautiful face. He stroked her cheek, ran his fingers over motionless lips.

"I love you," he said brokenly. "Don't leave me, Grace. Please don't leave me alone."

Pounding footsteps in the hall. Diego followed closely behind by Donovan. Donovan pushed Hancock aside and quickly worked to seal the wound.

He spared Rio a quick glance, full of regret and resignation. "It's bad, man. We have to move now. Chopper's waiting. Our only hope is to get her to a hospital so she can be stabilized long enough for her natural healing ability to kick in."

While Donovan spoke, he felt for a pulse. For a moment his fingers remained at her neck and then he cursed.

"Put her down, Rio," he barked.

Rio complied, easing her to the floor. His heart dropped when Donovan rose over her, his hands overlaid as he began to compress her chest.

"Hold pressure to that wound," Donovan ordered. "Make sure that airway is sealed." Then to Diego. "Give her mouth to mouth. We have to get her back."

Donovan pumped her chest and then lifted his gaze down the hall. "Where's the goddamn med pack? I need an IV yesterday!"

More footsteps in the hall, but all Rio saw, all he could focus on, was Grace and her fight to live.

He slipped into her mind just as she'd done to him.

Goddamn it, Grace. Don't you go out like this. You hang on. You can beat this.

No regrets.

The whisper was faint in his mind just as Donovan shouted for Diego to stop.

"I have a pulse. It's weak, barely there, but goddamn it, I have one. Get me that goddamn IV and let's move!"

I'd do it again. Never regret.

Rio wiped at the tears running down his cheeks.

Just hold on, honey. Please. For me. Don't give up.

Hurts.

The simple word tore his heart to shreds. Tears burned his eyes and scoured trails of acid down his cheeks.

Garrett and Nathan dumped the bag next to Donovan, and Nathan scrambled to get the IV set up. Donovan wasted no time. He inserted the needle directly into the jugular vein, taped it and instructed Garrett to hold the bag up.

He took another setup from Nathan and found a vein in her arm and plunged the needle in. He withdrew the needle, held the catheter in place, quickly taped it and tossed the other bag up to Nathan.

"There's a hell of a fight going on, so we have to be quick about this," Donovan said in terse tones.

Hancock rose, picked up his rifle and leveled a stare at Donovan. "My men and I have this. Farnsworth's security is a joke. We'll cover your exit."

Donovan lifted Grace while Nathan and Garrett held the IV bags high over her. Rio slammed into Hancock, driving him into the wall. "You have a hell of a lot of explaining to do, you son of a bitch."

Hancock smiled faintly. "We'll be seeing each other again, Rio. Count on it."

Rio shoved him away and then strode down the hallway, rifle up as he ducked around Garrett to take the lead. Nothing and no one would touch Grace without going through him first.

Once to the doorway leading to the helipad, they ducked and ran, sliding Grace onto the floor of the chopper before climbing in with her.

"Sam said he and the others will cover our exit and take care of things here. He said to take care of Grace and they'll catch up with us," Garrett shouted.

Nathan climbed into the cockpit and in moments the helicopter rose and flew low and fast over the water toward the mainland.

Donovan hovered over Grace, but it was Rio who held her in his firm grasp.

You're going to make it, baby. Don't let go. Just don't let go. Do it for me. I need you, Grace. I need you.

"I hope to fuck someone speaks Greek," Garrett muttered. "This could get hard to explain."

"I can get by," Diego said. "Languages are my thing. Besides, a gun is kind of a universal language all by itself."

"Fuckin' A," Garrett agreed. Then he turned to glare at his brother. "And don't you say a goddamn thing to my wife about my language."

"Nathan, give me an ETA," Donovan yelled. "She's barely hanging on with my patchwork job. We need to be there five minutes ago."

"I'm pushing the bitch as hard as she'll fly," Nathan hollered.

Twenty long minutes later, Nathan landed the helicopter right in the middle of the hospital parking lot. This time Rio gathered Grace in his arms while Donovan held pressure on the wound and Garrett and Diego held the bags as they ran for the entrance.

With the combination of what was obviously a seriously injured woman, the fact that every man was packing, and Diego's fractured Greek, they were quickly shown into a small area Rio assumed was their version of an emergency room. He just hoped to fuck he wasn't trusting Grace's life to a bunch of incompetent quacks.

The medical team worked fast, taking over, but Rio was reluctant to step back. At one point one of the nurses shoved him away with a stern glare that could only be interpreted as "get out of my way."

One of the doctors let out a stream of Greek aimed at Rio, who turned to Diego. "What the fuck is he saying?"

"He says they need to take her to surgery right away. He doubts she'll survive. He wants you to know the chances are little but that he'll do what he can to save her."

"Fuck that," Rio snarled. "You tell him his best isn't good enough. He'll goddamn save her or it'll be his ass."

Diego gave Rio a wry look and then turned to speak to the doctor. The message must have been adequately conveyed because the doctor paled and then began barking orders to his staff.

Moments later, Grace was wheeled past Rio and Donovan and the others. Rio stood there, feeling like the life had gone right out of him. He was heartsick over the thought that that might be his last glimpse of her. Broken, bloody, pale as death.

Donovan clapped a hand on his shoulder. "Come on. Let's go commandeer the waiting room and scare the shit out of anyone there so we'll have some privacy. We need to check in with Sam so he knows where to find us and make sure we don't have any casualties."

Rio nodded numbly and allowed himself to be pulled away. Nathan fell into step beside him and said in a low voice, "Shea is fighting for her too, man. I know you are as well. Grace is a survivor. She'll get through this."

"She has to," Rio said, darkness seeping into his soul. "I'm lost without her."

CHAPTER 39

RIO stood broodingly in the corner of the waiting room, staring out the window that overlooked the sea in the distance. It should be dark and raining, the sky filled with thunderclouds, but it was an absolutely beautiful Mediterranean day. Flawless, bright blue sky, the water dazzling like diamonds and winking in the sun.

Around him, the room had filled up with a steady stream of KGI members. Most left him alone to do his brooding. Terrence sat across the room next to Elizabeth, talking in soothing tones to the sobbing girl.

Rio should say something to her. Offer comfort. He wasn't a complete bastard. But what could he say to her? He was raw and hurting, knowing that this child lived because of Grace, and that at any moment Grace could be taken from him.

The hum of conversation that echoed through the room came to an abrupt halt. The hairs on Rio's nape prickled and he turned to see Hancock standing in the doorway, still in fatigues, blood—Grace's blood—still smeared on his shirt and his hands.

Hancock started forward, stopping a safe distance from Rio. He regarded Rio warily, without the innate cockiness that always accompanied Hancock's demeanor.

"Grace?" he asked.

"In surgery," Rio said shortly. "No word. They didn't give us much hope."

"Take a walk with me. There's a lot I want to explain."

He hadn't said "need," because Hancock was the sort who never felt the need to do anything. If he wanted you to know something, he'd tell you. But he never felt compelled to offer anything.

Rio's gaze drifted downward and Hancock emitted a soft laugh. "If I had any intention of killing you, you'd long be dead, my friend. I'm unarmed, which is saying a lot, since I walked in here with over a dozen men all ready to slit me from asshole to appetite."

Rio glanced toward Nathan, who was the closest to him and Hancock. "We'll be just down the hall. Come get me immediately if there's word on Grace."

"Will do, man," Nathan returned.

Rio followed Hancock into the hall and down the long corridor, ironically into a small chapel at the end. Hancock stopped a moment in the doorway, made the sign of the cross and then passed through.

Rio also paused, reached into his pocket for the rosary his mother had once given him. He made the sign and then kissed the beads and whispered a prayer.

"I'm not a good man. I'm not worthy in so many ways. But Grace is all that's good. She's one of yours. A gift to so many. She's my light and my hope. Please don't take her. I'll do my best to prove worthy of her and of the gift of her. Just please bring her back to me."

He walked farther into the chapel and settled on the front pew next to Hancock. For a moment, no words were exchanged. Then Hancock turned to Rio.

"Grace was never the target. She was just a means to an end."

Rio's lips tightened. "She wasn't the target and yet you

damn near got her killed. Hell, you might *have* killed her."

Hancock continued on in an emotionless tone. "Farnsworth was and always has been the primary objective. He was a slippery, cagey bastard who always had an eerie sixth sense when someone was closing in on him and he'd pull a disappearing act. It helped that he was one of the most paranoid bastards to ever live. He trusted no one. But he had a weakness."

"His daughter," Rio muttered.

Hancock nodded. "When she grew so ill, Farnsworth got sloppy. He would have done anything in the world to save her, and yet no one could give him what he most wanted. His contact in the government made sure he leaked information about Grace Peterson, whom the government also had a keen interest in."

"So you dangled Grace in front of him like a fucking carrot."

"Basically, yeah. The problem was that Farnsworth wouldn't do face-to-face meetings. If he did, it would have been a simple matter when he hired Titan. I could have gotten to him then and Grace would never have been involved. But the only way we were going to get close to him was if we handed Grace over to him. And in order to do that, we had to have her."

Rio shook his head. "Then why the fuck did you let us go that first time?"

Hancock looked away, toward the crucifix centered behind the small pulpit. "Because I owed you. You saved my life. I'm not completely without honor. I knew that Grace had been through hell. I knew she wouldn't be worth a damn if I took her to Farnsworth in her present condition. I wanted to buy her time because I knew it would damn well kill her to heal his daughter, and if she failed, she'd be dead anyway because he'd kill her in his rage."

"Who wanted Farnsworth?" Rio asked bluntly. "Who are you working for these days? Last I heard, Titan had ceased to exist even unofficially."

A crooked grin lifted Hancock's lips. "Don't believe everything you're told. I haven't completely lost all my belief in my country or the principles that made it great. Farnsworth was an evil son of a bitch who deserved to die. He was responsible for a lot of American lives lost. Military lives. Men and women who made the ultimate sacrifice for their country. He had no honor. He had no principles. Some would say the same for you and me, and yet we know that to be an untruth. What we did and do isn't always on the straight and narrow, but they are necessary things and they are for the greater good. The day I stop believing that is the day I die because I don't want to live in a world where I believe that good has no place in it any longer."

The quiet impassioned words cut straight to Rio's soul. It was as if he'd been taken back in time, so many years before when he and Hancock had fought so hard. For a cause. Because they believed in what they were doing.

"What now?" Rio asked softly. "Does Titan exist? Are you your own entity now?"

"We're there. We're always there. Rarely seen. But always there. We're a lot alike, you know. Titan. KGI. We see the world with different eyes. We fight for what we believe in. We do the jobs that no one else wants to do or has the means to. Some call us evil. Others call us heroes. But it's what we call ourselves that matters, wouldn't you say?"

In a completely twisted, ridiculous way, Hancock made perfect sense.

"For what it's worth, I'm sorry. I never meant for you or Grace to get hurt. I didn't fire the shot, but it came from one of my men. A man I trained. So it's my responsibility. He reacted without thinking, a mistake that will get you killed every damn time. I made an example of him, but it doesn't change the fact that the woman you love is fighting for her life because of a mistake made by one of my men."

Rio nodded. There wasn't much to say to that. The man had paid with his life. What else was there for Rio to do? Rage and hatred had no place in his heart right now. His focus had to be on Grace. His love for Grace. And his absolute faith that she would win the fight for her life.

"And now?" Rio asked. "What happens now? Farnsworth is dead. Grace and Shea will both still be hunted. We can sit here and talk civilly all day long, but if I ever see you coming for what is mine, I'll kill you without any regret."

Hancock smiled. "I'd think less of you if you didn't." Then he sobered. "My report will contain the following information. That Farnsworth was eliminated. His assets will be seized by the government. Many will celebrate. Included in the report will be that, regrettably, Grace Peterson died as a result of her attempt to heal Elizabeth Farnsworth."

Rio sucked in his breath and stared back at Hancock as he processed what it would mean for Grace to have "died" while trying to save Farnsworth's daughter. Freedom.

"It means you'd have to make her someone else entirely and that you'd have to stay off the government's radar. I'm sure you'd have no problem keeping her hidden in that damn jungle lair of yours. And I'm sure with the connections that KGI has, getting a new identity should be a simple matter."

Hope started a vicious beat in Rio's chest. A life. A normal life. All that Grace had dreamed of. Free of fear. Of always looking over her shoulder. She'd be dead to the rest of the world. Loved and forever cherished by him.

"What about her sister, Shea?"

"Without Grace, her value decreases. I'll do my best to dim any enthusiasm for Shea, but I can't guarantee anything. I have no doubt that KGI will keep her safe."

"Thank you," Rio said in a low voice.

It was hard to say to this man. But Hancock was trying to make amends. He'd tried to save Grace. He'd done what was necessary to accomplish the mission, and a lifetime ago, Rio would have applauded that drive and single-minded determination. He would have admired it. Would have aspired to have been like that. Machine, not man. The greater good above all else.

Hancock stood and started to walk away, and Rio knew, without a doubt, he wouldn't see Hancock again. Not unless Hancock wanted it. He'd fade back into the shadows. Back into a life steeped in gray. A gray world Rio himself had existed in before Grace had barged in with a burst of color, love and understanding.

"What about Elizabeth?" Rio called after him. "What will your report say about her?"

Hancock paused and turned around. "What would you like it to say?"

Rio hesitated and thought back to that innocent little girl who'd been so close to death before Grace had given her back her life. He lifted his gaze back to Hancock. "Tell them . . . Tell them that she died as well. That Grace was unable to save her."

Hancock nodded. "Tell Grace . . . Tell her that she's one hell of a woman. She had Farnsworth by the balls. Never quite seen anything like it. She's pretty damn fierce."

"I'll tell her," Rio said, feeling the first surge of hope creep over his shoulders.

"Safe journey," Hancock said before disappearing from the doorway.

"Safe journey," Rio murmured in the empty air.

Rio hurried back to the waiting room, anxious to know if there was any word on Grace. She'd been in surgery for three hours already and he had no idea how long to expect it to last.

As soon as he hit the doorway, he knew there was no word. Nathan looked up and silently shook his head. Rio bit back his frustration and blew out his breath, his shoulders sagging with fatigue and worry.

Elizabeth was sitting next to Terrence. The picture of the tiny little girl next to the mountain that was Terrence would be amusing in other circumstances. But then Elizabeth looked up and caught Rio's gaze. Sorrow swamped her expressive brown eyes.

Then to Rio's surprise, she pushed away the blanket Terrence had wrapped her in and got up. She walked to Rio, her face solemn, eyes sad. She stopped in front of him and looked up to meet his gaze.

"I know my father wasn't a good man. I'm sorry for what he did to Grace. She's such a good person. She's like sunshine and love all wrapped up in one."

Damn if tears didn't burn Rio's eyes all over again.

Gently he reached down and tucked her hand into his. "Come sit down and talk to me, Elizabeth."

She followed him to the far corner, away from the others. He sat and she stood awkwardly as if she had no idea what to do or what she should do. His heart broke when he looked at her, because she was trying so hard to be brave when her entire world had shattered around her.

"Come here," he said softly.

He held out his arms and she went willingly into his embrace. He hugged her to him and then lifted her onto his knee.

"You're right. Your father wasn't a very good man." He wouldn't lie to her. Elizabeth wasn't stupid. She knew what her father was. "But he loved you very much. Love will make you do all manner of things. He would have done anything to save you because he loved you that much."

She nodded solemnly. "I wished to be better so many times. I kept praying for a miracle because I wanted him to be good. I used to pray that God would make me well and that my father and I could go somewhere and start over. I—"

She bit her lip, but Rio could still see her entire mouth trembling.

"You what?" he gently prompted.

"I used to think that me being sick was his punishment for all the bad things he'd done," she whispered.

Rio hugged her tightly, his heart breaking for the burden this child had carried for so long. She was just a baby. Old beyond her years.

"Oh, honey, no. That's not how it works. Your father made choices. God doesn't punish you for the choices he made. You were a gift to your father. He loved you so very much. Bad things happen to good people all the time. It sucks. It doesn't always make sense. But look at Grace. She's been treated horrifically by people who want her for what she can do. She's good through and through. But she's suffered so much. It's not fair but then much of life isn't fair. It's how you live that matters. It's how you deal with the bumps in the road."

"I don't have anyone now," she said quietly. "I never knew who my mother was. I think my father took me from her when I was a baby. What will happen to me, Rio?"

He smiled tenderly and wiped the hair from her forehead. "I have an idea that I'd very much like to get your input on."

Her brow wrinkled and she stared questioningly up at him.

"What do you say, you and I go down and see if we can find something to eat and we'll talk over the proposition I have for you."

Her eyes lit up for a moment but then they dimmed, and she glanced toward the door as if expecting someone to walk through at any moment.

"What about Grace? I don't want to leave her."

"Terrence will call us the minute the doctor comes in if we're not here. Then we'll race back up as fast as we can so we can be there when she wakes up. Deal?"

Elizabeth smiled and bobbed her head up and down. "Deal."

CHAPTER 40

GRACE struggled through an endless sea of murkiness, shadows that seemed to reach out and wrap around her like vines. She warded off the encroaching darkness, wanting instead to savor the warmth of the distant light that seemed to grow dimmer all the time.

She knew she wasn't dead, but she also knew that she was dying. This was it. The epic battle between life and death. It all sounded so poetic but quite frankly it sucked and there was nothing particularly poetic about dying.

Rio?

It was a small whisper in her mind. She wasn't sure she had the strength to push it out, but she desperately needed confirmation that he was alive and okay, that she hadn't failed. And she needed the comfort of his presence because her mind was frighteningly blank. So dark and barren and *cold.*

I'm here, baby. Right here. With you always. Just open your eyes, Grace. I'm right here. Open your eyes and look at me.

Her brow furrowed and her nose scrunched up. He made

it sound so easy. She had no idea where she was. Somewhere between life and death, and yet he made it seem like all she had to do was open her eyes.

Her entire body was heavy. Understanding was slow to come, but with each passing moment, she became aware of more. She was cold because it was like a freaking icebox wherever she was. It was dark because she couldn't seem to pry her eyes open.

There were lots of sounds, harsh in her silent, dark world. Strange beeps. A whooshing sound. Distant buzzing, like conversation but not close.

Grace, I'm right here. Come back to us. Just open your eyes. You've been sleeping too long. You're safe now. You're with people who love you.

Shea.

Warmth spread, replacing some of the bone-deep chill. Rio and Shea both held her lovingly in their grasp. She was cradled in their arms, supported. Loved.

She tried. She truly tried to open her eyes, but it was as if someone had cemented them shut. She allowed some of the frustration to spill down the pathway to Rio and Shea.

It's okay, honey, Rio soothed. *You'll get there. Don't overexert yourself. Relax. Think of the happiest thought you can imagine. Then open your eyes so you can see it.*

That was easy. What she wanted most in the world was to see him. Know that he was alive. That he was here beside her.

She pushed everything away except the unerring desire to open her eyes. It was like rolling back a stone from a tomb. Heavy. Cumbersome. She'd never felt so weak in her life.

Her eyelashes fluttered.

Excitement coursed through her body, and she realized it was Rio's excitement.

That's it, Grace. You can do it. You are *doing it. Just a little more.*

It took every ounce of willpower she had to force her

eyelids open the rest of the way. For a moment all she could see was one huge blur.

But then her vision cleared and the first thing she saw was Rio leaning over her, his eyes filled with such joy. He was smiling so big that his cheeks dimpled. She'd never known he had dimples.

His hair hung limply over his shoulders, some of it falling forward into his face. Moisture welled in those deep brown eyes, and his hand shook as he lifted it to touch her forehead.

"Hi," he said softly.

She tried to smile and it was then she realized that something was terribly wrong. She couldn't move her mouth. There was a tube down her throat. She panicked, reaching, trying to yank it out. Then she gagged.

Rio grabbed both her hands and held them tightly, all the while yelling over his shoulder for help.

She was only dimly aware of what they were saying. She caught a few words from Rio. She'd woken up. She'd realized there was a breathing tube. She'd been more aware than maybe they'd thought she'd be. Or maybe it was that she'd come around before they expected.

Then from the nurse, talking to Rio about sedating her so they could remove the tube, but they had to wait for the doctor's orders. Had to be certain she could breathe adequately on her own.

She tried to protest, but she couldn't talk around that damn tube. All that came out was a muffled choking sound.

Rio turned back to her, still gripping her hands tightly. He put his lips to her forehead.

I need you to calm yourself, Grace. It's just a breathing tube. You've been in a coma and you weren't able to breathe on your own at first. They'll take it out. All will be well.

And suddenly her world went fuzzier. That panicked her too.

Rio!

Shhh, it's okay. They're just sedating you so the tube can be removed. They don't want you pulling it out and doing more damage. I'll be here when you wake up again. I swear it.

WHEN she woke again, her eyes came open immediately. There was no fight just to crack her eyelids. She felt stronger. Relief coursed through her veins until she was heady with it. She wanted to crawl out of the stupid hospital bed and do a double fist pump.

She was here. She was alive. She was going to make it.

She lifted her head, immediately searching for Rio. She frowned when she didn't see him anywhere. Figures. She was finally something other than a panicked, freaking-out nitwit and he wasn't even here.

Shea?

The response was immediate. She could feel her sister's relief.

Grace, you're awake. You're stronger. I can feel it. You're already so much better.

Thanks for being there. For all of it. I couldn't have done it without you.

It's over now, Grace. I can't wait to see you. You have to come for my wedding.

Wedding?

Grace felt Shea's beautiful smile, her absolute joy, and it warmed Grace to her very soul.

Nathan and I are going to marry at the same time that his older brother and his fiancée get married. We were the reason they waited as long as they did, so it's kind of fitting that we do it all together.

That's wonderful, Shea. I'm so happy for you. And of course I'll be there. Nothing could keep me away. Now go. I know you can't keep up a link for long. We'll talk later. Right now I have a man to track down.

Shea's laughter lingered in Grace's mind long after her sister left the conversation.

She was about to send out a demand to Rio to ask where the hell he was when her door opened and she saw him stick his head in.

His eyes brightened with joy and relief when he saw that she was awake and looking in his direction.

"Hey you."

She smiled. "Hey yourself. Where you been?"

"I brought someone to see you. I wanted to make sure you were up for it. She just wanted to peek in on you while you were sleeping."

Grace's brow furrowed and then Rio walked farther in. Elizabeth came in behind him, holding his hand, a shy smile on her face. As soon as she saw that Grace was awake, her face lit up. She dropped Rio's hand and ran for the bed.

"Careful!" Rio warned, not a second too late.

Elizabeth pulled up when she would have leapt onto the bed and instead stood beside it, jittering with excitement.

Then her smile turned down into a frown. "I was so worried for you. They told us you would die."

Grace smiled and then held up an arm to hug her. Elizabeth needed no urging and snuggled immediately into Grace's side.

"They were wrong," Grace said. "I have too much to live for to die now."

Her gaze found Rio's as she spoke, and his warm gaze stroked gently over her face.

He walked around to the other side of her bed, pulled up a chair and sat. He took her free hand, the one that wasn't occupied with holding Elizabeth, and he ran his fingers over the back of her hand and then her palm, over and over as if reassuring himself that she was here and alive.

"How are you feeling?"

She thought about it for a moment, mentally running down her body, testing what hurt and what didn't.

"Tired," she finally said. "Mentally tired. Like I'm burned out, you know? The mental fatigue is more overwhelming than the physical pain."

"That's understandable," he said gently. "You've been through a lot. It's amazing you still have your sanity intact."

Elizabeth snuggled harder into Grace's side and laid her head on Grace's shoulder. Her tiny hand crept over Grace's belly until she was wrapped firmly around Grace.

Grace snuck a glance at the little girl, who'd gained and lost so much in an instant. Her eyes were already closing, as if she too had reached her limit and now felt safe enough to rest.

Grace smiled and pressed a soft kiss to Elizabeth's hair. When she was sure Elizabeth was asleep, she turned to Rio, her gaze worried.

"What will happen to her? She has no one."

Rio smiled, slid their hands over to cup over Elizabeth's. "She has us."

For a moment, his answer didn't sink in, but when it did, tears pricked her eyelids and she blinked furiously as her vision blurred.

"And I have you," he said as he leaned forward to brush his lips over hers. "I have everything I could possibly want right here."

CHAPTER 41

IT was a frustration for Grace that the first time she was getting to see her sister in over a year was on her sister's wedding day. She wanted to come as soon as she'd been discharged from the hospital, but Rio had tucked her and Elizabeth away immediately and had insisted that Grace do nothing more taxing than eat and rest for several weeks.

While it had frustrated her, she had needed that time to heal. As did Elizabeth. She still grieved for her father, even knowing the sort of man he was, and she was dealing with guilt over her part in the whole sordid affair.

It had been a good time. Just the three of them. Rio had been so good to them both. She still got teary-eyed just thinking of how gentle and understanding he'd been with them and how he'd spoiled them so ridiculously.

Under Rio's gruff, tough-as-nails, badass mercenary exterior was a man with a heart of gold and a soft spot a mile wide.

Rio drove into the Kelly compound, and Grace marveled at its size and also how it resembled a military base with all the security. But she quickly forgot all about her surroundings when she saw her sister running to meet the vehicle.

"Stop!" she cried to Rio.

Rio braked, and before he'd come to a complete stop, Grace was out of the SUV and running as fast as she could to meet her sister.

They met halfway and Shea threw her arms around Grace. Shea was the smaller of the two and yet she engulfed Grace, squeezing like she was three times Grace's size.

Grace returned her hug, holding on. Just holding on.

Tears ran freely down Grace's cheeks. "I love you," she choked out. "I can't believe we're together. That we're here."

Shea's muffled sobs were lost in Grace's shoulder. The two sisters stood in the sun, hugging, laughing, crying and then hugging some more.

Around them, the Kellys gathered, all present for the double wedding. They smiled indulgently while the Kelly wives and wife-to-be sniffled and wiped at their eyes.

Rio got out and leaned against the hood of the SUV, smiling as he watched the sisters' reunion. Elizabeth snuck into his side and he wrapped his arm around her.

"They must have missed each other an awful lot," Elizabeth said.

"Yeah, they did," Rio said softly. "They've been apart for a very long time."

After several more minutes, they broke apart and wiped at each other's faces with their hands. Finally they gave up, laughing.

"Come on, there are so many people I want you to meet," Shea said as she pulled at Grace.

Grace turned to look back at Rio and Elizabeth.

"We're fine," he mouthed. "You go on. We'll catch up."

Shea dragged Grace toward where the others were gathered a short distance away. She beamed as she pushed Grace forward.

"Grace, I'd like you to meet my—*our*—family."

Grace nearly teared up all over again at the inclusion of her as family to all these others.

"This is Rachel, Ethan's wife."

The pretty brunette with soft brown eyes hugged Grace fiercely. "Welcome to our family, Grace."

"And this is Sam's wife, Sophie, and their daughter, Charlotte."

Sophie stepped forward, a toddler on her hip, and smiled broadly at Grace. "It's wonderful to finally meet you, Grace. We're so glad you're here and safe. Shea's been so worried for you."

Grace smiled back, her throat aching with emotion.

"This is Sarah, Garrett's fiancée, and my wedding mate. Nathan and I kept interfering with their wedding plans, so I know they're just happy to get on with it at this point."

Sarah laughed and punched Shea in the arm. "The wedding will be so much more special now that everyone is home where they belong. Including you, Grace."

Sarah hugged her tightly and then stepped back.

Then Shea took her through every single one of the Kelly brothers, all of whom she'd met or seen, but Shea insisted on introducing them when they were out of camo and not shooting at people.

When she got to the end, there was an older couple, their smiles as warm as the sun.

"And these two people are the most wonderful people in the world," Shea breathed. "I want you to meet Marlene and Frank Kelly. Or Mama and Papa Kelly, as they are often referred to. They spawned all those Kelly boys plus picked up more than a few strays along the way." She pointed in the direction of two men to the side. "Those are Sean and Swanny, two of Marlene's adoptees."

"You poor dear," Marlene said as she enfolded Grace in a hug. "You've been through so much and now this. This family is enough to overwhelm anyone. But welcome to our family. Your family. You're one of us now. Just like Rio, though he'd probably twitch at the thought. He's just as much my boy as any I gave birth to."

"Thank you," Grace whispered.

As soon as Marlene released her, Frank enfolded her

into a huge hug. She'd never felt so loved as she did right now, surrounded by all these people. Family. It boggled her mind.

Standing on Frank's other side was a young woman that he pulled forward. "This is Rusty. She's a Kelly too. The only Kelly sister to the horde of boys."

Rusty's face lit up and Grace could swear her eyes glistened with tears at the way Frank introduced her.

"She's going to UT," Marlene said, beaming with pride.

"Welcome to the chaos," Rusty said as she hugged Grace. "It's pretty crazy and overwhelming around here." Then her gaze softened as she stared at her family surrounding her. "But it's the very best kind of crazy."

"Let's all go inside," Marlene suggested. "We have a wedding to get ready for. I'm sure Grace is tired from her trip and would like a shower and something to eat. We're only down to a few hours, girls. Better get on the stick."

Everyone dissolved into laughter and then there was a chorus of "yes ma'ams" all around.

"NATHAN, Rio, I need to see you both for a moment," Sam murmured.

Rio and Nathan, who'd been standing together talking in Sam's living room while the women were dressing for the ceremony, turned in Sam's direction.

Rio frowned. "What's up?"

He motioned them away and they stepped onto the wooden deck that overlooked the lake in the distance.

"Resnick wanted to come. I told him no."

"What the hell? Shouldn't he still be in the hospital anyway?" Nathan asked.

Sam shrugged. "Probably, but I think he was more afraid to stay where he was vulnerable. He'd rather risk getting out so he can protect himself from any assassination attempts."

"You didn't tell him about Grace."

It didn't come out as a question. Rio said it fiercely, more of a demand than anything.

"I told him what Hancock put in his report. That she died," Sam said quietly. "Which is why I wouldn't allow him here. If he does ever come into contact with Shea, she can't let on that Grace is alive. It's not that I don't trust him—I don't fully—but I don't want any leaks where Grace is concerned and I know you don't either, Rio."

"Fuck no," Rio growled.

"He was devastated when I told him Grace had died. He feels responsible. He's tried to protect them since they were young. He's long suspected that he's their biological brother or at least half brother. Chances are Grace and Shea aren't even full-blooded sisters and maybe not even half sisters."

"It doesn't matter to them," Nathan said quietly.

"Yes, I know. But I wanted to tell you both. Rio, you'll need to get Grace out soon after the ceremony. I don't want to take a chance on Resnick not taking no for an answer."

Rio nodded.

Sam nudged Rio on the shoulder. "And hey, man, for what it's worth, I'm damn glad she saved your sorry ass."

Rio smiled faintly because he still couldn't think about what she'd done without a cold fist clutching his gut. The thought of losing her, even so many weeks later, sent him into an instant sweat.

Just as they reentered the house, Marlene swept into the living room, arms waving. "Okay, everyone, let's get this show on the road. Places everyone. Outside. Shoo shoo."

The men all laughed and then grumbled but good-naturedly fled outdoors.

It was a wedding fit for the lifestyle of KGI to a T. Although outdoors, the area where the ceremony was being held was between Sam's and Garrett's houses, but on the exposed sides, huge, bulletproof glass barriers had been erected, one facing the lake and the other facing the building referred to as the War Room.

Nobody let that get them down. The family had been through enough that no one took security lightly. Marlene had insisted on draping flowers from one end of the bulletproof barriers to the other. There was an awning with flowering vines from top to bottom, and rows of chairs lined the pathway from the house to the archway, where the preacher waited.

Rio ushered Grace into the back row and sat next to the open pathway, placing Grace on his other side. The wedding was small enough that neither bride was having attendants, but they'd immediately pounced on Elizabeth, welcoming the shy little girl into the fold and declaring that she had to be the flower girl for the occasion. Elizabeth had been so excited that she'd fairly danced down the aisle, sprinkling rose petals and honeysuckle as she went.

Nathan and Garrett waited at the end and smiled indulgently as Elizabeth took her place next to them. Then Shea and Sarah made their way toward their future husbands, their smiles big enough to light the darkest night.

Rio stared around him, soaking it all in. He squeezed Grace's hand, his heart so full of love that he could barely get out what he wanted to say.

"Do you think we can do this one day?" he whispered.

She cocked her head to the side and eyed him with one raised eyebrow. "Are you asking me to marry you?"

"Maybe," he hedged. He looked almost nervous. "If I were, what would you say?"

She smiled. "Well, hypothetically speaking, if you were to, I don't know, propose to me, I'd probably have to think about it for a while, but since this is all hypothetical, it's hard to know exactly what I'd do."

He frowned at her. "You just like to torture me, don't you? You know damn well I'm asking you to marry me."

He glanced around. At all the love, the unconditional love and support of the Kelly family. "I want this," he said in a quiet voice. "I want what they have. I want us to be *family*, Grace. You, me and Elizabeth. Nathan and Shea. I want our kids to grow up playing together. I want to know that if something ever happens to me, you'll have them to lean on.

"I know what I'm asking is a lot. You'd give up a lot. I'll always be overprotective of you and Elizabeth and any other children we have. We'll live in isolation in my home in Belize, where it's a veritable prison. You've had to become a different person, and you won't be able to just pop over to your sister's for a visit whenever you want. But no one will ever love you more than I do. I'll spend the rest of my life loving and protecting you with every breath I have."

Tears filled Grace's beautiful blue eyes. She reached up to touch his face and then leaned in to kiss him, uncaring of what was going on around them or that her sister was in the act of getting married.

"Yes, I'll marry you, Eduardo Bezerra. And no one will ever love you more than I do."

"I already know that," he said gruffly. "You nearly died for me and don't think I'll ever forget that."

"But you also gave me a reason to live," she said in a quiet voice. "You came to me when I was at my lowest point and you wouldn't let me give up. You saved me, Rio. You made me stronger."

He kissed her back, long and sweet. "I love you, Grace. I already love Elizabeth. I feel as though she's my own. But I'll also want to give her a few brothers and sisters down the road."

Grace smiled. "I'd like that. I think you'd be a whiz at changing diapers."

He grinned then. "Bet your ass I would."

TURN THE PAGE FOR A SPECIAL PREVIEW OF
MAYA BANKS'S NEXT KGI NOVEL

SHADES OF GRAY

NOW AVAILABLE FROM BERKLEY SENSATION!

P.J. RUTHERFORD cocked back her chair and flung her boot on top of the table in front of her. She adjusted her straw cowboy hat so her eyes were barely visible, and stared over the smoke-filled room to the band setting up along the far wall.

The waitress thumped a bottle of beer on the table next to P.J.'s boot and then sashayed away, her attention reserved for the male customers she flirted and chatted up.

P.J. wasn't a chatterer. She'd never spoken to anyone in all the time she'd been coming here. She couldn't really be called a regular, but yet, in all her irregularity, she was.

This was her place to unwind between missions. It wasn't what most would consider a place of rest and relaxation, but for P.J. it worked to throw back a few beers, inhale some secondhand smoke, go deaf from listening to bad cover songs and watch a few bar fights.

She winced when the guitarist riffed a particularly bad chord and then ground her teeth together when the mike squealed. These guys were amateurs. Hell, it was probably their first live gig, which meant she was going home half deaf and popping ibuprofen for the headache she'd be sure to have.

But it beat spending the evening alone in her apartment with jet lag. Although she wasn't even sure it could be considered jet lag. She'd been three days without sleep, so truly she could sleep at any time, but she was wired and still buzzed from the adrenaline the last mission had wrought.

She was wound tighter than a rusted spring and there was no give in her muscles tonight.

The big happy mush fest that had gone on at the Kelly compound, complete with double weddings and enough true love and babies and bullshit to make her green around the gills, hadn't helped.

Not that she was a cynic when it came to romance. She had her romance novels and she was fiercely protective of them, and of anyone giving her shit over reading them.

But sometimes the Kelly clan was a little overbearing in the sheer sugary sweetness of all that unconditional love and support. Did no one ever get pissed off and start a fight?

Now that, she'd pay real money to see.

The truth was, she just felt out of place, which was why she'd rather stick to her own team, let Steele take the orders from Sam or Garrett Kelly and she'd follow her team leader. The day Steele became embroiled in all that happy bubbly shit was the day she hung up her rifle and called it quits.

She liked Steele. She knew where she stood with Steele. Always. He didn't sugarcoat shit. If you fucked up, he called you on it. If you did your job, you didn't get any special accolades. Not for doing your fucking job, as he put it.

And she liked her team, even if Coletraine was one giant pain in her ass. But he was a cute pain in the ass and he was harmless. Plus he was a perfect target for cutting jokes and egging on. Easy. Too easy. He rose to the bait on too many occasions for her to count.

She was the better marksman. She knew that without false modesty. But it didn't stop a healthy rivalry between her and Cole when it came to sniper duty.

It pushed them both, made them better at their jobs, and it made the relationship between them easygoing and casual. Just the way she liked it.

The current song ended and she sighed in relief even as she reached for her beer. To her surprise a hand reached out and took the bottle from her just as a pair of booted feet—big booted feet—appeared right next to her chair.

She knew those boots. Ah hell, what was Cole doing here?

She glanced up with a scowl then reached for the beer he held just out of reach.

"Fancy meeting you here," Cole drawled.

"Don't make me take my feet down," she growled. "I was comfortable. This is my space. Go find your own."

Instead, he sat down, plunked her beer back in front of her and then held up a hand to the waitress, who wasted no time hurrying over.

"Bring me whatever you have on tap, sugar," Cole said with a wink.

P.J. rolled her eyes as the waitress fell for that fake charm. Cole was easy on the eyes for sure. Muddy blond hair, a newly grown goatee, which P.J. had to admit looked damn good on him. Blue eyes that could be mean as hell one moment and twinkling and carefree the next.

He was a badass, not that she'd ever tell him so. It suited her purposes to keep him down a few notches. Wouldn't do to have his ego blow up on her. She did have to work with him, after all.

"What the hell are you doing here, Coletraine?" she demanded after the waitress had left. "This isn't exactly your neighborhood."

He shrugged. "Can't a guy come in and check on a teammate?"

Her gaze narrowed. "Sure. There's Dolphin, Baker and Renshaw and you could always look in on Steele. I'm sure he'd looooove the company."

"Maybe you're just special," he said with a grin.

"Lucky me," she muttered.

But she couldn't control the peculiar butterflies floating

around her belly when he turned all that charm on her. Hell, she was acting like a damn girl.

The waitress returned and Cole tipped up his bottle, taking a long swig before he thumped it back down on the table. Behind him, the band had struck up another ear-piercing song and Cole visibly winced.

"Holy shit, Rutherford. I thought you had better taste than this. What the hell are you doing in this shithole anyway? Shouldn't you be at home catching some R and R? You haven't slept in what, three days?"

She cast a baleful look in his direction. "I could ask you the same question. At least I'm within a few blocks of my bed. Last time I checked you still resided in the great state of Tennessee. That's a long ass way from Denver."

"Maybe I like your company."

P.J. snorted.

For a long moment they sipped their beer in silence while the music clanged and more smoke filled the air. Cole's eyes suddenly widened when two girls in in the corners of the bar hopped up on an elevated step and began to do a slow striptease.

"Rutherford, are you a lesbian?"

She choked on her beer and then sat forward, letting her feet drop off the table and onto the floor with a clunk. She tipped back her hat so she could look him square in the eyes.

"What the hell kind of question is that?"

He gave her a quelling stare. "You're in a strip joint. What else am I supposed to think?"

"You're an idiot."

He gave her a mock wounded look. "Come on, P.J. Throw me a bone here. Tell me you aren't a lesbian. Or at least crush me gently."

"You're ruining my downtime."

"Well, if this is downtime, let's do it up right. Want to do some shots? Or are you afraid I'll drink you under the table?"

Her brows went up. "You did *not* just challenge me."

He gave her a smug smile. "I believe I did. First round's on me."

"They're all on you since this is your idea."

"Okay, but I'm guessing you can't get past three."

"Blah, blah. I'm hearing a lot of talk and no action."

Cole held up his hand again and the waitress walked up to the table.

"Can you set us up with some shots?" He turned to P.J. "You got anything against tequila?"

"I've only got something against bad tequila. Don't cheap out on me, Cole. You better get the good stuff."

"You heard the lady," Cole drawled. "Give us a setup in the best tequila you have."

The waitress looked dubious but she nodded and headed in the direction of the bar.

P.J. studied him from underneath her eyelashes. Despite her initial annoyance, Cole was intriguing her. What was he doing here? And why? She could swear he was flirting with her and the weird thing was, it was a rather delicious sensation.

A guy like Cole wouldn't have to look far to get laid. No way he came all the way to Denver just for a piece of ass.

The waitress returned, carrying a long board that had ten shot glasses. She set it on the table, took Cole's credit card and then looked at them both as if to say, *Have at it.*

Cole picked up one glass, handed it to P.J. and then took another for himself. Then he held it up in a toast.

"To another successful mission."

P.J. could drink to that. She tipped her shot glass against his and then they both downed the alcohol.

She nearly coughed as fire burned down her throat. Hell, it had been a good while since she'd had anything stronger than beer. She'd sworn off the hard stuff after her stint with S.W.A.T. and the aftermath of her leaving the unit.

She brought her glass down on the table with a thump and stared challengingly at Cole. He grinned in return and then scooped up another glass. She leaned forward to take her own, but this time they were both a bit slower to down them.

The music seemed to grow louder and the smoke got thicker. Her eyes watered, whether from the tequila or the smoke she wasn't sure. Cole was right about one thing. This was a sucky place to spend her first evening back home.

"What do you say we finish up our five shots and head to my place?" she said before she could change her mind.

He frowned slightly, and her heart sank. She hadn't read him right at all and now she was going to make a giant fool of herself. She was already preparing to excuse the invitation away with casual indifference when he spoke.

"If we're going back to your place, one or both of us needs to stop drinking now. How about I get us a bottle and we'll finish up there?"

She let out a sigh of relief that she hadn't even realized had welled up in her chest.

"You get the bottle. I'll meet you in the parking lot. You can follow me back to my place."

COLE went to the bar, motioned for the bartender and a few moments later left with a bottle and two shot glasses. Not that he intended on needing or wanting either, but he was going to make it look good.

He sauntered out to the parking lot, wondering if P.J. would even be there as she'd promised or whether she'd taken off.

She was a hardass. Hard to get close to. Hard to get any information from. He knew next to nothing about her personal life. She never slipped up and dropped hints. When they were on a mission, she had single-minded focus. And when the mission was over, she was always the first to bug out. No chitchat or social hour for her.

It had been surprising as hell to discover that she hung out in this joint. He would have guessed she hated people and that she'd never go out of her way to actually hang out in a place infested by them.

He didn't feel one iota of guilt over slipping the GPS chip into her backpack before she'd left. She carried that damn thing with her everywhere and it had led him to the parking lot of the bar.

To his surprise she was standing by her jeep, leaning back with a cool expression on her face. Her eyes were unreadable as she stared up at him.

He held up the bottle and flashed a grin in her direction.

She gave a half smile in return then threw her thumb over her shoulder. "Follow me and try to keep up."

Saucy little heifer. She had to make everything a challenge or a dare. It was okay, though. It wasn't worth it if it was easy.

He climbed into his truck and quickly maneuvered onto the highway behind her, making sure she didn't lose him. After a mile, she turned right into an apartment complex that looked like it dated back to the seventies. It was clean and seemed quiet, but Cole didn't like how dark it was and that there were no security gates.

How the hell did a woman whose job was all about security and protection live in a place like this?

He pulled into the parking spot beside her and slid out. She was already on the sidewalk waiting for him and before he could catch up to her, she turned and walked up the pathway to her front door.

He grimly surveyed the area and when she opened the door, he frowned harder because the door wouldn't withstand a simple kick. He walked through and then paused as she closed and secured the door. Not that it would do any good if someone really wanted in.

When she turned back to where he was standing, she frowned as she stared down at his hands.

"You forgot the tequila."

"I didn't forget anything."

Before she could react, he backed her up against her door, his body pressing in close, and he did what he'd been dying to do ever since the day he'd first laid eyes on her.

He kissed her.

THERE will be a time when I call for you, Talia. I'll expect you to come. Until then, you're needed here. Remain with your mother until she is strong and healthy again.

Talia Montforte shivered as the long-ago words slid through her mind. Words she'd never forgotten, though there were times she'd wondered if the prince had truly meant them. She'd gotten her answer a mere week ago when the royal summons had arrived.

Now, as she stared out the window of the private jet, the island grew bigger as they closed in. She was nearly there, and Prince Alexander "Xander" Carrera waited somewhere on that island. For her.

Anxiety clutched at her stomach. She flipped her long, dark hair back over her shoulder and thought not for the first time that she should have pinned it up. But his instructions had been explicit. What to wear. How to fashion her hair. Everything to the letter had been dictated in the summons.

And God, had it been lengthy. Her cheeks still buzzed with heat over the details. The questions. The medical exam. Her entire world had been upended the moment the messenger bearing the royal seal had appeared at her mother's home.

It was time, the message had said. There would be care provided for Talia's mother, but Talia was to come at once.

The last years had been turbulent years for her country. Xander's father had been assassinated. Talia had feared the worst for the royal family, but word had leaked that they'd escaped safely.

The rebellion still raged and there was yet hope that the usurpers to the throne would be ousted so that the royal family could be welcomed back. The country waited. Talia had waited, never expecting that she would be summoned to him in exile.

It had been difficult to leave the life she'd resigned herself to. Only in the beginning had she had even a whisper of regret that things wouldn't turn out the way she'd planned. She'd wanted to attend university. Travel the world. Eventually come back to her country to contribute to the growing industry and economy of the small island nation off Spain's coast.

Instead her mother had been diagnosed with cancer, and, faced with the inability to pay for the mounting costs, Talia had sworn off university and had taken any odd job she was able to land. Until the day Prince Alexander, or Xander as he insisted she address him, had arrived at her small cottage by the sea.

He'd swept in, issued orders for her mother to be transferred to a center in France that specialized in treating the form of cancer Talia's mother suffered from. He'd then insisted that Talia attend university in Paris. He'd put her up in an apartment that was close both to where her mother's care was being overseen and to the school where she studied. He'd even given her a monthly allowance and made sure that all her living expenses had been paid.

And why?

She still didn't know why.

The only thing he'd ever said to her was that one day

he'd summon her and she was to come at once. Of course she'd agreed. What person wouldn't? When faced with her mother's mortality, being able to ensure her mother's health and realize her dream of attending university, the promise hadn't seemed too much to give.

Now she wasn't certain, because now she had no idea just what she'd traded in her bargain with the prince.

She shook her head as the plane touched down. Oh, she knew. Or at least now she had a very good idea. And it was no matter because if faced with the same situation all over again, she'd do it once more, without reservation.

Her pride. Her body. Her very soul. None of it was too precious a thing to sacrifice for her mother.

And, if she were completely honest, she was intrigued by the request.

The missive had been short and to the point. But what had come after had opened her eyes to exactly what it was the prince was expecting of her.

Mistress. Lover. Concubine. Whore?

No matter what word she put on it, nothing changed the stark reality of her presence on this island sanctuary.

She was a toy. A thing. She was for his amusement, his entertainment. His desire. His whim.

The plane rolled to a stop and as she looked out her window, all she saw was the sparkling waters of the Caribbean.

"You may remove your seat belt and come with me, Miss Montforte."

She unfastened herself with trembling fingers then looked up to the staid-looking, gray-haired man who stood in the aisle waiting to assist her. She grabbed her handbag like it was a security blanket and slowly stood.

When she stepped onto the platform outside the plane, the bright wash of sunshine had her reaching for the sunglasses she'd stuffed in the pocket of her bag. For a moment she paused, soaking up her surroundings. The water sparkled in the distance and all around her was rugged landscape, mountainous toward the center and west, and flatter to the east. The sky was as brilliant as the water itself, and not a single puff of white marred the perfect sheet of blue.

A hand touched her elbow and she started, jerking from her silent assessment of her temporary new home. Six months. For six months she'd agreed to live in this place. To be whatever the prince wanted her to be.

The man who'd escorted her out of the car and onto the plane in Paris was now assisting her down the steps toward a black Mercedes parked just a short distance away.

She smoothed the wrinkles from the silk skirt, a gift from Prince Alex—no, she must remember that he was to be addressed as Xander. He'd been very specific on that matter. He'd purchased her an entire new wardrobe, and it was baffling how he'd chosen the exact sizes she wore. Everything from underwear to shoes.

The lingerie was to die for. Sinfully sexy and yet ultra feminine. Putting it on made her want to purr in delight and yet roar like a sultry seductress. She didn't even want to entertain what it all had cost. It would likely have paid for her mother's treatment twice over.

"His Highness awaits," the man said as he handed her into the backseat of the car.

In the front, another man wearing dark sunglasses glanced at her in the rearview mirror.

"Are you ready, miss?"

She nodded and then the door closed and the car immediately pulled away from the small jet.

They pulled onto a roughly paved stretch of road, but the further they traveled it, the smoother it became. She glanced curiously around, wondering at the inhabitants. If there was a town. She hadn't been able to see anything on the flight in. It had all looked frighteningly barren of any sort of human activity, but it certainly didn't suffer from lack of vibrancy of nature.

Lush, green. Sparkling sands. Rugged mountains. She'd even seen a waterfall as the plane had made its descent.

The road meandered around a curve and then turned out onto a point on the eastern edge of the island. She leaned forward, spotting formidable gates that opened as if by magic as they approached.

They continued in and she gasped softly at the private paradise that existed beyond those imposing gates.

There weren't words to describe the grounds. Immaculately rendered. Flowers, so many that the burst of color was a shock to her eyes. Plants, foliage. Fruit trees. Palms. Flowering vines and bushes.

And nestled among it all was a palatial villa with a huge water feature in front of the sprawling entrance. She couldn't call it a fountain exactly. It wasn't one fountain, but a huge series of them, intricately designed. It looked like the villa's own private waterfall and oasis.

As the car pulled to a stop, she was gripped by sudden nerves that nearly paralyzed her. Grateful that at least her eyes were hidden by the sunglasses she'd donned, she turned to see a tall man striding toward the car. He reached for the handle as the driver stepped out and opened her door.

"Miss Montforte," he said smoothly. "His Royal Highness bids you welcome to his home."

"SO she came," Xander murmured as he stared down at Talia gracefully exiting the car he'd sent to pick her up at the airstrip.

"Did you doubt she would?" Garon asked dryly.

Xander's gaze never left Talia as Sebastien took her arm to escort her into the villa.

"Who knows the mind of a woman?" Xander said. "I've seen nothing to doubt that she would ever go back on her word, but when faced with my expectations, it's only logical to assume that any woman in her position would have second thoughts."

Garon's lips twitched in amusement. "Indeed."

"She's still a virgin," Xander said, unable to keep the satisfaction from his voice.

"That pleases you."

Xander lifted an imperious brow. "Of course it does. I may not be her only, but I'll damn well be the first."

"Some might argue that what you plan to subject her to is a bit much for an innocent."

Xander could no longer see Talia. Sebastien had escorted her to the front of the villa where she would await him in the sitting room. He twitched with impatience to go to her, but it wouldn't do for him to seem eager.

He wanted this to be on his terms. She would never know just how long he'd waited for this time to come. She was his now.

"You're a damn hypocrite," Xander said with no heat. "You're dying to fuck her every bit as much as I am."

Garon's lip lifted once more. The slight arch at the corner of his mouth was the closest he got most days to actually smiling.

"I don't have the taste for innocents that you seem to have."

"She won't be so damn innocent when I'm finished with her," Xavier murmured. "Besides, I don't have a proclivity for virgins. Just one virgin. Her. I find I'm very possessive when it comes to Talia."

Garon gave a snort. "And yet you'll share her with your most trusted men."

Xander shrugged. "It's who I am. It's what I do. I haven't heard you complain once."

Garon seemed to ponder the matter a moment and then his expression grew more serious. "No, I've not complained. But the woman in question has never been someone important to you. Talia obviously is. Think about what you do, Xander. Sex is sex. Kink is kink. I like a good time and a beautiful woman as well as the next man. But I would hate to lose trust or a friendship because emotions got involved."

"Then see that yours don't."

Garon shook his head just as Sebastien entered the library. He inclined his head in respect toward Xander. "Talia waits below as you requested."

"Tell me, Sebastien, do you find her beautiful?"

Sebastien lifted one eyebrow, and then his eyes narrowed thoughtfully. "I'm uncertain of the point of your question, Your Highness. Of course she is a beautiful woman. Time has been more than kind to her. She's no longer a girl of eighteen but a lovely woman of twenty-two."

Garon stifled laughter at Sebastien's rather irreverent address. "Your Highness" only got brought out for sarcasm. Xander's security team was made up of men who'd been with Xander for many years. Even before working for the prince, they'd attended university together. Their friendship, trust and loyalty was unquestioning. Garon, Sebastien and Nico had been Xander's only friends during a time of unrest in his country, and in return they were the only people Xander trusted implicitly.

"Some would argue that twenty-two is still very much a girl," Garon pointed out. "Virgin. Untouched. She seems very unworldly for a woman who's spent the last four years in one of the world's most sophisticated cities."

"Are you trying to insinuate that Xander is a dirty old man?" Sebastien drawled.

Xander chuckled and Garon did that half smile again.

"I think it's been well established that I'm a hopeless hedonist," Xander said. "The question is whether she'll be able to accept that."

Sebastien sobered and glanced between Garon and Xander. "Is that what this is then? A test?"

Put that way, it sounded cold and clinical. No, nothing about his feelings for Talia could be considered cold.

"Perhaps?" he said lightly, unwilling to let his friends see the depth of his uncertainty or his indecision. "Perhaps it is a test of myself as well to see if this . . . lifestyle . . . is what I need or if it's something I've merely wanted and enjoyed in the past."

"We'll endeavor not to fuck it up for you," Garon said dryly.

Xander lifted an eyebrow. "See that you don't. She is to be spoiled and pampered. Her every need and whim seen to. She is mine—ours—make no mistake about it. She will be molded and taught. She will submit without reservation. But in return she will be treated and respected as the princess I intend her to be."

"Fucking a beautiful woman," Sebastien said sardonically. "Such a chore. I think we should ask for raises."

Xander's gaze sharpened. "You won't be fucking her, Bastien. You're going to worship her and pleasure her as you've never pleasured another woman."

"I have no problem with that at all," Sebastien said in a lazy voice that was full of satisfaction—and anticipation.

Xander checked his watch. "We've kept her waiting long enough. Go find Nico. I want a few moments alone with her and then I'll expect all three of you to make an appearance."